BALLAD OF THE BOW

S K A B Y

BLUEROSE PUBLISHERS
India | U.K.

Copyright © SK Aby 2025

All rights reserved by author. No part of this publication may be reproduced, stored in a retrieval system or transmitted in any form or by any means, electronic, mechanical, photocopying, recording or otherwise, without the prior permission of the author. Although every precaution has been taken to verify the accuracy of the information contained herein, the publisher assumes no responsibility for any errors or omissions. No liability is assumed for damages that may result from the use of information contained within.

BlueRose Publishers takes no responsibility for any damages, losses, or liabilities that may arise from the use or misuse of the information, products, or services provided in this publication.

For permissions requests or inquiries regarding this publication, please contact:

BLUEROSE PUBLISHERS
www.BlueRoseONE.com
info@bluerosepublishers.com
+91 8882 898 898
+4407342408967

ISBN: 978-93-5989-762-2

Cover Design: Shubham
Typesetting: Sagar

First Edition: January 2025

DISCLAIMER

This book is a work of fiction created to provide entertainment to fantasy readers and to explore imaginative possibilities, not to serve as a historical account. Names, characters, places, and events are either products of the author's imagination or are used fictitiously. Although the narrative is set in ancient China and references historical figures such as emperors to frame an approximate period for the narrative, the story is entirely fictional. Any resemblance to actual persons, events, or locations is purely coincidental and does not purport to represent historical accuracy in any manner.

Acknowledgements

Dear Reader,

Thank you for choosing *Ballad of the Bow*. It means the world to me, and I hope this tale transports you on an enthralling journey back to around AD 10, an era shrouded in mystery. Beyond stone carvings and inscriptions, bards from these times have passed down epic tales that blur the lines between the deeds of gods and men.

Monsoon trade winds have set many sails aflutter, transforming the coastal cities of numerous kingdoms into thriving crossroads of culture and commerce. Explorers, priests, and traders from as far as Rome, Africa, and Persia in the West mingled with East Asian realms in the crucible of culture - Tianzhu. This narrative begins in the Han dynasty and belongs to all these peoples and cultures.

No one writes a book alone.

This novel is curated from books, films, television shows, travels, the Internet, and life lessons I have encountered. I extend my gratitude to the authors of these books, the creators of the films and shows, the contributors online, and everyone who has traversed the path before me—a special thank you to all the archaeologists and historians who have provided insights into our existence from times immemorial. After all, we are what we are because of those who came before us.

I am immensely grateful to Blue Rose Publishers and their team (Deepika, Khushi, Rishav & Sagar) for making this book a reality, especially to editors Kushi and Jhanvi in marketing.

I sincerely thank my dear friends, teachers, and colleagues whose unwavering support has guided me through writer's block and has served as my sounding board, critic, and cheerleader. My gratitude goes to my family for steadfastly standing by me throughout two decades of writing and rewriting: my wife Alice, support from children Shannon and Sam, Sarayu, and especially Sasha, who dedicated considerable effort to editing the book into a coherent manuscript. Special thanks go to my dad, sisters, and everyone who believed.

To the indomitable spirit of adventure in every reader – *Battle speed, brothers!*

Yours truly,
S.K. Aby

Contents

Prologue 4
  # 1 Journey Across the Great Whites 5
  # 2 Camp of Horror 12

PART #1 ZHENGJUN 28
  # 3 ZhengJun Becomes Empress 33
  # 4 Prince Ao Marries XuPing 44
  # 5 Emperor Cheng Marries the Zhao Sisters 56
  # 6 Fang the Witch Visits the First Harem 66
  # 7 Hede Fools Palace Mandarins 93
  # 8 Fertility Rituals Gone Wrong 107
  # 9 WangMang Discovers the Tomb 121
  # 10 WoShi Finally Believes the Prophecy 128
  # 11 WangMang's Daughter Marries LuiKan 138
  # 12 WoShi Visits the Monastery 155
  # 13 Qian Runs Away to Save a Bird 173
  # 14 WoShi Meets the Prince 190
  # 15 The Boys Meet the Immortals 209

PART #2 SUJIN 232
  # 16 SuJin Meets the Emperor 235
  # 17 Batu The Hun Becomes Family 268

18 Valley of The Dwarfs 290

19 Batu Is Accepted by The Boys 305

20 Making of The Recurve Bow 329

21 Batu Teaches Archery 351

22 WoShi Meets Ailing Empress Wang 365

23 HuKui Is Captured 390

24 Bandit Attack 421

25 Ride into Changan 445

26 Boar Attack on HeGan 462

27 SuJin Meets Empress Wang 490

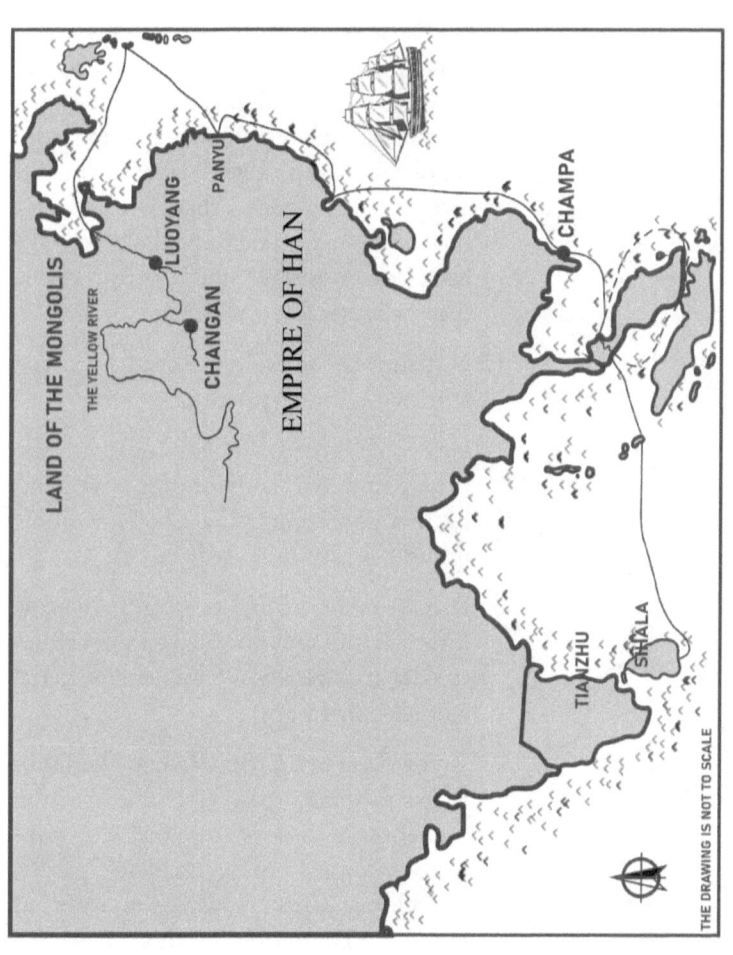

Recurve Bow Action

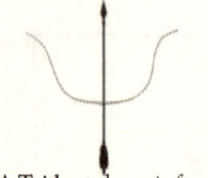

A **Trident** shape is formed just as the **Arrow leaves the bowstring**.

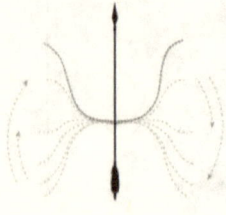

3 & 4. Limbs of the Bow oscillate after arrow release

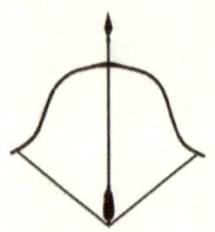

2. Bow **Drawn** to fire.

1. Arrow is **Notched**

A **Recurve bow** is unlike a regular (straight) bow because the shape of the bow changes significantly when it's drawn. The change in shape helps store more energy and deliver higher thrust and arrow speed on release than with a regular bow of the same length. As the bow snaps back, for an instant, the bow and arrow together resemble a **trident**.

1. **Notch:** The arrow is notched onto the string.

2. **Draw:** The string is pulled back with the arrow, and the ends of the bow bend backwards, curving fully. The bow is now under tension (refer to diagram).

3. **Release:** The string propels the arrow forward, and the bow's limbs straighten rapidly, transferring all their energy to the launched arrow.

4. **Arrow Leaves the Bowstring:** The limbs snap forward; however, due to the immense release of tension, the arms bend forward and oscillate briefly, resembling a trident with the arrow in motion. [**Therefore, in this book, the trident represents a launched arrow**].

5. **Rest:** The bow returns to its resting state, with the limbs and string in their original positions.

Sangachatvam – *Sanskrit* –
"Moving together, belonging to each other."

Prologue

	Generic Description
Qin	Ancient China, **before** the Han dynasty, came into being – pronounced as "Chin"
Tianzhu	Ancient peninsular India, referred by ancient Chinese as the land below the Shindu River
White Mountains	Himalayas
BaLi	Commander of the Qin Army, a devout follower of Lord AoYang, *Immortal #1*
Qin Shi Huang	Mighty Emperor of Qin, who unified China, before the Han empire came to being.
NaiLa	Qin Warrior, builder, *Immortal #2*
Anoman	Young apprentice of NaiLa, *Immortal #3*
AgDai	Qin warrior priest who is a stickler for rituals, *Immortal #4*
MiDai	Blood brother of Ag Dai and a warrior, *Immortal #5*
ZhuBajie	Qin Warrior Priest, *Immortal #6*
ShaWajing	Qin Warrior Priest assistant, *Immortal #7*
Sun WuKong	Qin warrior who stayed back in Tianzhu, *Immortal #8*
Lord AoYang	Warrior and Dragon King in Tianzhu
Lord Bing	Warrior brother of Lord AoYang
Lady GuanYin	Prince AoYang's Consort

#1 Journey Across the Great Whites

BaLi was certain they had crossed the borders of Tianzhu, too late for any pursuit. Hearing a shout up ahead, he nudged his horse forward and gazed down into a broad valley. He grunted in satisfaction, taking in the rolling green meadows, frothing streams, and glistening glaciers. Large herds of deer and mountain goats grazed peacefully, dotting the landscape.

The Great Whites loomed in the distance – an imposing physical barrier before the long ride home. The open vistas sharply contrasted with the jungles to the south, which BaLi had been forced to call home for many years.

He turned to look at his army winding its way up the narrow mountain trail. Their progress was slow, hindered by trudging slaves and carts laden with gold and plunder looted from the temples of minor gods. The slaves from the sultry plains fell ill, their bodies unaccustomed to the thin mountain air, but his soldiers hardly paused. The sick had to keep up, or they would be abandoned, stripped of their meagre clothing, and left to starve and die on the desolate mountain slopes.

BaLi's mind wandered back to their expedition in Tianzhu. He had experienced the adventure of a lifetime: discovering a fabled land and fighting fierce battles. Their incredible stories would echo in the courts of Qin when he reported everything he had witnessed to his mighty Emperor, Qin Shi Huang.

The journey through the southern jungles of Tianzhu had been gruelling. The Qin army lost their way and struggled as endless expanses of dense foliage obscured the sky, disorienting them as they wandered through the undergrowth. At times, relentless rain lasting days turned paths into streams, forcing them to seek shelter. Snake bites, strange illnesses, and infighting among the men took a heavy toll. The jungle would have claimed them one at a time but for their fortunate meeting with Lord AoYang. After that, everything changed.

In the war to support Lord AoYang, BaLi witnessed courage, honour, and sacrifice from warriors on either side. These battles did not pit unequal warriors against each other without a challenge; wars were fought from sunup to sundown, with rest at night to prevent any undue advantage.

In Lord AoYang, BaLi recognised a god, a true Dragon King. No ordinary mortal could embody such extreme righteousness or achieve such extraordinary feats.

In hindsight, meeting the Aryan Princes, Lord AoYang and his brother, Lord Bing, felt like destiny. BaLi's smile turned sour when he thought about Sun WuKong, his best friend and trusted confidant, who had stayed behind in Tianzhu to serve Lord AoYang. BaLi would have also gladly remained, but as the commander, he was responsible for leading his soldiers back to Qin.

Before their departure, Lord AoYang gifted the Emperor of Qin many treasures. He warned BaLi and his generals not to shed blood in Tianzhu and assured them that, upon reaching Qin, they would attain glory and wealth beyond their wildest dreams.

When it was time to say goodbye, BaLi asked Lord AoYang for a guide to cross the Great White Mountains. Lord AoYang, however, declined. Smiling, he said, "Don't worry, BaLi. You will reach home. You are destined to set karmic forces in motion with reverberating effects that will last an eternity. Go now, my friend, and build an empire. That is your true destiny."

BaLi approached Lord Bing and pleaded, "Good brother, we lost our way once in this land, and you rescued us. Let's be practical. We need a guide to cross the Great White Mountains before winter."

BaLi's lack of faith in his brother did not offend Lord Bing. "Look to the skies and trust Lord AoYang's words, for in it you will find direction. A warrior's words are cast in stone."

A few days into their march, Bali was stunned to see a giant eagle soaring low in the sky, screeching to announce its presence. Despite ridicule from his generals for following a bird, Bali remained resolute, directing the army to follow its path.

Every morning, the bird screeched to announce its arrival over their camp before flying ahead, indicating the path they needed to follow. With the bird setting their course each day, BaLi and his men swiftly crossed the scorching plains and could see the foothills of the great white mountains.

Problems began when one of the villages offered a few scouts beautifully woven red cloth and gold earrings as gifts. Upon the scouts' return, others ventured out to collect souvenirs. Soon, they began looting the vulnerable village, breaking their promise to the Aryan King. They pillaged the land and robbed temples.

Blood was spilt, slaves were taken, and it was too late for BaLi to intervene. Though bristling with rage, BaLi remembered his promise to Lord AoYang that he would not shed blood within Tianzhu. His generals argued that their Emperor, Qin Shi Huang, would approve bringing in skilled artisans from Tianzhu. Torn, he prayed to Lord AoYang, seeking forgiveness and guidance, and resolved to punish his generals.

The eagle stopped appearing in the skies.

Thankfully, they still had the fish machine that had guided them out of the jungle.

Lord Bing, the brother of the Dragon King, climbed a hillock of black rocks and sat in penance. That night, lightning bolts struck the hillock, and several boulders exploded, throwing up dust and debris. By morning, white mushrooms had sprung up everywhere, transforming the hill into a white landscape. Lord Bing collected strange metal flakes from the debris. The flakes stuck together when brought close. He fashioned a hollow fish using wood and tree sap, coating it with black metal flakes as scales. When placed in water, the fish always pointed north.

Before they departed for Qin, Sun WuKong handed over the machine to NaiLa, a disciplined warrior and loyal deputy of BaLi.

****

The scouts were uncertain whether to go through or around the valley and were waiting for direction from their commander. BaLi realised he would need a reading from the fish machine before they ventured further.

Dark clouds gathered beyond the valley, stretching like a massive curtain and blotting out all features except for the occasional glimpse of mountains when lightning struck. A thunderstorm was brewing. BaLi frowned at the clouds and commanded in his deep voice, "Summon NaiLa."

NaiLa rode up to him, and BaLi said, "Set up the fish machine and send a scout to confirm if a path extends through the valley."

NaiLa stroked the fish scales with a piece of leather while chanting the necessary prayers one hundred and eight times. After completing his chants, he placed the device inside the vessel. Immediately, the floating fish changed direction, pointing to the north. NaiLa placed an arrow eleven counts to the right of north, indicating the direction of their homeland. The arrow pointed straight into the valley.

BaLi gazed into the distance across the valley with unease. He did not want to enter this beautiful valley.

With a frown, NaiLa said, "Commander, it looks like we're heading for wet weather, possibly even snow. I should send Anoman to scout the pass beyond to see if a path exists." BaLi grunted, and with a slight bow, NaiLa excused himself, pausing just long enough to confirm that his attendant had safely packed the fish device on his packhorse.

The flat valley, bordered by snow-covered mountains, had small ponds edged with ice. It offered sufficient space to camp safely away from the steep sides, reducing the risk of rockfalls and avalanches. The mountains would protect them from cold winds, and rain would quickly drain through the streams. He couldn't fault the camping site, yet a heavy feeling sat in his gut.

He waited and watched as his army advanced into the valley. It was evening when the last stragglers passed him. His generals, hungry and impatient, murmured irritably as they waited, eager to descend into the cosy valley.

****

As BaLi looked around, he saw a large rock overhang and a deep crevice beneath it overlooking the valley. He would camp under it, as it would provide protection from the rain and allow him to watch over the valley. He had to figure out what was causing his unease.

He decided on a fire sacrifice to allay his fears.

His cook served him soup made from marmot meat and flat mushrooms picked on the trail. The man mumbled that he would bring venison once the hunters returned. Something unsettled him, but it was not hunger. After a few sips, he returned the bowl and told the cook he would have dinner after the fire sacrifice.

One of the scouts pointed to a distant movement against the stormy backdrop, and BaLi shaded his eyes. A man was galloping toward them at breakneck speed. BaLi scowled at the punishing pace Anoman had set for his horse. He hoped this hard push was necessary; otherwise, his mentor, NaiLa, would punish him severely.

The army strictly prohibited exhausting a horse except in battle, to escape, or carrying crucial information. Upon realising it was their scout, the generals quickly arranged themselves in two rows beside

BaLi to receive his report.

Anoman skidded to a halt in front of a bristling NaiLa, threw the reins of the heaving horse to a startled warrior on guard, and landed with one knee bent and his head bowed, all in one fluid motion. He waited for NaiLa to command him to report.

"Speak loudly, warrior. Let the commander hear your report." BaLi had to suppress a smile as the boy remained bowed but smoothly turned on the ball of his foot to face him.

With bowed head, Anoman reported, "Respected Commander, mighty generals of Qin, and teacher, I must share the appalling sight I witnessed. The waters of an entire lake are being sucked into the air by powerful, twisted winds. Rocks and debris fly around like daggers, and lightning pierces the clouds with a deafening roar!" He raised his head slightly and said sincerely, "I did not approach any closer, fearing that I too would be pulled into the great winds and unable to return to report." Many of the seated generals tittered at the summary.

Peeved by their mocking laughter, Anoman said, "I am reporting what I saw, and I recommend we look for shelter. Perhaps we should go back the way we came until the storm subsides!"

Anoman looked furtively at NaiLa and found him frowning in displeasure at his audacity to suggest a recommendation to an entire assembly of generals. Anoman gulped hard as he realised his mistake. His job as a scout was to inform, not to make decisions for the wise commander he so desperately wanted to please.

BaLi looked at the trembling horse, frothing at the mouth, then at the excited boy, and he knew Anoman's report was sincere. After all, his intuition was also against going down into the valley. He glanced at NaiLa and gave a slight nod.

With a surprised look at the commander's response, NaiLa turned to the boy sternly. "Anoman, you are an apprentice of the great Sun WuKong. Why does a storm make you afraid?" Anoman twitched uncomfortably, both angry and embarrassed. NaiLa continued his tirade: "Are you still a child on your mother's teat? Are you terrified of the rain and thunder?"

One of the generals said, "Can't you see the sky above us is clear? The winds are strong, but we are in an open valley. Should we be alarmed? What can any storm do but sprinkle some water on our backs?"

Anoman looked at the general and replied hesitantly, "Respected general, the spiralling winds are not behaving like a storm cloud. It is alive!"

The general pulled a clump of dry grass from the ground and let it fall. The grass blew away from them into the valley, and all the men seated smiled in comprehension. "Look at the direction of the wind, carrying the grass. The storm is blowing away from us."

Anoman mumbled, "What if the wind direction changes and the storm rebounds off the high mountains?"

BaLi said, "Apprentice, we cannot outrun a storm in these mountains. All storms, no matter how big, eventually pass. We shall cross the mountains once the storm blows over in a day or two."

BaLi turned to his generals and said grimly, "We fled Tianzhu like rats, shamelessly plundering the lands of our hosts." He paused and ominously added, "Outside its borders, no oaths bind me to the Aryan king. Send back the artisans with enough food to reach the lower settlements. This is my command."

BaLi noticed the silent communication among his generals; a showdown was imminent. Ignoring them, he told Anoman, "Apprentice, join me for the fire sacrifice."

He stood up, signalling the end of the discussion. His attendant took out a conch and blew into it three times, indicating a long break. A roar of approval rose from the valley below.

NaiLa dismissed Anoman, saying, "Before anything, go and rub down your tired horse."

2 Camp of Horror

AgDai had custody of the "live fire," the essential element for a fire sacrifice. He removed the flame carrier from the packhorse with his massive hands. It was his responsibility to keep the fire burning until they reached Qin.

The flame carrier was a cylindrical baked clay spindle with a spiral groove that held a smouldering hemp rope to preserve the "live fire." The resin-infused rope burned slowly and needed replacement just once a day. To carry it on a horse, the spindle had a cover that cleverly locked onto the base of the cylinder.

BaLi intended to build a fireplace in the name of Lord AoYang from the living spark at a temple in Qin. The rope had been ignited from Lord AoYang's blessed fireplace, a sacred fire that had been part of their elaborate preparations before battling a rogue king.

Lord AoYang's consort, Lady GuanYin, had given AgDai three tiny stone bottles of liquid lined with beeswax and sealed with corks. She told him the liquid was flammable and could restart a fire from an ember.

The original fire was taken from a tree struck by lightning, a gift from the Aryan gods for the fire sacrifice. As long as the fire burned, no one could defeat them in their battle. BaLi was the sole Qin warrior trained in the sacred invocations required to conduct the fire sacrifice, known as Yajna.

AgDai motioned to his brother MiDai to set up a fire behind a large rock, away from the wind. As they prepared to light a fire from the smouldering end of the burning rope, it began to drizzle. A drop of water fell on the smouldering cord, causing it to sputter and sizzle.

AgDai panicked! He shouted and cupped the ember to protect the holy fire. They had to nurse the fire back to life quickly.

BaLi pointed to a crevice on the mountainside. "Quick, under that rock overhang! Don't let the holy fire die!"

AgDai clambered up to the crevice and urged his brother, "Run! Get the bottle that Lady GuanYin gave us." MiDai darted to their horse.

The crevice was a cave, and AgDai moved deeper inside to prevent any draught from extinguishing the feeble spark. He handed the fire spindle to MiDai and took the stone bottle from him.

MiDai steadily blew a stream of air, desperately cajoling the tiny spark to stay alive while untwisting the strands of rope to give space for the fire to revive, but he was failing.

"*Battle speed, brother!*" MiDai screamed.

AgDai removed a blade of dry lemongrass from his waistcloth and pulled the cork stopper from the exquisitely made stone bottle. They were enveloped by the heavenly scent of a hundred flowers in bloom, yet he did not notice the fragrance in his distress. AgDai dipped the blade of grass into the jar just as Lady GuanYin had instructed him. With a sudden spurt, the liquid soaked the dry grass and crept towards his hand. He pulled out the wet blade of grass and gasped in surprise, "Is this water alive? Can water burn?"

He just had to bring the wet grass near the dying spark, and a blue flame leapt across, lighting the blade of grass. With a delighted cry of relief, the brothers lit the fire rope properly.

"What magic is this?!" exclaimed MiDai. "How can wet grass catch fire? What's this fragrance? It feels like we are in a garden. Is this the scent of heaven?"

AgDai said, "Let us set the fireplace here." MiDai ran out to get dry dung chips from their packhorse while AgDai nursed the flame on the wooden spindle. His eyes adjusted to the darkness inside, and he gasped in surprise. "Firewood! Plenty of it."

He raised his head to the heavens in gratitude. The cave was a regular camping site for shepherds during the summer and contained the remnants of many cookfires. Inside, it was spacious, featuring a high roof and a natural cleft that allowed light and smoke to escape. From the cave entrance, the shepherds could watch their sheep grazing below.

BaLi ran in and grunted in relief to see the glow of the smouldering rope. Brushing away raindrops from his tunic, he said, "Camping here is better than sleeping in wet tents down in the valley."

He called out to NaiLa to set up camp. The generals had gone down into the valley, followed by their assistants and pack horses, but they had asked some ardent supporters to stay back to report on discussions following the fire sacrifice.

AgDai set up a two-foot-wide by three-foot-long sacrificial fireplace lined with stones. Meanwhile, MiDai hurried in with a few dung cakes and said, "We have to manage by using embers from the dung cakes and not build a proper fire."

AgDai gestured to the firewood stack, and MiDai gasped, "Where in the heavens did this come from?" Men entered, carrying horse packs and dumping them inside the cave. One said, "NaiLa told us to leave it here and let the horses graze in the valley."

AgDai lit the fire as he had been taught, invoking the fire, wind, king of the gods, and the creator. The fire burned cheerfully bright, shadows disappeared, and they were enveloped in cosy light and warmth. BaLi looked around to find that most of his trusted confidants had stayed back with him, with a few others. His eyes turned to the mouth of the cave, where he found Anoman and a group of young warriors peering in to watch the fire sacrifice.

NaiLa told Anoman, "A warrior shouldn't neglect his weapons or horse. The animal can die because you exert it to exhaustion, and the cold of the night is extreme. Go and tend to your horse, rub him down, give him grain, and put on a blanket if necessary. Tomorrow, you can let him loose with the other horses to graze in the valley."

Predictably, Anoman's face fell, and he said, "I don't want to miss the fire sacrifice, and I shall take care of the horse later."

NaiLa, expecting dissent, was ready with a retort. He leaned a little into Anoman and whispered loudly, letting his friends hear, "Fine, shall I ask all your friends to join you? You can spend the night rubbing down every horse in the valley. That way, we can dispense with sentries at the periphery."

A cowed Anoman scowled at NaiLa, slumped his shoulders and dragged his feet as he walked past. He wouldn't cross NaiLa because the man always stuck to his word.

The fire ceremony was long, and with BaLi immersed in the rituals, the men posted by the generals saw no merit in staying back. AgDai politely requested on their commander's behalf that they wait until the fire sacrifice was complete to avoid insulting the invoked gods.

A young man savagely grinned and said, "You come down to the valley when you are done burning firewood. You are no Aryan priest, and we are not in Tianzhu for their gods to answer."

Something snapped inside AgDai at the man's audacity, and he reacted violently. He withdrew his double-edged sword in a flash and swept hard in a smooth arc that should have decapitated the warrior's head.

MiDai blocked his brother's blow in time, locking the deadly double-edged Jian sword within the metal splice of his knife's handle. An unearthly screeching sound echoed off the cave walls as metal grated against metal, and angry sparks flew around.

AgDai looked down at the knife in surprise, realising it had blocked his fierce blow. It was the dreadful, green-coloured knife gifted by Lord

AoYang to MiDai. He recognised the strange knife's handle, shaped like two frogs mating, with a bubble in the middle that resembled frogspawn.

MiDai locked AgDai in a firm arm hold, pivoted, and delivered a powerful kick to the man frozen in shock. He was sent hurtling across the cave, crashing to the ground with a bone-jarring thud. Struggling to his feet, he clutched his chest and coughed harshly. Seizing his narrow escape, the terrified soldier bolted, much to the amusement of the youngsters!

MiDai disengaged from a simmering AgDai and said, "Not here, brother. This place is sanctified with holy fire. Let that rat scamper out. If the gods are not eager to dirty their hands with his death, you can take his miserable life for insulting our commander."

When he saw that AgDai was still incensed, he lowered his voice and said, "Brother, please be patient. I know the mind of BaLi, and he has reached his limits in tolerating the insolence of these soldiers."

AgDai looked blankly at MiDai before replying, "Either the gods hasten his demise, or the commander declares war. I will not let that insolent fool live beyond another sunset, along with his master, who is behind this dissent."

An infuriated AgDai walked over to the sacrificial fire and sat beside BaLi, who seemed unconcerned, though the violent twitching of the muscles in his neck and face gave him away. He had seen and heard everything.

The wind picked up with a howl, and the occasional crackle from the fire broke the silence as BaLi continued the rituals in silence. Other than his trusted confidants, all the others were now down in the valley.

NaiLa's eyes opened in surprise when he realised BaLi was not making a simple fire sacrifice! He cleared his throat and walked towards the cave entrance, and all the men followed. These brothers-in-arms did not need words to communicate; they had fought side by side and lived their lives together.

NaiLa said, "Brothers, the inevitable has begun. Our generals have disobeyed Lord AoYang, our host, and insulted our commander with their insubordination. BaLi gave them a way to redeem themselves by setting the artisans free. However, none of them are ready for that; surely, a repentant general would have stayed with the commander and not insulted him further by ignoring the fire sacrifice. We have a battle on our hands to regain dignity."

NaiLa looked at each of his brother warriors, and they nodded in agreement. "Lord AoYang does not want the warriors who fought alongside him to die on Tianzhu's soil. On this promise, our hands were tied, and we remained mute spectators while every military commandment of loyalty was broken. We are now outside the borders of Tianzhu, within the White Mountains that belong to no man. We are outnumbered, but weren't we always!" he thundered.

AgDai said, "There is no need for all of you to get involved. My brother and I will send him to the netherworld before sunset tomorrow."

NaiLa motioned to BaLi, who was still at the Yajna fire and said, "Our commander isn't invoking the gods for a prayer to help cross the mountains. He chants the verses of a yajna with the sole objective of victory in war. Just as we fought once with the fire burning, we will ensure that this fire burns until we are done fighting. Let us live as legends. If we die, let men and gods acknowledge our loyalty and dignity."

AgDai flexed his muscles in glee. "At last! There are a few scores to settle." He added a few words on basic strategy, "The traitors know that they face death as soon as they disobey the commander. They are banking on BaLi's restraint not to act until we leave Tianzhu. They have been waiting to assassinate our commander since the first raid, but they fear Lord AoYang might respond with force if any death occurs within Tianzhu."

"Not anymore," NaiLa added. "Tonight, they will choose their leader from the three factions vying for command. Tomorrow, they will attack in force."

MiDai said, "Once we enter Qin, the law forbids revolt, but not here. We are neither in Tianzhu nor in Qin."

AgDai turned to NaiLa, "How do you know all this? Do we have spies in their ranks?"

NaiLa laughed and said, "No spies. Weak men talk! They play both sides to join the winning side. That is why, despite the overwhelming odds, all we have to do is eliminate the generals and their followers. The vast majority of the soldiers will stand down."

AgDai asked, "What will their punishment be? I mean, the rest of the soldiers."

NaiLa responded, "I don't know what the commander will decide. Probably, he may confiscate all the ill-gotten wealth."

NaiLa looked around, and all the warriors gave their consent, one by one. They would fight.

NaiLa exhaled noisily and said, "We have no choice but to attack tonight. We are outnumbered, but the chilly night will help. We need to take out the three leaders before we subdue the majority. This is not a mass killing. Find and eliminate specific targets. Each one of you will be assigned a kill list. Make it count."

"When our commander finishes the yajna, we go to war," AgDai whooped excitedly.

****

NaiLa went out to survey the valley. The drizzle had stopped, and although the wind up in the pass was strong, there was hardly any breeze in the valley, dotted with many cookfires. Unsurprisingly, the fires were grouped into three distinct areas.

NaiLa decided they would split up and infiltrate all three camps simultaneously to assassinate the offending generals and their cronies.

The air was colder than anything he had faced back in Qin. He turned back to the cave, and his jaw dropped in surprise. Despite the tense situation, he couldn't help chuckling at what he saw.

Anoman had the audacity to tie his horse and two pack horses under his care at the cave entrance. He was rubbing his horse down with dry grass and keenly watching and listening to everything happening inside, along with the other boys.

The boy was incorrigible, and now he realised why Sun Wu Kong liked him so much. He was a replica of that fun-loving, mischievous warrior.

AgDai, who had come out, locked eyes with NaiLa and shook his head, signalling him to leave the boy alone. NaiLa grumbled to himself, "I am his mentor. Why is everyone advising me?"

NaiLa loosened his bronze Jian sword and warmed up while reciting chants, just as Lord AoYang and Bing had taught him. Energy flowed into his body, and battle fury replaced trepidation. He was prepared to kill.

Two veterans, ZhuBajie and ShaWajing, clambered over the ridge from the valley. They were surprised to see NaiLa practising with his sword.

Disconcerted, ZhuBajie hollered, "NaiLa, this is Zhu, the priest." He walked forward, and NaiLa nodded and let them all pass. A few loyal men, mostly boys, followed ZhuBajie.

ZhuBajie told NaiLa, "There is a call to arms in the valley, but seeing you warm up, I guess you've already been informed. We're just a few who came of our own accord. After snatching back all the food we carried for you, the renegade generals let us go."

ShaWajing spoke, "They have asked us to inform BaLi that bowmen and scouts roam the periphery. They expect an attack tonight and will kill anyone entering the valley."

"Are you going to fight?" ZhuBajie asked, and NaiLa gestured for them to go inside.

NaiLa waited for more warriors to join, but none did. He assessed that their situation was dire. They were too few, with few bowmen, and all their food was in the valley below.

A little later, the winds stopped and changed direction, causing a freak cold spell to sweep through the mountains. As the wind blew across the valley, the temperature began dropping again, and NaiLa entered the cave, unable to withstand the intense cold.

The fire sacrifice had concluded, and the cave was filled with the pungent smell of burning hair. One by one, each warrior made an offering to the gods by chopping off a lock of their pleated hair and dropping it into the fire. When BaLi saw NaiLa, he motioned for him to make his sacrifice.

NaiLa held his sword up and flipped his head. His long-pleated braid whipped up and caught the honed edge of the blade, neatly snipping a lock of hair. He turned the sword, grabbed the falling lock of hair on its broadside, and angled the blade. The lock of hair slid off the entire length of the sword into the flames.

After all the warriors made their offerings, they turned to BaLi to elaborate on their battle plans. He gestured for the wide-eyed boys to step forward and make their offering.

The warriors were surprised. ZhuBajie was the first to recover, and he told the boys, "You are now drafted as warriors and will fight alongside the legends of Qin, men personally honoured by Lord AoYang. Be proud of your worth and implicitly follow the instructions given by your leader. Your life belongs to the commander." The excited youngsters came forward one by one, offering their hair as a sacrifice, bowing to BaLi first, and then swearing their oath of obedience to each of the assembled warriors.

Anoman was the last, and everybody turned to wait for him to make his sacrifice. He was making a show of it. Anoman patted his horse, which neighed and nuzzled its head lovingly against him. He walked purposefully towards the fire, holding his long braid of hair in one hand and a knife in the other.

In a demonstration of his delight at finally being drafted as a full-fledged warrior, he jumped high into the air, sailed out with his hands stretched, and, pulling one of his arms in, spun and landed softly, perfectly balanced on all fours. His head was bowed low before BaLi with the knife tip pointed inwards. A small piece of hair, which he had cut mid-air, separated into strands and floated gently into the fire. Just as the hair fizzled and sputtered, signalling the end of the yajna ceremony, the wind died, and a deathly silence descended.

BaLi spoke into that silence with a glum face. "I saw Lord AoYang, and he told me nothing. He is unhappy with my decision not to act on the errant soldiers."

The sound of something heavy dropping fast was their first warning. The sound increased to a mighty crescendo, and they couldn't hear themselves over it. Was it an avalanche? How could that be possible? There was no snow where they camped.

Anoman's horse neighed in fright, trying to seek the safety of the cave, but it collapsed with a loud, fearful neigh. The roar outside was so deafening that the ground shook, causing many to fall over. The cave entrance vanished! In the firelight, they saw a glittering white wall blocking their way out!

MiDai tossed wood chips into the fire. With the better light, they could see their plight; no explanation was needed. The cave was sealed shut by ice!

BaLi, the fearless commander of Qin, dropped to his knees and cried,

"My lord, what is this? Are we being punished for our crimes? You could have taken our lives, and we would have gladly died as warriors."

ZhuBajie reassured him, "Don't get upset with the gods, BaLi. Our men outside will dig and rescue us, so let us not despair." BaLi did not reply. He held his head down, knowing that the soldiers outside would happily abandon them.

The boxed-up cave filled with smoke, and their eyes began to smart. Some started coughing. They needed fresh air! In a flash, MiDai put out most of the burning firewood. He screamed for someone to climb up and punch a hole into the sealed-up cleft above.

Anoman clambered up the rock wall like a spider. The boy could find footholds where none existed as he hoisted himself through a narrow natural shaft until he reached close to the crevice opening. The snow blocking the hole was just an arm's length away, and he needed a stick to dislodge it.

NaiLa threw a spear that curved through the air and punched into the snow-filled opening next to Anoman. He shrieked, "Careful, that's too close!"

NaiLa said, "No time! Quick, you must work and open the hole before we all die from tainted air."

Anoman spread his legs below the opening, resting his back against the rock's wall. He poked and hacked at the snow, which barely moved. He shouted to those below, "This is not snow, but hard ice." The boy worked without pause, sweating profusely despite the cold. After hacking and clearing the ice bit by bit, he finally created an opening. Loud cheers greeted him as fresh, frigid air rushed in.

Looking at the pile of ice that fell into the cave, ZhuBajie said, "Can we call this a snowfall? It's just big chunks of ice. We are inside an avalanche that has come from nowhere."

Anoman descended from the narrow, high opening. In exhaustion, he uncharacteristically slipped and fell the last few feet onto the uneven cave floor, grazing the skin from his shins. His friends patted him appreciatively as he grinned weakly. "You were amazing, Anoman. Weren't you scared?"

Anoman rubbed his grazed shins and hooted at them, "Scared! Who? Me! In the company of Commander BaLi and legendary warriors like NaiLa and the Dai brothers? No way!"

BaLi looked at Anoman and realised the youngsters' blind confidence in them. He turned to his warriors watching him and said, "With such fine young men, we will make Qin great, like Tianzhu. I believe I finally understand Lord AoYang's cryptic message! He wants us to build an empire— a new one."

BaLi commanded, "Dig me out! The way out is the way we came in."

They were comfortable and snug in the warmth of the cave, and the warriors took turns digging and scraping into the ice, blocking the cave entrance. If food was available, they could wait for the ice to thaw.

NaiLa and AgDai dug hard at the cave entrance to remove the ice pileup. The avalanche of ice blocking their access was strange. It moved like large beads, and the more they dug through, the more ice pebbles rolled in.

Despite this difficulty, they worked long hours and reached Anoman's dead horse. The faint light from the open cleft above showed the skies brightening with dawn.

Hunger soon became a priority. They had not eaten anything since the meagre marmot soup the day before.

****

ShaWajing slashed into the dead horse, ignoring Anoman's wailing, as others joined in to help the veteran butcher the horse. The cold was so intense that the carcass, except for the liver, had already frozen. He passed the liver slices around, and the hungry warriors wolfed them down.

ShaWajing held up his bloodied hands to Anoman and said, "Boy, we are provided with food. At least we don't have to starve while digging ourselves out. Your horse died to save us from starvation. Honour that." But Anoman steadfastly refused to eat his horse.

ZhuBajie made a second fire for cooking, leaving the yajna fire smouldering, and said, "I hope our men see the smoke and rescue us."

The Dai brothers laughed, and MiDai said, "No way! They would have waited to exact revenge, but this strange cold is too much to endure. We are on our own."

NaiLa held up his fingers. "See, my fingers have turned blue. The ice pebbles are like hard stones, radiating cold. We must be prepared to wait a day or two for the cold to ease. Then we can dig a tunnel."

BaLi said, "No need to hurry!" His men were surprised, and BaLi clarified, "Look around! All the men here haven't looted Tianzhu; plenty of firewood, a heated cave, and meat sustain us. This is no coincidence."

After a heavy meal of roast horsemeat that Anoman steadfastly avoided, the men took turns digging into the icy wall without much success.

Two days passed, and they had little to show for their progress except fingers that had turned blue from the cold. The tired men slept early, except for ZhuBajie, responsible for tending the Yajna fire during the first watch. Anoman and his friends sat beside ZhuBajie and asked him, "Priest, how do we handle ice pebbles if more just keep rolling in?"

ZhuBajie pondered it for some time and said, "Well, NaiLa is the builder, and he will surely devise a plan. We must make an ice cocoon and scoop the pebbles from within." He looked at the eager eyes and said, "Pour hot water on them, start from either side, build to the roof and so on until we have a tunnel."

"Worth a try. I hope it doesn't collapse from the weight of pebbles from above," said Anoman

Zhu Bajie chuckled. "Yes, it's worth a try, especially since you are hungry and running out of nuts and dried meat strips that we have with us." He yawned. He woke Sha Wajing to tend to the yajna fire. The excited boys set to work while the senior warriors slept.

****

BaLi woke up with a start as someone shook him. "What?!" he exclaimed, rubbing the sleep from his eyes.

It was Anoman. "Commander, wake up, wake up! I want you to see this! We have made a tunnel out."

They waited until daylight and honoured ZhuBajie, asking him to be the first to crawl out into the open, waiting world. He excitedly squeezed through the short tunnel. Strangely, he did not go out entirely; he just paused at the entrance.

After much coaxing from BaLi, cajoling him to go out, ZhuBajie did the opposite. He withdrew into the cave, and his face showed shock. All they could make out from him was, "Gone, all gone."

BaLi grunted in disgust. "Of course, the rats would have sneaked away long ago."

ZhuBajie recovered and said, "Commander, the fire sacrifice saved us! We are not the ones condemned by the gods." Unable to understand what ZhuBajie was saying, the senior warriors crawled out one by one, and BaLi could hear their gasps of astonishment.

BaLi pushed aside eager men waiting to go outside, crawled through the tunnel, and emerged just below the rocky overhang. "Oh, my lord AoYang, what on earth is this?!" he said, with a hand over his heart.

The sky was clear, and waves lapped against the rocky sides of a lake beneath the tunnel. The broad valley had disappeared, and in its place was an unending lake of clear blue water, with blocks of ice floating everywhere.

The silence felt threatening compared to the chaos of man and beast they had experienced until a few days earlier. BaLi wouldn't have believed they were in the same place, but for the familiar mountain peaks, now covered in brilliant white.

NaiLa came and sat beside him, and BaLi asked the question that had been racking his mind since he had come out. "Do you think any of our people made it?"

"Look carefully into the depths, Commander. You can see them stuck below." BaLi peered into the water and sat back, horrified. NaiLa continued, "They are all dead. Soldiers, slaves, and beasts. Ice pebbles from the sky would have immobilised them. What we see is the melted waters above them."

BaLi exclaimed, "What a horrific death. Pounded by ice and sealed in a watery grave."

****

AgDai raised the alarm! A line of mounted men looked down at the lake from a distant ridge. One of the mounted men was gesturing animatedly at them.

BaLi groaned aloud, "What now, friend or foe?" The warriors scrambled to pick up their weapons, except for ZhuBajie.

ZhuBajie calmly told the warriors, "Friend! They are friends. Don't panic."

BaLi entreated ZhuBajie, "How in God's name can you tell they are friends?" Instead of giving reasons, Zhu pointed at the horizon.

A thoroughly mollified BaLi rubbed his eyes in disbelief. "Curses, Zhu, you are right, as usual. We are saved."

A giant eagle was lazily flying towards them.

Vinaasha Kale, Vipareetha Buddhi - *Sanskrit* -
"When your destruction is imminent, intellect forsakes you."

PART #1

ZHENGJUN

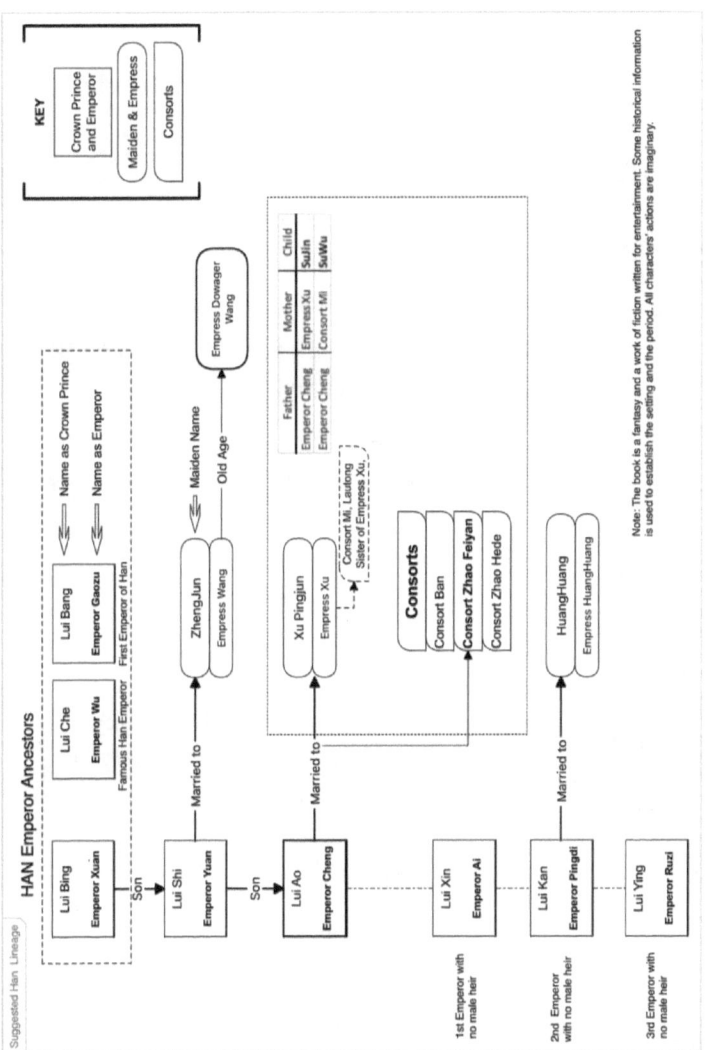

Important note to the reader: As soon as a Prince becomes an emperor, he takes on a new name—for example, Crown Prince LuiShi → Emperor Xuan, Crown Prince LuiAo → Emperor Cheng.

Generic Descriptions

Han	Ancient China ruled by the Han dynasty from LuiBang the first emperor.
HanKaoTzu	Imperial School for training bureaucrats, since the first Emperor
Chophouse	A house for peasants to buy/barter food or rent a mattress to sleep
Jiubang	A tavern that serves wine
TaoYin	WoShi (grandmaster of HanKaoTzu school) "modified" fighting style
Laotong	"Soul" Sisters officially bonded for life
Mandarins	Senior bureaucrats of the Empire, managing palace and affairs of state
Yima	Mother's sister or aunt
LuiBang	The founder of Han dynasty and first Emperor
Zhang Liang	The brilliant strategist of Lui Bang, set up HanKaoTzu School
Emperor Xuan	Father of Lui Shi and 10th Han emperor, since LuiBang
Empress Xia	Consort of Xuan
LuiShi	Son of Emperor Xuan
Sima	Dead consort of Crown Prince LuiShi
ZhengJun	Princess and Consort of Crown Prince LuiShi
Emperor Yuan	Same as Crown Prince LuiShi after he was crowned Emperor
Empress Wang	Same as ZhengJun, Consort of Xuan, later Empress Dowager Wang
ZhangHe	Powerful and experienced eunuch, supporting Empress Xia

LuiAo	Son of LuiShi and ZhengJun, Crown Prince
Fu	Consort of Emperor Yuan, mother of LuiKang
LuiKang	Son of LuiShi from Consort Fu
ShiDan	A trusted confident of the Emperor Yuan, to mould Prince LuiAo
Chunyu	Cousin and best friend of Crown Prince LuiAo
Yu	Bright officer working with Crown Prince Ao
XuPing Jia	Marquis of Pingen, friend of Emperor Yuan and Father of Xu PingJun
XuPing Jun	Consort of Crown Prince Ao, daughter of the Marquis of Pingen, later Empress XuPing
Mi	Beautiful laotong sister of XuPing Jun, XuMi
Ban	Consort of LuiAo, an intelligent and widely read girl
Emperor Cheng	Same as Crown Prince LuiAo becomes Emperor Cheng
WangMang	Nephew of Empress Wang and later commander of armed forces
Fang	Midwife and Witch, descendant of Zhang Liang the strategist
Feiyan	Consort of Cheng, sister of Hede
Hede	Consort of Cheng, sister of Feiyan
ShiXi	Palace eunuch helping Feiyan and Hede
WoShi	The powerful grandmaster of the HanKaoTzu school
JiaShao	The chief of dwarfs and security for the HanKaoTzu school
CaoShen	JiaShao's dwarf assistant and second in command of the dwarfs
WangGen	Supreme commander of the armed forces for Emperor Cheng
LiPing	Chief of palace bodyguards

LuiXin	Son of LuiKang, succeeding Emperor
Emperor Ai	Same as LuiXin, become Emperor Ai
LuiXing	Younger brother of Emp Cheng/LuiAo
CaoTeng	Eunuch, handle palace administration for Empress Wang, after Shi Dan
Yang Xiong	Scholar at HanKaoTzu, Scholar, Breaking Codes
Huan Tan	Scholar at HanKaoTzu, Ancient languages & philosophy
Lui Xiu	Scholar at HanKaoTzu, Geography, Astronomy, Land Sciences
SuJin	**Green Warrior**, leader of golden glow, the son of Emperor Cheng and XuPing, rightful blood born Crown Prince of Han.
SuWu	**Strategist** to golden glow, Mi's son with Emperor Cheng, elder, stepbrother of SuJin
Qian	**Black Death**, trained by the forbidden troops, scholar and knife expert, youngest sworn brother of SuJin
ChenHe	**Brick**, Muscular friend of SuJin, wrestler and Pit fighter, sworn brother of SuJin
SuFei	Grandmaster of the monastery in the mountains
HuKui	Successor to SuFei, militant scholar
Golden Glow	Represents sworn brotherhood of SuJin, SuWu, Qian and ChenHe, continuing from the time of the first emperor.

#3 ZhengJun Becomes Empress

Crown Prince LuiShi was troubled by his father, Emperor Xuan. He was grieving the death of his beloved Consort Sima, but his father was firm that he should take more wives to ensure the family lineage. The imperial court highlighted that procreation was his primary responsibility as a Crown Prince. After he protested vehemently in court, the Emperor relegated the task of finding him a suitable wife to Empress Xia.

His stepmother, ably supported by the seasoned eunuch ZhangHe, compiled and reviewed all eligible girls in the empire. With assistance from her favourite palace astrologer and bureaucrats, she meticulously scrutinised the family histories of all the girls in contention and the time of their conceptions from the official records. After all, the future Empress of the Han should not only be chaste and beautiful but also appropriate to NuWa, the goddess of "marriage arrangements."

Like everything else in the palace, selecting a new Princess proceeded along well-oiled lines. The palace Mandarins adhered to proper procedures for finding him a suitable bride by eliminating any girls whose horoscopes failed to complement those of a Han Prince. The extensive list was quickly whittled down to a few for Empress Xia. The selection process intensified, examining each girl to the most minor details. The Empress informed the Emperor and young LuiShi that the final choice was almost at hand.

Therefore, LuiShi did not acknowledge his chief bodyguard when he declared that the Empress had chosen fourteen-year-old ZhengJun as his consort. This feat was unparalleled in Han's history because her selection had included girls from nearly every noble family, encompassing hundreds of candidates.

"So soon?" LuiShi said, and his loyal bodyguard rolled his eyes in mock exasperation. He looked outside, where the bleak weather matched his mood. Thick black clouds were bunching together, and it would surely snow. He sighed heavily, dropping his shoulders in acceptance of his fate. He had to sire a male child for the sake of the empire, and then he could return to his grieving.

****

Empress Xia was not apprehensive about ZhengJun. Her efficient eunuch, ZhangHe, rated her highly for being a demure, obedient, and intelligent girl. The best part of his spy's report was that she was religious and a staunch Confucian. Many in her family were palace bureaucrats trained at the prestigious HanKaoTzu School, established by Zhang Liang, the brilliant strategist of the first Emperor.

ZhengJun looked around with wide eyes. Empress Xia glanced at her and told her assistant, "She is completely out of place. Paint her face and change her gown."

ZhengJun's parents conceived her when the star of Kuan Ti, the God of War, shone brightest in the night sky with the crescent moon. An excited astrologer verified the authenticity certificate accompanied by the constellation drawing from the imperial records, confirming everything was in order.

ZhangHe, the overzealous bureaucrat, had gone one step further and checked on the antecedents of the officer who had recorded the document and found him sincere. ZhengJun's parents hired him to witness the conception in their sleeping quarters. Although her parents had hoped for a male child, to their disappointment, they had a girl. The celestial alignment of ZhengJun's conception was the most auspicious for an Empress of Han, and no Princess in the past was born with such astrologically robust credentials. If the astrologer's predictions were to come true, one of her progenies would become a demigod warrior.

The symbol formed in the skies at her conception, with the crescent moon, resembled that of a staff with three sharp prongs, the trident of a mighty God. By a quirk of fate, a smudged symbol of the constellation appeared as a prominent birthmark on ZhengJun's arm. Empress Xia abhorred war. She hoped that LuiShi's son would be an avatar of the peaceful and serene golden god, Buddha of the West, fervently worshipped by Emperor Wu during his reign. Sea-faring merchants had brought news of many temples and priests of the golden god worshipped in the kingdoms of the southwest bordering Han.

With such potent portents favouring ZhengJun, the court selection for the Princess was a sham. However, ZhangHe ensured that all palace rituals and ceremonies were followed. No one should doubt her authenticity, especially when she became the mother to a mighty emperor. The lingering worry for ZhangHe was the young Prince, LuiShi. He seemed disinterested in life after his Consort Sima had passed on to greener pastures. Would he accept ZhengJun?

As ZhengJun prepared for the confirmation ceremony, ZhangHe informed the Empress that the court physician had rigorously examined all potential brides. The examinations included checks for virginity, dental health, skin condition, hair quality, and menstrual regularity for fertility. Unprompted, ZhangHe noted the strict scrutiny ZhengJun had undergone. Unlike several other candidates who had failed and were discreetly dismissed, ZhengJun emerged without any blemish.

A eunuch announced the arrival of the new Princess. The Empress smiled to herself. She was tired from all the excitement of the past few weeks, but she prided herself on finding a bride for the Crown Prince. Her husband would be proud of her choice: ZhengJun.

She waved her hand impatiently to begin the last ritual to confirm ZhengJun as the chosen bride. The shoe fitment ritual started with much fanfare and music. The smaller the feet, the better the catch for a Prince. The size of the feet was always the talk of the city in every marriage! Tiny feet were considered an essential aspect of beauty in Han, and most women had the bones in their feet broken and bound into clubs to fit small shoes.

Since childhood, ZhengJun had naturally tiny feet, but her mother took no chances. She always tightly wrapped her feet in strips of linen to prevent them from growing. Thankfully, she had not outgrown her last shoe.

ZhengJun trembled as a cloth was placed as a partition over her feet, hidden from everyone. The maids removed her cowhide sandals and untied her bound feet, hidden under the cloth. She stopped in surprise when the strips wrapping her feet were longer than usual. Confused, she felt ZhengJun's feet with her hands and found them not deformed or broken but naturally tiny.

The maid looked up at ZhangHe, surprise written on her face, and he groaned in dismay. Somehow, he had come to believe that the child's feet weren't an issue, but now they seemed oversized. He regretted overlooking such a crucial detail; not everything could be perfect for the Princess, who had been chosen by destiny.

The maid massaged ZhengJun's feet with warm oil while she relaxed, gently pressing them on pressure points. The heat from the oil eased her stiff muscles, and she giggled, much to the amusement of the women watching her, curious to know the size of her feet.

The junior eunuch overseeing the massaging bowed to her and said, "Princess, this oil is tilled from mustard and sesame seeds collected by the nomads in the steppes. Palace maids perfume the oil with the essence of jasmine flowers." ZhengJun smiled happily.

Her foot was wiped dry and dipped into warm goat's milk to soften it for the shoe-fitting ceremony. ZhengJun watched in delight as maids danced and brought in colourful shoes while flutes and string instruments played. The court ladies laughed as shoes were taken around before they were placed before ZhengJun. Among them, a pair of tiny golden shoes, known as the golden lotus, was held stiffly on a platter by a young palace attendant. The shoes belonged to a goddess and were kept at the temple.

ZhangHe looked towards the Empress for permission to unveil the future Princess's feet one last time for the ceremony before they would be hidden forever from the public eye. She nodded, and the room's chatter quietened. He sat down at ZhengJun's feet as the maid pulled away the cloth with a flourish.

The women and eunuchs craned their heads to look at her feet. ZhangHe could not bring himself to look at ZhengJun's feet and, with trepidation, he looked at the Empress. There was a collective gasp amongst the gathered ladies, and ZhangHe wilted when he saw the surprise in the Empress's eyes. Unable to handle the ridicule he would face from his peers, he bowed in shame and glanced at ZhengJun's feet. Although sitting comfortably, he recoiled and fell, landing awkwardly on his back.

The feet before him were not large! ZhengJun's feet were small, dainty, and pink! Startled, he croaked at ZhengJun almost accusingly, "Why are they so small?!" The assemblage burst out laughing.

After showing her feet to the women gathered, ZhangHe wrapped them in fresh silk strips for the shoe ceremony while he kept shaking his head in disbelief. Sitting on her raised couch, Empress Xia smiled as she watched the proceedings. She was caught up in the disquiet of ZhengJun, emerging as the most beautiful woman in Han on the merit of her feet.

Unable to handle her joy, the Empress closed her eyes and recited her favourite romantic poem, swaying in delight. The Empress opened her eyes when the onlookers gasped loudly. ZhengJun's foot had slid into the smallest embroidered shoe. Not a whisper escaped the gathering as all of them, including ZhangHe, looked towards the Empress for permission to try on the golden lotus.

The situation was extraordinary! No one had ever heard the golden lotus shoe fitting any Princess before, and the anticipation grew as the audience began to prattle animatedly. The Empress had expected the ceremony to end with one of the smaller shoes, but now it seemed ZhengJun might fit the golden shoe! The tension was palpable, and the musicians hesitated, unsure whether to continue playing or stop. Sensing the moment's gravity, they paused, reading the mood to avoid misstep.

Legend has it that the exquisitely made slippers, woven with gold threads and precious stones, belonged to Hengo, the goddess of the moon. The golden shoes were brought from the moon temple for the shoe ceremony, but this was the first time anyone tried them.

The young attendant bowed low to Empress Xia and ZhengJun and extended the tray towards ZhangHe. He lifted the shoes off the tray and, after touching the footwear to his eyes in religious fervour, held ZhengJun's feet and tried to slip one on, but it did not fit. The audience groaned, and the Empress exhaled slowly, disappointed. She was about to end the ceremony when ZhangHe began removing the silk bands he had wrapped just a while back. The onlookers gasped! ZhangHe discerned the golden shoes would fit once the silken bands that padded her feet were removed.

Young ZhengJun pulled her leg away from ZhangHe. "No, I will not wear the golden lotus." She shuddered, "It belongs to the goddess Hengo." She ran towards Empress Xia and kowtowed before her. "Please, I beg you, Empress, let me remain in ordinary shoes."

ZhangHe reminded the Empress, "Highness, the shoe must be tried on. Although it is a first, tradition cannot be broken." ZhangHe attempted to hold young Zheng Jun, but as she pushed him away, her hand became stuck to the strings of colourful glass beads that adorned her neck, breaking them. The beads hit the wooden floor and bounced everywhere, filling the audience chamber with the sound of hard hailstones falling on the stone pavement. Zheng Jun had ruined her painted face and dishevelled her hair.

Empress Xia narrowed her eyes a fraction, disapproving of the mess before her. That was enough. ZhangHe pushed ZhengJun down and hissed at her, "Don't show your tantrums before the Empress."

The Empress cleared her throat. "ZhengJun, let me help you wear the golden lotus since you feel my palace attendants are beneath your position." When they heard the Empress, the palace attendants holding ZhengJun released her and respectfully withdrew.

The Empress told ZhengJun sternly, "Han tradition cannot be ignored in any situation. May this be your first lesson." The Empress stood up. The fight had left ZhengJun, and she collapsed on the floor. The ladies gasped at this breach of protocol. It was unheard of for an Empress to perform such a lowly task on a daughter-in-law.

The Empress got off the couch, smoothed some imaginary crease on her dress, and, as if on cue, all the ladies, including the assembled bureaucrats and attendants, fell to their knees. It was an acknowledgement of the great honour to be bestowed upon an ordinary girl, already famous in the eyes of many!

ZhangHe extended the shoes to the Empress, lowering his forehead to the floor. She lifted the golden shoe from his hands and quickly slipped on the first shoe. Thoroughly chastised, ZhengJun lifted her other leg so the Empress could slide in the other shoe, hoping to reduce the embarrassment.

The Empress returned to her couch and sat, mechanically adjusting her hanfu, while maids repaired ZhengJun's face and hair. The golden shoe fitting ZhengJun's feet was unorthodox but ample proof of the heavens' mandate on ZhengJun as a Princess and a future Empress. The texts of the HanKaoTzu school library foretold a tumultuous time for the Han empire in the coming years. It all began when a Princess walked in the shoes of Hengo, the goddess of the moon. It would take a Prince born from ZhengJun's progeny to save Han by sacrificing his throne.

Empress Xia asked ZhengJun to walk around the room wearing the exquisite gold-embroidered shoes. She was impressed by what she saw! ZhengJun bent her knees slightly and swayed with small steps to maintain a lady's proper balance and poise. The Empress clapped her hands in delight, sure that her choice would entice LuiShi, the Crown Prince. After all, what more does a man want than a woman with tiny feet? Undoubtedly, the Prince would be happy with his wife, or the gods would ensure he was.

Empress Xia, in her uncontrolled happiness at the possibilities ahead, jumped up, clasping her fingers, and declared, "I want ZhengJun to be known henceforth as Princess Wang, my name. Let her womb bleed, and her birth cries bring forth a powerful Prince for Han." She looked around as the ladies-in-waiting roared their approval and smiled as the court scribe scribbled down what she had said onto a scroll. The day was historic, and she was sure that she had played her part in full to the demands of the gods.

ZhengJun was awed by the sheer variety of drinks served in her honour and realised that the palace kitchen was working ahead of unfolding events. Food was an integral part of imperial life. She watched as the ladies-in-waiting sampled the six clears: water, sour wine, sweet wine, mellow wine, Yi wine, and Ye wine.

The extraordinary events of the day and the copious wine consumed loosened the women's tongues, and they laughed and engaged in animated talks. As soon as the excited but tired Empress left the room, they dramatised role plays of the shoe ceremony, much to the chagrin of an embarrassed ZhengJun.

After resting in her inner chamber, Empress Xia summoned the new Princess, made her sit next to her, and held her hand. ZhengJun, slightly drunk, curled her feet luxuriously into the thick bear rug.

"Do you know why you were chosen?" the Empress asked her.

"My celestial mistress, I am to become a good wife to the Crown Prince and give him an heir that Han will be proud of," ZhengJun replied earnestly.

The Empress laughed and leaned forward to kiss ZhengJun's painted forehead. "Yes, yes, dear, that and others as well. First, you should learn how to survive court politics. You are destined to be a powerful Empress and must differ from a simple concubine. An Empress must understand what is happening in the empire and beyond and be involved in court politics. You must provide the Emperor with unbiased and perhaps distinct perspective to his courtiers so that he can rule effectively."

"Now, before you manage the Prince's bedchamber, I want you to look beautiful, and I want him to be pleased with my choice. We need to train you in all matters that a man wants, starting from the bedchamber and, in your case, everything beyond the borders of Han."

"To leave your mark as the future Empress, you should be well-informed and surrounded by trustworthy people. The welfare of the Emperor and the empire takes precedence! Become ruthless. Eliminate anyone who goes against you or the empire once you become the Empress. Situations change quickly. You won't have time for a second chance."

She looked at a shocked Zheng Jun and said, "Never regret past decisions! The Emperor doesn't make mistakes."

****

Crown Prince LuiShi married ZhengJun a day after the spring festival concluded. The marriage was not as grand as his first marriage to consort Sima, and the list of invitees was reduced to just a few hundred. However, the wedding was remembered for its excellent food and arrangements because the bureaucracy had gone all out to please the bride chosen by Hengo, the goddess of the moon.

For a week, the Emperor paid for food and wine in all the taverns and temples in the capital city, effectively extending the spring festival. ZhangHe sourced sword dancers, fire-eaters, acrobats, and musicians to perform in the streets to entertain the commoners. Despite its simplicity, everyone enjoyed the wedding, and a pleased Emperor hailed it as a bond between the Han and the imperial bureaucracy.

Crown Prince LuiShi handed ZhengJun to the Empress to train her in palace etiquette. They both agreed it would take at least a year, which was acceptable to LuiShi.

ZhengJun stayed with Empress Xia in her palace and was trained in domestic administration by palace Mandarins. The eunuchs and cooks trained her to care for her husband's every comfort. ZhengJun took her training seriously, and unlike earlier Princesses, she discreetly spoke to LuiShi's favourite cooks and servants to learn about his likes and dislikes. She found out that LuiShi was a stickler for order and cleanliness.

Not satisfied with the army of servants who attended to LuiShi, ZhengJun selected and trained a new set of servants and cooks. She gave them a distinguishing blue uniform with a gold-embroidered imperial insignia.

The Empress, pleased with her prodigy, officially sent her to LuiShi's palace six months before the year they had agreed upon for training. She was formally sent in a procession of drums and flutes in a palanquin, followed by her servants and personal guards in uniform, who became the talk of the nobles.

LuiShi initially did not acknowledge ZhengJun's presence but grudgingly approved of her efficiency and the unobtrusive care she took to make him comfortable.

The food she served him was exotic and delicious. She used unique recipes, including quail hatchlings dipped in garlic sauce, horse rib chops greased with pork fat, and dog sausages in blood dumplings. LuiShi's favourite was steamed fish and goat soup, which was light yet filling during winter evenings.

Palace mandarins and army officers frequented LuiShi's palace and were served the same grand food as the Crown Prince. In time, she began receiving inside information on palace politics, which she conveyed to a surprised LuiShi.

A year later, ZhengJun had a son, and an ecstatic Emperor named his grandson LuiAo. Within a few years, LuiAo became Emperor Xuan's favourite.

Emperor Xuan was proud of his grandson because he was intelligent, well-mannered, and obedient—a rarity among the palace brats. In fact, by the age of six, LuiAo accompanied the Emperor to all important meetings, and he always made significant decisions with LuiAo on his lap. Unsurprisingly, Emperor Xuan named LuiAo the next Crown Prince after LuiShi, his son, became emperor.

Emperor Xuan regularly visited his grandson LuiAo's sleeping abode and later feasted on the exotic preparations made by ZhengJun. It was the happiest time of his life, relishing exotic food and relaxing with his grandson.

The Emperor's reluctance to visit his consorts in the evenings caused them much heartburn and embarrassment, so they treated him to a culinary extravaganza unheard of in the empire. The best chefs in the country prepared exotic dishes and invited all the palace dignitaries for a grand feast. Unfortunately, Emperor Xuan ate a purple mushroom, suffered severe food poisoning, and died in excruciating pain.

Soon after, Dowager Empress Xia paved the way for Crown Prince LuiShi to ascend as Emperor Yuan. Zheng Jun took the name of Empress Wang in a pompous ceremony that had the capital celebrating a complete moon cycle.

#4 Prince Ao Marries XuPing

Crown Prince LuiShi officially changed his name to Emperor Yuan, as required by imperial mandates, and he took many consorts and concubines to strengthen military alliances. A sparse royal harem would reflect poorly in the eyes of ordinary citizens and visiting dignitaries.

Emperor Yuan frequently visited Consort Fu because he favoured her son, Prince LuiKang. Kang excelled in warfare, was an exceptional horse rider, and was passionate about the fine arts, especially music.

At the same time, ZhengJun was concerned because Prince LuiAo had turned into an impudent brat. She nominated ShiDan, a senior eunuch and confidant of the emperor, to mould Prince LuiAo into a worthy Han Prince. As the head of households, ShiDan was granted sweeping powers to restrain the Prince.

Emperor Yuan was convinced that if his wayward firstborn, LuiAo, were to succeed him, it would lead to the downfall of the Han Empire. He decided to wait for the right opportunity to make LuiKang the Crown Prince.

LuiAo patronised brutal fights staged for him in the fighting pits of Changan, where condemned men fought to the death. He exclusively acquired girls and exotic dancers from neighbouring kingdoms and sold them to the nobility and gambling houses, earning more money than most traders in the city.

Despite his powers, LuiAo remained wary of ShiDan, his formidable imperial protector and bureaucrat. The eunuch had several times confined him to his chambers and dispatched his unruly friends to the imperial army. He avoided using the royal bodyguards to carry out his nefarious activities lest word of them reach the Empress, his mother, through ShiDan. However, spies kept ShiDan updated on his activities.

Matters escalated when Prince LuiAo's cousin died after falling from his horse during training. To show respect for the Han Prince and the Lui clan, the Emperor imposed statewide mourning for an entire moon cycle and tasked Prince Kang with overseeing the mourning within the palace.

No one was allowed outside the palace without specific instructions from Prince Kang. Crown Prince LuiAo grew bored with the lamentations and prayers when his cousin and friend Chunyu entered, telling him that two celestial beauties were visiting the Empress. He speculated they were making a courtesy call after visiting the deceased Prince's residence.

LuiAo's face brightened with delight. There seemed to be potential for entertainment while he was stuck inside the palace walls. He quickly gathered his friends and rushed to the Empress's palace, where he saw two beautiful girls and an older woman leaving his mother's palace with bodyguards following them.

One of his friends remarked, "Chunyu is right for once. They are indeed heavenly beauties. Look at their long hair and the alabaster colour of their skin. Alas, they are consort class and not concubine. Let us go back. Our Crown Prince cannot have all of them," he lamented in jest. His friends laughed, but LuiAo took it as a taunt.

The Crown Prince gritted his teeth and replied, "I will decide who becomes a consort, concubine, or mistress."

The boys quietly fell in line behind the girls and listened to them talk animatedly about the luxurious palace, the beauty of the Empress, and the other ladies-in-waiting. The girls were stunning beauties who displayed the sophisticated mannerisms of the nobility. One of the girls' mothers chaperoned the two maidens.

Their nervous bodyguards had already identified the Crown Prince stalking them and deliberately slowed their pace to increase the distance between the girls and the Prince.

Crown Prince LuiAo, being a natural bully, ran ahead and waylaid them. The guards instinctively blocked his path, but when the Crown Prince glared at them, they bowed low and reluctantly stood down. The terrified girls hid behind their mother, who shielded them and pleaded with the Prince to leave them alone.

The Prince demanded that the girls be courted in the palace gardens. To his surprise, the mother refused and told him she would seek help from the Empress if he continued to trouble them.

Prince LuiAo avoided taking liberties within the palace walls, but spurred on by the prospect of ridicule from his friends, he yanked one girl's hand and pulled her forward. The terrified mother shrieked.

The other girl rushed in, hissing like a cat. She tugged at her friend's hand and kicked the Prince in the shins. The commotion brought the guards running, and frantic horns signalled a situation involving royalty to the barracks.

Chunyu realised things had gone too far and forcibly released the girl's hand from Prince LuiAo. The Crown Prince turned on him in unrestrained fury. Chunyu pleaded, "Prince, they are your mother's guests, for heaven's sake. Let's get away from here before it is too late. There are too many witnesses." It was the appropriate action, but Prince LuiAo hesitated.

Sensing his plea to Prince LuiAo had worked, Chunyu turned toward the girl who had kicked the Prince and smiled. She smiled back at him sweetly and bowed her head in gratitude. This nonverbal exchange did not escape the Prince's notice. Blinded by rage and unaware that Chunyu was sincere, he hit him. The girls screamed in unison as the quickly converging imperial soldiers seized Chunyu and dragged him down to the ground by his long-pleated hair.

ShiDan and LuiKang arrived and commanded the guards to stand down. The mother and the girls moved behind ShiDan, who quickly inferred the situation. ShiDan scolded the Prince, "When will you learn, Crown Prince? Why have you brought your antics within the palace walls when a state of mourning is in force? You are troubling a royal guest—family members of the Marquis of Pingen! Your father's dear friend."

In an effort at bravado, LuiAo replied, "ShiDan, I was just inquiring about their well-being. Am I making any indecent approaches? I want to discuss state matters and discover what happens in Pingen. Isn't this true?" He turned towards his friends, who bobbed their heads in agreement. A dumbfounded LuiKang looked at the boys helplessly. No one would foolishly venture to speak out against the rogue Crown Prince.

A sceptical ShiDan sighed and watched one of the girls rubbing her reddened wrist while looking at LuiAo with loathing.

LuiKang glared at the LuiAo's friends and said, "Elder brother, I understand you have approached the daughter of the Marquis of Pingen with the good intention of seeking their opinion on imperial governance there. I will convey happy tidings to the Emperor that you have at last taken an interest in the well-being of the people."

LuiKang added sarcastically, "Though it had to start with frightening little girls." The boys smiled at the deliberate quip against the Crown Prince. Prince LuiAo was livid with rage but could not go against his younger brother, who was in charge of the palace during the mourning period.

Before he could retort, Prince Kang said, "Now, let me ensure that the girls and the lady reach home safely." He smiled without humour and added, "Safe!" Prince Kang gallantly approached the relieved girls and their mother and led them away.

ShiDan worried that the hot-tempered LuiAo might retaliate against

Prince Kang for insulting him. He warned him, saying, "Prince Kang is the Emperor's favourite! Do not trouble him over your loss of face without dire consequences. I will make amends."

ShiDan confirmed the capture of numerous girls as slaves during a recent conquest and stated, "Now leave!"

ShiDan organised an exotic dance party for the Prince that evening. Unfortunately, the mayhem they caused disturbed many in the palace who were still mourning. The Emperor was quietly informed of the breach of his decree by his favourite son, LuiKang.

Emperor Yuan became furious when he learned that Crown Prince LuiAo indulged in drinking and revelry despite his decree for official mourning, and he decided to act.

The Emperor reprimanded Empress Wang for her blind affection for her son, overlooking his reckless behaviour. In conclusion, he stated, "ZhengJun, I will not forgive a slur on my friend's family. If LuiAo does not atone for the crime to the satisfaction of the Marquis of Pingen, I shall demote him to a mere Prince and send him away."

Anxious, the Empress summoned ShiDan and Prince LuiAo. ShiDan noticed with satisfaction that Prince LuiAo was not his usual smug self; he appeared subdued and very receptive as his mother explained the consequences of not publicly apologising to the women of Pingen.

Seizing the opportunity, ShiDan admonished the Prince, labelling him a womaniser and a lout. He cautioned that a demotion from Crown Prince would alienate all those loyal to him, and his mother would lose her position of power as the first Empress. LuiKang would rise in the eyes of the people and bureaucracy as Crown Prince, and Consort Fu would become the first Empress.

ShiDan predicted a grim future for the troubled Prince. "Fearing revolt or subterfuge from you, Consort Fu would surely send you away from Changan, and you would be assassinated." LuiAo looked up in shock, but it was clear that he believed his mentor.

Empress Wang said glumly, "I loathe my son bowing his head to a lowly marquis, yet we have no choice. LuiAo must apologise to the Marquis of Pingen and his women, swallowing his pride." The Empress added, "My son's gesture towards the Marquis of Pingen should be such that the Emperor has no option but to overturn his decision."

LuiAo's face lit up with a smile. "What if I obey my father and am not personally insulted by a public apology?" Although ShiDan was cynical about Prince LuiAo's solution, he waited for him to continue.

"Allow me to marry Xu PingJun, the daughter of Xu Ping Jia, Marquess of Pingen and brother of Emperor Xuan's first wife, consort Sima."

Empress Wang was left speechless, covering her gaping mouth with her hand, while a surprised ShiDan smiled and nodded. "Of course, it will solve everyone's problem if you marry the girl from the family you have wronged," he said.

****

Although XuPing initially resisted the union by threatening her mother with suicide, she ultimately capitulated to marry the man she loathed with all her heart. She sacrificed her happiness to honour her father and enhance her family's standing in the imperial court. A delighted Marquis, Xu Ping Jia, formally conveyed their acceptance to the royal palace. Her sole request was for her laotong sister XuMi to accompany her to the palace.

Price LuiAo monitored the progress toward the wedding, which could bring him closer to his father. He was determined not to displease his father ever again and lose his position to his younger brother. Palace Mandarins began the matrimonial process by routinely asking the royal astrologer to compare the conception time for a divine marriage settlement.

Prince LuiAo entrusted one of his clever officers, Yu, to manage the palace astrologer. It was not uncommon for marriages to be abandoned due to a mismatch in the astrological constellations, sometimes influenced by corrupt bureaucrats. His instructions to Yu were clear: bribe or threaten the astrologer, secure celestial approval for the marriage, and thwart any attempts by Prince Kang or Consort Fu to stop the alliance.

It was common knowledge that once the dice were cast in front of witnesses from both families and the astrologer expressed any disagreement, the marriage was as good as abandoned. Nobody would risk the life of the Crown Prince for a mere girl. Officer Yu asked the astrologer to throw the dice a day earlier by invoking the gods so that the outcome could be manipulated. He subtly conveyed his intent to influence the result in exchange for monetary benefits.

The astrologer anticipated that Prince LuiAo or Prince Kang would approach him. Now, with Prince LuiAo reaching out, the outcome had to be manipulated for the marriage to happen. He had faith in his trade and skill; however, politics often overruled when it came to royal births and marriages. He wouldn't have reached the position of chief palace astrologer if he had not respected political overtures.

The astrologer asked Officer Yu to return that evening while he made final preparations for divination. Officer Yu agreed, saying, "Oh, you work too hard. I will bring refreshments from Empress Wang's kitchen."

The astrologer bowed and replied, "That would be a treat! And don't forget that exceptional food cannot be described without wine." They laughed together, clearly understanding each other's intentions. It was a foregone conclusion that some considerations would be paid along with food and wine.

As soon as Officer Yu left, the astrologer's assistant asked, "What is the purpose of this meeting, teacher, if you will only speak what they want to hear?"

The astrologer looked at him and said, "Patience, you will learn! However, you are right that nobody is above destiny! Good or bad, as astrologers, we will inform them of what the future holds."

He added thoughtfully, "There is no need to predict the outcome for the unblemished flower of Pingen. She will bloom for a day or two before being crushed under the feet of the wicked Crown Prince."

The assistant's eyes widened in shock, and the astrologer said, "Ensure that the dice are polished and shining for tomorrow. Get it blessed by the priest and bring back incense from the temple."

****

Officer Yu arrived just as the sun ducked below the horizon. He reminded the astrologer, "Tomorrow, there's no need to invoke the goddess NuWa. Go through the suitable gestures in the presence of both the families and the mandarins, and tell them that the marriage will be auspicious for the Crown Prince."

The astrologer scoffed at Officer Yu. "You think I don't know it's forbidden to invoke Nuwa, the goddess of marriage, twice? Invoking her twice will have serious repercussions for me!"

Officer Yu shrugged his shoulders and said, "Just reminding you."

The astrologer was pleased with Prince LuiAo's generous gifts, which included silk, gold, and grain, and promised Officer Yu auspicious tidings the next day. After discussing palace gossip and downing a few bowls of rice wine, they began the divination process.

The astrologer spread his board and arranged seashells on markers that indicated the conception constellation for the prospective bride and groom. He rummaged through his belongings, searching for his regular dice kit. He paused in frustration; his assistant had taken his ivory four-sided dice for polishing and to the temple of Nuwa to be blessed for tomorrow's ceremony.

Despite his drink-addled mind, the astrologer recalled his teacher advising him not to stop divination once a marker was placed on the board. He remembered that he possessed a set of dice given to him by a woman at the market. It was a strange gift for an astrologer, but he accepted it because of its excellent craftsmanship.

Unlike the regular rectangular four-sided dice with square ends, this dice had tapered ends, enabling it to spin like a top. With the outcome already decided, it did not matter which dice he used.

Throwing caution to the wind, the astrologer took the dice from a leather pouch that resembled a human scrotum. He looked at the leather and, for a moment, imagined that what he held was human skin but dismissed it as the effect of the drink he had consumed. The dice were shaped to look like male and female figurines.

Despite an intense feeling of foreboding that enveloped him as he held the strange dice in hand, the drink in his belly and the shiny gold coins that were gifted outweighed his morbid thoughts. He did not wait for his assistant to return.

After invoking Nuwa in his mind, he cast the dice, and it tumbled limply onto the board. He did not throw it properly! The astrologer moved the seashells, revealing a grim future for the union. Typically, he had to provide numerous explanations about the outcome, but what lay before him was too clear. Every single variable was in place for a definite prediction. Death was inevitable!

A heavy feeling settled in his gut. Forbidden to throw the dice twice, he paused in confusion. How could a divination have no room for ambiguity?

What would he tell Prince LuiAo? This was one marriage he shouldn't proceed with. He retrieved the dice and examined them, wishing to throw them again to change the depressing destiny awaiting the unfortunate couple. The goddess of marriage would be upset if the dice were thrown twice, as it would be equivalent to calling Dizang personally, the God of death and ruler of all ten hells.

He looked at Officer Yu, patiently waiting for him to make his prediction. Thinking of Dizang, he flung his hands out in frustration. The dice slipped from his hand, and he watched in mounting horror as they bounced on the board and started to spin.

Officer Yu scrambled to his feet with a cry of surprise as the two dice spun eerily around each other. It seemed an invisible force made them spin. After what felt like an eternity, the two spinning dice broke apart in opposite directions and came to rest.

At first, the astrologer doubted that he imagined the dice spinning, but that hope was immediately extinguished. Yu exclaimed appreciatively, "I haven't seen anything like this before."

The astrologer went through the motions, repositioning the shells according to the second dice throw. Although the counts differed, he was horrified when the seashells took the same positions as before!

Officer Yu was alerted by the astrologer's anxiety and his overall change in demeanour. He sent a message to the Prince, who arrived within the hour and demanded the outcome of the divination.

Trembling, the astrologer declared that this marriage should not happen as it was unsuitable for the royal family. Curious, Prince LuiAo asked for details. The astrologer spoke gravely, asserting that the child from this union would not become a Prince despite taking a position on the board that denoted a powerful destiny. He added gravely that the marriage should be called off because XuPing, the soon-to-be consort, was destined to die.

At first, Prince LuiAo's eyes reflected shock but soon gleamed in merriment, and then he laughed outright. "Is this the misfortune you've predicted for me?" He snickered, "I get to marry the girl who can solve all my troubles, and then she conveniently dies, and her brat disappears?" He looked at his palace officer meaningfully, and they burst out laughing.

Prince LuiAo motioned for the jug of rice wine and took a long swig.

He narrowed his eyes and said, "Perhaps we can persuade her feisty friend to bear a royal brat and cast her aside, too."

Prince LuiAo told the astrologer, "If you think I will brood like my father over his first wife, Consort Sima, you are mistaken. I will ensure an inexhaustible supply of beautiful women enters the palace harem. Surely, the eunuchs wouldn't be bothered if a few died."

Having loosened the knots of wine, the astrologer stated calmly, "Prince LuiAo, disaster is in store for you if you proceed. The influence of Erlang Shen, the nomadic God with the third eye, is involved in this union, and his influence on the child is substantial. The boy, your son, will grow up in abject poverty and misery, destined to be a commoner or peasant. I don't know how that is possible at this moment." Prince LuiAo ignored the astrologer completely, and Officer Yu accompanied him out.

The astrologer had broken a celestial rule by throwing the dice twice, and his days were numbered. Ignoring Prince LuiAo's vile threats, he wrote down his predictions and sent them to the Grand Master WoShi of the HanKaoTzu School to be handed over to the Empress.

A month later, the palace priest conducted the marriage of Prince LuiAo and XuPing Jun. A newly appointed palace astrologer attended the festivities. Unfortunately, a failed robbery resulted in the murder of the former palace astrologer.

XuPing and her laotong, soul-sister XuMi, moved into the palace. It was a foregone conclusion to many that beautiful Mi would soon become another conquest of the Crown Prince's lecherous advances.

Knowing her husband well enough, the new Princess, XuPing, cleverly circumvented this. She ensured that her dear friend Mi served Prince LuiAo's mother, Empress Wang and was not at the harem when LuiAo came to visit.

****

The mothers of XuPing and Mi were close friends who became pregnant around the same time. The two families made a social contract to marry their children to each other while they were expecting – a socially accepted and legally arranged marriage before the babies were born to bond the families.

Despite their wish for a boy and a girl, the babies were both girls. The two families wanted to maintain their bond and decided to make their daughters Laotong sisters. A Laotong is a solemn promise to care for each other for life.

Both families formalised the relationship by placing their seals on the contract. They were named Xu Ping and XuMi. After examining their astrological birth details, an official marriage matchmaker declared they could become Laotong sisters.

XuPing and Mi were close friends, having known each other since infancy. By the time they reached their teenage years, they had developed a sign language for communication. They could understand each other without verbal cues, much to the annoyance of their friends and parents.

#5 Emperor Cheng Marries the Zhao Sisters

Three years had passed since their marriage, and XuPing was paranoid that her husband, Crown Prince LuiAo, would reject her if she became pregnant. Pregnant women were moved to a separate mothers' area of the harem, and LuiAo rarely returned to the women he had discarded.

One of his conquests, consort Ban, an educated girl, claimed he detested crying infants. She had initially entered the imperial harem as a junior concubine and bore him a son. Unfortunately, the infant died a year after birth. She had the second position in the palace hierarchy, just below XuPing, because the Crown Prince trusted her with intellectual and palace matters.

XuPing made desperate attempts to avoid impregnation by using herbs and medicines, but she failed and became pregnant. Until her return from the mother's area, she would have no control over the Prince's and the harem's activities, which could be disastrous.

XuPing sacrificed her self-respect and married LuiAo to benefit her family, and she wanted those privileges to last. After XuPing became the first wife in the eyes of the gentry and bureaucracy, her family members made significant strides in the military and administration.

She sent word for her laotong sister Mi, who was serving as a lady-in-waiting for Empress Wang, her mother-in-law. XuPing held Mi's hand and, with tears in her eyes, said, "I am pregnant, and they will send me to the separate area for young mothers. My husband may no longer favour me, and our family might lose their position in the administration."

Mi wiped XuPing's tears and said scornfully, "How does it matter? Surely, this lewd man will bring in more innocent girls with or without your absence." She was curious about why she had been summoned and asked, "Why did you call me sister? Surely, not for telling me this!"

XuPing looked into Mi's eyes and said, "Take my place here in the royal bedchambers as my laotong replacement."

"How dare you!" Mi spat at her sister. "Sleep with that detestable man! You know I disliked your lecherous LuiAo since the day I saw him." She choked and cried, shivering in disgust at the thought of getting intimate with a man she hated.

"What do we do? All my sacrifices for our family will be in vain. We need to remain relevant until LuiAo becomes emperor." XuPing wept. "Once I become the first Empress, I can directly manage the elevation of our family members."

"I need someone I can trust to dissuade him from promising another woman the position of first wife. At least until I deliver my child and return." She held Mi's hands and said, "Women live a cursed life under such tyrants, Mi. We are laotong sisters, two bodies and one soul. If not you, who can I turn to save our families? At least in our next lives, let us be born as men."

Overcome with emotion, Mi used sign language and told XuPing that she would be back after considering the proposal.

Mi knew LuiAo was biding his time to humiliate her because he had inquired about her whereabouts with the harem eunuchs. Women were commodities to the Crown Prince, and the number of women he ravaged, bought and sold in the markets was abhorrent. She was fortunate to be working for Empress Wang, but once LuiAo became emperor, her time would be up. She prayed and offered incense regularly for the long life of Emperor Yuan.

Mi was aware that XuPing was a noblewoman, and her motive was to protect and enhance the prestige of their families. Mi's brother was doing well in the military, and she had to ensure that XuPing succeeded in continuing as the first wife to protect his position. After a day of pondering, Mi reluctantly agreed to the proposal, although it was revolting to be with LuiAo, the wretched husband of her dear friend.

The next step was to convince LuiAo to consider Mi an equal laotong replacement for XuPing as a consort; however, this would be strictly for XuPing's absence from the harem. How do you negotiate with a Crown Prince who owns everything and everybody?

They confided their plan to Consort Ban, who was shocked. It was an open secret in the harem how much Mi hated the Crown Prince, and she recognised the sisters' desperation and motives and negotiated a counterproposal.

Consort Ban said, "I will agree to this hateful proposal on one condition: If a son is born to Mi from LuiAo, he shouldn't be considered an heir to the throne. The recognition of a Crown Prince should remain with a son born to XuPing or myself."

Mi responded, "Of course! That goes without saying. I don't want to get pregnant with his child and will leave the harem as soon as Princess XuPing resumes palace duties." She agreed emphatically to Consort Ban's proposal and said, "Can you imagine my son sitting on his lap and smiling at him? Preposterous! I do not want any child from LuiAo, let alone be a challenge to my sister."

Princess Ban and XuPing convinced LuiAo to take Mi as a laotong equivalent to the first wife. The strange request surprised the Crown Prince, but he did not negate it. This proposal directly threw the petite Mi, whom he lusted after, into his lap, and he was determined to shame her. On consort Ban's insistence, the eunuchs in the harem documented the agreement, and the ladies put their seals on it.

Consort Ban did not divulge to the laotong sisters that the Crown Prince had told her about the astrologer's dreadful prediction: XuPing would die, and her child would be lost. If Consort Ban eliminated the threat that Mi would produce a male child with LuiAo with a claim to the throne, her legacy would be secured.

****

LuiAo became fascinated with a reluctant Mi, who did nothing to hide her loathing for the Crown Prince as he sadistically ravaged her. He taunted her as frigid in front of the other women in the harem and tortured her by beating and whipping her. LuiAo promised her that he would impregnate her and unceremoniously discard her but keep her child to become his bedchamber slave to wash his backside.

Within two months, LuiAo impregnated Mi, but she faked her moons by cutting her hand and using the blood to confuse the eunuchs. She wished to take her life but would not give despicable LuiAo the satisfaction of exacting his revenge.

With more and more stories of the brutal assault that Mi had to endure and the torturous screams of pain that chilled every woman in the harem, Mi became a symbol of laotong sacrifice, and her stature in the harem grew. Women were the property of their husbands, and they had to endure and suffer cruel ill-treatments, but Mi was enduring torture and intense mental agony for her laotong sister.

The harem eunuchs were unforgiving and would kill any woman who raised her hand against the Prince, and they kept a close watch on Mi for any signs of resistance or breakdown. Mi suffered in silence, as it was not just her but Princess XuPing who would be demoted if she retaliated against the sadistic Prince.

Prince LuiAo was tired of Mi, who was as cooperative as a corpse while he tortured her. The discussion in the harem was that XuPing would be relegated to a lowly concubine if Mi dissented. The eunuchs had already placed bets on how long Mi would silently endure her torture before she retaliated.

It was sheer providence that when things were becoming intolerable for a battered and injured Mi, Emperor Yuan asked the Crown Prince to travel into the Han Empire and visit the outer-lying provinces on his behalf.

Princess XuPing formally asked permission to return to her parent's residence in Pingen, along with her laotong sister, to deliver her child and recuperate. LuiAo was distracted by the journey ahead and readily agreed, lost in the details of exploring the Han Empire. It was an adventure for him, having hardly left the palace in Changan.

LuiAo left with Consort Ban, promising Mi that he would taste local flavours throughout the trip and come back with new ways to torture her. He chose Consort Ban to accompany him because she was educated and could inform him about their travel and cultural details that he would otherwise miss. Furthermore, Consort Ban enjoyed making notes and drawings of their journey and collecting stories from the locals while he could pursue his pleasures.

****

During their journey home, Mi confided in XuPing about her pregnancy in sign language and her desire not to disclose this to the imperial household. She requested XuPing to let her complete her pregnancy, deliver the child, and return to serve Empress Wang.

Upon arriving home, XuPing informed her parents about Mi's pregnancy. There was no way Mi could conceal her pregnancy from the palace eunuchs and soldiers who had accompanied them for long. XuPing Jia, the Marquis of Pingen, and his wife discussed the situation. If XuPing gave birth to a girl and Mi delivered a boy by laotong contract, Mi would become a legitimate concubine to the Han throne, a situation unacceptable to the Marquis.

With the help of the Marquis's trusted men, Mi left Pingen in secrecy to go to a friend's home in Nandan County. Although the Marquis's family tried to hide Mi's disappearance, the eunuchs soon realised she was missing. Unable to get credible information on her whereabouts, they tortured the stable hand and learned that she had gone to Nandan County.

They organised a team of guards to pursue her, but the Marquis took personal responsibility for her safe return. He promised that Mi would be back as soon as XuPing was to return to Changan. He argued that Mi was an ordinary woman and servant to Princess XuPing and was not officially tied to the Prince in any capacity. The eunuchs had limited authority because Marquis XuPing Jia's official status surpassed theirs. As the Princess's father and Emperor Yuan's friend, they had to obey his instructions.

The eunuchs waited impatiently at the Marquis's residence in Pingen and contemplated vile ways to punish Mi once they returned to the palace. They planned to make her an example for every woman in the harem who disobeyed the eunuchs, boasting about this to the Marquis's household staff.

Princess XuPing gave birth to a stillborn boy a few months later, and the Marquis's household was heartbroken. The palace eunuchs blamed their arduous journey to reach Pingen from Changan. After the miscarriage, they wanted to return to Changan, but the Marquis was noncommittal about this proposal. Princess XuPing was depressed and desperately needed time to regain her mental strength. He reminded the eunuchs that the Princess had time until Prince LuiAo returned from his expedition.

It took XuPing many moons of pining to get over her loss, and the restless eunuchs asked her to prepare for her journey back into Changan. The eunuchs sent word to the marquis to return Mi in time for their travel. The Marquis had no excuse to offer this time and reluctantly agreed. He sent word to his friend in Nandan to send Mi back as soon as he received his message.

It took another month before Mi finally returned, flushed and happy. The senior women in the Pingen household and their servants quickly deduced that she had delivered a baby and became a mother. It was not long before the information reached the eunuchs' ears.

Mi was forced to undergo a physical examination, and it became apparent to the eunuchs that she had indeed delivered a baby. They demanded the whereabouts and gender of the baby.

She told them that she had ruptured her water sac and lost the baby. She could have died but for the presence of Fang, a midwife. Mi said that she had lost a stillborn girl, but the eunuchs were not convinced because her glowing face and demeanour did not match that of a mother who had lost her baby.

The timing of her abortion and lactating breasts was inconsistent with the date of conception. They did not torture a smug Mi to uncover the truth because the eunuchs realised that such an elaborate cover-up required the blessings of the Marquis family.

To put matters to rest, they decided to investigate independently and make the Marquis the scapegoat for the severe lapses he had willingly committed against the Han empire. They confided in the local imperial guard, a confidant of the Marquis, and ordered him to be on standby upon their return. Everyone wanted to be part of the party that returned with a Crown Prince, so all senior eunuchs and soldiers left for Nandan County, leaving three junior eunuchs.

A few weeks later, the Marquis was informed by scouts that the Crown Prince had returned to Changan. He forced the reluctant eunuchs to return to Changan with his daughter and Mi. He promised the eunuchs that he would send search parties to find their colleagues and guards and hoped they were not waylaid by armed gangs of bandits that had recently plagued the Pingen countryside.

Despite the Marquis's efforts, no trace of these men was found, and he promptly reported this to the emperor, asking him for reinforcements to tackle the recent bandit menace in Pingen.

****

Emperor Yuan fell ill with a severe rasping cough. The court physician advised him to rest in his bedchamber to recuperate. Usurping exclusive access to the emperor, Consort Fu demanded that he make Prince LuiKang the Crown Prince. She put on a charade of blowing hot and cold, much to the Emperor's discomfort, prompting him to send word to ShiDan and WoShi for their opinions.

ShiDan, a stickler for Han principles, insisted that Prince LuiAo remain the Crown Prince, considering the tradition of naming the first legal-born son the Crown Prince. He reminded the Emperor that he would have to suffer the wrath of his ancestors if he broke their long-held tradition.

The vacillating Emperor died that night.

Soon after, Crown Prince LuiAo ascended the throne as Emperor Cheng.

Empress Wang ZhengJun became Empress Dowager Wang.

Consort XuPing became the first Empress XuPing.

Emperor Cheng declared to the court that he trusted Prince Kang with his life and made him King of Ding Tao. On the advice of WoShi, the imperial strategist and grandmaster of the HanKaoTzu school, Empress Dowager Wang took over the administration of the empire until her son became experienced in palace affairs. A relieved LuiAo, now Emperor Cheng, welcomed this decision as he wanted power without responsibility.

Emperor Cheng loved the company of Prince Kang, his stepbrother, and frequently summoned him to Changan or sent him as his emissary to discuss state matters. Empress Dowager Wang disliked Prince LuiKang because he took the advice of palace mandarins who were earlier aligned with Consort Fu.

Anticipating a coup against her son, Empress Wang consulted her brothers for a solution. WangFeng, the Marquis of YangPing, suggested that the Wang family needed to consolidate their power in the military and administration to ensure protection for Emperor Cheng. Empress Wang agreed and elevated all her six brothers to the rank of marquis to support Emperor Cheng from within. She quietly introduced her brothers into the administration to manage the empire and placed them in strategic positions above the palace bureaucrats.

With the administration diligently managed by the Wangs, Emperor Cheng spent his time enjoying music, dance, wine, and women. During a state visit, two exceptionally talented and beautiful girls entertained him. He was fascinated by Zhao Feiyan's dance and demanded that she accompany him back to the palace as a concubine.

Feiyan reminded the Emperor of the laotong sisters in the palace and requested that her twin sister, Hede, accompany her. Emperor Cheng decided to make both the Zhao sisters his wives. He asked their family to solemnise the wedding immediately and finalise the compensation they wanted in exchange for the brides.

During his extended stay, their father demanded that since Emperor Cheng did not have any male progeny, the first-born child of either of the sisters should be made the Crown Prince. Enamoured by the seductive sisters, the newly crowned Emperor readily agreed to this promise.

The Zhao sisters worked hard to please the Emperor and became the Emperor's favourites in the harem; he hardly visited Empress XuPing or Consort Ban. The low-born Zhao sisters openly demonstrated their animosity towards Consort Ban and derogatorily referred to Empress XuPing as an empty well in the desert. They were rude and intolerant of everything related to XuPing, the first Empress, because they perceived her as their primary competitor. Although the Zhao sisters spread many rumours of infidelity about Empress XuPing, the eunuchs reported otherwise.

Emperor Cheng reduced the privileges accorded to a bewildered XuPing to appease the Zhao sisters and constructed a separate palace for them away from the original harem. The new palace was exceptionally grand, built by the best artisans using beautiful furnishings and decorations from the treasures of annexed kingdoms. The palace was made with red panelling and gold engravings and designs and furnished with the finest furniture and cushions.

The Zhao sisters, skilled in the art of seduction, surrounded themselves with beautiful slaves while the cooks prepared dishes infused with renowned aphrodisiacs. Their ultimate victory would be realised when one of the sisters conceived.

Despite their best efforts, the Zhao sisters did not get pregnant, which pleased the Empress Dowager Wang. She did not want an heir from the uncouth dancing girls to ruin the pure Han bloodline; however, the Emperor's impotence was a reason for concern. She called her son and told him in no uncertain words that the Han seed in him was potent because he had recently impregnated Empress XuPing. She urged him to spend time in the chambers of Empress XuPing and Consort Ban because the wombs of dancing girls were rotten and weak.

Empress Dowager Wang divulged the details of the prophecy that plagued the Lui clan since the first emperor: the Han could lose the mandate to rule from the heavens if three successive rulers failed to produce a legitimate heir or male offspring. Did he want such troubled times to start with his rule?

She told him that the gods would change the course of the Yellow River three times, and the empire would fall into anarchy, bringing widespread destruction through drought and famine.

To soothe his anxious mother that the prophecy won't begin with him, Emperor Cheng disclosed the palace astrologer's prediction that he would have a son but did not mention XuPing's death or that the child would be lost subsequently.

#6 Fang the Witch Visits the First Harem

The Zhao sisters feared Dowager Empress Wang, who was the final authority within the palace administration. She would have thrown them out if it weren't for her son's infatuation with them. Empress Dowager Wang's regal and refined demeanour was a stark contrast to their upbringing in the countryside, making the Zhao sisters feel small and insignificant in her presence.

When Emperor Cheng, on his mother's advice, desired to pursue more concubines, the Zhao sisters offered their handmaidens as concubines. However, when one of the girls became pregnant, they panicked and quietly disposed of her.

They convinced Cheng that he would soon have an heir if he spent all his time with them, and he agreed. A year later, there was still no sign of an heir. Empress Dowager Wang summoned XuPing and Consort Ban and rebuked them for neglecting their duties. She commanded them to perform their primary palace duty by getting impregnated with the royal Han blood or face replacement by other fertile concubines.

Thoroughly chastised, Empress XuPing and Consort Ban deliberated on their predicament with the women in the first harem. Mi was the first to articulate their situation openly by blaming Emperor Cheng. She said, "Royal Highnesses, surely there isn't any problem with your wombs. Both of you and others have conceived in the past." Mi lowered her voice so that none of the eunuchs could overhear them and said, "I think it is a problem with the Emperor's virility. He has spent a lifetime spreading his seed across the realm, and his seed must be water."

Consort Ban vigorously nodded, and an encouraged Mi added,

"Undoubtedly, the Emperor produces weak water these days. How else can so many women go without getting pregnant? We need to ensure that the gods are appeased and that he has the virility to impregnate one of you when he returns to the first harem."

"How?" was the moot point that hung unanswered.

A glum Consort Ban responded, "You have a powerful argument, Mi, but what can we do if the gods have decided otherwise?" She sarcastically added, "Our husband has loose undergarments that drop at the sight of the Zhao sisters." Mi giggled at Ban's saucy comment while XuPing held her blushing cheeks.

Mi smiled at Ban and said, "We have a way out, but it is not conventional. We need ShiDan on our side; otherwise, we are doomed." The ladies looked at her curiously, ready to seize any opportunity that came their way.

"We need Fang, the midwife from Nandan. Some people call her a witch, but I can assure you that she can help. She has the magic and herbs to restore a man's virility," Mi declared confidently.

Whispering, Mi added, "We need a little Prince in here with ladies running after him, definitely not a Prince who runs after the girls without his undergarments." Her cheeky reply took some time to register. Consort Ban giggled uncontrollably at Mi's audacity, and XuPing joined in the laughter.

"A tiny man, a little warrior," said Consort Ban with a snort. They made jokes on behalf of their Emperor and giggled uncontrollably.

Smiling, XuPing extended her hand and said, "For the sake of our families, the Han people, and the Han Empire." They held hands in a silent pact to bring Fang, the midwife.

Although sceptical, ShiDan finally catapulted after the Princesses' persistent pleading, especially from the first Empress XuPing. Much against his wishes, he agreed to try their suggestion and send word for

Fang. His primary concern was that witchcraft and magic in all forms were banned within the palace.

****

It took over a month to locate and bring Fang to the palace in response to Shi Dan's summons. A middle-aged woman with streaks of white hair and tattoos covering her wiry body immediately took charge of the proceedings, showing no awe of royalty.

Fang told ShiDan, "We need an invocation ritual for the gods, followed by a fertility ritual. However, before that, I need to see the divine knots I must untie for the union to succeed and for the child to descend."

ShiDan enquired, "Descend? You mean to be born?"

Fang nodded. "However, you want, eunuch, it doesn't matter."

Fang smiled at Mi, showing her blackened teeth, and said, "Your cousin's son, SuWu, is doing well. He is a lovable toddler who is curious about everything and asks many questions. He is destined for greatness." Except for XuPing, nobody else understood why Mi burst out crying.

"Was she so attached to the infant?" ShiDan asked XuPing, little realising that Fang was referring to Mi's son. XuPing gave ShiDan a sheepish smile; within her heart, she felt guilty about her laotong sister's sacrifice. She had spoken to Mi many times in the recent past to declare the existence of her son to Empress Wang, but she refused. Mi detested Emperor Cheng so much that she would rather have their son grow up as a commoner than bring joy to the empire. Moreover, she was committed to ensuring that the son of XuPing became the next Han Prince.

XuPing was aware that the punishment for hiding a royal Prince would lead to extreme torture and death, and all the maids and eunuchs of the harem would be executed, starting with affable

ShiDan. Despite these imminent threats to life, XuPing resolved to disclose the boy's existence to Empress Dowager Wang if she did not conceive soon. This attempt with Fang, the midwife, would be her last try.

Deep in her thoughts, she missed most of what Fang said but noted the expression of bewilderment on ShiDan's face. It was not an easy ritual, and ShiDan asked the midwife with genuine concern, "Fang, what you ask is difficult. We will need months to source the ingredients."

Fang was cross with ShiDan and waved her hands irritably. "Don't fret, eunuch! I am not asking you to deliver all of this tomorrow. Send word to the coast and get the ingredients."

ShiDan looked at her in surprise. Few commoners would dare to order a senior eunuch around. He asked, "How do we present the elixir to the emperor? The Han Empire is rooted in Confucianism, and I do not know how to keep these rituals a secret. There are more spies than people in this porous palace, where every secret is gossiped."

Fang turned to him with her hands on her hips and asked ShiDan, "Do I have to do everything here myself, or can you manage some part of the work?"

Stung by her sarcastic response, ShiDan asked, "What's your price, midwife? You would demand a large reward if the Empress's womb became fertile again. Let's discuss that as well."

Fang smiled, showing her black teeth again. "Reward! A payment to bring forth a warrior son of the heavens... Can this empire afford it? I am doing this service to the Han because it is my destiny to bring forth a giant killer, a purebred warrior! For that, I don't want to be heaped with some colourful dirt dug up from the earth." She laughed loudly, shook her index finger at ShiDan, and said, "However, I will take my payment in full when I perform the rituals the second time."

ShiDan looked at her in confusion. "Repeat the rituals a second time?

What for? Can't you conduct the ritual for both the consorts together?" he inquired.

Fang squawked at ShiDan. "What do you think the Zhao sisters will do when they find out the fertility rites work? Of course, I will have to repeat it for them." ShiDan looked at her in fear, and Fang waved her hand in disgust. "You don't have to be an astrologer to glean this, old man. That is why I have doubled the requirements for all ingredients you need to source." ShiDan was stunned into silence, and Fang did not pursue that line of conversation. Instead, she dived into the procedures to appease the gods.

The midwife explained that first, they needed to satisfy HouYi, the deity of archery, and his dear wife, Cheng'e, the Goddess of the Moon. They also needed to remove the influence of WuGang, who endlessly cut the moon to size, and appease Zhu Rong, the god of fire, and Xi He, the goddess of the sun.

Fang spread her leather chart, which had become blackened with age. After invoking the gods one by one, she moved her shells on the ancient chart, marked in a strange language. She ran the dice through XuPing's hair and made her throw the dice.

Sitting back on her haunches, Fang exclaimed, "Tut-tut! There is a significant arraignment in the union of XuPing and the emperor. This block is causing astronomical disharmony, preventing the birth of a god-king waiting to cross seven heavens." She looked at a baffled ShiDan, but her expression showed she was not surprised.

She sat back on her hips and said monotonously, "I can untangle it for a short while, just enough for a single union." Looking keenly at XuPing, she asked, "Do you want to go through this, Princess? It will cost lives, and your son will be a great warrior, more than just a Crown Prince." Before an apprehensive XuPing could reply, Fang continued, "I must inform you of the perils of bringing a giant into this world, a god that destiny will bow to."

XuPing moved close to the midwife and said with humility, "Yes. The empire needs an heir; otherwise, my dear sister's sacrifice will be in vain."

Fang smiled and nodded in understanding. "Don't worry, girl. I know. It was a necessary question to confirm my rituals." She referred to XuPing, a Han Empress, as a mere girl, much to ShiDan's discomfort. It was clear that Fang was not concerned with titles or royalty.

Fang turned to Consort Ban, who was shivering in fright after hearing the midwife say that the union would cost lives. "I guess you won't be too keen on these rituals. I shall concentrate on this girl here, but rest assured that you are included."

The midwife created a male doll representing the Emperor and two female dolls representing XuPing and Consort Ban. She instructed ShiDan to gather their hair and nails and wrap them in the dolls. The midwife would use the dolls in a month-long ritual to appeal to QuanYin, the fertility goddess.

ShiDan had to source ingredients, including live exotic animals. He was miffed with Fang and expressed his displeasure. "What are you planning to do? This is not a royal wedding, for heaven's sake! I need months to buy and bring live animals for pens near the seaports. I cannot keep such grand arrangements a secret in the palace," he growled.

Fang did not get flustered. "I know. Tell them the truth. Spread the word that the first harem is preparing to welcome the Emperor to bring forth a son. You have three months to prepare, and I need that time to prepare the girls."

Consort Ban, who seemed to have contained her fear, told an irate ShiDan, "Chief eunuch ShiDan, the Empress Dowager Wang has commanded that the first harem produce a male heir for Han. You need to say that we have hired a midwife to purify and make the wombs of the Princess fertile. The palace and people want assurance of the continuation of the lineage from the first emperor. We have tried everything before, haven't we? Surely people will welcome a different approach."

ShiDan sighed and said, "So be it. May the gods help us."

Fang smirked, "The gods *want* it, eunuch. That is why I am here!"

After arranging with the port masters to import exotic animals to Changan, ShiDan took three weeks to reassign servants and eunuchs from the harem who were not loyal to him. In the meantime, he leaked irrelevant information about the preparation of the fertility rites. Consort Ban had warned him that a sudden cessation of information from the first harem would make people anxious, especially the Zhao sisters.

Fang made XuPing and Consort Ban consume a cocktail of bitter herbs for the first seven days, which caused them severe diarrhoea. They were prohibited from eating anything but leek soup and herbal tea, which the midwife concocted. Every day, after a simple purge, they had to make a fasting prayer followed by penance to the deities of HsiShih, the goddess of face cream, and QuanYin, the goddess of fertility.

Their baths were elaborate. The day began with a mud bath using clay dug from deep under the riverbed, followed by a hot oil massage to make their skin supple. Servants rubbed their bodies vigorously to stimulate blood flow. Finally, they lay in a stone basin filled with sweet-smelling milk and spices to make their bodies smell good. Their hair was washed with the essence of jasmine and dried in incense smoke.

Fang's assistants made them dance to exotic steps to gain poise and be seductive in their walk and appearance. Many ladies in the harem joined them in these physical activities. It was wholesome fun for all of them; however, there was no let-up for the two Princesses, who were pushed hard to exhaustion.

Initially, the eunuchs were curious onlookers but soon lost interest, and spies reported the midwife's activities as harmless physical exercises. XuPing and Consort Ban began to look more alluring than any other girls in the harem, with fair, glowing, almost translucent skin and shiny, black, silky hair. The routine had to continue for at least four moon cycles before meeting the emperor.

ShiDan had to pay an enormous bribe to the eunuch responsible for trimming the Emperor's hair to source his hair and nails before they were burnt to avoid misuse in witchcraft.

Once all the ingredients were provided, a pleased Fang delegated the daily routine of bathing and exercising the Princesses to Mi. The midwife and her assistants had to prepare a special paste with distilled jasmine and flower extracts mixed with brown hut-shaped mushrooms with thin, long stalks from the mountains. This paste would be applied to XuPing's body after the fertility rituals. Inhaling the drying concoction would induce mild hallucinations to attract a mate.

Another tonic had to be prepared to increase the Emperor's virility. This exotic preparation contained the semen and shavings of a rhinoceros horn, an extract of dried tiger genitalia, ginseng, saffron, pepper, nutmeg, oyster sauce, the essence of ginkgo biloba, ground shavings of deer antlers entering the mating season, and Reishi mushrooms. The Emperor was to regularly consume this concoction for eight weeks before he visited the first harem.

The tonic had to be prepared with clarified butter on a no-moon night, away from all murderous weapons like knives, spears, and arrows. This was necessary because the celestial couple Hou Yi and Cheng'e could stop loving each other, making the tonic toxic. On Fang's instruction, the tonic had to be prepared inside a dark tent so that no light, including starlight, could alert the gods. To keep ZhuRong, the god of fire, unaware, they had to heat rocks in a fire, carry them away from its glow, and drop the hot stones into the mixture in total darkness.

ShiDan was in a quandary because magic was banned in the palace, and he was unsure if potions that increase virility were considered magic. Fang told him that the ritual was not black magic but a method to make the tonic without the influence of any god. In the coming days, she would individually appeal to each major god, imploring them to be passive to the birth of an heir. Once their influence is removed separately, the celestial block can be overpowered to pave the way for a mighty warrior's birth, but just once!

Nevertheless, this was too much responsibility for ShiDan, so he approached Empress Dowager Wang for a final decision. Her spies had already updated Empress Dowager Wang, and she was enthusiastic about the preparations. "ShiDan, I don't see a problem with dances, fasting, baths, and potions. However, keeping the conservative Confucian priests in the dark would be prudent." She added thoughtfully, "We have prayed and sacrificed to the gods without success. Perhaps this midwife can help us appease the gods. If nothing else, the Princess will be motivated to get my son away from the clutches of the Zhao sisters; they are street scum!" she exclaimed, her eyes burning with hatred.

ShiDan bowed in relief. "The midwife is confident she will succeed in this endeavour and give us a Crown Prince. She claims this son will be a great warrior from beyond the seven heavens. It's as prophesied, she says."

The Empress looked startled. "Are you sure that's what she said?" ShiDan nodded.

The Empress cautioned ShiDan, "Before you give any concoction to my son, ensure that many food tasters verify the effects for his well-being. Since the deaths of many emperors have been attributed to poisoning, the army has demanded a complete purge of the palace to safeguard future emperors. I just about stopped it last time when my husband died, but be warned that I will not stop the army if my son dies. No one will be spared."

ShiDan bowed and said, "The concoctions will be tested on me before it is given to the emperor." The Empress Dowager nodded, satisfied.

The Empress frowned thoughtfully and asked, "How will you make my son drink this vitality elixir?"

ShiDan grinned sheepishly and said, "Forgive me, Empress, but I plan to give it to him through the physician attending the Zhao sisters. Tell them the truth; it's something to increase the Emperor's virility," The Empress slapped her thighs and laughed.

****

Empress Dowager visited the first harem and was surprised to see the radiant Princesses. They appeared younger and incredibly beautiful. Thrilled by this transformation and believing the midwife's actions would bear fruit, she instructed palace mandarins to pay the Zhao family blood money in full. She did not want the last official obstacle to remain when the Princesses became pregnant, aiming to eliminate the Zhao sisters.

The father of the Zhao sisters accepted the money without a murmur, relieving all claims on his daughters. He did not want to annoy the powerful Empress Wang. He told his family members that if his daughters were to become pregnant, it should have happened already.

Hearing this disturbing development, the Zhao sisters became anxious to devise a way to prevent the Emperor from leaving them for the first harem. They gladly accepted the virility potion from their physician.

Frustrations finally broke through a few weeks later. While trying new clothes, Zhao Feiyan threw her cloak away and screamed at the attending eunuchs. She demanded, "Can't any of you tell me one good way of getting rid of that hateful and pompous XuPing?" She kicked the tray that carried clothes, silk rolls, and spindles before bursting into tears.

The oldest eunuch, a tailor who had made clothes for Empress Fu, suggested, "ShiXi! You need ShiXi. All of the high-ranking eunuchs in the palace today are from the glorious time of Emperor Yuan, and ShiXi recruited them."

Zhao Feiyan looked at him with narrowed eyes and signalled for him to speak. "ShiXi got ousted along with Empress Fu when the Wangs took over. Empress Wang brought in her family above the eunuchs, but all the eunuchs and palace administrators are indebted to ShiXi." He paused and added quickly, "There is no one more cunning in palace politics than him, and if you want to dispose of someone ..." he did not say anything further, but Zhao understood.

"Bring him to me," she said softly.

ShiXi visited a pensive Zhao Feiyan, who was sipping tea. Without any prelude, she asked him, "Can you help me dispose of Empress XuPing? I want my husband to remain with me." She added politically, "Of course, by officially exposing to the court how corrupt and wayward XuPing is. Unfortunately, I am unable to prove this with my ineffective spies." The meaning of what she wanted was evident, and the old scheming Mandarin smiled in pleasure. He had missed political intrigue since he lost clout after Consort Fu was sidelined, but here was a chance to enter it again. The high of a political victory lasts longer than the high of black opium applied to the gums.

ShiXi bowed deeply and said, "Princess, my life's purpose is to serve the empire, and this is a small request you have asked of me. I consider it my duty to help make you the first Empress. Please be assured of my discreet services and your eventual victory," he said.

Zhao Feiyan smiled and said, "So we understand each other perfectly."

"Of course," he paused and added artfully, "Please reinstate me fully to serve you better after I give you the first victory." Feiyan smiled for the first time in many days.

ShiXi learned what was happening in the first harem through his contacts in the bureaucracy. When he informed the Zhao sisters about the impending fertility rites, which could be interpreted as witchcraft, Zhao Feiyan squealed in delight.

She was about to summon the Emperor when cunning ShiXi stalled her and asked for patience. "Let us begin by slowly filling the Emperor's ears that evil black magic is practised inside the palace walls. Let us storm in and capture Empress XuPing and Consort Ban red-handed when the ceremony is at its zenith. The Emperor can't ignore such damaging evidence. Your revenge will be complete, and you can decide how they die."

Zhao Feiyan felt a thrill go down her spine as she hugged her sister. She laughed happily and told ShiXi, "You are indeed a fox, just as I was told. Be useful to me, and I shall reinstate you to your old position." This pact was sealed without a written agreement.

****

The whole of Changan was aware of the upcoming fertility rituals at the palace because a pair of one-horned rhinoceros was brought from the kingdom of Java. It was a rare spectacle that could not be missed, and the animals attracted many visitors to its pen, including the bureaucrats and the wealthy. ShiDan had to deploy imperial soldiers to prevent people from getting too close. People cheered for Princess XuPing and Consort Ban when they visited the rhinos. With the high public support, reports on the impending witchcraft were watered down and ignored by the bureaucracy.

Fang began rituals on the seventh day of the seventh month of the lunar cycle by offering special prayers at all the major temples. The previous night, hundreds of lanterns were set afloat in the canals, crisscrossing Changan to alert the gods and urging the people to pray for a Crown Prince. The air of a festival enveloped Changan, and all the temples were crowded with women and children praying earnestly for a Crown Prince. ShiDan had arranged to distribute incense and lamps freely at the temples, and priests ensured that prayers continued through the night and into the next day.

The much-anticipated rituals began at sunrise. ShiDan was too nervous to stay inside and politely waited outside the harem hall. He explained that if something went wrong, it was ideal for him to control the situation from outside the entrance.

When Fang asked for the Princesses to assemble, Consort Ban lost her nerve and opted out with an apology because she dreamt that a monster would be born to her. Although ShiDan was upset, Fang did not blame her for opting out of the rituals.

Fang tied the clay and straw dolls representing the first Empress and the Emperor at the waist and discarded the doll representing consort Ban into the fire. Consort Ban flinched as the doll burst into flames.

Fang gestured to her assistant, who shut all the doors. Eunuchs stood guard to prevent anyone from coming in or going out. Another assistant threw incense into three charcoal braziers and fanned the embers. Thick plumes of smoke erupted as she carried a censer around the room, wafting exotic-smelling smoke over each of the assembled women and eunuchs.

XuPing sat on a stool atop a raised wooden platform encircled by an intricate lattice of sacred symbols crafted from rice flour. Her lips trembled, her nostrils flared, and her eyes were as wide as those of a deer caught in a tiger's jaws. She had surrendered her body to Fang to endure the fear and pain of the witchcraft, to die and be reborn.

She looked piteously at Consort Ban and Mi, who sat close to the platform to reassure her. They smiled encouragingly at XuPing, and she sighed heavily in acceptance of her fate. Fang spoke to her softly while she removed all her clothes and draped her in lily-white silk, sashed at the waist. The smoke from the incense made Princess XuPing appear like a fairy emerging through the morning mist.

Fang said aloud, "First Empress of Han, XuPing! I ask you: Are you ready to bring forth a child of the gods?" XuPing nodded, and she continued, "I shall disintegrate you and mould you back from the primordial mist to give immense power to your womb. There is no turning back once we begin, and the consequences are severe for any disruption."

XuPing was nervous. She closed her eyes after opening and closing her mouth as if to say something. Trembling, she opened her eyes and said fiercely, "I need a son. I'd rather die than be an empty vessel and bring shame to my family. Let the gods hear my laments and bless me." Tears streamed down her fair cheeks, and she sat up in determination.

Fang nodded but did not smile. She shook the smoke censer around the Princess and chanted prayers in a foreign language. The smoke made the Princess cough and her eyes water, but the midwife seemed unaffected. She motioned to her assistants, who came over with two large bowls and upended blood from the freshly slaughtered rhinoceros over a whimpering XuPing. The women of the harem collectively gasped at the sight of the blood flowing down XuPing. The midwife assistants mashed the coagulated blood over XuPing's face and body. Many fainted, and some screamed in fright and tried to run away, but eunuchs stationed by ShiDan at each door turned them back. No one could leave the hall until the ceremonies were complete.

The harem watched spellbound as the Empress transformed from an exquisite white flower to a bloodied, skinned animal in the throes of death. Or was it a primordial being in the frenzy of birth?

Fang held a green-black knife and whispered invocations to a dark god. She slashed Xu's blood-soaked robe, ripping it piece by piece, and the wet cloth was burned in the brazier. Consort Ban's eyes narrowed in curiosity to see the strange knife with a handle shaped like two frogs mating, back-to-back, with a bubble in the middle representing eggs. The midwife covered every part of the Empress's body with blood using the knife as a brush, including the soles of her feet and the spaces between the toes.

Blood smudged and disfigured the intricate drawings made with rice flour covering the platform, turning it brown with black blobs of congealed blood.

Consort Ban told a dazed Mi, "Fang is transforming our Princess into a mass of living flesh drawn from the primordial essence."

Nobody moved, transfixed by the gory rituals.

Once Fang was satisfied that XuPing's entire body was covered in blood, she took rice dough and mixed it with blood. She kneaded it into small, flat discs, stuck them over the Empress's eyes, nose, and ears, and plastered her lustrous hair, leaving her mouth open to breathe.

Consort Ban whispered aloud, "She is now a primaeval womb, ready to receive the seeds of the emperor."

Fang meticulously arranged white flower petals over the fast-drying blood, creating a ghoulish scene. Princess XuPing resembled a scaled creature from some dark realm of the occult, becoming a mosaic of brilliant white with thin dark lines of blood streaking in between.

Fang motioned to her assistants to add exotic dried flowers and black stones to the burning embers. Eunuch physicians recognised the flower of the "fly in the sky", a medicinal plant many holy men used to converse with the gods. The black stones were resin from the poppy's sap. Knowing what was in store, they quietly moistened their hanfu with spittle and held it pressed to their nostrils.

Thick grey smoke rose into the room, burning the physicians' eyes. Despite their covered nostrils, the potent smoke drugged them, and they felt themselves drifting up to the roof. In their drugged state, they saw the splotch that was the Princess swell and shrink, beating like a heart pulsating with energy.

Strangely, Fang and her assistants were unaffected. When everyone in the room was caught up in spasms of deep delirium, she took out many thin brass needles from a box. They had handles with tiny frogs crossed back-to-back, and the physicians felt the frogs slither from the handle onto her hands.

Chanting loudly in a foreign language that echoed in their heads, she moved her fingers as if to concentrate some dark energy on the clay dolls. The physician watched in disbelief as blue smoke snaked from the dolls onto the needles, and the needles glowed as if heated in a blacksmith's fire. The dolls charred and disintegrated into ash before their eyes.

Fang opened XuPing's mouth, rubbed black poppy gum on her lips, and made her inhale more of the smoke. The disoriented Princess resisted weakly. Fang Mang hissed at her, "You cannot change destiny without suffering. Your son is ready to descend from the heavens." XuPing relaxed, and the midwife helped her lie flat on the platform.

Fang jabbed a needle into Princess XuPing's womb. She screamed and arched her back like a drawn bow, then fell slowly onto the platform, writhing in pain.

Through the hallucinating smoke, Consort Ban laughed hysterically and asked Mi, "Is it pain or pleasure?"

I drawled, "Poor XuPing. I can feel every emotion she is going through. It's extreme pain, and she can't handle it. Isn't this too high a price for a son?" She wept copious tears while holding Consort Ban, who laughed hysterically.

Fang punctured XuPing's womb with needles at particular nerve points, energising her life force, and XuPing screamed with each jab. Each time her body arched, it looked like the mosaic of flower petals on her body exploded into individual pieces before merging back onto the limp form of the Empress.

After what seemed like an eternity, the profusely sweating Fang gently pulled out the needles. The Princess whimpered and raised her hand as if to stop someone from leaving.

Fang's assistant sprinkled water to extinguish the smouldering embers. As the potent smoke cleared, people began to breathe normally and recover their senses. However, the Princess remained unconscious, lost to the world of the living.

The sliding doors were opened to dissipate the smoke. The rituals were complete, and the hall flooded with light.

Fang gently bathed XuPing's body with warm milk and powdered spices, filling the air with a fragrant aroma and moved her from the platform to a straw mat. XuPing looked incredibly beautiful, with ruby red lips, alabaster skin, and lustrous black hair. Unlike the other women in the harem, she wore no makeup or jewellery. She was curled up like a newborn!

Fang's assistant lit incense, filling the vast palace chamber with sweet-smelling smoke. In her drugged trance, XuPing piteously called out to the Emperor to see their beautiful son.

Fang sat cross-legged near Princess XuPing, waiting.

Consort Ban, recovering from her drugged state, was bewildered by the brutality of the gruesome rituals. She held a weeping Mi, who was distraught over what her laotong sister had just undergone. Consort Ban asked Mi, "I agree that XuPing has undergone intense pain and misery to rejuvenate her womb. Where is the Emperor to impregnate XuPing?"

Mayhem erupted as imperial soldiers stormed in, and the Emperor barged in with the Zhao sisters.

Feiyan screamed in disappointment, "I think we arrived a little late to catch them in the act."

The Emperor looked at a supine XuPing and asked, "What are you doing naked on the floor?" He paused in surprise, realising she was lying in a stupor from which she could not answer. He looked at her again and exclaimed, "How did she become so young? What magic is this!"

Feiyan shouted, "Not magic, my lord. This is witchcraft, and you are looking at the proof. She is trying to entice you with witchcraft." Emperor Cheng looked closely at XuPing, and she mumbled, "Look, my dear, our son! Isn't he beautiful? He will become a warrior." ·

The Emperor tore his gaze away from XuPing and found Consort Ban among the women. He beckoned to her, and she prostrated herself before him. Feiyan looked at Ban and said, "She is part of this, my lord. She must be executed now, along with XuPing." Feiyan was upset to find the Emperor was hesitant to act.

She pleaded with him using words coached by ShiXi. "My lord, remember, your forefathers had framed the mandate of heaven in moral and cosmic terms. It is demanded that an Emperor's rule be just and carried out with the prescribed rituals of our ancestors to ensure natural and human order. They have indulged in witchcraft, disturbing the natural order of man, and should be executed without any delay."

The Emperor was not alone in wondering how an uneducated Feiyan could make such an intense and profound statement.

Feiyan was confident that Empress XuPing would be executed for her transgressions. She wanted to ensure that Consort Ban was also killed. In this upheaval, she wanted all her rivals removed, paving the way for her to become the first Empress.

Thankfully, before he could comment on Feiyan's astute insight, there was another commotion, and more palace eunuchs rushed in. They covered the naked Empress in silk cloth as ShiDan approached the Emperor and kowtowed before him.

Emperor Cheng said, "ShiDan, get up." ShiDan sat on his knees and nodded to Emperor Cheng, conveying that everything was under control.

On a signal from ShiDan, the eunuchs lifted a supine XuPing, hesitating to ask the Emperor for permission. ShiDan roared at their indecision, "Take her into the palace and leave her in her bedchamber."

After a long pause, Emperor Cheng asked, "ShiDan, what is happening here? Is Consort Ban part of the witchcraft to keep me impotent?" His accusations were profound, and his bodyguards took defence positions to prevent anyone from escaping.

ShiDan replied calmly, "Far from it! My lord, this is no witchcraft. Look around! The rituals were done in the presence of the entire harem, and brave XuPing endured a painful fertility ritual just for you. Empress Dowager knows that the Han seed is potent, and the problem lies with the women, who cannot produce an heir." He gestured towards Fang and said, "We have engaged a midwife to strengthen your women's wombs. If anything, I implore you to see this as nothing more than an innocent transgression of a woman's intense desire to conceive your child."

The Emperor was aware of what was happening in the palace for a long time through his spies, especially the appreciation of the ordinary people for the harem's efforts to perform a fertility ritual. Moreover, he trusted ShiDan, the man responsible for putting him on the throne in the first place, by pleading with his father. He asked, "Is my mother, Empress Dowager, aware of this?"

"Yes, my Lord", ShiDan replied, "The great lady has overlooked the unconventional procedures in pursuit of any chance to make your woman conceive."

ShiDan added slyly, "It is not enough that you conceive one son. The Han Emperor needs many sons, and if this ritual is successful, we should repeat it for all your Consorts," effectively taking the wind out of the sails of the allegations made by the Zhao sisters.

Emperor Cheng smiled and dropped his shoulders in resignation. He declared, "Witchcraft is not allowed in the Changan palace. XuPing will be punished with banishment to a house outside the palace, and she will no longer be the first Empress. Feiyan will take her place as the first Empress." Feiyan squealed in delight, and the courtiers, soldiers, and everybody else bowed their heads in submission to the new Empress.

He looked at Consort Ban, who lay prostrate on the floor. He asked her gently, "Ban, what about you?"

She opened her palm upwards in an apparent request to speak, and he nodded. She addressed the Emperor in a firm voice, "My Lord, I am not fit to grace your bedchamber anymore. Now, you are in the company of beautiful women like Feiyan. I request your kind permission to be a lady-in-waiting for the Empress Dowager Wang and continue to serve you by pursuing knowledge, history, and books."

Surprised by the request, the Emperor relented, "Yes, you will become my mother's lady-in-waiting and report anything of concern directly to me." The Emperor turned to look at the midwife.

ShiDan followed the Emperor's gaze and said, "Do you want her executed, my lord, for misleading the palace ladies?"

Fang laughed aloud, saying, "Do you execute someone who gives the Empire a Crown Prince, eunuch?"

The Emperor looked at the midwife curiously. Consort Ban interrupted whatever he wanted to say. "My lord." He looked at her, and she requested permission to speak in private.

The Emperor walked toward the one woman he trusted implicitly, took her aside, and inquired, "What is happening here, Ban?"

Consort Ban ensured no one was overhearing them and said, "Do you remember the journey into the border areas we undertook some time ago?" He nodded, and she continued, "During that journey, you told me about the prophecy that would befall Empress XuPing. You said that she would give birth to a boy, who would, in all probability, become a street urchin, and Empress XuPing would die soon after."

Emperor Cheng frowned. "Yes, but what has all of that have to do with this?" he inquired.

"Everything," replied Consort Ban. "Everything, because that midwife told us that Xu's son would be a great warrior and cleverly suggested that he wouldn't be a Crown Prince, and bringing him forth would cost lives, meaning XuPing. That was when I decided to back out. Fate has plans for you that do not include me."

She called him "Dear Ao," referring to the endearment she used in private. "If XuPing becomes pregnant, it proves this midwife is here to fulfil destiny." Emperor Cheng looked at Consort Ban with wide eyes. She nodded and said, "She is powerful, and we can use her services to make the Zhao sisters pregnant and get you another son to become Crown Prince."

Emperor Cheng looked perturbed and walked over to Fang, instructing his bodyguards to move all the onlookers away from earshot, but Feiyan shrugged off the command and followed him. Trusting Consort Ban's intuition that this was a woman not to be trifled with, he was very candid. "When did you meet the palace astrologer? He did not live long after my marriage to XuPing."

Fang was equally candid. "His fate! He threw the dice on himself. If your question is, did the astrologer tell me anything? The answer is no. Knowing what destiny has in store is not one man's ability; it is known to many mystics."

She prophesied to the Emperor, "A son you will have, but he will not sit on your lap." Looking at a startled Emperor, she added, "I thought we would meet earlier, but this wimp of your passion kept you imprisoned in her bed chambers." Feiyan began protesting, but the Emperor lifted his hand and silenced her.

Fang derided the Emperor, "Your harem life would have improved if you had raised your hand earlier."

The Emperor waited expectantly. He was sure that Fang would tell him something more. She mumbled faintly to the Emperor, "Empress XuPing has suffered for you, and she deserves a son. You know that her suffering will end soon."

The Emperor asked, "What about my son? Will he disrupt my rule?"

"The boy is destiny's child from beyond the seven heavens, a warrior. He is here to fulfil a prophecy made by the first Emperor of Han to the immortals. He is not here for you."

Fang accused the emperor, "You won't get to hold him because of the curse of three pious girls. You and your friends defiled them while your bodyguards murdered their family at the temple of fire." Emperor Cheng's mouth went dry, remembering the incident that had gone wrong long ago.

He took off his gold and jade necklace, threw it at Fang and said, "Take whatever you want, but go," he said.

Feiyan realised they were in the presence of a powerful sorceress who could probably help her conceive and said, "My Lord, I would like to keep her with me for some time. I want to ensure her corruption has not gone too deep into the harem."

Emperor Cheng replied, "No, she goes free! No one will stop her against her will."

****

Feiyan was distressed by the Emperor's refusal to execute XuPing. That evening, she intentionally made herself unavailable to him, citing the moon cycle for both sisters, despite the Emperor's need for comfort.

Dejected, Emperor Cheng's thoughts drifted sympathetically to Princess XuPing and what she had gone through to beget a son for him. It was an incredible sacrifice that no other Princess had made. He regretted demoting her from the first Empress and decided to calm her.

He summoned ShiDan and expressed his desire to meet XuPing secretly. ShiDan escorted the emperor, accompanied by LiPing, the chief of palace bodyguards, to meet XuPing. They passed through the servants' gates unchallenged. ShiDan and LiPing were not to be trifled with, and nobody checked on the third person accompanying them.

They walked to a modest house just inside the palace compound. ShiDan and LiPing stopped at the entrance while Emperor Cheng entered the house. He paused. Did he feel a presence, someone slinking away? Was it the midwife? The air smelled of freshly picked jasmine flowers, calming his mind.

He had no difficulty locating XuPing's bedchamber, as the corridor was well-lit with small lamps. He found XuPing sleeping, covered by a woollen blanket.

Small lamps lit the warm room brightly. An exotic fragrance emanated from XuPing, who looked drenched in sweat. He pulled the blanket away and found XuPing sleeping with her head down. He hesitated and looked at her lily-white skin glowing, rekindling the same romantic feelings he had when he saw her earlier. He paused, unsure of himself, when he heard her murmuring his name. Her voice sounded hoarse, unlike XuPing's soft voice.

He turned her light body over, gasping in surprise. "Feiyan, how did you get here?" His mind was playing tricks, but he did not care. Beautiful Feiyan looked at him and whispered hoarsely, "Come, my husband, come into my arms. You are so cold. Let me give you, my warmth."

He was overcome with lust and hugged her. Her exotic perfume overpowered his senses, and the touch of her soft body enhanced and heightened his desires. He was drawn into her embrace like the fly caught in a bright, hot flame, and all his apprehensions evaporated.

****

LiPing challenged someone coming out of the house. ShiDan was astonished to see that it was Fang, the midwife. She waved LiPing down. "Don't be ridiculous, soldier. You're challenging a harmless old woman."

She looked at ShiDan and said, "I was just in time to finish applying the medicinal cream on the Princess. It will make the Emperor see whatever he desires."

She frowned, looking at LiPing carefully and chuckled. "I did not realise that both of you are here together! The ways of the gods never cease to amaze me. I wanted to speak to both of you and here you are. The Emperor will take some time to come out, so you should listen to me. Your destinies are tied to the one whose life begins even as we speak."

A flustered ShiDan replied, "I am troubled to see you here, midwife. You are meddling in imperial affairs."

Fang let out a small laugh and said, "Let me make some things clear to you, eunuch. I am a descendant of Zhang Liang, the first Emperor's strategist, and if anybody should be concerned about the future of Han, it should be me." Her words made no sense to ShiDan. She said sternly, "Don't ask me to explain what you don't need to know. Suffice to know that I am interested in the child to be born."

ShiDan asked her, "What are you? A witch?"

"No, you idiot. I am flesh and blood." ShiDan balked at the disrespect Fang gave a senior bureaucrat of the imperial Han.

ShiDan asked, "Where is the Emperor?"

"In the making, in the making," she said.

She looked at the stars and asked, "What is special about the seventh day of the month?"

Comprehension dawned on a shocked ShiDan. "Oh, by the hair of the sun god, on the seventh day of the seventh month, the Empress is... we don't have a eunuch to record the time of conception?" he wailed.

Fang chuckled, "Yes, our Emperor! At least he is good at something." ShiDan and LiPing joined her in laughter.

ShiDan reconfirmed to LiPing, "A Crown Prince is in the making as foretold." Fang said, "As foretold. Ensure that I am allowed to monitor the mother-to-be." A while later, Emperor Cheng came out in a hurry. He said quietly, "I am done here. No one must know I was here."

He moved towards the palace, and they followed in silence. He stopped mid-stride and commanded them, "Keep her under house arrest. When a child is born, I want to be present." ShiDan and LiPing bowed their heads.

****

Late the following day, XuPing got up from her mat, smiling. She had dreamt that Emperor Cheng was with her the night before. She sat up and saw the midwife squatting in a corner, applying poppy resin to her gums. She recoiled in shock and asked, "What are you doing here, Fang?" She looked around the strange room and asked, "Where am I?"

Fang replied calmly, "You are outside the harem. You are carrying the seed of a god inside you."

Fang folded her palms into a single fist and bowed low. "Allow me to bow to the mother of a celestial Emperor." She prostrated before a surprised XuPing and tapped her forehead on the floor three times in devoted obeisance.

XuPing decided to share the glad tidings with her laotong sister, and she rushed out to find imperial soldiers blocking her way. She was under house arrest, and the soldiers did not stand down at her command because she was no longer an Empress.

All her pleading with them was in vain, so she insisted on meeting ShiDan. He could explain the misunderstanding to Emperor Cheng.

ShiDan was ready with his answer: "Princess of Han, you are pregnant, and you have many enemies. The Emperor has commanded us to protect you because of a prophecy that the child will be abducted."

Feeling guilty for XuPing's predicament, ShiDan gently said, "It is best for you, my lady, to remain protected. I will send Mi to keep you company."

XuPing wailed at ShiDan, "How do you know I am pregnant!"

ShiDan said, "Let's wait for a month, Princess. The Emperor is convinced you are carrying his son." A month later, Xu Ping missed her moons, and he informed an ecstatic emperor, who asked ShiDan to continue to hold Xu Ping in secrecy to thwart the prophecy.

To ensure complete secrecy about XuPing's pregnancy, none of the servants were allowed to leave, and they, too, were forced to undergo house arrest. Except for a few of ShiDan's loyal eunuchs, Mi and Fang, no one from the outside world was permitted inside.

Princess XuPing was depressed and weeping most of the time, lamenting the injustices she had suffered and the ignominy of her existence. Mi was concerned about the health of her unborn child, and in an attempt to distract her, she confessed her secret: "Do you know that Chunyu and I are together?"

Xu Ping exclaimed in horror, "They have spies everywhere, Mi. Both of your heads will roll when the Emperor learns about this."

Mi was not bothered. "I don't belong to him. With Chunyu, I feel all the emotions of a woman in love. He said he would speak to the Emperor at the appropriate time and free me."

XuPing wiped her eyes and giggled. "You were always brave but foolish. It doesn't matter, sister. Let one of us experience love in this life." They hugged each other and cried.

Mi wiped her eyes and said, "Thank you, sister, for not judging my choice. After we die, I hope we are reborn as swans in some distant lake with no humans or wild animals to hurt us. We can fly over human settlements to avoid their cunning and deceit."

Mi requested Chunyu to help her laotong sister regain her lost status and plead with the Emperor to reinstate her as the first Empress. Although Chunyu knew the Emperor was infatuated with Feiyan, he readily agreed to help Xu Ping. He slyly added that he needed money to look impressive in the Emperor's company. Mi lavished him with gifts and treasures smuggled out of the palace to please her lover.

****

General WangGen, the Emperor's uncle and brother of the Empress, fell ill. WangMang, a minor officer and nephew of Empress Dowager Wang, rushed to his bedside and cared for him. WangGen was impressed by his diligence towards the Wang family and his rigid, straightforward lifestyle. He spoke to Empress Dowager Wang, recommending WangMang. "This boy is of Wang blood and can be groomed to become a trustworthy bureaucrat under you. The Wangs will never let you down."

Empress Dowager Wang, who was looking for a personal assistant to help her navigate the bureaucracy, appointed WangMang as an officer. She was impressed by his diligence and devotion to work. WangMang took it upon himself to report dissidence and rumours to the pleased Empress.

#7 Hede Fools Palace Mandarins

General WangGen fell ill again, and it was a foregone conclusion that he would not survive. Rumours within the palace were abuzz that Chunyu, a close friend of Emperor Cheng, would succeed as the armed forces commander. To build a loyal clique, Chunyu began interacting with the commanders and gifted them artefacts stolen by Mi.

WangMang had hoped to become the next commander, replacing General WangGen. However, when Chunyu came into serious contention, he became desperate. He approached the Empress Dowager and said, "Empress, I have information that Chunyu is gathering generals in anticipation of replacing your loyal brother, WangGen. I fear that our Emperor is considering someone outside the Wang family for the commander position."

He carefully worded his concern to the Empress Dowager as a warning, "The power and influence of the Wangs will dissipate if someone outside the Wang family controls the military. Let other offices go to different clans, but not the armed forces. I dread for the life of our Emperor and the Wang clan if a coup occurs within the military." The Empress looked at him in alarm, and he continued. "We should not face the extermination of the Wang clan, especially in a situation when the Han Empire is without a Crown Prince to secure the future." There, he had done it. He had overstepped his limits and commented negatively on the emperor. It was treason!

WangMang did not realise that he had struck the very concern the Empress Dowager was battling, considering such an eventuality. She replied, "Loyal nephew, you are, of course, right. Someone outside the Wang controlling the armed forces poses a substantial risk." She turned to him and said, "I want you to spy on Chunyu and gather any information that can implicate him. Every man has secrets that can be used to create his downfall. I will handle it appropriately, and the gratitude of the Wangs will be yours."

She added, "Make haste but be discreet. My brother is sinking into the eternal sleep he has earned with diligence and hard work, and we need to act before he joins our ancestors." WangMang commissioned spies to monitor Chunyu day and night to uncover any transgression. He told his men that the Empress wanted to ensure that Chunyu, the future general of Han, was under investigation to confirm his loyalty to the Lui clan.

Within days, he discovered Mi and Chunyu's affair and acquired incriminating evidence of their secret meetings. Additionally, many generals expressed surprise at receiving expensive gifts with citations engraved on them, which gave irrefutable proof that they originated from the imperial palace.

WangMang gleefully reported on Chunyu to the Empress Dowager Wang, and she was pleased. Then she moaned in despair, "Chunyu is a traitor but a childhood friend of the Emperor, and he will forgive him of all indiscretions."

WangMang said, "Let me charge him with treason and get rid of him. You can always blame it on me, acting zealously as a Wang to protect the Emperor."

Using the Empress's seal, WangMang deployed the forbidden troops to detain Chunyu at his home. They discovered more treasures that had been embezzled from the imperial palace.

WangMang tortured Chunyu until he disclosed that he received the gifts from Mi to reinstate XuPing as Empress. On further torture, he blurted out about the house arrest and pregnancy of XuPing to a surprised WangMang.

WangMang was unwilling to believe that the Emperor could impregnate any woman, so he tortured Chunyu until he declared that he was the father of XuPing's child. WangMang reported all the sordid details to the Empress, who was distraught. She told WangMang to keep this information under wraps until she discussed matters with ShiDan.

WangMang was displeased and asked the Empress, "Mother Empress, what is the purpose of keeping XuPing alive? She should be immediately executed for unfaithfulness to our Emperor."

The Empress disagreed, saying, "ShiDan told me that the Emperor visited her the night after the fertility rituals, and she has been under house arrest since then. ShiDan says that Emperor Cheng has placed her under house arrest under oath not to divulge this information to anyone." WangMang was not pleased to hear this.

"What about Chunyu and Mi?"

"Execute the traitors!" she commanded WangMang. WangMang woke up Chunyu, who had fainted from the torture and cut him into pieces in front of a screaming Mi, who was then beheaded. Their bodies were chopped and sent to the kennels.

Empress Dowager Wang confronted her son with the details of the treason by Chunyu and Mi and their execution. The Emperor was shocked that his mother did not seek his permission to execute his dear friend, and he was agitated.

Empress Wang questioned the Emperor about XuPing's pregnancy, her virtue, and Chunyu's involvement. The Emperor turned on his mother angrily and warned her, "Do not doubt the purity of XuPing, a chaste Han Princess. No man has been with her other than me. It is prophesied that our child would be abducted. To thwart such an attempt, I will keep her under house arrest until his birth."

Realising that her son was very emotional, the Empress dropped the discussion on XuPing but insisted that a Wang be in charge of the military. After much persuasion, WangMang was declared the commander of the armed forces.

****

ShiXi was sure that with his current information and devious plan, he would get enough favour from the first Empress Feiyan to be reinstated as head of the palace administration. "Royal Highness, I have some disturbing information to share. However, if you approve, I also have plans to mitigate the situation."

Feiyan said, "The Emperor is troubled that his friend Chunyu and mistress Mi were executed without his consent. He hasn't gotten over that shock and is depressed."

ShiXi said, "I know, but I didn't come here to inform you of that."

Hede excitedly asked, "Is XuPing dead? Did the old hag finally execute her? I am expecting that after the unforgivable deceit by her laotong sister."

ShiXi said, "Shall we talk in the garden? The sun is up, and we can catch some heat." Feiyan quietly walked into the vast palace garden, signalling her eunuch bodyguards to stay put.

ShiXi did not mince words. "I am sure you know that XuPing is under house arrest with soldiers guarding her. Did you know the guards are there to prevent anyone from entering rather than leaving?"

Feiyan impatiently enquired, "Isn't that the same, preventing people from entering or leaving?"

ShiXi whispered, kneading his hands. "Is it? If people are stopped from coming out, you won't know what's happening inside," he scoffed and added triumphantly, "XuPing is in an advanced stage of pregnancy." He struggled to suppress his smile of victory as the sisters looked back at him in shock. Their world came crashing down when they heard that their archenemy was pregnant.

"Who is the father?" asked Feiyan, but she knew deep within that it was the Emperor.

ShiXi said, "On the night of the fertility rituals, ShiDan told the Empress that he was there with the Emperor, and no one has entered the house since then. XuPing is above reproach."

Hede looked at his sister accusingly. "The day we sent him off, miffed at him for sparing XuPing?"

Ignoring their turmoil, ShiXi said, "Ah, the fertility rituals work. The witch is indeed powerful." It seemed the sisters had not heard him; they were weeping.

After some time, Feiyan recovered enough to ask in a small voice, "What do we do now? You said you have a plan to save the situation." The haughty sisters had wilted upon learning that XuPing was heavy with a child.

"We need a miracle to save us from disgrace," wailed Hede.

"I can provide a miracle if you can play a small deceit," ShiXi said and continued. "Having a child without witnessing the impregnation will not go down well with the administration, especially after Mi's betrayal. Surely, the Emperor will overrule such talks by saying he was protecting the newborn from abduction."

ShiXi smiled. "We have to make the Empress kill XuPing through WangMang. I will create sufficient doubts about the father of XuPing's child since the conception was not witnessed. WangMang is a stickler for rules and will convince the Empress to remove her to protect her son's name. The imperial regime won't tolerate even a rumour to tarnish the Emperor's name."

The two sisters listened intently and agreed with ShiXi's assessment. Feiyan asked, "She should have executed her already. Why is she waiting?"

ShiXi said, "Han legacy! Her priority is to ensure the continuation of her lineage at any cost. At least XuPing is pregnant, and her son swears by XuPing, and ShiDan is a witness."

A tear rolled down Feiyan's face. "If XuPing is pregnant, the father is Emperor Cheng. I have no doubts about that! That haughty woman is too loyal to cheat!"

Hede asked, "What's your escape plan for us?"

ShiXi said, "If the Emperor impregnates someone in the harem and the eunuchs witness it, Empress Wang will quietly eliminate XuPing to avoid rumours of impotence against her son. I hear that WangMang pleads with her to eliminate XuPing to prevent a blemish on the Emperor's masculinity, but she steadfastly refuses to listen to him."

The Zhao sisters looked at him in confusion.

ShiXi explained again, "You wanted my help eliminating XuPing? I am offering you that opportunity. All you have to do is manage a few weeks of deception."

Hede enquired, "How? Explain."

"We need Hede's bedchamber eunuch and servant to declare that she has missed her moon cycle. This will force the Empress to kill XuPing and remove all embarrassment to the Emperor." Hede was already shaking her head in disagreement, but Feiyan's eyes narrowed, thinking ahead.

Hede said, "The eunuchs are experienced and too thorough for us to fake missing a moon."

ShiXi continued as if he hadn't heard her: "Soon after, one of you will get pregnant, and everything else will be forgotten."

In impatience, Feiyan stomped her foot. "ShiXi, if we knew how to get pregnant from an impotent husband, we would have done it already." She did not complete her thought, her voice trailing as her mind quickly put the missing bits in place.

She beamed when she finally declared, "Of course, we ask the witch to help us get pregnant, just as she helped XuPing."

ShiXi agreed. "She is competent. She can provide the herbs to fake missing moons."

"Will she help us?" Feiyan asked cautiously

"Of course, she will. I was head of the palace administration for my effectiveness. I spoke to her before I came here," he said confidently, radiating the aura of a man who had figured everything out.

Feiyan was impressed. "What did she say?"

ShiXi pulled on his long moustache and said, "She must give your sister potent herbs to suppress her moons for three months. She will have the same symptoms of morning sickness and nausea, all in line with a pregnant woman." The Zhao sisters listened quietly, and Feiyan interrupted.

"Why Hede, why did you choose her?" asked Feiyan

"You can protect her better, as you are the first Empress when the pregnancy fails. Women experience false pregnancies all the time, and the onus for verification lies with the eunuch physicians. Moreover, after she stops the herbs, she will need at least three moons to become fertile again."

"So?" asked Feiyan

"Hede will be declared pregnant by the eunuchs, and it will be independently verified by the physicians belonging to the Empress. They will not leave it to just the harem physician for confirmation. In the meantime, you can go through the fertility rites," ShiXi summarised.

Feiyan asked, "Why will the Empress kill XuPing? Why can't we get pregnant without all this subterfuge if the witch is ready to help us?"

ShiXi chuckled. "Once XuPing delivers a baby boy, it won't be possible for the Empress to suppress the momentous news, especially since the Emperor acknowledges her. XuPing will be promptly reinstated as the first Empress."

"We don't have time to waste. We show Princess Hede as pregnant and the seed of the Emperor as powerful. That will give the Empress hope and force her hand to eliminate XuPing."

"What about me? I want a son, too," said Hede.

ShiXi said, "Yes, of course. Mercifully, you will not have to go through the entire fertility rite. All you need is womb rejuvenation. The mandatory celestial appeasement will be done for you through your sister."

Feiyan asked ShiXi, "What has she demanded as payment?"

ShiXi smiled, "Gold, grain and bronze ingots. She negotiated a transport ship with a crew to take her to some south kingdom. I agreed on your behalf." The Zhao sisters smiled in appreciation at ShiXi. Indeed, he was efficient. It was an ingenious plan.

****

A month later, Hede missed her moon. A day later, this information spread like wildfire through the palace, and it was no surprise to Feiyan when the Empress Dowager's eunuchs came to examine Hede. She was advised bed rest, and physicians attended to her every need. A jubilant Emperor visited her and sat beside her, always inquiring about her health and well-being.

Ten days passed before ShiXi was summoned by a worried Feiyan. She hissed at him, "You promised that the Empress would act, and now we can hardly move without these physicians interrupting us on what to eat and what not. Do you have any encouraging news?"

ShiXi waved his hand, dismissing her concerns. "Most physicians are unanimous in their diagnosis that Hede is pregnant, except for the old palace doctor, a friend of our ShiDan. He will declare his diagnosis after Hede's third moon."

Worried, Feiyan bit her nail and asked, "What?"

"Will he find out about the herbs Hede is taking to suppress her moons?"

"I don't know, Empress. This is one aspect you must manage. Too many unfamiliar faces are attending to her, which is beyond my control." ShiXi added, "I suspect that ShiDan has asked the head physician to delay the confirmation of Hede's pregnancy to buy time for XuPing."

"Which means the Empress will not kill XuPing until Hede misses a third moon?" ShiXi said without humour. "They want to be sure the baby is fixed in her womb."

Two days after Hede's scheduled second moon, the experienced physician examined her but could not determine anything. However, other physicians criticised the court physician for incompetence and demanded that he be replaced. Empress Feiyan replaced the physician, and the newly appointed palace doctor declared Hede pregnant, and the palace burst into celebration.

****

When LiPing, the Emperor's bodyguard, called on ShiDan at night, he expected happy tidings of a son born to XuPing. He eagerly enquired, "Do we have a Crown Prince in our midst?"

Realising that LiPing had a crestfallen face, ShiDan inquired, "What happened, my friend?"

LiPing hesitated and said, "One of us has to take a risk, maybe die for Han."

"What are you saying? What happened?"

"WangMang has instructed me to get rid of XuPing and her unborn child and dispose of their bodies."

"How can that be?" It was more of a plea than a question. "You work for the Emperor, not WangMang."

"I know, but I cannot disobey the order given by the supreme general of the armed forces. He holds the official seal of the Han, granting him powers to execute anyone. This command originates from Empress Wang," he said to a physically wilting ShiDan.

"I need to provide proof of the execution to WangMang," LiPing said glumly.

"You have to take XuPing away from here, ShiDan. Live out a life in secret. I have brought some money for you. Wait for a year, and we will decide what to do next. We cannot stand by and watch XuPing and our Crown Prince murdered. I will burn down the house, leaving some charred bodies inside," he waited for ShiDan to absorb what he said.

"I don't understand LiPing. Why kill her? What does the Empress gain?" ShiDan asked in unease.

LiPing shrugged and said, "We don't have time to debate. Come," and a dazed ShiDan followed him.

While hurrying towards XuPing's house, ShiDan's frustration peaked, and he blurted out, "Why, for god's sake, tell me why?"

LiPing sighed. "Hah, the Empress wants all the blemish on the harem to be wiped out with the death of XuPing. WangMang believes that XuPing is fooling everyone. He claims that Chunyu is the father of this child." At last, ShiDan understood the grave situation they were in.

ShiDan asked LiPing to wait outside with his men and rushed into XuPing's bedchamber. He looked at a glowing XuPing, heavy with a child, and realised her delivery couldn't be far off. It was not one wasteful death, but two if they did not act.

XuPing smiled at him and welcomed him, "ShiDan, what are you doing here at this time of the night? Am I to be shifted back to the harem for the delivery?"

ShiDan knelt, composed himself, and told her about the execution order. She was traumatised beyond reason, and her beautiful eyes widened in disbelief. ShiDan had to repeat it before she could comprehend that he was telling her in earnest.

"Why?" she screamed in terror. "What did I do other than get pregnant for my husband?"

ShiDan tried to explain, but she was frightened and inconsolable. "Why do these cruel people want my baby's life to be snuffed out? First Mi, now me. When will their lust for blood end?"

Hearing the commotion, Fang ran into the room and brandished her knife at ShiDan. As soon as she saw that ShiDan was unarmed and nobody else was in the room, she dropped her hand and asked ShiDan, "What happened? I thought someone was attacking the Princess."

Before ShiDan could reply, XuPing pulled the knife from Fang's hand and held it in front of her threateningly. She reached the door to escape, not believing that ShiDan was there to help her.

Hearing the commotion, LiPing arrived with two guards. They saw a dishevelled XuPing threatening ShiDan and wailing hysterically. LiPing sent the guards back to block the exit.

Realising she was trapped, she boxed herself into a corner, brandishing the knife in front. She jerked as the baby inside her womb gave a violent kick, and her water broke.

Nobody spoke, and ShiDan watched her until he calmly said, "Princess, listen! We are here to take you out to safety." She snarled at him, and he pleaded, "We don't have time to waste."

Fang said firmly, "Her water broke; we need to deliver the child."

With tears streaking down her eyes, XuPing said, "I don't want my son to descend into this evil world. I'm taking him with me. I call upon Dizang, the god of death, to curse the Han empire to rot and ruin!"

ShiDan screamed, "No, Princess, don't do it! Listen to me," he shouted in vain as she plunged the knife into her midriff. With a gasp, she collapsed. Blood seeped from the wound, staining her robe while they stood frozen.

Fang was the first to move. "Oh, I did not foresee this. I did not see this at all," she said. She ran towards XuPing and, looking down at the blood-soaked and dying XuPing, exclaimed, "Oh, god, what kind of torture did you put yourself under, you silly, brave girl?" ShiDan and LiPing fell to their knees in deference to the Princess taking her own life.

Fang grasped the knife's handle firmly and wrenched it out with a loud grunt. XuPing screamed in agony as the instrument of death released its victim with a squelching sound.

"It won't be long now," Fang said aloud.

XuPing shivered and said, "I feel cold."

Disgusted by Fang's behaviour, LiPing shouted at her in anger, "Leave her to a dignified death, witch. She won't live whatever you do."

ShiDan and LiPing dropped their heads in respect for a dying XuPing. XuPing screamed again, and LiPing and ShiDan rushed towards the slumped Princess.

They stopped in horror! Fang had sliced XuPing's lower stomach in a moon-shaped crescent, and her hands were inside her. Princess XuPing lay shivering in the throes of death, gasping for breath.

The midwife pulled the baby out and cut the umbilical cord with the black knife. Holding the baby by its legs, she gave its backside a gentle slap, and the little bundle stirred to life with a cry. Fang ripped the dress over XuPing's bosom and put the baby's mouth on her breast. XuPing looked with wonder at her baby sucking, and Fang pulled and placed XuPing's hands around the baby.

XuPing looked at Fang and smiled. With a shudder, XuPing's tear-laced eyes glazed into stillness.

Fang sat on her haunches. "A boy, just as it was prophesied. Why am I not surprised? A Prince from the heavens." She called for her assistant, who was waiting outside the entrance.

Fang pulled the baby away from his dead mother, and the baby howled in fury. A young girl, a wet nurse, took the infant and held him to her breast, and he quieted down.

ShiDan angrily told Fang, "You knew this would happen?"

"Of course not." She wiped the blood off her hands on XuPing's gown and said, "What do you think I am, a witch!"

"Where did the wet nurse come from? If you did not know this would happen?" ShiDan demanded.

"Oh, her! I brought her in from the streets two weeks ago. Her child is dead, and I promised her a Prince. XuPing doesn't have much milk in her breasts, and a warrior needs a lot of milk to grow strong."

She stood effortlessly and told ShiDan and LiPing, "This is no ordinary boy. He is a child of destiny." She looked at them intently and said, "I demand that you honour him and keep him safe. The gods will be merciful to you in your afterlife." ShiDan and LiPing fell on their knees in obeisance to the Prince.

The infant slept, and the wet nurse wiped his body clean of his birth blood mixed with his mother's blood.

Fang held LiPing and ShiDan by their arms. "We must look after his wellbeing until he can fend for himself. He needs teachers and friends. We are answerable to hundreds of men and women who have worked for this day through the ages. Many have paid with their own lives, like his mother here."

"I am taking the boy to safety," Fang said.

She looked at LiPing and said, "Let all the soldiers outside come in to confirm her death. Cover her stomach where I cut into her." LiPing took a woollen blanket and covered XuPing's body.

Fang placed her hand on LiPing's chest and said, "No witnesses."

When they came out, all the eunuchs and servants under house arrest were waiting. Many were weeping, realising that the Empress was executed.

Fang blew out the lamps and crouched beside the front door with the nursemaid. LiPing covered them and asked his soldiers to gather inside XuPing's bedchamber. He followed them, read out WangMang's command with the imperial seal, and gave them their instructions.

In the meantime, Fang and her maid slipped out of the house.

The house inmates were gathered at LiPing's command to swear an oath of secrecy. LiPing drew his sword and clubbed an old woman at the nape of the neck with the hilt of his sword. She collapsed without a sound. The other inmates screamed in terror, realising their fate. Together with his soldiers, all of them were swiftly hacked to death.

LiPing said, "I shall sever the head of the Princess." He hacked XuPing's head and held it up for all to see. The soldiers kneeled one last time to their Princess in respect. He wrapped the severed head in a silk cloth and handed it over to a soldier. "We are done here."

LiPing commanded, "Break the house and burn it. Ensure the fire doesn't spread."

8 Fertility Rituals Gone Wrong

Emperor Cheng did not take the death of his Consort XuPing lightly. He crumbled upon hearing the news, much to the embarrassment of his doting mother. The Emperor was, however, convinced that he had not lost his son when astronomers proclaimed that a long-tailed pheasant with four tails that turned clockwise had appeared in the sky, heralding the birth of a god.

The old prophecy about his son living beyond the death of his mother gnawed at him, but multiple sources and spies confirmed that a fully pregnant XuPing was indeed beheaded. How can an unborn infant survive?

Hede had her moons and bled soon after. Empress Dowager regretted that she did not wait long enough to confirm Hede's ghost pregnancy, and now she had lost XuPing as well, and her son was devastated.

Much against the wishes of his mother, Dowager Empress Wang, and the Zhao sisters, Emperor Cheng, asked the court to come up with an eligible candidate to be nominated as the next Crown Prince.

Emperor Cheng selected Prince LuiKang's son, LuiXin, as the Crown Prince. After his time, he would ascend the throne as Emperor Ai. The Zhao sisters were appalled, but he reassured them that he would rescind the appointment if an heir were born to them.

Feiyan was convinced that ShiDan was deliberately stalling the fertility ceremony. Fang had agreed to the rituals but wanted payment upfront. She also wanted a fully furnished and manned ship that could sail the oceans for her return journey to the kingdom south of Han.

ShiDan told Feiyan that the midwife had charted bones to divine the time for the fertility rites, but she said it was not time because of XuPing's death. She would conduct the fertility rituals in a couple of years.

Feiyan was angry and summoned Fang. "Two more years to wait! Witch, no one refuses the Empress. You could die before you complete the fertility ritual. Aren't any of your assistants competent?"

Fang patiently assured them, "It is not my reluctance, Empress of Han. It is the gods' will to delay the rituals for a more auspicious time. I am but their servant." She added vociferously, "My word is as heavy as bronze, and I will not die until I perform the rituals for you. You are destined to go through the fertility rituals, same as XuPing."

Feiyan offered Fang a house in the sprawling palace, but she refused. She said it was too stifling and wanted to be in the city to offer regular prayers in the temples. With the Emperor's command that she was free, there wasn't much Feiyan could do to detain her, so she often sent her money and gifts and kept watch on her through spies.

A year later, they lost track of her, and ShiXi executed several spies for their negligence. Fang, however, left a sealed scroll stating that she would be back when the time was right. Imperial spies painted portraits of her and posted them on the docks, promising a reward for locating her, but she had disappeared.

****

It took the palace bureaucrats more than two years to locate her. She was in Changan. Her change in appearance from a ragged woman to a well-dressed noble lady threw the spies off. They were looking for an old woman in the poorer quarters of the docks and the markets.

One of Fang's assistants gave a wool overcoat to a tailor, overlooking the Empress's insignia inside the coat. The tailor was instructed to cut the heavy woollen cloak into small overcoats for children. The tailor alerted the palace soldiers, and the assistant was caught. During interrogation, she confessed that the late Empress XuPing gave the coat to Fang.

ShiXi sent spies to investigate what Fang was up to before they confronted her.

ShiXi learned that the old midwife had travelled to monasteries, engaging in religious discourses and debates with scholars. Her topic of interest was Tianzhu, a land far away favoured by the gods. They had returned to Changan six months ago. Fang and her assistants stayed at a rundown chophouse on the city's outskirts, which served food.

Spies reported that she spent time with the orphaned children, teaching them whenever they had time off from the kitchen. The inn's mistress had a soft corner for destitute children, feeding and clothing them in exchange for work. Spies said the chophouse was a nook for poor scholars visiting Changan for monastery work, and many renowned scholars visited the place to meet other like-minded people.

ShiXi summarised, "Cheap labour, employing children, especially orphans." He lost interest in the chophouse when he was informed that no one from the palace, not even the lowest bureaucrats, ever visited it.

After ShiXi updated the Zhao sisters, Feiyan summoned ShiDan and told him about Fang. "You should approach Fang and ask her to begin the fertility rites for us."

ShiXi added, "Do remind the hag that she is under imperial surveillance. She will be slain if she tries to escape."

Uncharacteristically, ShiDan couldn't suppress his sarcasm while addressing the Empress. "Sure, and after you slay her, who will conduct the fertility rituals?" ShiXi glared at him for his breach of conduct.

Feiyan wasn't offended and said, "That is where you come in, ShiDan. Go, convince her. The empire needs a Crown Prince."

Fang saw ShiDan dismounting from his litter and hailed him without surprise. "Ah, I was expecting someone from the palace once my assistant disappeared. I believe it had to be you for the negotiations. Is it because both parties trust you, or is this visit entirely your initiative?"

ShiDan smiled, holding his palms together in greeting, and said, "Can we talk somewhere private? Maybe next to that stream?" He gestured to a small canal nearby.

"Excellent, old man. I need a stroll to warm up my aching bones. I cannot stand the cold of these northern provinces."

They walked in the sun for some time without speaking before ShiDan said, "Imperial spies watch you."

Fang said, "I know."

"Why haven't you run away?"

"I have no plans to leave for some time: unfinished business, a sacrifice to the fire god for his devotees."

"Oh, if you are not leaving, I need to negotiate and confirm a fertility ritual."

"First, free my assistant as a goodwill gesture."

Shi Dan bobbed his head. "Let me speak to the Zhao sisters."

After some thought, she said, "The ship I requested needs to be docked with all the gifts loaded before I begin the rituals. I need to go elsewhere; my work here is almost complete."

ShiDan asked, "Do you plan to take the child?"

The midwife's façade cracked momentarily, but she quickly composed herself. "I wish I could take him, but his destiny lies here. He and his brothers will be trained to become warriors in this city."

ShiDan turned and looked at her in surprise. "Brothers? Is the child safe in Changan? So close to the palace?"

"What safety can I provide to a child of the gods? Let them work towards his protection," she said callously. "The boy needs friends and teachers, and I, for one, am determined that he learns what poverty and hard work entail. Nothing goes to him in a golden bowl."

Shi Dan winced, appalled by her response. "For heaven's sake, Fang, he is a Prince of Han! He needs to grow up in comfort."

"No. Let the boy learn the value of friendship. Let him starve for knowledge. Let him fight and get hurt. The child must learn how unfair life is." Fang reiterated her stand.

ShiDan sighed in resignation. "How is he?"

"The toddler is obedient, very acrobatic and a ball of energy. Like all children his age, he finds joy in everything."

ShiDan smiled and said ruefully, "XuPing would have been proud."

"Yes," replied Fang, "He is a fine boy."

"Can I see him?"

"No." ShiDan scowled at that reply.

"If he comes to you on his own accord, excellent. Just treat him as any other street urchin. They think I am their mother's sister and address me as Yima."

Fang told ShiDan that she entertained the children with stories of courage, compassion, and great sacrifices. Fang had paid the grandmasters of a few monasteries to send their best teachers to Changan to instruct the boys in counting and writing. She had also organised travelling troupes of acrobats and knife throwers to visit and perform in Changan. They would camp nearby and provide training to the youngsters and their children.

When they entered the chophouse, a small boy skipped and ran toward them. In a halting, childish voice, he asked Fang, "Can we serve food, Yima? We have fish stew and boiled turnips." He snuffled loudly while staring at ShiDan. He wiped his nose on his dirty hands, smearing them on a thoroughly soiled and torn hanfu.

Fang waved him away and said, "Not now, SuJin. This is a great man from the palace, and I must speak to him." The boy looked at ShiDan with eyes as wide as pancakes.

"Is he the emperor?" he asked, and Fang laughed.

"Of course not!" Fang said. ShiDan had tears in his eyes, suspecting that this was the Prince, but Fang did not acknowledge his inquiring gaze.

A voice called from the kitchen, "SuJin, if the guests don't want food, come and help me clean the bowls."

The small boy ran back, shouting, "Coming!"

****

ShiDan handed over the green-black knife, the hilt featuring two frogs mating back-to-back to the Zhao sisters.

Feiyan nodded in recognition, "I have seen the knife with the witch. Why did she give it to us?"

ShiDan said, "Before the fertility ritual can commence to bring life, the blood of another life needs to wash away the debt of death, tainting this holy knife."

Feiyan angrily stamped her foot and commanded, "Speak clearly so I can understand, eunuch!"

ShiDan nodded and said, "Fang demanded a human sacrifice to appease an unknown god of revenge with this black knife. The last fertility ritual was disrupted when XuPing was executed. A cup of the blood of the sacrificial victim needs to be added to the aphrodisiac."

ShiDan added, "Since the Emperor has already taken the elixir to increase his virility, he needs to be given this aphrodisiac just once to activate his life force."

The Zhao sisters looked horrified, but ShiXi bobbed his head. "Of course, I have heard these occult ceremonies have their prerequisites."

Hede asked, "We will pay her more. Let her get the sacrifice done."

ShiDan shrugged with indifference. "I asked the same question. She said it's not for her to make a sacrifice."

Hede told Feiyan, "Sister, everything looks uncertain. Let me undergo the fertility rituals, and you stay out to protect me." Feiyan and ShiXi nodded in agreement.

"When will she be ready? Asked Feiyan.

ShiDan said, "She asked us to prepare such that the rituals culminate on the seventh day of the seventh month."

****

A week later, ShiDan called on LiPing, the head of palace security, at a local tavern late into the night. LiPing was surprised to see his old ally, who looked frail and thin.

ShiDan pulled a pouch from his waist, took a dab of black paste, and rubbed it on his gums. LiPing exclaimed, "ShiDan, you... an addict of black opium!?"

ShiDan laughed mirthlessly, "Yes, that is why I am here. To tell you that I will die soon. There is a lump below my stomach that is growing, feeding on me from the inside and killing me. My physician has mercifully been blunt with me in not giving any hope. Should I care if my body dies of opium or sickness?"

He spat and wiped his mouth on his sleeve, which was riddled with similar stains, a sure giveaway of a drug addict. LiPing did not respond, and ShiDan continued, "I have a small pouch of poison to snuff out my life when it becomes... unbearable. I am a dead man walking and will be one of the few who get to decide when he dies."

LiPing was sympathetic to ShiDan. Death was nothing new to the commander. "As you say, friend! Death is a certainty for everything that lives. At least you get to choose when to embrace the black void."

After a long silence, LiPing asked, "So, why did you seek me out?"

ShiDan said, "I am sure that you know where the boy is, and with me gone, I want you to promise to protect him at the cost of your life!"

LiPing said, "Of course, old man, I am sworn to protect the imperial family at the cost of my life. This boy is the Crown Prince in hiding."

ShiDan touched LiPing on his sleeve, tears in his eyes. "Thank you! This is all the assurance I need."

****

Preparations for the fertility ritual began earnestly on the first day of the seventh moon cycle. The second harem was spruced up; the floors were scrubbed clean, the wood was waxed and polished, and new silk tapestries featuring red and gold symbols of luck and good fortune were hung.

Hede was immersed in a tub of warm but smelly mutton fat while Fang supervised maids massaging her skin to make it supple. Feiyan entered with ShiXi, holding her nose and asked the midwife, "Why is my sister in this foul-smelling bath? Wasn't XuPing immersed in milk with sweet-smelling spices?"

Fang was unperturbed and said, "Each woman needs specific treatment based on her body. You are a devotee of the goddess of face cream and beauty; you should know better." When Feiyan did not respond, Fang continued, "Beauty treatment depends on skin type. Your sister needs fat to make her skin glow since it is dry. Let me clarify that this is not part of the fertility rituals; it is merely a treatment to make your sister alluring to the Emperor."

Fang turned to ShiXi and said, "I need my knife anointed. Once I begin, we can't stop the rituals without suffering severe consequences." ShiXi nodded, understanding what Fang meant.

ShiXi motioned for Feiyan to come away, just out of earshot. She asked, "What about the sacrifice? Isn't that what the witch was hinting at?"

ShiXi replied, "Yes, she wants the knife bloodied before anything. Not to worry, though. We are holding the youngest son of a lesser noble who was thrown into the dungeons for conspiring to kill his father. He will be the sacrifice now that his family has disowned him." Feiyan shook her head in disgust.

"Princess, please give me the knife. Let's finish this quickly."

Following her command, a maid brought Feiyan the green-black knife wrapped in red silk. Feiyan marvelled at the intricate designs on the knife while ShiXi took the thick red silk cloth. "We must bring the craftsmen who shaped this masterpiece to Changan. I want to gift the Emperor an armour made of this metal." She turned the knife back and forth.

Feiyan extended the knife to ShiXi, who bowed his head without looking up to receive it. His hands were covered in red silk cloth, and she dropped the knife into his outstretched hands. The knife slipped, and he instinctively reached for it. The knife cut deep into his palm, drawing blood. It clattered to the polished floor, jolting everyone.

ShiXi muttered curses and tried to stem the blood with the silk cloth that had wrapped the knife.

Fang asked in a concerned voice, "Did you just cut your hand on the sacrificial knife?"

ShiXi responded lamely, "No, no, this is an accident. I am not the sacrifice."

He looked up to find Fang watching him with a blank face. She sighed and said ominously, "The knife chooses its victim."

ShiXi pleaded with her, "The knife cut me by mistake. How do I change its implications?"

"You mean to ask, how can you change fate?" Fang shrugged and said, "Eunuch, maybe you can replace the sacrificial victim with someone of equal stature and pray that the gods accept your offering."

Feiyan looked at a cowering ShiXi. "We can't sacrifice you. Do what you must to find a replacement."

****

As was his practice, ShiDan meditated and prayed in the temple of the sun. His participation in a human sacrifice disturbed him, and he pleaded with ShiXi to make it look like an execution. Just as he opened his eyes, a palace eunuch from the harem hailed him.

"Master ShiDan, you are requested to attend the no-moon ceremony early tonight. Eunuch ShiXi has sent a litter for you." ShiDan frowned. The sacrifice had been advanced a day earlier. Wouldn't the collected sacrificial blood not spoil?

ShiDan reached the clearing in the bamboo grove and found it bustling with activity. As he trudged in, he felt a spasm in his lower stomach. He grimaced in pain, and ShiXi hailed him, "ShiDan, my friend, welcome. You seem to have reached the end of the road."

ShiDan immediately became apprehensive; something put him on guard despite his pain. He wished he had informed LiPing of his whereabouts. He looked around for the convict to be sacrificed and realised that no such person was present—he was the sacrificial victim!

A clammy feeling in his stomach aggravated his pain. Doubling over in agony, he reached frantically for his opium pouch, wondering how he could escape from this precarious situation. Instead of the opium, he grabbed the pouch that held the poison—the poison that his physician had given him in case he decided to take his own life.

In the throes of fear, he knocked the grey powder into his hands before he realised his blunder. He dropped the pouch with a shudder. Disoriented, he reached into his belt again to retrieve his bag of opium. ShiXi screamed, "Now! Now, you idiots, take him! He is pulling out a knife!"

Two men rushed at him, and one pushed him hard, propelling him towards a tree stump prepared for his execution. He saw a brass cup glinting in the twilight. As he tumbled forward, he instinctively reached out for support, grabbed the cup, and dropped the powder into it. A foot landed heavily on his head, and his neck struck the jagged edge of the tree stump, crushing his windpipe.

Poison fell into the cup, and he desperately tried to speak. "Stop! Poison!" but all that came out of his mouth were garbled sounds. ShiDan shrieked, more in his mind than with his mouth, when a green-black knife sliced into the side of his throat, draining his lifeblood into the cup.

****

The sun rose over a palace in mourning on the eighth day of the seventh month. Emperor Cheng had died the previous night in the arms of his consort, Hede.

A jubilant Hede told Feiyan she was sure about her impregnation, but the happiness was short-lived. The eunuch attending the Emperor screamed in terror, alerting guards and doctors. The Emperor began sweating profusely and frothing at his mouth before losing consciousness.

Palace physicians rushed to revive him by voiding his stomach, but he did not wake up. The symptoms pointed to a well-known poison that physicians administered to terminally ill patients to stop their heart.

****

Li Ping rushed to the summons of the Empress Dowager and found WangMang already there. The Empress looked haggard, and her eyes were bloodshot as she lay back against the cushions, staring at the wall. Heads would roll for the witchcraft conducted, and LiPing was the main executioner in charge. WangMang was adamant that all executions must be done before the next regent took over the empire.

WangMang was curt in his command. "Execute every person involved in this unfortunate incident, especially the witch."

LiPing replied, "Yes, commander. For your ears, ShiDan informed me that the Emperor sanctioned the fertility rituals. We are trying to locate ShiDan. He has gone missing."

WangMang was about to say something when the Empress Dowager stirred from her slouch of despair. She exclaimed, "ShiDan, missing! It adds credence to the physician's diagnosis that my son was poisoned. That eunuch is loyal to my son, and he will know what happened. Find him!" she commanded.

LiPing retreated to gather all the eunuchs and servants involved in the second harem. However, he couldn't find either ShiDan or ShiXi, the principal organiser of the fertility ceremony. It took his men two days to finally locate ShiXi. They caught him while he was fleeing the city in disguise.

Under torture, ShiXi confessed everything. LiPing killed all of the men involved in the same clearing where ShiDan was murdered. They recovered the severed head of ShiDan from a shallow pit, and LiPing organised priests to chant all the relevant prayers to ensure a good afterlife for his friend.

LiPing did not have the authority to arrest Princess Hede, so he returned to the Dowager Empress and reported. The Empress ordered, "Bring Hede to me. Let her explain how my son died before I execute her."

LiPing reached the chamber of Hede. She was sitting on folded legs, holding the same cursed double frog-hilted knife, and her eyes were bloodshot from lack of sleep. She slashed her wrists and held her bleeding hands up to LiPing. "I was waiting for my summons to die."

LiPing's soldiers rushed forward, and he had to shout, "Stop! Let the woman die as she wants." LiPing asked her, "Princess, I need to tell the Empress Dowager how the Emperor died. Can you tell me?"

Hede gave him a tired smile. "I don't know what happened except that I am pregnant." At the incredulous look on LiPing's face, she continued, "I deserve to die because my crime is that I faked moons to get innocent XuPing killed. She was carrying the son of our Emperor. I killed them, and that is my regret."

Disoriented by the loss of blood, she fell to her side, blood pooling on the floor. LiPing took pity on her and lifted her frail body in his hands. He whispered into her ears, "XuPing's son lives." Her eyes fluttered open in shock, and she smiled in relief as her body went limp. The serene smile did not leave her pale face in death.

****

WangMang reported to the court, "I could not interrogate Hede personally because she took her own life to evade capture. I questioned Feiyan, and she confessed to knowing everything that happened with our Emperor Cheng. By the Empress Dowager's command, I have demoted her to a commoner and tasked her with protecting her husband's tomb in the imperial gardens.

"Since we could not punish Hede for her crimes against the empire, I have commissioned priests to chant in reverse from the Book of the Dead. Let her soul inhabit the deserts, crying for water from every traveller there but receiving none." Empress Dowager Wang nodded her head in appreciation.

WangMang continued, "I take responsibility for not personally caring for Emperor Cheng, although he did not allow me to manage his eunuchs. I am stepping down as the commander of the armed forces."

A hushed silence greeted WangMang on his momentous

announcement. It was sensational! Nobody willingly moved out of the supreme commander's post.

WangMang looked at WoShi, the grand teacher at the imperial HanKaoTzu school who had been summoned to the court. "Grand Master, let me become your student once again, continue my education in Confucianism, and learn to improve the governance of the empire." WoShi smiled and nodded his acceptance. He did not have a choice to refuse when the supreme commander made a request.

The Empress looked at WangMang and addressed him fondly. "Dear nephew, you are not responsible for the demise of my son inside his harem. We all know that you led the affairs of the army with dignity. Now that we have lost my son, do I have to lose one as loyal as you?"

She looked at CaoTeng, the newly appointed eunuch for palace administration after ShiDan, who announced her decree.

Cao Teng read from a scroll that bore the seal of the Empress. "I accept WangMang's decision and order his resignation from all official posts. However, if the Han Empire wants him back, he shall be reinstated to his original position as supreme commander."

#9 WangMang Discovers the Tomb

WangMang was not new to the HanKaoTzu school. He excelled there as a student before joining the imperial administration. He had come to the vast library to read historical documents and identify effective policies from previous dynasties.

He studied scrolls on legalism and scientific progress during Qin Shi Huang's reign. He explored the history of the Zhao dynasty, which predated Qin, and learned how they thrived.

His objective was to combine the best of ancient philosophies with Confucianism and present it to his aunt, Empress Dowager Wang, to herald a new and effective administration for the Han.

WangMang's insatiable thirst for scrolls led him to an older section of the ancient library, where he stumbled upon a room brimming with cobweb-covered materials and a sealed door.

He contacted WoShi to open the door. WoShi explained that this section predated all the newer rooms, as they expanded the library with more rooms as scrolls accumulated. They attempted all the keys to fulfil WangMang's request before realising that no key existed for that section. Upon closer inspection, they noticed that the brass lock depicted four warriors with weapons.

WoShi was surprised by this inexplicable discovery and did not want to open an ancient, sealed room. WangMang threatened to bring in imperial forces under the command of Empress Dowager Wang to open the door. He promised WoShi that he would rebuild the entire library and add more rooms to accommodate the overflowing manuscript storage if he could read what was locked inside. WoShi reluctantly agreed to open the room, provided he examined it first.

With no other options left, WoShi asked his assistant, a dwarf, to force open the lock. Despite the ancient locks on the outside, the inner room was empty. A broken wooden shelf contained documents and deeds of gifts and grants for the construction of the school, which was all that was found inside.

WoShi felt relieved. He greeted WangMang and informed him that the entire school's archives were open to him. After reminding him of his promise to add rooms and increase the imperial grant, he left the library. Despite all these innocuous gestures from WoShi, he left a scholar to supervise WangMang's activities under the pretence of assisting him.

WangMang walked in and looked around. The room was of older construction, with clever recesses just below the roof, allowing light and air to enter. He couldn't believe someone would lock a room containing a list of construction materials bought to build the school.

After a thorough second look, he decided to use the room for his reading, as it was well-secluded from the main library. He had the room cleaned and settled in.

WangMang was a frugal man who spent little on food and luxuries. He stayed in his room, eating cold meat and drinking tea while students took their lunch break. The bored student assisting WangMang showed impatience as the sun crept past its zenith.

Without lifting his head from the scroll he examined, WangMang said, "Don't worry, I will not tell WoShi. You can go for your lunch."

WangMang groaned at the exuberance of youth as the boy ran away before he finished speaking. The boy seemed oblivious to WangMang's influential position in the imperial bureaucracy, and he was disappointed that such apathetic students would soon join the bureaucracy.

A little later, he heard a scraping sound near his feet. He looked down and found a mouse nibbling on a piece of meat he had dropped.

WangMang frowned but decided against disturbing it, reminding himself to tell WoShi about the rodents in his library that could ruin his ancient scrolls.

WangMang returned the next day and the next. It was an icy winter day, and the scholar assigned to spy on him shuffled his feet, anticipating the lunch break. It had become a habit for them to communicate nonverbally about lunchtime. WangMang was in a mood to wind up his library visits, so he generously gave the boy a few copper coins and asked him to feast with his friends.

It was winter, the sun had gone down early, and the boy had not returned to light a lamp when WangMang heard the familiar scraping sound of the mouse. The mouse had become friendly with his constant gift of titbits. WangMang threw a piece of meat, and it sat back joyfully to nibble at it. He moved to stretch his stiff back, and his dagger slipped from its sheath and landed on the floor with a thump. The mouse scurried off, went to the shelf, and disappeared behind some neatly stacked documents he had examined earlier.

Curious, he moved the bundle of brittle scrolls and found a small hole in the back panel. WangMang stepped back in astonishment, realising the hole extended to an open space beyond. He measured the room's length with his foot, went outside, and measured his steps again. He was extending his walk by over twenty steps—a concealed room!

WangMang lit a lamp, and after emptying all the scrolls on the shelves, he examined the wall behind. He found fragmenting wooden pieces wedged on one side of the shelf while the other end was hinged ingeniously on concealed pivots. The entire shelf was a door. WangMang pierced away the wooden wedges with his knife. He pulled hard on the shelf, and it moved. He needed privacy to explore, but the boy had returned.

The next day, he returned with his bodyguards and sent the boy away early for lunch, giving him a few coppers. His bodyguards followed the boy to a local chophouse.

WangMang pulled open the shelf and faced a small, low-set doorway. The door led to a room resembling a shrine, and he had to bow his head to cross the threshold. The floor was cleverly recessed to provide height to the room once inside.

Four mummified warriors in full armour sat in two rows. A clay fire pot was in the centre. Beyond, he could see a high altar with three idols.

The warriors paid homage to the deities, even in death. Their bodies were desiccated yet untouched by rodents or worms. They seemed to have died from deliberate starvation. What was once a makeshift temple is now a tomb.

He found a fifth body on the floor, but somehow, it had undergone severe ravages of decay. He looked again and wondered if they knew each other, as the fifth body was out of place while everything else was in symmetry.

The fifth man had undoubtedly died of violence. The end of a green-black knife was sticking out of his stomach and was possibly a ritual suicide. Lighter patches around him could be long-gone bloodstains. Rats and worms had made a meal out of him.

He walked over to the altar ahead. Three exquisitely crafted idols glowed, strangely devoid of dust, and he felt a strange hum from them that calmed him. He counted nine steps up to the platform where the idols were placed, almost touching the ceiling. Diffused sunlight flooded in from a beautifully crafted recess. Unlike other rooms with thatched roofs, this room had a wooden ceiling.

WangMang tested the steps for strength with his leg, and the wooden structure broke. It had become brittle with age. One of the idols toppled down, and he lifted it. It was a heavy, gold metal alloy! It was a female deity, with one palm extended out in a strange greeting—a goddess! WangMang did not like goddesses! He kept the idol where it had fallen, not bothering to replace it on the high altar. He scrutinised the two other idols and realised the hum he had felt earlier had stopped.

The idols on the top shelf depicted two muscled men holding unusually long recurve bows. He marvelled at the skilled craftsmanship of those who created such lifelike idols, which featured details like scars and creases on their bodies. Indeed, the craftsmen would have seen these gods in the flesh. How else could their images be so authentic?

WangMang walked around the room, examining every corner, but he found nothing empty except a large pile of terracotta tiles embedded with copper strips. He looked at the floor and saw the mummies sitting on whatever had been assembled. Strange! The shrine appeared partially built before someone sealed it.

How had this shrine existed for so many years without discovery?

It dawned on him that he was beholding a god unseen in Han or the annexed kingdoms since the first Han Emperor. WangMang wondered how that was possible. The school was built during the first Han rule, and these idols predated the Han Empire.

WangMang frowned when he noticed a pendant hanging on the idol, which seemed out of place. The pendant was exposed when the female deity toppled from the pedestal.

He reached up and held the medallion. It felt warm, and then he was frozen in place. Energy surged into him like a mighty waterfall. He couldn't breathe, and neither could he let go!

He heard a voice that said, "Keep me close. I will guide you to greatness."

Images of him sitting on the imperial throne flashed through his mind, yet WangMang hesitated. His chest tightened to bursting, and he screamed, "Yes, yes!" The vice-like grip that had immobilised him gave way, and he gasped as life-giving air filled his lungs. He was left holding the pendant, its brittle leather strip having broken away.

WangMang examined the golden disc. It had inscriptions in a strange language and an image of a man sitting in meditation on a tiger skin engraved on it. Tiny bright stones, twinkling like real stars, were embedded above the god, forming a constellation.

He turned the disc over and smiled blissfully at the face of a fearsome goddess with many hands holding weapons and the severed head of a demon. He lovingly cleaned the medallion's surface, and the presence within the pendant whispered about the untold glory coming his way.

The voice told him that nothing else in the tomb was valuable. It warned him not to disturb the deities and to leave everything untouched, as it was destined for destruction.

Lost in thought, he closed the shelves and left the library much later than usual. He ran into WoShi, who asked about the boy he had given him as an assistant.

"He left for lunch and did not return," replied WangMang.

WoShi snapped, "I found him battered by your goons. Don't deny it. We saw the goons accompanying you this morning."

WangMang was blunt. "They might have been a little rough, but I did ask my men to delay him."

WoShi asked, "Why? What is so important that you have to beat up a poor scholar? If I remember correctly, you were as helpless as he was some time ago in this school?"

WangMang ignored any reference to the boy. "I will come again tomorrow." WangMang emphatically knotted his interlocked hands and said, "Good day, master," unequivocally ending the conversation.

#10 WoShi Finally Believes the Prophecy

A dwarf servant ushered WangMang into WoShi's presence, where he greeted his famous student with a resigned nod. WangMang squeezed his hand over a shiny pendant hanging around his neck, and his brows knitted before he pushed it deep into his hanfu.

He smiled at WoShi's inquiring expression and said, "Teacher, I have been interpreting philosophies until yesterday. Today, I am seeking the help of your brilliant scholars."

His response perplexed WoShi, "Scholars? How can scholars help you master age-old philosophies? You have to do that yourself."

WangMang harrumphed. "I thought I could find gems of wisdom within the older philosophies, merging them with Confucius's teachings to create a new philosophy for the betterment of Han—something practical, yet radical to take us forward."

Ignoring WoShi, who was pondering a response, WangMang said, "I realised that I don't have to do everything myself. Scholars can swiftly retrieve relevant philosophies for implementation in the bureaucracy if they are instructed properly."

WoShi asked him, "New philosophy? For what? The HanKaoTzu school is steeped in Confucianism and Taoism and has successfully trained the best bureaucrats, haven't we?"

"Ah, this school is a tomb if you don't know! We need to move away from age-old philosophies that have failed. I am searching for a philosophy that binds the rich and the poor." WangMang earnestly added, "Now that requires the brightest minds to combine the best of past and existing philosophies to forge a new philosophy for a greater Han—something that will result in fewer disgruntled city inhabitants and a more productive peasant class."

WoShi was concerned about the overly exuberant WangMang. "What happened here yesterday? You seem like a different person."

WangMang grinned and said, "Oh, I am a new man. I shall share my reasons along with your scholars. Summon them."

The gentle chiding was infuriating for the grand teacher, but he couldn't refuse a high-ranking bureaucrat like WangMang. "Alright, my scholars need a challenge and money. I shall call them to hear you, but if they refuse to join you, please accept their choice gracefully."

A radiant WangMang beamed enthusiastically. "Of course! Although, I very much doubt they will refuse my offer."

WoShi cautioned, "Whatever your plan, don't mistreat my scholars like you did yesterday," and snapped at his dwarf servant, JiaShao. "Summon everyone available."

WangMang interjected, "Not everyone, half-man; you just need to call three of them: YangXiong, HuanTan, and LuiXiu."

The dwarf looked at WoShi for instruction.

WoShi stared at WangMang and said, "Those are our best scholars!"

WangMang replied, "I know." WoShi gestured to his dwarf assistant to fetch them.

WangMang looked at the retreating dwarf with a creased forehead. "Dwarfs are secretive creatures, and this school has quite a few—a whole clan for the upkeep of this large estate! Do they still go on their annual visits to their ancestral lands on some mountaintop?"

WoShi grunted and said, "They are not secretive; nobody wants to mingle with these unfortunate people. By employing dwarfs, every able-bodied man is available for the imperial army. The last place you want to find men of fighting age shouldn't be at a school when war demands resources."

WangMang was wary. "They listen to everything spoken here. Is it safe?"

WoShi assuredly stated, "They keep to their kind. These dwarfs have been with the school for generations and are not intrusive or controversial. Do you recall any breaches of information from this school through the dwarfs?"

WangMang agreed, "No."

WangMang casually inquired, "How far back do they go? Were they here when the school was constructed?"

WoShi snorted, "I doubt that! Maybe five or six generations. One of our illustrious philosophy teachers was a Lui and a dwarf if you can recollect."

WoShi speculated, "Maybe since his time, they congregated here."

The three scholars rushed in at their master's summons. WangMang smiled warmly as they walked in and greeted him with deep reverence. It was evident that they held him in high esteem.

WangMang greeted each of them courteously with a preamble.

"HuanTan, you changed the water wheel to pound rice using large hammers. Your work has provided the army and the palace with a large quantity of flour. We are pleased with it." HuanTan looked surprised at the praise he received from the commander and blushed happily.

"LuiXiu, you are the author who merged Confucian thoughts of materialism and legalism into practical laws that could be implemented to govern an empire." After acknowledging LuiXiu's appreciation for the praise, WangMang turned to the last scholar.

YangXiong is deeply influenced by Taoism, which teaches that a person can embody both good and evil. Thus, an individual's behaviour relies on his power and the opportunities presented to him.

Therefore, we must regulate individuals through laws and penalties to uphold a fair society.

WoShi couldn't hide his shock when WangMang mentioned each scholar's specialities. "What do you want from this group?"

"I want to show and tell what I need from them," WangMang grinned at WoShi as he turned and walked towards the library. WoShi and the scholars followed WangMang as he led them to the previously locked room. He spun around and asked them, "Are you afraid of ghosts or the dead?"

WoShi replied, "Don't be silly. We consecrate this ground. The dead won't frighten anyone here."

WangMang replied, "Really! All your lives will change in a few moments."

WoShi looked at WangMang quizzically as he emptied the shelf on the wall and exclaimed in exasperation, "Now, what?"

WangMang pulled the secret door, and it creaked and swung open.

WoShi looked wide-eyed at WangMang when he turned back triumphantly. He said, "I leave you alone for a few days, and you find something that none of us has seen in our lives."

"What's inside?" he inquired nervously. Instead of a reply, WangMang moved aside and asked them to enter. WoShi fell to his knees as soon as he crossed the threshold.

WoShi prostrated on the floor and mumbled, "Zhang Liang and the four wise men, you honour this wretched man." The scholars looked at WoShi and the mummified bodies with unrestrained curiosity.

WoShi was inconsolable. Nobody had seen him shed a tear or lose his composure like this before. "Please accept my apologies for not believing the legend, teacher. I am truly sorry!"

WangMang looked at WoShi and said, "Zhang Liang, the founder of the school of all people— who else?" He shook his head in disbelief and exclaimed, "Now we know the whereabouts of the fabled immortals. They are just dead people, hidden away."

HuanTan examined them and remarked, "Giants, powerful physiques, but starved to death! Hairy and muscled, I can't imagine they are of Han stock. Look at the size of their swords! Surely, they must have left clues about what they ate and how they practised their war skills to wield such mighty weapons. Imagine a whole army of such strong warriors."

LuiXiu exhaled and said, "By the breath of the most wicked demons, imagine what havoc a small army of these men could do to the enemy."

WoShi pleaded for reverence. "They are men of gods! You are privileged to be in their presence."

WangMang smirked and said, "Yet I am the first to enter here, not you, the grandmaster, or anyone before you. They are just a pile of dead skin and bones."

WoShi sniffled and said, "Don't disparage them, WangMang! They held the power to forge an empire!"

"Really? Then, by entering this tomb first, maybe it's my destiny to forge a new empire." He said this with an unabashed grin.

Pinching his nose, YangXiong said, "There is a peculiar smell in this room, similar to what lingers after a lightning strike. Maybe something here in this tomb attracts lightning! It could be why thunder and lightning are always prevalent near the school."

HuanTan remarked, "There is something here that these men did not want the first Emperor and the bureaucracy to discover. They wanted someone—maybe a specific student or grandmaster—to find the tomb in later generations. Otherwise, why build this temple in the middle of a school?"

YangXiong added thoughtfully, smiling at WoShi, "Perhaps a combination of a grandmaster and a student."

"I am the student who found this tomb! Now, the reason we are assembled here," WangMang said impatiently. The voice in his head urged him to leave the tomb.

WangMang said, "Our bureaucratic policies are flawed, leading to poor governance. We need an infusion of old and new thoughts to strengthen Han. The peasants are less productive today, facing challenges due to flawed policies, while the corrupt bureaucracy oppresses the commoners. Day by day, the rich seem to get wealthier, while the peasants get poorer." The young scholars nodded vigorously. WangMang was echoing their very thoughts.

WangMang looked at WoShi once before turning to the scholars. "Together, we can devise a new doctrine to administer this vast empire. Are you willing to work for that?"

Holding their fists out in acknowledgement, the scholars bowed and said passionately, "Of course, great commander, we will serve you and the empire."

HuanTan asked WoShi, "Is that alright, teacher?"

WangMang responded before WoShi could say anything. "Our teacher has agreed to spare you in the empire's interest. He has work now. Surely, he has to hide this tomb." He smiled charmingly at WoShi.

"I no longer find anything appealing here. This school is nothing but a tomb! We shall build another one!" WangMang's arrogant and overpowering demeanour surprised and worried WoShi.

WangMang told the scholars, "You may move into rooms reserved for senior bureaucrats near my accommodation. Do not hesitate to request anything for your comfort."

WangMang turned to WoShi. "Leave everything here as it is. It is my command."

As WangMang walked past WoShi, he purposefully pushed the face of the pendant for WoShi to see. He beamed triumphantly when the old teacher baulked. WoShi realised that it had been taken from the tomb. With a flick of his shoulders, WangMang adjusted his hanfu and walked away as WoShi watched him leave in despair.

****

A few weeks later, WoShi's dwarf guards woke him up in the dead of night. YangXiong was waiting to speak with him. A tousled WoShi asked, "What happened? Why now, in the dead of the night?"

YangXiong replied, "I can't be seen with you, master."

WoShi yawned and gestured to JiaShao. "Tea?"

After sipping the hot brew, YangXiong said, "Ah, how I miss the tea made here — strong and refreshing."

He looked around to confirm that no servants were nearby to overhear them. WoShi reassured him, "Go on. What's spoken here stays here. You know that."

YangXiong relaxed and said, "We believe an infant of imperial lineage is being raised somewhere in obscurity."

WoShi snapped out of his sleepiness, and YangXiong smiled. "Shocking! Isn't it? A Prince who holds the heavenly mandate to rule. All the rebels of the empire will flock to him, and we could have a bloody war in the streets. The empire, as we know it, will collapse and fragment.

WoShi's face went ashen, and his hands trembled. He carelessly put his teacup down, spilling the tea. "How can you be sure that an imperial child is growing up outside the palace? No Prince or infant can escape the eunuchs."

YangXiong disagreed. "Master, now that the Zhao sisters are gone, palace servants are disclosing sordid details that have remained secret all this time. Reports mention not one but two infants, both fathered by Emperor Cheng. Although it seems improbable, circumstances and witnesses indicate that these infants exist. Military spies are searching everywhere for them. I hear they are paid extra to kill any boy between the ages of three and six in the nobility without an imperial document confirming the time of conception."

Shaken from his pensiveness, WoShi said, "There are hundreds of children among the nobility without documented conception time. Moreover, this certificate can be bought from a corrupt officer."

YangXiong replied, "Yes, indeed. That is why any child with a reasonable doubt about their birth or adoption will die."

WoShi exhaled loudly. "So, many innocent children will die! For what? Who is doing all this?"

YangXiong sidestepped the question and asked, "Teacher, why did it not surprise you when WangMang opened the hidden door? You were taken aback, but it did not seem a total surprise."

WoShi did not reply, and YangXiong passionately said, "Teacher, I work in the palace now. We have verified many of the prophecies from the early days, including those related to Empress Wang. They are facets of a single prophecy, unravelling rapidly even as we speak."

WoShi's eyes narrowed, and his bushy eyelashes bunched together. "I find it difficult to believe all this."

Yang Xiong said, "This school, the tomb, and Zhang Liang are all connected to the prophecy." He gave WoShi a crooked smile and added, "A succession of three emperors will die without a progeny, and the Yellow River will turn three times."

He leaned forward to look WoShi in the eye. "The current Emperor Ai could be the first of three. He is afflicted with a strange illness. The Yellow River is silting up. We have many incidents of boats and ships going aground." WoShi was taken aback by this disclosure.

"What are you implying, YangXiong?" WoShi exclaimed.

"The Han is thrown into turmoil when the Yellow River changes course and successive emperors fail to produce male heirs. This confirms part of the prophecy. By extension of the same prophecy, it also affirms that the son of Emperor Cheng is alive. Isn't this the school where the boy will come?"

WoShi asked him, "Why would he come here? So close to the imperial palace?"

YangXiong replied, "As grandmaster, you know the boy will come here to learn. The tomb is here for him. That is why you were not surprised when WangMang opened the secret door."

Although very close to the truth, WoShi denied it, snorting in disbelief. "What nonsense! Just because we unearthed a tomb. What about WangMang? What's his take on all this?"

YangXiong said, "Strangely, WangMang doesn't care. He believes the boy is no threat to him because he won't be able to prove his royal conception."

WoShi nodded in agreement, "That's true." After a few moments of disquiet, he asked, "What do you want, YangXiong? Why are you telling me all of this?"

YangXiong nodded. "When the boy comes here, send word to us. We must prevent the prophecy from unfolding and save Han from chaos."

WoShi arched his eyebrows and said, "Kill the boy?"

YangXiong smirked and replied, "You taught us military strategy. What is one life worth compared to thousands that could cripple the empire?"

When YangXiong left, JiaShao, the dwarfs' leader, who had been listening in clandestinely, approached WoShi and said, "It's time,

Master WoShi."

WoShi shook his head in disbelief and said, "As preposterous as it seems, events are falling into place. We can't deny the tomb in our midst."

He looked at the dwarf and asked, "Can we trust YangXiong?"

"No," JiaShao replied emphatically. "Their loyalties have changed. We can expect spies to check on the antecedents of all novices joining the school."

WoShi harrumphed and said, "I've lost my sleep."

In the following days, WoShi methodically executed the plans handed to him by his teacher, who had received them from his predecessor. They were following the plans written by the first teacher, Zhang Liang!

#11 WangMang's Daughter Marries LuiKan

WoShi made discreet inquiries within the Lui clans and among the nobles to locate adopted children aged four to ten. He quickly abandoned his search because people became apprehensive of him when many adopted children died.

Years passed since the night Yang Xiong met him, but the children continued to turn up dead. WoShi suspected this to be the work of the dreaded forbidden troops, deployed by someone high up in the imperial bureaucracy to ensure secrecy. He suspected his scholars, now working with WangMang, to be behind these murders because spies did not have the wherewithal to go through imperial birth records to identify adopted children.

JiaShao, the dwarf chief, confronted WoShi. "Master, we can't sit idle, waiting for the boy to come to us. What if he needs help? We must find him."

WoShi snapped at him in irritation. "You know that I have searched everywhere for the boy. Let him come to us if such a boy exists." JiaShao looked at him with reproach.

WoShi apologised for snapping at JiaShao and gently asked, "What has happened now that you are reminding me of this search?"

"Three emperors will die without a successor," JiaShao said ominously, "I am here to inform you that Emperor Ai has succumbed to his illness just as YangXiong said."

WoShi sat up in shock. "What!"

"He is the first of the three if you believe the prophecy. The boy is out there, somewhere."

****

On the advice of senior mandarins, Grand Empress Dowager Wang brought nine-year-old Prince LuiKan to Changan and crowned him Emperor Pingdi. WangMang was elevated to regent to rule the empire until Emperor Pingdi came of age.

WangMang used spies to spread misinformation that the Lui clan had lost the mandate to rule. They informed the populace that WangMang abhorred power and wealth and was more of a sage sent by the heavens to revive the empire to its former glory. The propaganda worked, and people hailed WangMang as Han's saviour, a champion of the poor.

****

WangMang had an appointment to meet Empress Wang, and he preferred to walk across the vast palace from the east gate, keeping the courtiers waiting. He could have taken a sedan chair, but he preferred to walk within the palace walls like an ordinary man. Of course, his spies would ensure that the commoners heard an exaggerated version of how he walks to meet the Empress.

The massive imperial complex contained the main palace for the Emperor and dowager Empress and significant residences for many others, including consorts, concubines, eunuchs, and high-ranking bureaucrats. An army of servants and bodyguards supported them, making the palace a city unto itself, housing thousands of people.

Walking to the Empress's court would take time, allowing him to contemplate what he intended to tell the Empress Dowager.

His spies informed him about Cao Teng, head of palace officials, who frequently beseeched the Empress to reduce the regent's powers. While WangMang had support in the armed forces and the bureaucracy, his influence among Empress Dowager Wang's courtiers was limited. To neutralise CaoTeng's influence, he had to consolidate his hold on the young Emperor Pingdi.

A hush fell over the court as he strode in. CaoTeng was on his knees, appraising the Empress with some detail. The royal bodyguards beside the Empress Dowager sharply knocked the wooden floor with their spears, and all heads turned towards him. WangMang, as regent, took precedence over everyone in court.

WangMang knelt in reverence before Empress Dowager Wang. "Your Highness, two emperors have died without an heir, and the ominous prophecies are partially fulfilled." He paused for effect.

The Empress sighed heavily and demanded, "What do you think will happen, Regent? Many times, these prophecies don't materialise?"

WangMang turned to include the courtiers and said, "Most of our villages and cities are on the banks of the Yellow River. We have reports that the river is bringing in unusual amounts of silt from the mountains. Our scholars believe the silt will soon block the river and change its course."

Many courtiers cried in concern, "Regent, that would be disastrous for the people living on the riverside!"

WangMang said, "Not just them, all of us will be affected."

After ensuring he had the full attention of the alarmed courtiers, WangMang added, "Once the river chooses a different path, it will bring drought to the villages along the dry riverbed and breach the shores elsewhere, inundating fields and flooding villages. Crops will fail due to drought and floods, leading to famine, disease, and death for tens of thousands of our people in each province." The entire court gasped in shock.

WangMang painted a bleak future. "Now, imagine the chaos if the river turned three times. The peasants would rise, shouting that the heavenly mandate to rule was lost to the Lui. We could face rebellions across the empire, with a clamour for a new dynasty." The courier howled, and everyone in the court began discussing the implications.

The Empress lifted her hand, and her bodyguard struck his spear on the floor. The buzz in the court ceased. With her eyes wide in shock, the Empress asked, "What do you suggest we do, Regent, to prevent such a bleak outcome?"

WangMang said, "I implore you to choose a fertile girl as the consort for our young emperor. Let the cries of a newborn Han Prince break the evil effects of this vile prophecy."

"Is that all?" asked the Empress.

WangMang shrugged, saying, "We break the prophecy and limit the damage. That would be the quickest and simplest remedy." Her courtiers nodded, and the Empress agreed.

The Empress asked, "Who do you suggest we choose as the Empress to avert this tragic situation? I will surely consider your counsel."

WangMang bowed and said, "We must find a noble girl with a proven lineage and a fertile womb. I take it as my responsibility to scour the empire and identify eligible noble ladies for your final selection."

He glanced at CaoTeng and smiled before delivering the final blow. The palace was abuzz with rumours that WangMang wanted his daughter to marry the emperor, having arranged many occasions for them to meet and bond.

WangMang turned to the Empress again and saw her forehead creased in thought. "By custom, the Emperor would have one consort as Empress and eleven concubines. I have already started a selection process by identifying eligible noble ladies."

Empress Dowager gazed at her nephew with softened eyes. "It would be a relief for me if you could shortlist eligible girls for young LuiKan." She shrewdly asked, "Now tell me, why did you come to my court?"

WangMang said in a hurt voice, "There is talk in the imperial corridors that I am garnering too much power as regent. This is not true. I am trying to consolidate the Han blood and thwart a dangerously unravelling prophecy."

He looked at CaoTeng in the eye and said, "To prove my good intentions, I declare that all eligible girls in the Wang family, including my daughter, are not to be considered for selection."

WangMang's declaration surprised Cao Teng, while the Empress was furious and expressed her displeasure vehemently. She said, "Your daughter, HuangHuang, is my child and my blood. Excluding her is not wise. I reserve my decision on this matter. Let the selection process begin."

Cao Teng was confused but happy with WangMang's declaration. He knew that if the Emperor married HuangHuang, the regent would practically become the emperor, having the power to overturn decisions made by Empress Dowager Wang.

****

CaoTeng waited outside the audience chamber until WoShi, who had sent a petition to WangMang for funds, concluded his audience. When WoShi came out, he said, "Did you hear that? In my wildest dreams, I did not expect WangMang to exclude his daughter from snaring the young emperor. Surely, the Empress would have chosen her."

WoShi replied, "HuangHuang is a kind and overly sweet child, unlike her father."

CaoTeng agreed, saying, "That child of his differs from her father. She had a good upbringing and is a lady. I hear she is a scholar and well-educated in Confucian values. Maybe WangMang loves his daughter and doesn't want her to marry LuiKan. If he dies, her life could be ruined." WoShi gave a noncommittal grunt.

CaoTeng asked, "I feel bad for her. Shouldn't she be excluded for the greater good of the Han empire?" He looked at WoShi for approval; he grunted again and continued his walk.

CaoTeng rushed ahead, blocking WoShi in the corridor. "What is the matter with you? Did you not hear anything I said?" He then asked, "I look forward to your point of view, WoShi. You are a master strategist!"

WoShi laughed blandly, "CaoTeng, you are a novice in WangMang's style of politics. HuangHuang will become the first Empress, one way or the other," he said to a stunned CaoTeng.

He walked ahead, turned back, and told CaoTeng, "...and soon."

****

A month later, young girls chosen by WangMang thronged the temple of NuWa, seeking divine blessings to be selected as LuiKan's consorts. At the same time, the Empress Dowager was visiting the nearby temple of the Jade Emperor.

The Empress was surprised to find a large crowd protesting before the NuWa temple, demanding that WangMang's daughter be included in the probable list.

She summoned the temple priest and asked why people demanded HuangHuang's inclusion when WangMang, as a father, had voluntarily removed his daughter from the probable list.

The priest answered, "The people are wise, Your Highness. WangMang has produced many sons, which is a sign of virility, suggesting that HuangHuang, his daughter, has a fertile womb. Moreover, HuangHuang's kindness and good qualities make her the most suitable candidate to become the next Empress."

On seeing that the Empress was present nearby, people began screaming praises for WangMang's daughter, comparing her to Empress Dowager Wang. Empress Wang made her offerings to the Jade Emperor and returned to the palace. To her annoyance, the crowd followed her, demanding that HuangHuang be included in the probable list as people's choice.

Empress Wang called for CaoTeng and asked him, "Is it true that the people's choice is Princess HuangHuang? What do you have to say about this?"

CaoTeng replied carefully. "Empress Dowager, I think we should respect WangMang's wishes as a father. Let's not include his daughter in the list."

Empress Wang's face became resolute as she said, "WangMang is a servant of Han. A demand from the people of Han will be binding on him."

CaoTeng flinched helplessly, and Empress Dowager asked, "What is your opinion about the girl?"

CaoTeng replied truthfully, "She is a lovable and cultured child. She would be a perfect choice as Empress, except for her father's position of influence. Together, they would wield considerable power over the empire."

He openly confessed his fear to the Empress, "With a binding marriage, WangMang's control over the empire would be complete."

Empress Dowager replied in anger, "Preposterous! I am Han by marriage and a Wang before that. The Wangs have always served the imperial Han with honesty. Why, WangMang himself gave up his position as commander-in-chief of the armed forces, didn't he?"

She paused for a moment and said, "CaoTeng, bring HuangHuang to me. I shall adopt her as Princess Wang. By adopting HuangHuang as Princess Wang and marrying her off to the Emperor from the house of Lui, I can ensure that WangMang's promise remains unbroken."

In a final desperate attempt, CaoTeng passionately suggested, "Empress, shouldn't we include her in the list of probables for a fair selection?"

Empress Dowager sat straight in her chair and hissed at CaoTeng, "I have spoken, bureaucrat. Make it happen."

Young Emperor Ping and Princess HuangHuang were married with much pomp and ceremony befitting an Emperor of Han.

****

A year later, copious rains in the mountains brought down heavy silt, clogging the river basin and blocking the water flow, causing the Yellow River to change course. The fertile northern settlements that produced millet and rice dried up, resulting in famine and drought. Thousands of ships and boats sat aground on the dry riverbed, and people revolted against imperial rule for angering the gods.

Angry peasants lynched government officials and bureaucrats, forcing WangMang to deploy his army to excavate and remove the massive silt dams, allowing the river to flow again.

In a show of austerity to the people, WangMang turned out all redundant consorts and their servants from the palace. While the servants found jobs elsewhere, the older women who had lived in luxury all their lives had nowhere to go. Many were robbed and killed, while others couldn't bear the hunger and cold of the streets. The consorts took their own lives, littering the main road to the palace with their bodies.

****

The low-level palace bureaucrat overseeing the imperial gardens was supposed to treat Feiyan as a servant responsible for maintaining her husband's tomb, but he treated her respectfully. Despite her low station, Feiyan ensured immaculate attention to duty and maintained an Empress's regal poise. She interacted with palace bureaucrats as if they were insignificant, and the bureaucrats feared she would be readmitted to the palace once LuiKan came of age because HuangHuang was sympathetic to her.

The bureaucrat looked at a large pile of dried leaves and twigs and asked why she was not burning them. Feiyan told him she would burn them on the anniversary of her husband's death.

Feiyan stayed nearby in a small, thatched hut, burning leaves and twigs at night for warmth. Empress HuangHuang clandestinely delivered food and grain to her, which at least prevented her from begging for food in the palace kitchens.

She ate sparingly and saved on what she could preserve, anticipating a hard winter. She was the last of the Han imperial consorts alive and did not know how long the kind Empress would support her.

After the bureaucrat left, she breathed deeply, savouring the solitude of the vast garden. She wiped a smudge of dirt from her delicate face and noticed four young boys watching her. She was accustomed to people watching her toil in the imperial gardens; seeing an Empress with soiled hands always amused the commoners.

A superb dancer, every movement she made had rhythm. She seemed to float like a goddess as she swept the fallen leaves from the lawns. A perfectionist, she kept the garden and surroundings of her husband's tomb spotlessly clean.

Autumn days were short, and she planned to have her only meal after work. An hour later, she finished and returned to the tomb, where the boys were still there. That was strange! Usually, people lose interest quickly and leave.

She settled down on a stone step, and they marched determinedly toward her. She said before they reached her side, "I have nothing of value."

The boys gazed at her intensely, awed by her beauty and imperial poise. Feiyan was aware that she still had that effect on men. She glowered fiercely at them when the stout one cleared his throat nervously to speak. He bowed with excessive exaggeration, displaying both respect and nervousness toward her as an Empress. Amused, Feiyan sat up straight from her slump and took a regal pose like an Empress at court.

"I am ChenHe, a humble servant of the imperial Han. This is SuJin,

SuWu, and this here is Qian," he said, pointing to a frail young boy. Despite the cold, the boy was sweating profusely from nervous fear. His features indicated he was from somewhere east of Han.

The older tall boy, SuWu, came forward and patted him. "That will do, ChenHe." His shoulders slumped in comic relief. Feiyan realised that it was a childish dare given to ChenHe to speak to her first.

SuWu addressed her with the poise of a gentleman from the court. "My lady, we came to speak to the true flower of this garden. We apologise if we have vexed you by following you around like bees."

Feiyan felt her cheeks flush, and she told him sternly, "That was rude of you, stalking a lone lady."

SuWu's cheeks turned red with indignation, and his earlier confidence faltered as he protested, "My lady, it wasn't rude. It was our respect not to disturb you while you toiled. We were waiting for you to take a break so that SuJin could speak to you." He gestured to a younger boy standing beside him.

SuWu said, "You work so hard and long without rest. We prayed to the trees and the wind not to drop any more dry leaves."

Feiyan's cheeks flushed a fiery red at the lavish praise, and she smiled. "Did you pray to the trees not to drop their leaves in autumn?" She laughed lightly and said, "I am a dancer trained to be graceful in my movements. Our movements are so coordinated that when I dance with my sister, people forget to breathe and sometimes faint." She giggled as she reminisced about her experiences as a dancer.

SuWu said, "Our teachers emphasise conserving strength by minimising movements while delivering precise, powerful blows. We didn't understand what those words meant until we saw you sweep the lawns."

SuJin, the other younger boy, interjected. "There is harmony in your movements, Empress. You would have made an accomplished warrior." Feiyan arched one of her eyebrows like a dancer, and she found it endearing when the boys' jaws dropped in awe.

She asked them in mock anger, "What? You are honoured to watch a woman sweep? I am used to getting accolades for dancing, not sweeping. Who are you? What do you want?"

The boy, introduced as SuJin, stepped forward, compressing his lips with tension and looking at her with unnerving intensity. He had an uncannily familiar aura, and she stared at him when realisation struck her. He had the unmistakable features of Cheng, her late husband. He had to be the son of XuPing, her arch-rival.

She held up her hand to her mouth to stifle an involuntary scream. She said, "Cheng's son? Are you my husband's son?"

He nodded and muttered, "Mother."

She spoke quietly, tears streaming down her face, "I am not..."

The boy knelt on the dry grass and said, "Consort to my father, sister to my mother." She burst into tears and gracefully fell to her knees beside him.

"Your father is buried inside! He would have been so happy to see you. He died searching for you." Feiyan pulled SuJin into her arms, and he wept with her.

Feiyan patted the tomb, calling to her buried husband, and said, "Chengdi, here is your son." She sobbed and said, "He called me mother! My heart is full."

Feiyan's tears embarrassed SuWu, prompting him to change the topic. "Empress, how did you recognise him? You are the only one who has done this!"

She sniffed before regaining her composure and said, "A woman knows her husband's child." Her radiant smile was like a rainbow that burst through dark clouds. She stared at SuWu intensely and said,

"You, too, have Han bearings and look like SuJin's brother. Are you a Han descendant?"

SuWu said, "I don't think so, Empress. I'm just an orphan."

She smiled and said, "No, you are a Lui too. Someone named you SuJin and SuWu - "Pure Gold' and 'Great Explorer.'" The boys looked at her in amazement.

Feiyan turned to SuJin and said, "Your mother was the beautiful and royal XuPing, and I hated her for her haughtiness. In the end, we are all silly women. I wish I could go back and correct our foolishness."

She patted SuJin and said, "The witch must have spirited you away as an infant before they set the place on fire."

She looked up and held his hands. "Why are you here? Do you want me to help you get back to the palace?"

SuJin grinned and said firmly, "No."

Feiyan was relieved and said, "I trusted people who had their self-preservation in mind. Now, I am powerless." She looked up with trepidation, but the boy seemed not to care.

In a squeaky voice, Qian, the smallest among them, said, "SuJin wouldn't fit in the palace. Imagine a fat and pompous SuJin in a sedan chair, whinging and mewing his way into Tianzhu." ChenHe and SuWu giggled.

SuWu told a smiling Feiyan, "We informed him about his royal lineage a few days ago. Our master HuKui revealed our destiny because the Yellow River turned."

SuJin said, "I came here to see my father's tomb. I did not expect to see you, Mother. Little Qian, who sees visions, was adamant that I would meet you. We are honoured, Empress."

Feiyan looked at Qian intently, "He must be clairvoyant. Is he related to Fang?"

Qian said, "You mean Yima? I don't know, but these last few years, I have seen visions that somehow turn out to be true. I hear strange voices telling me what could go wrong."

She stroked SuJin's head and pulled him close. "I had to see you, son. It is destiny!" Feiyan wept heavily as she kissed him on the forehead. "Be victorious! Forever and ever! I bless you with the authority of all the mothers who should have doted on you."

She pulled away, wiping her cheeks, and addressed all four. "Do not be swayed by the power and luxury of the imperial palace. It's a cage with spikes that will eventually impale you."

"Your father told me about a prophecy that you will free all Han ancestors from their pact with the gods. He mentioned that the gods may revoke the "mandate to rule" for the Han if you don't leave. You, SuJin, owe it to your father. Make him proud. He lives within you."

SuJin told her, "I will, Mother. Your blessings will protect us."

"You are so pretty, mother. Now I know why they call you a flying swallow. I hadn't realised that sweeping could be so graceful!" She laughed aloud, and to the boys, her laugh was like wind chimes tinkling in the breeze.

She sighed, "Poems, too. Many were smitten by the beauty of all your father's women, but we had eyes for your father and fought over him foolishly!"

"Come, dine with me, all of you. A part of you is my husband, and I want to serve you. Your father had many faults as a man, but I cannot fault him as an emperor." She guided them to her hut. They chatted happily, telling her about themselves while she cooked. She served them rice with dried fish.

SuJin said, "We haven't tasted such divine rice in our lives." The boys, devouring the hot rice, agreed. SuWu said, "Check the aroma. It must be palace rice." Feiyan fussed around the boys like a hen with her chicks.

She did not eat with them because there was not enough rice. The hungry boys made a short story of all the rice she had. She watched them eat hungrily in fascination, enjoying every moment and answering all their questions about imperial life.

Feiyan told SuJin, "Son, I do hope you visit your grandmother, Empress Wang, before you depart for Tianzhu. That old lady must see you and realise she is not above the gods. Too many of us died because of her."

SuJin disagreed, saying, "I don't want to meet her. She created WangMang."

Feiyan snorted, "Stay away from that treacherous man. Trust your instincts."

With his stomach full, ChenHe said, "Don't worry, Lady Feiyan, I will protect him. I am ChenHe, a descendant of General Zhao of Xiangshan. I will take care of him or forfeit my life." The intensity of his formal declaration and childish determination made Feiyan smile.

She gave him a slight bow and said, "Yes, my lord, do that to secure Han's future. You have this mother's blessing and gratitude for this service." She said gravely, "I just wish we had more valorous men like you to care for us all." The praise from an Empress made ChenHe proud. He puffed his chest out and grinned at his friends.

Feiyan reminisced, "Oh, how I wish I could spend a lifetime mothering you boys silly, but I must go, and so should you. Destiny awaits us."

The boys were sad to leave her, and Feiyan asked SuJin to wait. "I have something to give you," she said. She went to the only piece of furniture in the hut—a small wooden casket with no imperial markings. She pulled out a false panelling and opened a red silk bag. She handed SuJin a beautiful green-black knife with a double frog at the hilt and said, "This now belongs to you if I am right."

Feiyan hugged and kissed each one of the blushing boys.

She held SuJin by his shoulders and told the others, "I am sure all of your ancestors are somehow related to this prophecy. Beyond those reasons, never forget that SuJin is the true blood of the Han—a Crown Prince. Promise me you will take care of him with your lives." The boys solemnly nodded.

Qian said, "We are sworn to protect each other, Empress. We are sworn blood brothers."

SuJin and Feiyan held each other long, and ChenHe had to pry them apart. SuJin whined like a child and told Feiyan, "I will return after training. We will take you with us."

Feiyan interrupted him, placing her fingers on his lips. "No, son. Promise your mother that you won't return. I will not allow your precious life to be jeopardised for a spent life like mine. As your father's consort and mother, I wish you success because hope is what you give us. Destiny has chosen you for greatness!"

"Now go! Be victorious! Forever and ever!"

They said goodbye and parted. SuJin and his friends walked into the fast-fading light. He turned back many times to see Feiyan watching him steadfastly until a curve in the road hid them from each other.

When news came in that Feiyan had flung herself into a burning pile of dry leaves near the tomb, nobody, not even SuWu, dared to inform SuJin about it.

****

WoShi's thoughts turned to the boy whom JiaShao was adamant they find and train—the primary purpose of the HanKaoTzu school!

The HanKaoTzu School diligently compiled fighting techniques, documenting them with drawings and including weapons training throughout the centuries. Records indicate that the school traced the origin of hand combat training to YueNu, a woman renowned for her sword fighting.

WoShi developed his intense form of martial TaoYin, heavily influenced by the erstwhile LuiAn. The scholar-Prince is credited with blending different hand combat forms into the current approach of slow TaoYin, which is characterised by deep and precise movements.

Since the days of Emperor Cheng, imperial bureaucrats, army officers, and aristocrats have frequented the fight pits, and substantial bets have been placed on the outcome. The pit fights included weapons and exotic fighters with varied skills from all over the lands who fought opponents and condemned men.

Dwarfs from the HanKaoTzu school were regular patrons of the pit fights and were aware of other facets of a fighter that WoShi and his predecessors ignored. They insisted on specific foods, including fruits, vegetables, and meat. The dwarf's endurance qualification was a freestyle attack from three sides, and the fighter had to outlast the time allotted for two rounds in the fighting pits.

****

Pleas from JiaShao, the dwarf leader at the school, to WoShi had become frantic as the Yellow River changed course to find the elusive imperial Prince. He argued that it would take the school many years to train a warrior, and the training had to commence when the boy was young.

WoShi desperately wanted to dismiss the existence of such a boy, but the tomb within the school was a living affirmation that suggested otherwise. How was he to find this boy that imperial spies could not?

He needed help, and the best person to help him was old SuFei, a reclusive scholar living out his last days in the Taoist monastery. SuFei would know if scholars were providing training to a boy outside the HanKaoTzu school. The journey to the monastery was arduous, passing through forests reputed to be infested with rebels and bandits.

The debatable question troubling WoShi was whether SuFei would help his arch-rival, WoShi!

#12 WoShi Visits the Monastery

WoShi reached the monastery safely, albeit after an eventful journey dressed in the everyday clothes of a scholar from Changan.

The mercenaries he hired fought against bandits in the forest. Although two of his men lost their lives in the initial attack, they chased the rest away, leaving four of the brigands dead. They were attacked despite clearly showing they were well-armed and not carrying goods. Thankfully, the fight broke up quickly when the bandits lost resolve.

"It must be the horses that attracted them," said the captain of WoShi's bodyguard in exasperation as they prepared to bury their dead. The captain glanced at WoShi's horse and said, "The novel leather strips attached to the saddle of the horse to hold the feet in a metal brace... maybe they were after that!"

"What was it called, anyway?" WoShi grunted. "They're called stirrups." Stirrups made horse travel much easier by keeping the legs elevated like in a sedan chair rather than letting them hang loose.

WoShi, however, wondered why they were attacked. Bandits loot for gain, and this did not seem like an attack motivated by profit. It was an attack by daylight, and they had not gone after the pack horses, but he kept his counsel.

To reach the monastery, WoShi had to climb a high mountain. He asked his guards to wait in the village below. He then hiked up the narrow path, rubbing wet grass and dung on his clothes to look like a travelling scholar.

It did not seem wise to announce that the Grand Master of the HanKaoTzu School had come to visit when he wanted anonymity.

Therefore, he had to wait until cranky SuFei, the Grand Master, gave him an audience. WoShi wondered if old SuFei could recognise him from their younger days. Rumours suggested that the master had become somewhat... senile.

WoShi was admitted to the monastery when he stated that he had come to meet the grandmaster. He spent his time in the cookhouse, separate from the main building, recalling his student days as a novice scholar. Nothing had changed, he mused, since his time here as a student; the drudgery was the same! The food was bland, and the straw beds were still lumpy. He spent time in their modest library and garden, patiently awaiting his summons.

The inmates gradually warmed up to him, and over many conversations, they discussed the crisis looming in the palace at Changan. They guilelessly asked him about the talented boys at a chophouse in Changan. They were surprised when he admitted he genuinely did not know the boys.

Intrigued, WoShi sponsored wine and meat, which finally loosened their inhibitions, and the inmates included him as one of them. The scholars who had last come in from Changan bragged to the other inmates about the young boys at the chophouse. Each tried to add his exaggerated version of the boys' innate abilities. WoShi listened in and gleaned that some of the boys were astonishingly acrobatic and proficient in using weapons, astronomy, and TaoYin.

It was a tall tale, and WoShi smiled. Acrobatics, he could believe. They probably picked up the rudiments of somersaults and juggling from the glut of street performers visiting Changan. These days, peasants acquire swords and bows to protect their villages and crops from bandits. However, he could not digest astronomy, and, the surprise of surprise, TaoYin! Now, that requires a knowledgeable teacher! How could young boys working at a chophouse manage that? Preposterous!

No student could gain more knowledge in Han than at the HanKaoTzu school. For a moment, he contemplated whether one of those boys was the Prince he sought but dismissed the thought. An imperial Prince wouldn't stay at a lowly chophouse and stoop to menial chores in a kitchen.

The following day, WoShi heard excited commotions and learned that the monastery's second in charge, HuKui, had arrived. Soon after, scholars became overtly hostile and avoided him. He wondered what had happened when SuFei summoned him.

****

WoShi was ushered into a sparsely furnished room with a single window. The room had a straw bed, a low table with a blackened oil lamp, and many scrolls stacked to one side. A stove with a smouldering husk was near the window, and a novice fanned the smoke outside with fist-sized poultices of tightly wrapped grain and herbs kept on heat.

Despite the smoke, the rank smell of an inmate who stayed inside most of the time overpowered his senses. One side of the wall was sooty, indicating that the resident spent long hours reading and writing in the dark. SuFei sat on the floor behind a low table, and a young man sat beside him. WoShi gave them a friendly nod without eliciting any response. They were hostile!

SuFei's voice was thin and high-pitched with age. "WoShi! Something unique must be happening in Changan to trick you out of your luxurious cocoon." WoShi was surprised because he was sure no one had identified him until yesterday.

"How did you recognise me, master SuFei?" he asked, recalling the frostiness earlier in the day.

SuFei angled his head towards the man seated beside him. "Meet HuKui. He has just returned from Changan. He would have been here earlier, but you were crafty and confused him by walking to the monastery. The rich don't walk!" SuFei chortled and broke into spasms of cough.

WoShi looked at the young man curiously. HuKui was in his prime, lightly bearded, and tied his hair in a bun atop his head, unlike the current trend of braiding hair. Unlike regular scholars, he bore scars on his arms, and his hands were heavily calloused, like a farmer's or maybe a warrior's. He was probably a rebel.

HuKui spoke in an icy voice, displaying his hostility. "The people you beat up belonged to our village, and you killed many. Their families want revenge."

WoShi was dumbstruck before he realised HuKui was referring to the bandit attack they faced on their way in. "Why attack me? I am an old man travelling to seek SuFei's help, your master. Who are you to stop that?"

HuKui said, "We monitor the mountain roads for strangers, especially your kind. They attacked you because you were a high-ranking official at the cursed WangMang's court. We must prevent whatever evil you plan to unleash here."

SuFei interjected and said, "WoShi, why come in secret if you want to meet me? My scholars wish to kill you immediately, but I asked them to wait until I spoke with you."

It upset WoShi when SuFei said, "I didn't want them to act in haste, just as they got rid of your guards in the village." WoShi glowered at HuKui, who stared back in defiance.

SuFei continued speaking, ignoring the unspoken duel before him. "You would not have undertaken this journey without a purpose. If we were a threat, you could have sent in the army. Why would a senior imperial officer travel in secret?"

WoShi said, "I am not one of WangMang's henchmen. I am a scholar and your guest."

SuFei giggled, and WoShi found the tone evil. "You are an imposter. WangMang crawled out of your school. Or am I wrong? Recently, a few more of your elite scholars have joined him to heap misery on the people. Do you deny this?"

WoShi remained silent. Arguing seemed pointless. He had to pick SuFei's brain and escape these misinformed scholars, who were determined to right a wrong he was not part of.

Ignoring his silence, SuFei continued, "I always thought the greedy aristocracy was the ultimate evil. Can you imagine scholars plaguing this empire? Men with knowledge but whose rule is inept. Your learned men are wreaking havoc across the empire with their flawed policies."

"WoShi, before we kill you, I need to know why you came here. I won't be inconsiderate when history is written."

More directly, HuKui stated, "We want to know if we are compromised!"

WoShi's expression changed, and he sneered at HuKui. "So you are up to something illegal here while speaking saintly about errant scholars, eh?"

"What if I told you I don't have faith in WangMang's policies and am not involved? Will you believe me?"

"No" was the prompt and firm reply from HuKui, followed by another emphatic "No" from SuFei.

"Why not? What have I done to earn your hatred? Or, for that matter, what have I done to anyone here?" he inquired in disbelief.

"Well, if you were indeed against WangMang's policies, he wouldn't have made you remain the head of the most powerful school in the realm—a school from which all these detestable creatures have crawled out. Why, even the gods are against this outrage. The Yellow River has turned, and now don't tell me you know nothing about the prophecy of doom," he ended his talk with a rasping cough. He grimaced in pain and held his chest.

A novice moved behind the coughing SuFei. The boy handed two heated, sweet-smelling poultices to HuKui, who gently massaged his master's back.

WoShi realised HuKui was probably SuFei's successor, but why choose a militant young man over other sedate and experienced scholars? What was he doing in Changan? Unless, of course, they were planning a revolt. Whatever the case, he was in a dangerous place. He had to calm the situation quickly and escape if he couldn't earn the old man's trust. He took a direct approach.

WoShi waited until SuFei recovered from his coughing spasm and spat phlegm into a bowl. He said, "Hear me out! I am a teacher. Hundreds of students from the HanKaoTzu school join the Imperial administration every year. We are the storehouse of knowledge for the empire, as our students alert us to every new teaching and piece of knowledge they discover." Although they looked uninterested, he knew SuFei and HuKui were listening. "What these students become later depends on their talent and destiny. Some become scholars and monks as well."

WoShi added, "Except for better grants from the imperial coffers, there is not much difference between your monastery and my school. Many of your scholars teach at our school." He paused when three men cautiously joined them, blocking the door, perhaps to prevent him from escaping. He noticed that one of them was wounded in the upper arm from a sword thrust. WoShi recognised him as one of the bandits who had attacked his party earlier.

WoShi's eyes hardened; he may have to fight his way out. He turned to SuFei and said sternly, "I am here on an important mission and would like to discuss it with you, not in the presence of hired goons."

No one moved. WoShi further stressed, "Our master hinted at this situation long ago. You are duty-bound to obey him."

SuFei responded icily, "Either you tell me in their presence, or you don't tell me at all. I cannot promise your safety either way. The usual rules of courtesy don't apply to you. You are a spy." Silence greeted his outburst, and he heard swords being drawn.

SuFei raised his hand and flicked his head, signalling for them to leave the room. The men looked at HuKui in disbelief as they walked out in frustration. HuKui scowled at SuFei.

SuFei told HuKui, "Why did they draw swords? I want to hear him out. He came to meet me." Then, ominously, he added, "I don't care what you do to him later."

WoShi said, "The novice." HuKui motioned to the boy, and he ran out.

Unlike SuFei, WoShi was a scholar and combat master. He was not intimidated by violence but maintained the pretence to his advantage.

SuFei looked at WoShi. "So, you are here to spy on the Prince. WangMang or the Empress – who sent you?"

WoShi was shocked. "Revolt on behalf of Prince LuiKan? Don't tell me that small boy is planning a peasants' revolt against WangMang. He is too young for this."

WoShi looked from SuFei to HuKui as they exchanged puzzled glances. He wondered how a monastery, a place of learning and holy men, had become militant and, surprise of surprises, involved in imperial politics!

HuKui's brows creased in bewilderment. "We are not talking about LuiKan." WoShi looked confused.

"Didn't Master SuFei say, Prince?"

SuFei sighed and said, "Tell us why you came here, WoShi."

WoShi elaborated so that HuKui could understand. "Zhang Liang devised the grandmaster position at the HanKaoTzu school with an ulterior motive. Certain rituals must be passed on from one grandmaster to the next, including an oath to train an imperial boy who would come to the HanKaoTzu school. We were also told about immortals waiting for his arrival."

WoShi paused, and HuKui bobbed his head impatiently, urging him to continue. "Frankly, I did not believe all this despite subtle indications that such a boy would turn up in my lifetime. I stoically ignored all signs as I was getting on in age and was more interested in identifying a successor who could handle imperial politics and manage the school with aplomb."

WoShi paused briefly before he disclosed, "We found a tomb inside the school library."

Despite this momentous disclosure, HuKui looked unaffected and said, "Go on."

I believe that four of the well-preserved bodies are immortals. It seems they ended their lives in a ritual involving ingestion of slow poison and fasting. They are seated in reverence before idols of strange gods. Two muscular males and a goddess, all with sharp features and big eyes. They are not of Han origin."

SuFei smiled and said, "A fantastic story."

HuKui sniggered and added, "What an improbable story! A tomb inside a school, undiscovered for centuries. I am surprised that he did not mention dragons." SuFei chuckled, but it ended in violent coughs, so HuKui had to attend to him quickly.

After SuFei recovered, HuKui ridiculed WoShi. "Tell us, Grand Tutor. What else did you find in this tomb besides these immortals, who appear to be quite dead? Treasures of untold value and scrolls of magic?"

WoShi's face had turned red with anger, and his eyes glowered. He desperately wanted to hit HuKui but breathed slowly to calm himself. This conversation was not yielding results. He decided to stop before he mentioned WangMang and the medallion. "Another body lay on the floor, out of place, and I think it's Zhang Liang. His stomach was pierced by a green-black knife, surely in a ritualistic suicide."

"A black knife? You mean a bronze one covered in soot?" HuKui asked for clarity.

WoShi shrugged his shoulders. "It's a dark metal blade, black and green with age, and the handle is made to look like two frogs are mating on it."

HuKui stared at WoShi and said, "Fanciful! Do you expect us to believe all this?"

SuFei chuckled despite his heavy wheezing. "I told you the man would try to talk himself out of this, but this is a new low, even for him! Except for that part with our teacher, the rest is wonderfully made up!"

WoShi decided to try one last time to convince them. He said, "Look, SuFei. I am here to find a boy with imperial lineage, maybe under training with one of your scholars. I have checked most of the noble households without success. I don't even know if such a boy exists in the first place."

HuKui asked, "Once you find such a boy, what do you plan to do with him?"

"Since Zhang Liang, every grandmaster has been instructed to expect a child of destiny to enrol at the HanKaoTzu school. The very purpose of HanKaoTzu school is to train him."

WoShi ignored HuKui and appealed to SuFei. "I need to find and prepare him for his journey over the white mountains into Tianzhu. This is part of our secret vows to our teacher. Time is running out! I came here seeking your help to locate him."

SuFei complained ruefully, "Out of all the scholars, why were you chosen to head the school? Many were better than you, including me, as I am vastly more experienced. " SuFei was upset that his teacher had selected WoShi as his successor to lead the great HanKaoTzu School.

WoShi said, "I can tell you today, SuFei, why that happened. In my search for a successor, I must prioritise a trait beyond knowledge, just as our teacher chose me to lead. I'm seeking a successor who makes decisions instead of waiting and negotiating, especially in uncertain situations."

SuFei coughed, spat phlegm, and said, "Don't flatter yourself, WoShi. I am sure this beautiful story about the tomb in your school and whatever else you said will impress many, but I know you as an opportunist. I am convinced you are here to quell a rebellion brewing in the countryside against this corrupt and inept rule."

HuKui signalled to SuFei for permission to speak. He addressed WoShi, "Grand Master of the HanKaoTzu school." HuKui's use of 'Grand Master' to address WoShi shocked SuFei, who looked at his successor in disbelief. Ignoring his master, he continued, "The boy you are searching for is a servant at a chophouse in Changan. His name is SuJin."

WoShi's face turned pale in shock. "A servant? Our Prince!" Before he could grasp the significance of this information, a monk knocked on the door and entered the room, placing three bowls of tea on a bamboo tray.

SuFei looked at the steaming cups and smirked, "About time. I'm getting tired of these rotten talks."

WoShi asked HuKui, "Are you certain about the boy? Who has verified his antecedents?"

HuKui replied before SuFei could interject, "You can verify all of it in person when you meet him."

SuFei turned towards HuKui, snarling. Trembling with rage, he said, "Traitor! How dare you say that WoShi will train the imperial prodigy? Don't you dare steal my revenge?" SuFei drooled and warned HuKui of dire consequences, saying, "Don't take the path my master took by trusting him. I will ensure that you regret it!"

HuKui bowed to SuFei and spoke with deep respect. "Master, we came across the boys a few years ago because Fang wanted the best scholars to train the Prince from a young age." She wanted the boys to enrol at the HanKaoTzu School for higher learning, but you changed that."

HuKui said, almost whispering, "All this just to spite your rival?" He added, "HanKaoTzu school is the logical culmination of SuJin's training. Our prejudices should not cloud our minds. Fang is a descendant of Zhang Liang, and we have someone here who is clearly instructed on what to do with SuJin for his training." He ignored SuFei, leering at him like a deranged man, and said, "Who are we to judge someone Zhang Liang chose centuries ago?"

"Have you, too, become a face reader, like him?" SuFei asked. "Deciding on hearsay? A tall story he spun out about a tomb and immortals. How can immortals have a tomb, HuKui? Why aren't they alive to train him?"

HuKui said, "Master, look ..." but SuFei stopped him with a raised hand.

"Enough, HuKui. I want you to stick to our plans. A myth this man has spun enamours you. Just as he did to my teacher."

WoShi intervened and said, "Listen to HuKui, SuFei. Destiny will set the course. Nothing else will."

SuFei sneered at WoShi, "Even as you wait here, clamped tight within the jaws of death, you think destiny will change fate." He laughed hysterically like a madman.

Discouraged and disillusioned, WoShi reached for the teacup. HuKui graciously bowed and handed him a bowl of tea. HuKui's demeanour was vastly different from when they met earlier.

HuKui nodded and smiled at SuFei when he handed over a bowl of tea to his master. SuFei told HuKui, "I enjoyed this intrigue, but now I've had enough. Let me rest."

WoShi sipped his tea and said, "There exist forces greater than us, SuFei. I pray that you heed them before our time is up." He emptied his cup and smacked his lips in appreciation. The tea was excellent, in stark contrast to the low-quality brew served in the cookhouse.

SuFei rudely responded, "Forces at play, bah! I will read out your fate, WoShi. I shall outlive you, and I shall repeat this at your funeral. You haven't chosen a successor, like me. Let that fancy school end with you. We will burn it down for producing corrupt bureaucrats."

Something was unfolding, and WoShi struggled to comprehend it. He was sure HuKui and SuFei were communicating silently.

To subvert his mind, urging him to flee the place, he asked HuKui again, "Are you sure about the boy?"

HuKui dipped his head in acknowledgement. "Anyone who meets him will confirm that he is a son of heaven—a jade warrior if ever there was one: humble, diligent, pious, and extraordinarily talented!"

WoShi was not influenced by HuKui's claim about the boy's abilities. "I apologise, but I have my doubts! Perhaps we are discussing different boys. I have encountered my fair share of royal brats. They tend to be lazy, entitled, and whiny. Your description does not align with my image of a Han Prince."

SuFei had mellowed down after the silent communication with HuKui. He said, "The Yellow River has turned, and WangMang has proved to be an oppressor with bizarre policies. We shall train the boy here, away from imperial eyes, in this monastery. When the time comes, he will lead a revolution and overthrow this corrupt regime."

With eyes burning with conviction, SuFei added, "The common man will follow him, and the army will stand down when they know their true Prince is claiming his rightful throne." Startled, WoShi was about to respond, but HuKui gestured for him to remain quiet.

SuFei was wheezing heavily and was exhausted. HuKui called for his attendant to take over and guided a crestfallen WoShi into the sparse and unkempt garden.

Sitting on a stone bench, they looked at a group of swallows manoeuvring together in the sky. HuKui said, "The birds are gathering to migrate."

HuKui cocked his head to listen, then turned to WoShi. "SuJin spoke to Empress Feiyan before her death. She gave him a green-black knife with double frogs on the hilt."

WoShi's eyes widened in shock, "A second blade, a twin!?"

HuKui bobbed his head slowly. "You could have made up any story, and I assure you I would not have believed it. However, when you mentioned the frog-handled knife, I realised you were sincere. No one can imagine and describe such a bizarre knife."

"Ah, that is a relief, but I don't think SuFei agrees with your assessments. We must convince him one way or another," WoShi said.

HuKui said, "As a matter of fact, SuFei will not trouble us anymore."

WoShi looked at HuKui with narrowed eyes. He shrugged. "It was either him or you. Your intention convinced me. I turned the teacups. He drank the poisoned tea."

WoShi was stunned, "What? They will easily implicate you."

"Will they now?" remarked HuKui.

I asked one of the talented boys at the chophouse, SuWu, how to kill you. He suggested we should carry out a bandit attack. In case you escape and reach the monastery, we need to poison you enough to make you very sick but not die. We planned to end your life in the village below, making it appear as if you died from an illness. Anyone coming in search of you would be effectively convinced."

WoShi was shocked, "That's brilliant! A boy, you say!"

HuKui watched the swallows and said, "A face reader like you."

WoShi corrected him, "A strategist! We try to think logically about what the opponent's plans are."

HuKui said, "Hmm, still a face reader."

WoShi ignored that comment and asked, "SuFei, he will suffer."

"Maybe not... he is very sick."

WoShi asked HuKui, "How did you know I was coming here?"

HuKui shrugged, "Rebels are gathering. We have people at all the stables, and most guides to these parts are sympathetic to us. We were ready when you made inquiries, but I was informed a day later."

HuKui said, "Serving the Han Prince is my destiny. He is my priority. Fang recruited me to serve him until he can decide for himself."

"How about your men? Surely, they will not forgive you for this," WoShi remarked.

HuKui grunted. "Maybe, if they find out. The monk who served us tea is my man."

"I have organised scholars with exceptional skills for the children at the chophouse, but it is not enough. The boys need formal training." He looked into the garden and said, "Surely, the elite HanKaoTzu school is the logical answer. Zhang Liang knows what awaits them in Tianzhu. I should have realised this earlier."

HuKui exhaled heavily, saying, "Scholars cannot transform boys into warriors without a conscience. That requires the cold martial training of the aristocracy."

WoShi mocked HuKui. "Did I just witness the murder of a grandmaster by his most trusted scholar right here? Anyone can become a cold-blooded killer if they believe in their cause."

HuKui cocked his head, listening to running feet. The bells tolled, announcing the death of a monastery inmate. They watched stoically as monks ran helter-skelter, and one of them came running towards HuKui.

****

A few days after reaching Changan, WoShi approached WangMang to request an audience with the emperor. He wanted to discuss increasing school funding and enrolment. WangMang considered it trivial and agreed to allow WoShi to meet the emperor.

A month later, WoShi crawled on all fours into the court, kneeling before the young Emperor and Empress Dowager Wang. The boy Emperor's face was hidden behind strings of beads falling from his hat, preventing anyone from gauging his emotions. Courtiers had to make do with how the beads shook to decide on an action unless the Emperor spoke, which would then become a law.

WoShi looked at the Emperor and imagined a bored boy waiting to hear an old man speak, and he changed his address to interest him. "Son of heaven, I thank you for the privilege of meeting you to beg my plea. I want this empire to grow to greatness under your rule. I wish to train boys your age to serve you when you come of age."

Empress Wang interjected, "WoShi, you need not grovel so much. State your petition."

WoShi smiled warmly at her and said, "Our esteemed regent WangMang has introduced a golden rule of equality between the nobles and the peasants." He paused as the sycophant courtiers screamed praise for WangMang's glorified rule.

WoShi continued, "We need more schools to ensure a successful future for Han. Our school recruitment is primarily based on personal recommendations for the children of noblemen and high-ranking bureaucrats. There are very few direct openings for the children of commoners. Let's invite novices from remote monasteries and other talented children to study at the HanKaoTzu school."

WoShi quickly added. "Once these trained boys leave the school as low-level bureaucrats and return to their villages, they will spread the great deeds of the Emperor and the Regent. The enmity between the rich and the poor will dwindle over the years. We will have many poets, artists, inventors and maybe philosophers."

The boy Emperor Pingdi was ecstatic at the suggestion and clapped his hands. WangMang asked, "Grand Tutor, how will the selection process be?"

WoShi answered, "Great regent, I propose that imperial bureaucrats who work for you select candidates. I will add my recommendations."

WangMang was pleased and said, "I recommend to the Emperor that we recruit deserving commoners and monk novices." He beamed as if it was solely his idea, and the courtiers cheered praises to WangMang.

The Emperor interceded, a first for him in the presence of the all-powerful WangMang. One of his bodyguards banged his sword hard on his shield for silence.

The boy Emperor said, "What is wrong with having schools in every county as well? We will have more scholars, which will benefit the empire." The boy Emperor's addition to his suggestion disturbed WangMang.

He turned on him and authoritatively said, "This is an imperial policy decision, Your Highness. It will be prohibitively expensive to cover every county of our vast empire. Moreover, we are already building a special school for bureaucrats here in Changan exclusively for imperial service."

WoShi waited to leave the suffocating throne room now that they had decided in his favour. He was sympathetic to the boy emperor, but there was only so much he could do.

The young Emperor was almost in tears at WangMang's gentle rebuke, which alerted the grand Empress Dowager. She firmly said, "The Emperor has spoken." A snubbed WangMang covered his frown and promptly bowed his head in acceptance.

WoShi asked for permission to speak, and the Empress agreed. WoShi stated, "The regent has a strong reason, and the Emperor has a lenient view of his people. I suggest we establish schools to teach words and to count. Let the better students come to the imperial school for selection as bureaucrats." WangMang immediately accepted the face-saving proposal.

The boy Emperor leaned forward, and his assistant hastily crawled up next to him as the boy whispered something. Four bodyguards detached themselves, rushed up to a surprised WoShi, and held him by his limbs to carry him close to the throne.

The soldiers paused while two palace servants rushed forward, sprinkled odoriferous sprays of cloves and nutmeg into WoShi's nose and mouth, and covered his clothes in musk. Palace protocol forbade body odour and bad breath from bothering the Emperor's sensitive nose.

"Grand tutor, what is your rank today?" asked the boy Emperor as WoShi swung awkwardly in the air.

The context was entirely off, causing WoShi to pause before responding, "Your Highness, I am a highly ranked sixteen for most accomplished achievements", he said as he exhaled the pungent fumes of spices in distaste.

He struggled intensely to suppress his cough. Indeed, with over six feet of distance from where the Emperor was seated, there was no need to sweeten his breath. He hated the experience but remained passive as brute force held him in place.

The boy Emperor Pingdi said, "You are worth more to the empire."

WoShi bowed, "I am your servant, highness. I am here to do your bidding."

"What will you offer me in return for your plea?" the boy asked, and WoShi looked confused.

Emperor Pingdi continued, "You shall present me with a warrior my age."

Sensing that their Emperor wanted to say more, the bodyguards pulled WoShi closer. The boy spoke softly, "When the time is right, I will ask for many warriors as my bodyguards, so train more." The Emperor rattled the beads to signal that he had finished speaking

The Emperor's assistant bellowed. "WoShi, the grandmaster of the HanKaoTzu school, I appoint you to rank twenty, a full Marquis." The Empress Dowager daintily clapped her hands in genuine pleasure, and WangMang replaced his scowl with a forced smile. The official court criers hollered and relayed the imperial order to the entire court.

WoShi's promotion was significant because it was an imperial decree that made him a Marquis, and only the Emperor could rescind it, practically elevating his position above that of a Marquis.

#13 Qian Runs Away to Save a Bird

The bureaucracy spread the word in the counties that the imperial school at Changan was recruiting students from commoners and novices who were educated. Applicants for enrolment as student scholars poured in through the school gates, many of whom had letters of recommendation.

As days passed and no information was forthcoming from HuKui, WoShi seriously considered visiting the chophouses to find him. While he brooded, a flustered bureaucrat approached him. "Marquis WoShi, we have some unusual recruits for your evaluation."

LuiXiu, who was present there, was annoyed. "Don't you know trivial matters of novice recruitment shouldn't be brought to the grandmaster? I am here for that. Tell me about it."

The bureaucrat was unfazed and said, "Yes, Master LuiXiu, I wouldn't disturb you for selections, but these boys from a chophouse in Changan are special. They are more knowledgeable than some of our long-term students." WoShi sat up hearing that.

WoShi said, "I will see them." LuiXiu followed WoShi outside, glaring at the bureaucrat. It was a bright day, but the wind was cold and biting, and LuiXiu wanted to return to the warmth of the fireside.

The bureaucrat held out a tablet of wax, which had words imprinted with a hot stylus and dusted with chalk for reading. WoShi stroked his long beard as he read through a write-up describing "The Red Bird of the South" constellation. He took the next tablet, which recounted the basic Legalist Qin philosophy.

"You are right in calling me. This is an extraordinary account for beginners," WoShi told the bureaucrat. "We should recruit all of them immediately if their written and oral knowledge is this good."

LuiXiu approached the boys and quizzed them, asking, "How many of you are here? Who is your teacher?"

One boy answered, "Master, eight of us have come today." A chill went down WoShi's back, but he showed no emotion while scanning the children to see if he could identify the Han Prince.

LuiXiu asked, "Where is your teacher?"

The boy replied with a grin, "He is admiring the drawings on your school walls." The children giggled. Prospective recruits had a tradition of drawing on the walls.

WoShi told the bureaucrat, "Find their teacher and ask him to see me."

A few hours later, the bureaucrat let a red-eyed HuKui in. He held his fists together in greeting and bowed low. He had a long staff and wore a dirty sheepskin overall. The smell of dung emanating from him made LuiXiu wrinkle his nose in disgust.

He mumbled to WoShi, "How did this shepherd train sheep to write essays?" WoShi roared with laughter.

"Great masters, what do you need to see me for? I am HuKui, a teacher from Zhangzhou, which is east of here."

WoShi asked, "Tell us, HuKui. Did you or someone else train these children? They are quite advanced in their education, especially in describing constellations. Few laymen know this in Han."

HuKui looked perplexed, "My students? They haven't come in yet. I came here to plead for more time to bring them in."

WoShi looked at LuiXiu and said, "Have we mistaken him for someone else?"

The bureaucrat asked HuKui, "Aren't you from the chophouse in Changan?"

"Of course not!" HuKui fumed, "Are teachers here hard of hearing? How often do I repeat that I am from Zhangzhou..."

LuiXiu interjected, "Yes, we know it is east of here."

LuiXiu glowered at the bureaucrat, "You are an idiot. You've brought the wrong man!"

LuiXiu asked HuKui, "Where are you staying?"

"At the temple of the sun courtyard, just outside the school," answered HuKui.

The bureaucrat was adamant. "No, he is from the chophouse. Let me get someone to identify him." He went outside to bring in the student who had identified HuKui as their teacher.

HuKui seemed genuinely offended and complained in the bureaucrat's absence. "I just told him I slept in the temple courtyard. I can't afford the warmth of a luxurious chophouse?" LuiXiu snickered in polite sympathy.

The bureaucrat returned with a sheepish face and said, "The children have all gone back. We need to wait until tomorrow."

HuKui told LuiXiu, "Changan is colder than I thought. It must be the hearts of the rich. Do I not get served tea?" The bureaucrat glared at him, crossed his arms, and gestured for HuKui to leave.

"How many children did you say you brought from Zhangzhou?" LuiXiu asked casually.

"Six rascals, Master, but I am left with four now. Two of them ran away. Ha, you wait until I get my hands on them," he said ominously. He sheepishly added, "I have restrained the other four in a monastery, two days' walk from here. Once you agree, I will bring them here."

LuiXiu looked at HuKui and exclaimed, "Your wards are not with you? Why didn't you bring them?"

"Master, Changan is too expensive for me. I cannot stay overnight here. How can I afford to bring the boys."

LuiXiu said, "Bringing in your lads will take time, and we will finish our recruitment before that." He turned to WoShi and said, "We have the wrong man. There is a mix-up. We don't have time to assess these boys." He was about to push HuKui out when WoShi stopped him.

"It's all right, LuiXiu. Remember the Emperor's decree. Let's be lenient towards peasants coming in a few days late from outside the capital."

He turned to the bureaucrat and said, "Let's give them a fair chance. WangMang intends to raise the commoners to the level of the nobility over time, and it has to start somewhere."

LuiXiu was uncomfortable with the Marquis mentioning WangMang's name. He reluctantly turned to HuKui and said, "We cannot assure you the selection of your boys just because they have come a long way from Zhangzhou. The boys must pass imperial scrutiny, just like the others," he warned.

HuKui fell to his knees and clenched his fists, begging LuiXiu, "Master, the lads are better than me at their age. I don't have money to care for them anymore. Surely, you can accommodate them in this large school."

LuiXiu told HuKui, "Bring them. We are interested in scrutinising all prospective students who apply for admission to this school. However, you must be ready to take the boys back if they don't meet our expectations or if you turn up late."

As HuKui was leaving, WoShi called and gave him a handful of coins. "Next time you come here, ensure you have cleaned up. The same goes for your wards." HuKui folded his hands in gratitude.

****

LuiXiu participated in the novice interview and tested the children from the chophouse the next day. He spoke to their mentor, an old scholar, who clarified that many poor scholars stayed in the chophouse when visiting Changan. They taught the orphans for a discount on food and lodging.

LuiXiu was unconvinced! The knowledge demonstrated by the children had to come from systematic rote learning and couldn't be imparted by random scholars who took the trouble to teach. He summoned HuanTan and YangXiong.

The three scholars took a keen interest in the eight lads from the chophouse and spoke to them on various subjects. In addition to words and numbers, the children could wield swords.

Informed of the happenings outside, WoShi stayed in his room, nervous and uncertain. He let fate determine the selection process while wondering about HuKui. It was clear that HuKui had separated the Han Prince and his three friends from the rest of the children at the chophouse. Why?

The imperial bureaucrats examined the children for birthmarks and tattoos that could identify them as slaves or as belonging to bandit clans. After much discussion, imperial scholars declared the selection of all the children from the chophouse and sixteen other students from various counties for that week.

****

ChenHe jogged along the ridge of the third slope of sacred Huayin Mountain, stopping to catch his breath with his hands on his hips. They had been climbing since morning, and his friends, who had sprinted ahead, urged him forward. ChenHe glanced at the towering southern peak before falling back dramatically as if he had fainted.

SuJin ran back to ChenHe. "Stop acting like you are in a street play, ChenHe. You aren't even winded. We have to catch up with Qian and return to the school before they conclude the selection of novices."

ChenHe gasped in short breaths and said, "You catch him and come back. Why do we all have to climb if we are going to come down again? I will wait here."

SuJin gave him a disdainful look. "Wasn't it your idea that we all came looking for little Qian? He ran away, but you remained quiet until he had a good head start."

ChenHe breathed hard and growled, "The little dreamer! I did not believe he would run away so far. I am tired and hungry and don't want to climb mountains."

SuJin replied, "You should have thought of this before." SuJin pulled up his stocky friend and pushed him forward. When they reached SuWu, he said, "*We stick together and protect each other, always.*"

SuWu grumbled unhappily. "When HuKui finds us, he will give us a beating we won't forget anytime soon. He had planned for us to attend the selection process for many days, and we slipped away on his big day. I hope he has gone in with the other boys. At least let them get selected."

SuJin was unperturbed. "We can join the school next year; what is the hurry? Do you think they will teach us anything besides words and counting, which we already know?"

SuWu said, "Yes, of course. They will teach us many new skills at the big school." He turned to ChenHe and asked, "Come on, ChenHe, tell us why Qian ran away. I don't believe he had any issues with joining the school."

ChenHe, panting, said, "It was one of his visions. He said we needed to feed the eagle before going to the school."

"Why didn't he tell us all this, ChenHe?"

ChenHe accused the older boys. "He is the youngest. The two of you would've bullied him and made him follow you to the school. He said we had to do it, come what may!"

He whined, "At least you could've left me behind and travelled faster. *We stick together and protect each other, always,*" ChenHe ridiculed the older boys.

SuWu responded harshly, "We are no longer children."

"Not yet adults, either," quipped ChenHe and SuWu sighed in exasperation.

They trudged up the next hill and finally caught up with a tired and hungry Qian at the base of the towering south peak. He was sitting glum and forlorn beside a small pool of water. Qian looked up at his three best friends and smiled wearily. Nobody spoke as they collapsed next to him. It had been an exhausting chase on foot, with hardly any food between them for two days.

"We need to eat," said ChenHe.

SuJin asked Qian, "Can we go back now?"

"No," he replied. "You have work to do."

SuJin pointed at himself and asked, "Me?" Little Qian nodded.

SuWu's eyes narrowed as he critically examined Qian's ripped hanfu and fresh blood oozing from cuts on his body. Qian gave him a weak smile and said, "It's okay. I have washed the wounds with clean water."

SuWu furrowed his brows further and asked, "Why are your fingers bloody?" He looked at the sheer granite cliff and gasped, "Don't tell me!"

Qian broke down and wailed loudly, sniffing hard. "I couldn't do it! The birds nesting on the cliff have sharp claws. I had to come down quickly or be thrown off the cliff." The boys looked at each other in confusion.

ChenHe hugged the petite boy and growled at his brothers. "Enough of the adult talks. If you want us to believe your *"We stick together and protect each other always,"* do what little Qian wants. He has asked nothing unreasonable. Just scale a cliff to feed a bird!"

SuWu was furious and yelled at ChenHe and Qian. "You're a glutton, and you're a dreamer. The two of you planned to get us here beforehand! Now, you want the Prince to climb a vertical cliff to feed a hatchling?"

SuJin, who was listening to the exchanges, was shocked and exclaimed, "What!"

Snarling, ChenHe stood up and punched a surprised SuWu, who fell. He straddled him and punched him in the face. SuJin stepped in, pulled them apart, and slapped ChenHe.

SuJin turned to a bristling ChenHe and said, "I am ashamed you tricked us! SuWu has a reason to be upset!"

With tears streaming down his face, ChenHe held his cheeks and shouted, "Shut up, you pompous Prince. If Qian has a dream, we make it happen. The reason is unnecessary! All his dreams have reasons!"

SuJin looked at Qian, who was watching him with apprehension. "You must feed a baby eagle high up on the cliff. I don't know if its mother is dead or is taking time to return, but it's starving! The bird is connected to you and will save us."

Blood dripped from SuWu's nose and torn lips as he was about to storm off. SuJin said, "Wait. I'm coming with you."

Qian cried and said, "I am sorry, but the "voices" in my head told me to get away immediately, and you would follow. They said we were in grave danger."

Wiping the blood from his face, SuWu sarcastically remarked, "There's no danger in climbing a vertical cliff, but there's a big danger in going to school!" Having recovered from his anger, SuWu sighed and asked, "What's done is done. Tell me, why should we feed an abandoned hatchling?"

Qian looked at SuWu and said, "I don't know why, but we must do it. I feared you would talk SuJin out of coming away if you didn't find a logical reason."

ChenHe lambasted the Prince. "Of course, SuJin acts like a Prince from the palace. Once he decides, he won't change his mind. We thought he would refuse, especially with HuKui making a big deal about joining a fancy school." ChenHe put his meaty hands on his hips and said, "As if we aren't getting the best education at the chophouse!"

SuJin jumped to his feet, angry. "I've had enough; come, SuWu, let's make it down before nightfall."

Qian opened a cloth pouch from his waist belt and took an exquisite fourteen-sided Liubo dice. He offered his proud possession to SuJin. "Take it, SuJin, but feed the bird."

"I couldn't make it up because the mother birds were attacking me on the cliff." Qian's pitiful gesture of offering his prized possession deeply affected SuWu. He knew that giving away his precious possession was like cutting off a limb for Qian.

SuWu hugged him fiercely and said, "I am sorry, Qian. I didn't realise how important this was to you." The small boy bawled.

SuWu told SuJin, "Don't worry about HuKui. I left a message saying that we are on Huayin Mountain. Maybe he will wait for us at the monastery below. I told him we would meet him there if he came after us."

SuJin was touched by Qian's offering of his prized possession, which was gifted by a bladesmith after watching him throw knives. He looked at SuWu and asked, "What now? Shall I climb the" mountain?"

SuWu said, "Yes, my thoughts, exactly. Let's respect his dreams, and we are here anyway." Looking up at the towering cliff, SuWu asked, "How do we handle hostile birds with talons?"

****

SuJin and SuWu went on a hunt and returned with three fat bamboo partridges. Leaving one partridge aside, they made a quick meal while Qian explained where the eagle's nest was, just above a rock jutting from the cliff. SuJin hung the partridge on his chest and began climbing the sheer cliff. He securely fastened SuWu's armour of woven bamboo slats to protect his back from a bird attack.

Watching him climb up the cliff, ChenHe was awestruck. "Is he walking down a street or climbing up a cliff? How can he be so effortless? Are footholds magically appearing for him?"

SuWu, still smarting from the blows he received from ChenHe, said, "Maybe the pompous Prince practised strength training outside the kitchen, unlike someone we know." ChenHe smiled sheepishly at him in surrender. SuWu added, "Next time you hit me, I will hit you back and trip you down a cliff,"

Qian shrieked as a bird flew close to SuJin, threatening him. However, it veered away when SuJin flashed his knife. SuWu had advised SuJin not to climb directly to the nests but to go parallel, ascend higher, clamber down to the nest, drop the partridge, and get down quickly.

They watched in fascination as many birds shrieked and swooped at him. The bamboo vest SuWu made began to fray and fall apart. Eventually, SuJin discarded the cumbersome vest and started climbing faster.

The boys ran back from below the cliff to the lower hilltop farther away to watch him ascend. He was a mere speck in the sky, and they couldn't make out much.

SuWu mused, "Maybe at such heights, he is closer to the gods, who may subdue the attacking birds?"

ChenHe remarked, "I just want him back safe on the ground. I'm so scared that I've forgotten my hunger."

They waited and watched on the cold mountainside without taking their eyes off the cliff. After what seemed to be an eternity, Qian said, "I can't handle this tension. Let me climb." Just as he was about to run off, ChenHe said, "I see movement." It was SuJin!

The lads dashed back to the cliffside, and SuJin jumped the last few feet, landing in a somersault. "That was exhilarating! I will do this more often!" He smiled at Qian.

"What happened up there?" asked SuWu.

SuJin wasn't even breathing hard as he excitedly explained his climb. "I got the stench of decaying meat and a strong, pungent odour of bird droppings once I reached the protruding rock. I found a massive eagle nest on that rock." He stretched his arms wide to show the size of the nest. He continued, "It was empty, but I heard a feeble screech from below. A large chick had fallen out and was stuck between two boulders. It was weak, so I pulled it out and returned it to the nest." SuJin showed the bruised areas where the bird's talons had gripped him and his arms where it had pecked him.

"I gave it the partridge, and it screeched at me."

"I cut the partridge open, and the bird hungrily gobbled up the innards and later the meat, ignoring me."

"How about its mother?" Asked ChenHe.

"That is the curious part. It looks like the mother had abandoned it."

"Abandoned, like us," said ChenHe

"Will it survive?" asked SuWu

SuJin looked glum as he said, "I don't think so! It's a big bird and needs food to regain its strength. A partridge won't do." Qian was distraught when he heard that.

"The bird screeched at me when I began climbing down. Probably demanding more food."

Qian insisted, "We must do something. That bird must survive."

SuWu asked, baffled. "Was this your urgent need, Qian? To feed an orphaned eagle?"

SuJin remarked, "SuWu, Qian may be right! This is no ordinary eagle! In a few years, it will develop into a massive bird, large enough to snatch a goat or a child." ChenHe whistled in amazement.

SuWu pointed to the ripped hanfu and the bruises on SuJin's hands and said, "Why did it hurt you?"

SuJin smiled and replied, "It's a bird, SuWu, with talons and a beak. It had to hold me someplace!"

They set snares that night and took turns keeping a fire burning to chase the bitter cold away. At first light, Qian rushed to check the snares. Sometime later, SuJin got up and mumbled, "I hate this cold. I can handle anything but the cold" He stretched, rubbed his frozen body to increase the blood flow, and exclaimed, "Qian has brought in a few hares! At least we won't go hungry."

SuWu looked at the trussed-up hares near the fireside and asked, "Where is he? Did he run away? again!"

ChenHe said, "Don't panic, he will be back! Qian feels that a hare is too meagre for our bird to survive. He has gone hunting!"

SuWu was sarcastic. "Hunting with a knife? What does he have in mind, a bear?"

Later that day, Qian trudged in, leading a sheep. Surprised, SuWu quizzed him, "Where did you get the sheep?"

Qian collapsed to the ground, tired. "I stole it from a shepherd near the monastery. Dragging it up was the hard part." ChenHe offered his friend the roasted leg of a rabbit he had kept aside for his best friend.

SuWu sighed loudly and said, "My word, you are determined to ensure the bird survives! What about the voice in your head? You said we were in danger!"

"I don't hear them now," he said.

Early the following day, SuJin and Qian climbed the cliff just before dawn to avoid bird attacks. They had butchered the sheep, making it easier for them to carry. The eagle chick greeted them with familiar shrieks and opened its mouth, expressing its hunger. They dropped the large carcass of the sheep, and the bird climbed onto it and pecked at the flesh. It was too weak to tear into the meat.

ChenHe had packed the offal of the butchered sheep in its skin for the eagle. Qian picked up a piece of offal and offered it to the eagle chick, who hungrily gobbled it up with a screech. Then, Qian pushed the remaining offal into the butchered carcass.

SuJin remarked appreciatively, "The cold up here will keep the meat fresh for days."

Qian stuffed a few fallen feathers of the mother eagle into the belt of his hanfu. The bird shrieked, and he said, "Appreciating decent food, eh! It's up to you now, little one! You learn to hunt and feed yourself while we go to school!"

Just as they clambered down, they heard loud voices. HuKui was reprimanding SuWu and ChenHe. On seeing Qian, HuKui raged and rushed at him, delivering him a few lusty blows with his stick. SuWu and SuJin tried to mollify him in vain. He would not be satisfied until he had beaten Qian. The three brothers pleaded with him to share the punishment, and finally, he relented. HuKui slapped and thrashed each of them relentlessly, and none whimpered, except for Qian, who hollered. With his anger spent, HuKui threw the stick away in frustration.

HuKui said to no one in particular. "I am doing my best to enrol you in the imperial school, and you ran away to save a bird that came in your dream? I had to beg and buy time with the bureaucrats. I don't know if that is enough to get you in." He snarled at Qian.

The boys rubbed their bloodied backs with each other's spit. HuKui felt uncomfortable and remorseful about beating them. He explained to them he had to change tactics. Instead of declaring himself as a scholar at the chophouse, he donned the dress of a scholar who had just come in and introduced himself as a scholar from Zhangzhou, holding his students outside Changan.

Although he had trouble when a boy identified him as a scholar from the chophouse, he managed the situation. He practised with the boys the places and names of the people of Zhangzhou as they hurried back to Changan.

HuKui abruptly stopped as they entered the city. A fire had ravaged parts of Changan toward the chophouse, and smoke rose from the area. His gut clenched in fear, and he turned and looked at Qian. "Did you know anything about a fire?"

Qian looked blank. "What fire?" HuKui realised the boys had no idea about his suspicions. He decided not to go to the chophouse but took them to a soup kitchen near the school. He rented sleeping mats, using WoShi's name.

After quickly settling the boys, HuKui went to the burned-out chophouse. He stood with the onlookers at the edge and did not go forward to inquire. He knew that spies would be listening for anyone overly concerned.

HuKui listened to whispers that everyone, including the children, was mercilessly slaughtered before the assassins set the chop house on fire, although the fire was made to look like an accident.

HuKui returned and told the boys what he saw. They were inconsolable at the loss of their foster mother and friends. HuKui forbade them from going to the chophouse, as imperial spies would be looking to round up stragglers.

HuKui bitterly asked Qian, "If your vision told you that imperial guards would come and kill, why did you not save the others?"

A weeping Qian sniffed loudly, saying, "I did not know all this would happen. The voices told me that SuJin had to rescue the bird, or his life was in danger. They did not tell me about any fire that would burn down our home."

SuWu told HuKui, "Stop blaming Qian. Had you not followed us, I suppose you would have been dead like the others?" HuKui shook his head in agreement and looked at SuJin.

ChenHe said, "I want to leave this place. It is frightening," and the others agreed.

HuKui agreed, saying. "Yes, it is too dangerous for you in Changan. We will not go to school. Let us go to a monastery far away." The boys wholeheartedly agreed.

"Now, I need to mourn my friends," HuKui said, tears streaming down his cheeks. He trudged to a nearby jiubang to drown his sorrow in drink. SuWu accompanied HuKui to prevent him from making a ruckus. Surprisingly, HuKui was quiet. He drank and sobbed, murmuring the names of the dead in prayer.

A stocky dwarf approached them and spoke to a dull HuKui. "I am JiaShao. I work with WoShi, the school's grand tutor. The imperial scholars will wrap up and leave tomorrow. You need to get the boys admitted to the school before they depart."

After many attempts to snap HuKui out of his misery, the middle-aged dwarf dipped his head to SuWu and excused himself. His parting words to HuKui were, "The HanKaoTzu is their destiny."

SuWu deeply contemplated what JiaShao told HuKui as he guided a drunk but silent HuKui back to their sleeping quarters.

He spoke to his brothers, who were grieving.

****

When news of the accidental fire at the chophouse reached WoShi, he paled and returned to his residence.

When the bureaucrat ushered in four boys from Zhangzhou, LuiXiu was gentle. He asked SuWu, the oldest, "Where is your master, HuKui?"

"We came in yesterday, but unfortunately, our master had too much to drink, and he hasn't gotten up yet." SuWu added, "We came in alone, looking for a job."

LuiXiu nodded at SuWu. "Job? Don't you want to become a scholar?"

"Not exactly, Master," he replied with a crestfallen face. "That's what our master wants us to do. We know who we are and can't compete with the rich and smart city students. Please give us a job as servants here, and we shall work hard for our keep."

LuiXiu frowned. He remembered feeling inadequate when he joined the school on a noble's recommendation. "I, too, am from a village, a poor noble's son, yet here I am. Success depends on aptitude and hard work, not city or village upbringing."

SuWu said, "Please, master, we don't want to return with our master. He thrashed us and threatened that we would be sold as slaves." They lifted their hanfu and showed the angry welts on their backs that had scabbed poorly. The brutality of the strokes on SuJin and Qian did not surprise LuiXiu. He expected as much.

LuiXiu gave the boys wax tablets and administered simple word and number tests. The boys' performance was minimal. They fared adequately on basic questions but did not attempt any difficult ones.

LuiXiu told them, "Go back and come with your teacher."

After the boys left, the bureaucrat assisting the selection process said, "We lost eight of our best recruits. Why not take these boys instead? They are poor and can become minor bureaucrats in some far-flung provinces. Moreover, they can stay away from that brute of a shepherd."

LuiXiu agreed. "Hmm. I was thinking about that. I feel guilty that we snuffed out so many lives. We could have taken time to identify the one special boy instead of sacrificing all of them. Unfortunately, my fellow scholars did not want to take any chances with destiny. They wanted the nest burned with the boys, their mother and all the scholars gathered there."

This candid and callous disclosure shocked the imperial bureaucrat, and his eyes opened wide. However, he kept quiet, realising that he was in the presence of a dangerous man.

LuiXiu told the bureaucrat, "There is no need to inform YangXiong and HuanTan that we enrolled these four. These boys are peasants, and their scores are just below acceptable."

After a pause, LuiXiu added, "When that smelly shepherd HuKui comes in, we will tell him he has been selected as a junior teacher."

The bureaucrat expressed his shock. "Hire the shepherd? He is a brute!"

"Of course! We need someone to wield the stick mercilessly on wayward students."

#14 WoShi Meets the Prince

The sun had just risen, and WoShi was practising his style of TaoYin next to a gurgling cascade of water flowing down from a pile of moss-covered rocks. WoShi was depressed since the day the chophouse went up in flames. He held himself responsible for the deaths of so many gifted children.

He contemplated the disturbing information the dwarfs had just told him. WangMang's spies had found the foster parents of concubine Mi's son. Although they had tortured and killed the parents, they couldn't locate the son, who was abducted as an infant by the midwife who delivered him.

His unrestrained thoughts disrupted his breathing, and WoShi unusually missed a step. Thankfully, practising in his private garden had its benefits. No one could see his mistakes!

The grand master of the imperial school lived in a secluded house with large rooms and courtyards that had existed since the first emperor. Sprawling gardens and orchards, fringed with tall trees and bushy bamboo groves, separated his residence from the school estate on three sides. At the end of his vast garden was a wall of shops opening onto a busy market.

The grandmaster's residence and enormous bamboo forest were closed to students and teachers. Dwarfs guarded them against trespassers, and after the Emperor elevated him to Marquis, the imperial bureaucracy forcibly assigned a few servants to his residence.

The cluster of low-roofed outhouses where the dwarfs lived was near the wall of shops, hidden by thick bamboo groves and shrubs. A few of these thatched houses had entrances to tunnels and underground chambers, which were revealed to WoShi when he took over as grandmaster. The dwarfs had handed over a set of silk scrolls, the legacy of his master and many before him. In time, he would have to do the same for his successor. The dwarfs were the true custodians of the estate.

WoShi wondered about the role of the dwarfs in Zhang Liang's prophecies because they were deeply involved but mentioned nowhere. He was amazed that Zhang Liang's plan was still in motion centuries later. WoShi read through the scrolls, which he had ignored until the tomb was discovered inside the school. The scrolls contained instructions on what he had to do if the prophecy unravelled during his time.

JiaShao was a spiritual man and leader of the dwarfs. He told WoShi, "We feel privileged to be alive during the time of our Prince while fulfilling the oaths of our ancestors. The Prince is a living god. We will gladly lay down our lives for him." WoShi was not impressed by JiaShao's enthusiasm and downplayed the prophecy.

JiaShao reminded him, "The second Emperor in succession without a progeny is on the throne. The Yellow River had turned south. All ominous signs indicate that WangMang is ready to seize the throne. What more do you want, grand tutor? A divine message in the sky for you to read?"

WoShi glared at the dwarf, and JiaShao vehemently declared, "You probably won't believe that message either." The dwarfs had a hearty laugh at WoShi's expense; they weren't subservient to the grandmaster in private.

Many more dwarfs had entered Changan in anticipation of the Prince's arrival. They were everywhere, integrated into Changan's businesses and bureaucracy as support staff, diligent and silent in their work yet listening with wide-open ears. The vibrant dwarf's network across Changan ensured that the school received the freshest produce while he was served the latest information and the juiciest gossip. The dwarfs loved gambling and were always found at the fighting pits.

The outhouses had large caverns and tunnels below them. The tunnels beyond the caverns were deliberately low and narrow, leading outside the school. With many sharp turns and narrow clefts, they would slow any pursuit. The dwarfs were a formidable force within the labyrinth because a few could hold off a large army.

All this intrigue spans many generations. WoShi's thoughts turned to the present. HuKui had not contacted him since he joined the school as a junior tutor a few weeks ago. He pondered why a Han Prince had to go to Tianzhu. What was his virtuoso that the gods needed so badly? He would probably get his answers when the boy returned from Tianzhu—if he returned! WoShi had little hope that an imperial offspring could become a warrior, and he would have to look to the other boys to train.

He tripped again. Disgusted, he stopped practising.

WoShi left the garden for a bath in a wooden tub, a luxury he indulged in most days. His servants scrubbed him clean, brushed his hair, and gave him fresh clothes. He didn't trust his servants, as the dwarfs had identified quite a few as imperial informers.

WoShi was upset when his servant entered and informed him about a persistent guard who demanded an immediate audience. He came out of the bath and glared at the dwarf. To his chagrin, the guard stomped his foot and said, "Master, come! There is a ghost prowling in your garden. We want to show it to you before it melts away." The servants who overheard this fled, screaming in fear.

WoShi asked his servants to remain inside the house and followed the dwarf. As he led him inside the outhouse, the dwarf moved a wooden panel, revealing steps descending into the caverns below. The tunnel was well-lit with lamps, and the chief of his guards was restlessly hopping from one foot to the other. When JiaShao saw WoShi, he bowed. "Master WoShi, follow me. Quick!"

"JiaShao, what is so important?" he asked. The burly dwarf did not respond and rushed down a tunnel as fast as his stunted legs permitted. WoShi followed him and muttered, "Dwarfs, they have a mind of their own and make lousy servants."

JiaShao replied, "I heard that. We are not your servants, WoShi. We are here for a purpose, just as you are." WoShi shuffled behind him, wondering what they wanted to show him.

JiaShao motioned for silence while a dwarf quickly applied lampblack around WoShi's eyes. They gestured toward a recently excavated vertical shaft where he could look out. The lampblack was meant to conceal his eyes as he peered through a slit.

Water seeped all around, and sunlight streamed through the opening. WoShi looked into his garden, where he practised TaoYin. He was inside the moss-covered rock formation with the stream flowing over it.

He was surprised to see a young boy practising TaoYin, diligently following his steps, right down to the pauses he had made. He grimaced when the boy repeated his mistakes.

The boy was a prodigy, having learned all the moves from mere observations. However, the teacher in him frowned at the boy's shallow breathing and overt focus on limb movements. The boy stomped hard at the imperfections on the ground he was supposed to navigate. Too many errors!

Who was he? What was he doing in his garden, and why had he not noticed him before? How did he slip past the guards?

The youngster improvised on WoShi's moves. It was amusing how he transformed TaoYin's graceful and intentional movements into a silly dance. WoShi smiled when he realised that the boy was not impressed by TaoYin's slow and deliberate moves.

Like a squirrel sensing danger, the boy froze, alert to movements and melted into the nearby bamboo grove like a ghost!

WoShi ducked back into the main tunnel and faced a grinning JiaShao, "Why did you build this tunnel? To spy on me? I don't need anyone to watch my private practice!"

JiaShao gaped at him. He was expecting questions about the boy. "I assure you that the tunnel was already in existence."

WoShi turned his head and pointed at a pile of fresh mud recently dug up and heaped near the shaft.

JiaShao chuckled and said, "Oh that! Master, we made the tunnel wider to accommodate you. The lookout slits have always been there. Baked clay bricks support the rock formation as a foundation, and the water flows above it.

The dwarf chief grumbled. "Bah! You are asking all the wrong questions." With a big smile, he added, "We have a reasonable idea of who the boy is. Do you?"

Although WoShi guessed who the boy was because of JiaShao's excitement, he responded in jest, "Tell me, who is this sneaky boy?"

JiaShao swung his stunted hands around at the smiling dwarfs behind him in exasperation. In a haughty voice, he said, "Let it be repeated at every fireside that the great chief JiaShao pointed out the son of destiny to the blind master of the Imperial School."

WoShi laughed. "Did the boy declare who he was to you?"

JiaShao said, "No, but we know him. Let me clarify that we don't watch your boring Tao Yin. How do you people even swat a mosquito?" JiaShao grinned and added, "We found footprints in our sand traps, and it took us an entire day to locate him. He is tricky, a flicker at best. He explores the garden but comes here daily to watch you."

WoShi frowned and said, "Thank you for showing me what the boy is capable of. It will go a long way in understanding his training needs." He wiped the lampblack off his face and said, "Tell me, how do you know he is the Prince we seek? Maybe this is some other boy brought in by HuKui."

JiaShao turned again to his grinning dwarf colleagues and said, "Let it be repeated at every fireside that the great chief JiaShao showed the blind grandmaster his student, but the student was ahead of the teacher by one class," the dwarfs burst out laughing.

WoShi politely laughed along with them, and JiaShao said, "The boy has already picked up your technique and changed your slow TaoYin into a dance.".

"Utter nonsense," WoShi exclaimed. "TaoYin is for the mind. He has learned it all wrong somewhere, and his modifications will result in a sound thrashing."

JiaShao was unsympathetic to WoShi's assessment. "Whatever! You need to make him the best warrior out there. Do not cram his head with useless knowledge from the scrolls. Let his friends do the reading."

WoShi did not bother to reply to the uneducated dwarf, who thought formal education was a waste of time. He cleaned himself as best as possible and said, "I need to bathe again."

He looked at the dwarfs listening in and said, "Let it be repeated at the fireside that after listening to JiaShao, the grandmaster had to bathe twice to clean his eyes and ears." JiaShao beamed unabashedly at the dwarf's unrestrained laughter.

****

WoShi began his TaoYin practice the next day while stealthily searching for the boy in the foliage, but he could not find anyone. Sitting on the ornamental stone, he said, "Come out. I know you are in there."

A boy timidly scrambled down a tree, headfirst like a lizard, and stood reverently before him with his hands clasped. He was tall and wiry, unusual for a Han boy.

The boy bowed his head and said with humility, "Few people can spot me when I hide. You have good skills, Grand Master. What gave me away?" he asked.

WoShi evaded the question, "Who are you, boy?"

"I am SuJin, a novice, master."

WoShi grunted and said, "I won't ask you what you are doing here because your teacher will take you to task for trespassing into the grandmaster's residence."

The boy smiled and said, "Only if you tell them, master." WoShi chuckled.

WoShi made a few basic moves in TaoYin while varying the pace of his movements. He gestured for SuJin to repeat what he had just done. To his surprise, the boy mimicked his moves, including the change of pace, reasonably well. Impressed, WoShi stroked his long beard absently. This boy was indeed a prodigy.

After trying more complex movements together, WoShi grunted in pleasure. It wasn't often that a teacher witnessed such devotion and concentration in a student.

WoShi said, "Excellent, you have learned what I did, but do you know why?"

"Not really, master. Forgive me for my ignorance. I studied with different teachers, and the fighting techniques were obvious. The purpose of TaoYin was always beyond me," his direct answer pleased WoShi.

"Our style of TaoYin binds mind, breath, form and movement, so don't underestimate its power when adapted to fighting. I have modified it to suit combat, making every limb a weapon for attack or defence. The HanKaoTzu style focuses on honing the student's mental abilities to throw a punch that aligns with the senses, like an eyelid closing when dust blows into it."

"You need to learn to react without thinking, which requires harmony in your breath and acute awareness of your surroundings, putting to work all five senses, not just the eyes. Developing such an ability requires training until all your muscles align with your senses. It will take years!"

SuJin listened in rapt concentration and said, "I will practise, master. Please teach me."

WoShi snorted happily, saying, "That I will."

WoShi explained, "A true warrior won't fight unless he has to. If he does engage in a fight, he fights to kill; there is no other way. Every fighter has an innate style that has defects. The last thing you want is a maimed opponent who knows how you fight. His revenge will be your death."

WoShi asked, "Am I clear on this? You fight to kill or don't fight at all!" SuJin nodded cautiously.

With a grunt, WoShi continued, "The objective is not to land a blow on an opponent but to deliver it at a precise nerve point, with the right angle and power to maximise damage. The weapon can be your fists, daggers, or swords. Anything, for that matter, can become a weapon!"

SuJin absorbed everything he heard, and WoShi said, "Let me be clear: I won't train you to spar. You will train to kill. Strength with speed, agility with balance, and to strike accurately."

"Our first lesson will be to unlearn - instinct!"

SuJin was shocked. "What! How can you unlearn instinct? Isn't that what we use in a fight?"

WoShi shook his head in disagreement. "Far from it. Instinct can be used for defence, but a fight to destroy your enemy needs planning, and no plan can be made on instinct. You must know your opponent, their circumstances, and their motivation before facing them."

SuJin wasn't convinced. "What happens in a surprise attack?"

"Usually, a surprise attack points to intelligence failure; maybe your strategist is to blame, or your enemy is smarter than you think," WoShi grunted. "There's no option but to escape, regroup, and replan!"

"I don't understand, Master WoShi," said SuJin.

WoShi nodded, "You will. That is the purpose of training at the HanKaoTzu school. We will train your mind, too."

WoShi continued, "For now, it suffices to know that killing is not the objective of a warrior; every death should be necessary for a favourable outcome for your team or your emperor."

"A warrior is not a murderer. We don't kill for personal gain."

SuJin was taken aback by a philosophy he had never heard before. "So, a warrior won't fight for revenge or glory?"

WoShi smiled and said, "Never! Such sentiments are for the commoners." SuJin exhaled through his mouth, flapping his lips noisily.

"How about my brothers? Will you train them?"

"Some of your lessons may be together, but each will be honed with skills that suit their inherent strengths. However, the philosophy lessons will remain the same. We can't have warriors thinking differently."

"How about weapons?" SuJin probed.

"What about it? I thought I explained to you clearly -you are the weapon."

WoShi made SuJin practice a single move - moving forward in horse stance and extending his arm to touch the end of a leaf. After repeating it a few times, SuJin was distracted, and WoShi said, "Mind over everything. You must do this blindfolded soon, and I will add weights to your arms."

SuJin hesitated and sheepishly said, "Master, you are older, and I am younger. I have practised various martial arts forms, and trust me, I am very quick with my moves. Your style is too slow, and frankly, I don't think this skill is useful."

SuJin expressed his opinion without arrogance, and WoShi motioned for SuJin to strike. SuJin gently feigned a strike to the chest and then whipped a blow to WoShi's face; however, he found himself lying flat on the ground. The back of his head hurt from the impact he sustained in the fall. SuJin was shocked! He barely saw WoShi move, and the force of the blow was tremendous.

Suppressing his pain, SuJin grimaced and gracefully somersaulted to get back on his feet. However, his feet did not land on the ground. Instead, he was whipped forward, and his face slammed into the ground, breaking his nose.

SuJin groaned and curled up into a foetal position in meek submission as WoShi hit nerve points on his arms and legs. SuJin screamed in agony and tapped his fingers on the ground in complete surrender.

"Tomorrow, we start again," said WoShi. Nursing his face and holding his bloodied nose, SuJin hobbled away, groaning in pain.

The dwarfs greeted WoShi with wide grins as he returned to his residence. "That was impressive. You will be a sensation in the wrestling pits. Together, we can make a lot of money!"

WoShi coldly replied, "I avoid fighting desperate men."

JiaShao confronted the marquis and expressed his displeasure. "What did you teach our Prince today? How to take a beating? He is not a peasant for you to bash up, Marquis! Your job is to teach him. His beautiful face will have bruises. Which maiden will marry him if you disfigure him?"

WoShi said, "Didn't you tell me some time ago, I think yesterday, that your job is to protect the boy, and my job is to teach?" JiaShao was not happy to be reminded of that.

WoShi smiled at JiaShao and said, "I've always wanted to beat up a pompous royal, and it feels good." JiaShao looked at him in shock, but WoShi smiled and quickly reassured him. "We made progress today. The first lesson SuJin learned was that you don't learn enough. The second lesson is not to take anyone lightly, especially an older man with more experience. Third, don't be overconfident in your abilities against an unknown opponent. Lastly, life is always unfair to those who haven't practised," he paused and added to insult JiaShao, "... or educated."

****

WoShi felt rejuvenated and charged with a sense of duty after meeting SuJin. He had a dinner of pheasant soup, rice with spiced tofu, and vegetables, and then he sat back to enjoy a cup of tea. He let out an exasperated sigh when his dwarf guard announced HuKui. Following the recent upheavals in his sedate life, guests constantly seemed to drop in at ungodly hours, and WoShi wondered if he would ever return to his routines.

HuKui staggered in, reeking of rice wine, and flopped onto the floor. WoShi looked at him in disgust.

Contorting his face into an exaggerated expression of anguish, HuKui said, "Despite years of training with me, the boys were bonded. After one session with you, the Prince can hardly walk or speak." He paused to burp loudly, and WoShi stroked his beard furiously. "He insists that he wants separate classes with you. Now, SuWu wants to learn military strategy, Qian wants to learn astronomy, and the fat one wishes to become a cook."

"They aspire to train and become what they are good at." WoShi bristled angrily and spoke, "I am the master here, and you are a junior teacher. I will train, untrain, disband, or do anything I want with the boys. Do I make myself clear?"

"Now get out! For any official matters regarding the training of boys, I expect my subordinate teachers to seek me out at the school, not at my residence."

"Now leave! I don't want to hear your whinging or see your gut filth on my floor."

JiaShao barged in with armed men. He looked at WoShi and said, "Master, just nod. I shall arrest this drunk and throw him into the dungeons. No one belittles our marquis."

"Thank you, JiaShao. HuKui was leaving."

JiaShao said, "Very well, master. We shall escort this man out of our premises." He gestured to his men, who pulled HuKui on his unsteady legs and pushed him out of the house.

WoShi heard HuKui throw up outside his house and JiaShao cursing loudly, "Ugh, it stinks!" This lout has emptied his vile evening on my leg."

****

The following day, WoShi heard loud arguments outside his house. A dwarf peeped in and said, "Master, HuKui is trying to come in. JiaShao is in front, threatening to skew him with his spear." He grinned and added, "He wants your permission to beat him up for yesterday."

WoShi groaned, "Drunk again! HuKui?"

The dwarf frowned and said, "He looks all cleaned up today! His matted hair is brushed, and the man looks presentable."

"Ask him to go away." The dwarf bobbed his head and went out.

A little later, JiaShao came inside and said, "The man is mad! He brought a novice student along to plead for an audience with you. Says it's a matter of life and death."

WoShi grumbled, "I don't want my day spoiled if HuKui is in one of his moods; check if he is inebriated. If he is, throw him in the dungeon for a few days."

JiaShao gleefully grinned and rubbed his hands before he frowned. "He is not drunk!"

WoShi grunted and said, "Ok, send him in. Just him."

HuKui demanded tea from WoShi's servant before sitting down.

WoShi asked him, "Ok, tell me, what do you want?"

HuKui frowned and, wetting his lips, said, "I don't want anything! I came to apologise for yesterday."

He admitted with embarrassment, "I overreacted a little yesterday. A bit, I think."

"You overreacted a little?" WoShi repeated with a pained look

"Yes, a little, I guess."

"A little."

"I guess."

WoShi glared at him, but HuKui did not meet his eyes. He was concentrating on checking the ends of his dirty nails with interest, biting them and spitting the broken pieces out.

WoShi exhaled hard, "What do you want?"

HuKui's expression darkened before he said, "First, you need to accept my complaint. Your guards poured freezing water all over me last night. I mean, just because I spat on their garden and maybe a little on the leg of your bull-headed dwarf, the one with two mouths and a half ear on his head."

WoShi was not amused. "Yes, they have strict instructions from me to evict all drunks from the school. They have been extremely tolerant of you. Perhaps you are using your position as guardian to the boys and taking undue advantage."

"It sobered me up," complained HuKui. When he saw WoShi's eyebrows gathered into a frown, he hastily added, "It made me think. I woke up the boys, and we talked."

SuWu, older brother to SuJin, explained that it's better to be trained individually by you, as the boys have very different abilities.

"SuWu, the one who strategised on how to poison me?" asked WoShi

"Shh, he doesn't know that it was for you. Let's keep that to ourselves, shall we."

WoShi wondered aloud, "Are you sure that SuFei chose you to lead the monastery of scholars?"

HuKui did not smile. "I lost friends, my family in that fire. Let me mourn for a little longer."

WoShi was not convinced. "I, too, was affected by that incident. Now we have work to do. If you want to mourn, go to the temple and make offerings. There is no need to make a tragedy an excuse to drink all your life. You are a teacher, and you went overboard yesterday."

HuKui said, "I have already forgotten yesterday's incident, except for that bullfrog of a dwarf. We have scores to settle."

WoShi sneered at HuKui, "Be careful about what you say. That bullfrog has big ears. He is a known pitfighter! I would be careful around him, or you'll wake up in the pits to face him."

HuKui gulped in apprehension, "Really! A pitfighter, nobody told me that."

"Absolutely! Do you think I will joke on such matters? Why do you think he is around to protect us?" HuKui sat back straight, and WoShi asked, "So, why did you come here?"

"I brought SuWu. He wants to speak to you. The boy is their spokesperson. They listen to him."

WoShi said, "Bring him in." HuKui brought in a skinny boy with a solemn demeanour. It did not escape WoShi's notice that he had features resembling SuJin's, and he was a year or two older.

The boy bowed reverently to WoShi and stepped back for the elders to converse.

HuKui said, "I have scouted and found a training ground for the lads. It is in the abandoned gardens of a Prince who was ordered back to his fief by Emperor Wu a hundred and fifty years ago. Nobody goes in there anymore."

WoShi asked, "Weapons training?"

"Yes, they will eventually need it."

WoShi said, "Spies have a low opinion of TaoYin, as do most students. However, weapons training would alarm them. Taking the training off of our grounds is a clever idea."

WoShi considered it and agreed. "I shall ask the dwarfs to find the best weapon masters to train them. It will be a good cover if word spreads that gambling dwarfs are training boys to fight in the pits for profit."

WoShi asked SuWu, "What do you think about this arrangement, boy?"

SuWu bowed again before responding, "I am a student master. I will listen and obey whatever you decide for me." The boy looked awed to be in the presence of the grandmaster.

WoShi grunted and said, "Then obey. I asked for your opinion, didn't I?"

SuWu smiled sheepishly and said, "Our training in the estates shouldn't be consistent, that someone notices our regular disappearances or detects a pattern to our absence. I can work on a schedule for that. Further, it would be helpful if someone watched the peripheries. Engaging the dwarfs will help."

WoShi encouraged SuWu to continue. "We want to excel in your teaching master while we pick up weapons training in hand-to-hand combat, archery and the blades."

"Why is that?" WoShi asked

"Grand Master, SuJin asked me to explain your words, and he is excited. You are teaching him to fight an opponent using his mind. The weapon and the method are incidental. This form of fighting is a unifying style for facing an opponent of unknown skills."

"I am impressed," he said, adding, "What else?"

"I am here to plead with you. Please accept me as your student for strategy. The older students say you are the empire's best teacher."

HuKui asked SuWu, "Explain why?"

"In a war, hundreds of infantrymen move on commands from their generals. Bowmen are deployed on specific terrain and asked to fire at a particular time. Units are asked to advance or retreat based on flags and enemy movements."

"All of this happens from a single mind, the strategist." SuWu paused and said, "I want to be the strategist!"

WoShi was impressed by the boy's ambition and said, "That is the last part of the strategy, where you commit your resources to action. However, I will consider your request. You may go now, boy."

"He is good, eh?" HuKui remarked as soon as SuWu left, and WoShi grunted.

"I thought you would like him. He is my favourite! The boy has a sensible head on his shoulders."

****

WoShi began their formal training. In addition to their classroom training in philosophy and sciences, he individually instructed the four boys, honing their innate strengths. He made them spar with each other in freestyle and specific sequences to teach them how to manage and camouflage their weaknesses. He also used bamboo to simulate swords.

SuJin was a gifted boy who was exceptionally talented at handling situations and weapons, particularly swords. His blinding speed, acrobatics, and balance were incomparable to anyone WoShi had seen. WoShi put metal rings around his wrists and ankles to increase his endurance and slow him down.

HuKui insisted that SuJin restrain his capabilities to mediocrity while learning from various weapon masters who taught him myriad styles of sword fighting. Despite toning down his reaction, he didn't fool any of his masters. He also grasped the various nuances of using a weapon within days. JiaShao insisted on paying the master extra for an oath to remain quiet about this prodigy.

SuWu's sword skills were ordinary compared to SuJin's, but he worked hard as SuJin's sparring partner. He compensated for his inferior skills with clever fakes. Despite this, he did not win against SuJin; nobody did. SuWu preferred archery, and although SuJin was a slightly better archer, they competed fiercely.

SuWu loved discussing war strategies with scholars, and they played simulated war games. The only class that SuJin liked to attend was history.

SuWu soon became WoShi's favourite student. His knack for strategy and organisation stood out, and they discussed imperial politics, mainly how to address Hun raids in the border towns. Sometimes, HuKui joined in their heated discussions that sometimes lasted late into the night. Typically, these discussions ended with heated exchanges and HuKui storming out.

The dwarfs were particularly impressed with SuWu. JiaShao and CaoShen, his deputy, regularly took him out into Changan to read the minds of merchants and traders and haggle their purchases. Invariably, after a good day, they ended up in the fighting pits, where SuWu evaluated fighters and figured out subtle rigging to help JiaShao place bets.

ChenHe was a chubby, lovable boy who could be found near the kitchens, helping the cooks. Frustrated, WoShi handed ChenHe's training to JiaShao, who enthusiastically trained him to use the heavy staff with rings, mace, and wrestling. At the dwarf master's insistence, the kitchen servants took ChenHe to Changan to carry their sacks of goods and pull the carts to develop his stamina in exchange for treats.

JiaShao did not lose hope and was determined to transform ChenHe into a warrior to fight beside SuJin. He got lucky when a pit master challenged ChenHe to a bout with their inexperienced wrestler. After a gruelling fight, ChenHe won. The pleased pit master rewarded ChenHe with a few coins to treat himself.

The freedom to buy treats whenever he wanted changed ChenHe's approach to wrestling. He trained with renewed vigour and begged JiaShao for fighting bouts with bets. Sensible JiaShao allowed him to win a few bouts before pitting him against experienced wrestlers at higher stakes, which resulted in him getting thrashed. JiaShao had to pay back the money he had bet on ChenHe, but he refused to sponsor him without training. This forced ChenHe to train earnestly with the dwarf masters. JiaShao was confident he would present a skilled wrestler in time.

Qian, the youngest of the four, was drawn to the library, where he spent time poring over scrolls. WoShi trained him, but he hated the rote practice. Despite the dwarf's best efforts, Qian always found ways to slip away and return to the library. HuKui told WoShi about his time with acrobats and his love for blades, and WoShi discovered that the boy was a marksman, throwing knives.

JiaShao, realising that Qian's talents lay elsewhere, advised WoShi to send him to train with the forbidden troops. These troops specialised in infiltration and assassination. WoShi acted upon this advice.

WoShi had to use his bureaucratic influence to enrol Qian into the forbidden troops. He had to swear an oath with the boy that he wouldn't assassinate any imperial authority without authorisation from the emperor, queen mother, or regent through the military commander, failing which Qian would sacrifice his life voluntarily or die a thousand deaths in their torture cell. Equivalent life would be exacted on WoShi's near and dear as Qian's mentor.

Qian did not discuss his training with anyone during the few days he visited them. The first lesson he was taught was to remain silent and listen. He revealed that their library contained accounts of previous assassinations, and the stories he heard from his master and tutors were daring and bold.

#15 The Boys Meet the Immortals

SuJin and SuWu turned into strong, wiry young men in five years.

Burly ChenHe continued to fight in the pits, and JiaShao fed him a diet of meat, snake oil, and vegetables to maintain his bulk. JiaShao trained him to use a heavy staff with metal rings to enhance his rib-crushing strength.

ChenHe sported a mangled, half-chewed ear and had scars all over his body. His battle rage was famous in the pits because once he was primed, he never backed down. He was known as the "Brick."

On strict instructions from WoShi, the dwarfs ensured his freestyle bouts weren't pitted against condemned men who fought to the death. The pits were deadly, and despite every precaution, ChenHe was beaten many times, once almost to death.

No one knew what was happening with Qian because he stopped returning to school a few weeks after joining the Forbidden Troops. They had not heard about him for years and had forgotten that he existed.

Therefore, WoShi was surprised when the master of the elite forbidden troop summoned him to take Qian back. The old master asserted that Qian was one of their better students, known as the "Black Death."

WoShi asked the forbidden master, "Why such a name? Did he kill people?" The master laughed and said, "It's for the better that you don't ask us anything, and we don't tell you anything." The master added, "We have a problem confirming Qian into our ranks."

"Why? What happened?" WoShi enquired.

Of late, demons plague his dreams, preventing him from sleeping. He hasn't slept for many days, indicating regret and a troubled conscience. We believe in sleeping without guilt because the responsibility for our actions, both before man and God, lies with our imperial masters. We are faultless in the eyes of our war god, Kuan Ti. Without this mental clarity, we will fail or compromise our assignments."

WoShi wholeheartedly agreed, "Of course! Remorse can be dangerous for the work done by the forbidden troops. A weapon can't have a conscience."

The old master gave a short bow. "Thank you, Marquis, for understanding your ward's situation. You must resolve whatever plagues him and send him back. He is ready to take the blood oath to join us." Looking sympathetically at Qian, the master added, "Medicines don't seem to work on him."

WoShi enquired. "A cure could take years, and what if he doesn't want to return?" The master of the forbidden troops smiled at WoShi and said, "It's for the better that you don't ask us anything, and we don't tell you anything." He gestured towards the door, indicating that their conversation was over.

As they were about to leave, the forbidden master said, "We mentioned his name here to remind you of the forbidden troops." Although this seemed like an offhand statement, WoShi knew it was a promise of intense violence if Qian did not return.

WoShi noticed that Qian was covered in well-healed scars and fine cauterisation. He realised that the apothecary and physicians of the forbidden troops were very competent.

On their horse cart, returning home, WoShi asked, "Why did they let you go? No one leaves the forbidden troops."

Qian nodded and said, "Yes, not even if they're dead!" After a long silence, he said, "I saved the master from assassinations within the group. Twice!"

WoShi was shocked and looked at Qian. "The voices! They helped me thwart the attacks."

WoShi did not want him to reveal more and said, "You've grown, become taller and stronger, but you look haggard. Is it the lack of sleep?"

Qian rubbed his temples and said, "Yes, it's a lack of sleep because the voices in my mind refuse to stop talking." He opened up to WoShi despite WoShi asking if it was prudent to disclose what he endured with the forbidden troops. "I am trained to blend in and look ordinary and neutral. People on the street should easily forget me. I learned to mimic them and blend in with nature as well. It's exhilarating to lie motionless for hours in the woods, watching wildlife up close."

"Is that a tough challenge? Lying still?" enquired WoShi with a hint of condescension.

"Well, one of our challenges is to stay camouflaged while a deer is let loose with grain thrown all around. Without alarming the animal, we must retrieve a silk thread tied to its leg in a slipknot."

WoShi looked at him, stunned. "You did that!" he exclaimed.

Qian forced a smile despite his fatigue. "I have done this a few times. There are techniques to achieve it. I started by sleeping near the deer for many days. The tick bites are unbearable."

WoShi was surprised and said, "Oh, I now know why they want you to return."

Qian responded, "I haven't slept in quite a while. I spend my time reading ancient scrolls and journals of assignments undertaken by various troop members. They meticulously record each assignment, and it's a fantastic read. After every assignment, successful or otherwise, an imperial record-keeper is called in to document and record everything, just like you do at the HanKaoTzu library. They have scrolls that have recipes for deadly poisons and a few antidotes. I have memorised many of them, especially the antidotes."

"Isn't that forbidden? I mean, taking their recipes?"

"I did not ask whether it was right or wrong! The teachers and students there don't care for words and depend on their master's word-of-mouth. The recipes are kept along with the scrolls. If you need any poison, physicians prepare it at the apothecary."

WoShi grunted. "I guess that none of them knows how to read and write, and you haven't told them you can read words."

Qian smiled. "We are taught not to say anything we are not asked for, especially in casual conversations."

"You just told me."

"Yes, I did. I wanted you to know this."

"You want to go back?"

"Yes. My master believes that I will come back when I am ready. They have immense patience for these things."

Perceptive WoShi asked, "You have told me many things, and it's deliberate. Why?"

Qian disclosed his fears. "I have a bitter rival within the forbidden troops. He is good, very good. If I don't return and my master dies, he might come hunting."

WoShi was appalled. "He won't be satisfied with merely your death. He will go after people close to you." Qian nodded.

Qian massaged his temples again and groaned. "Grandmaster, help me sleep. I dream a lot, and spirits speak to me, keeping me awake."

WoShi organised sleeping draughts from the local apothecary, but just as the forbidden troop master said, it didn't help.

****

Qian's sleeplessness worsened at school. He spoke to SuWu about it. The description of Qian's dreams made no sense: dead men, their bodies still preserved, whispered about a secret hideaway in a lush valley that they had to visit. The voices also demanded that three deities be taken back to Tianzhu.

"What deities?" asked SuWu

Qian told SuWu, "Two men and a lady. It's the goddess who demands that she be returned to Tianzhu. I feel it's her influence that makes me see visions."

SuWu shrugged his shoulders. "Strange, if a goddess wanted to return to Tianzhu, she could go there instantly. Why trouble you?"

"Us," Qian clarified, and SuWu frowned. "The goddess wants *us* to attend to unfinished business here. We have to release the immortals."

A few days later, SuWu repeated Qian's strange dreams to WoShi.

****

The Hun tribes allied and raided the vast borderlands of the Han Empire along the Great Wall. Overland trade had ceased, and many peasants were killed while their women and children were taken as slaves. Vast tracts of fertile land lay uncultivated as the influx of refugees continued into the border towns. The imperial army was ready to march into the steppe to put down the menace and force the Huns to negotiate.

JiaShao approached WoShi, who appeared listless after his talk with SuWu. "The imperial forces need recruits to man the borderlands, and they may come to the school. We should move out with the boys for a few months, at least until after the torch festival. We have sent most other students back to their villages."

WoShi looked up. "Where to? It seems things are coming to a head."

JiaShao ignored WoShi's worry and continued, "I will take them to our village. They can help us farm and hunt boars, and we will fish in the mountain lakes. I spoke with SuWu, and he said the boys are all for it."

WoShi protested, "The torch festival is in the middle of the first lunar month and many months away. I cannot let them take such a long break."

HuKui supported JiaShao, saying, "They need to see the world outside, especially the villages. They must understand what Han is like in the countryside – simple, happy people despite a hard life."

WoShi protested, "What if they get used to life as a commoner? Will they abandon the expedition?" WoShi begrudgingly agreed to let JiaShao take the lads and asked HuKui to accompany them.

The boys jumped at the prospect of travelling, anything to escape the monotony of training. Qian nodded his head at SuWu in gratitude.

****

WoShi gathered everyone early in the morning to declare that the training for the Golden Glow was complete. He wore a gold, silk-embroidered Hanfu with the imperial badge of a peacock in regal colours on his chest, reflecting his bureaucratic status. Two scrolls hung on stands behind him, one proclaiming him a marquis and another confirming the Emperor's appointment of him as a grandmaster.

A table beside WoShi held idols of Guan Yu, the god of war; Kuei Xing, the clever yet unattractive dwarf of exams; Guan Gong, the god of strategy; and a tiny idol representing a scholar. Tuhu, the dwarf's butcher, doctor, and surgeon, served as the priest for the ceremony. He lit lamps, burned incense, and arranged food offerings before them. JiaShao and HuKui sat beside WoShi, dressed in their best clothes, and the four boys sat facing them.

WoShi formally welcomed the gods who were called upon and the teachers present to witness the ceremony. He added, "On instructions from my teacher and his teacher before him, the idol of the scholar you are unfamiliar with is that of Zhang Liang. With this ceremony, and as his spokesman, I declare your training and the purpose of the HanKaoTzu school complete."

A gust of wind blew out all the lamps, throwing the room into darkness. They relit immediately, with the flames burning brighter. What was astounding was that even the rising smoke from the incense had a clear break. Quite inexplicably, Zhang Liang's idol crashed to the floor, and Tuhu's hands shook as he set it back upright. They all looked at each other in bewilderment, and HuKui stared at SuJin, who shrugged his shoulders.

A visibly frightened Tuhu completed the invocations to bless the gathering. WoShi was also shaken by what he had just witnessed but firmly continued, "Normally, this ceremony is done in the presence of all our students and guests from the bureaucracy, but we are forgoing it this time."

WoShi looked at the boys and declared, "Your training is complete. There is nothing more I can teach you." He checked the scroll for the exact words he needed to use and said, "I release you, *Battle Speed warriors*." Each boy stepped before WoShi, fell to his knees, and kowtowed to their teacher.

WoShi looked at HuKui and JiaShao and nodded his head.

HuKui said, "I release you. Battle Speed warriors." The boys got up, fell again to their knees, and kowtowed HuKui.

JiaShao said, "I release you. Battle speed warriors." The boys got up, fell to their knees again, and kowtowed to JiaShao.

Qian shouted, and everyone looked at him anxiously, but he was smiling. "Can you hear the silence?" he asked, clarifying, "The voices—

they have left me."

WoShi looked worried, and HuKui asked, "Are you sure, Master WoShi? We seem to be dealing with supernatural powers?"

The grand master nodded assuredly. "I am as much in the dark as you, HuKui, and that is why we must follow what my master instructed us to do in his scrolls."

WoShi declared to the apprehensive students, now warriors. "The time has come for you to face your destiny." Although JiaShao's eyes widened, he remained quiet. Something inexplicable was happening, and he did not dare express his fears.

"Come," WoShi beckoned to the boys. Everyone followed him except Tuhu, the priest who did not want to get involved.

WoShi paused outside the library and squinted at the bright rising sun.

JiaShao stood beside WoShi, looking up. "It hasn't rained for a few weeks. There isn't a cloud in sight. What's your worry, Master?"

WoShi sighed heavily. "JiaShao, I was looking at a normal day one last time. We are entering the unknown, and I wonder how our boys will react once we disclose our last secrets. Will they remain together?"

JiaShao said, "Ah, I understand. After they return from the village, Qian will join the forbidden troops. What prevents the others from changing their priorities once they see a different world? Will they abandon the journey to Tianzhu?"

HuKui nodded in comprehension. He said, "It's out of our hands! Our job is done."

SuJin stepped forward and told WoShi. "I will not travel with JiaShao, master. I shall remain by your side until it is time to leave. We are the golden glow. '*We stick together and protect each other, always*'." Oddly, his brothers remained silent. SuJin's eyes widened in shock at his friend's refusal to acknowledge their oath.

WoShi asked Qian, "What else did the goddess tell you?"

"She implores us to free the immortals using the spark from the skies."

HuKui curiously asked, "Was she alone?"

Qian answered. "I'm not sure, master. I sensed two other mighty beings towering into the sky but were silent. I was plagued by the whispers from four fierce men who demand obedience to the goddess." WoShi and JiaShao looked at each other dumbfounded. Qian continued, "I don't know what happened, but they are silent."

WoShi's legs buckled, and he sat down. After composing himself, he told the boys, "This vast empire was founded by a peasant guard with the help of a disillusioned strategist, Zhang Liang. Their success was not mere fluke; they had help from immortals."

SuWu interjected, "But master, that is pure conjecture. A myth!"

WoShi replied, "I wish I still had that doubt, but for you, it will become a certainty in a few moments!" WoShi strode towards the inner room.

He unlocked the door, stopped, and looked back at the boys, similar to what WangMang had done many years ago. Trembling, JiaShao said, "Master WoShi, destiny's crossroads are just a few steps away. Last chance! Are you sure about this?"

WoShi acknowledged JiaShao with a smile. "Friend, it's time for us to step back! Look at the boys one last time before we push them into the hands of destiny."

SuWu impatiently said, "Let's face it, master. If all of you have seen whatever's inside and managed to remain composed, we will surely be the same."

HuKui said, "Don't be so logical, SuWu. I became a changed man after WoShi showed me what's inside."

WoShi pulled the wedge while holding the crumbling shelf, and it swung open to reveal the shrine inside. With a loud moan, Qian collapsed into a dead faint!

SuWu exclaimed. "Oh, my! This place is just as Qian described. It was no random hallucination! He was called here."

A hushed silence followed. Nobody ventured into the shrine. JiaShao sat down on his stunted legs and tried to wake the unconscious Qian. He looked at ChenHe and said, "Go, get some water. We need him to make sense of all this." The boys, frightened, sat down and touched their foreheads on the floor in reverence. No one entered the tomb, as it was a privilege assigned to Qian.

JiaShao sprinkled water on Qian, and they brought him back to his senses. The boy sobbed as the others crowded around him. SuWu rubbed his back in reassurance. Sniffing heavily, Qian regained his composure and motioned for SuJin to enter the room.

SuJin looked at Qian in embarrassment and said, "I did not dream of this place. You did. It's for you to enter."

"No, SuJin. They want you, but the four of us have a deeper connection. I'm sorry that I just realised this." SuJin stared at Qian for some time before getting to his feet. He bowed his head at the entrance and walked in.

The others followed, and muscular ChenHe lifted Qian to his feet. They came in last. JiaShao did not enter the room. He hovered near the entrance, peeping in and hopping from one leg to another.

The shrine had a profound effect on SuJin. He was confronted with irrefutable proof of his destiny. He tried to stifle the tremble in his hands. This was reality! He stared at the immortals and fell on his knees, tears streaming down his cheeks. He mumbled, "Help me. I don't know what to do!"

SuJin reverently paid his respects to the mummified warriors and the deities by touching his head to the floor. The others followed suit beside him. JiaShao kneeled outside the door.

ChenHe was the first to sit back on his knees. He spoke in astonishment, "Qian, you are unbelievable! The dreams and the ghosts! You told us the goddess would be lying on her side. Look, it's the deity; she has fallen to the side."

WoShi could not contain his disbelief and asked. "All of you knew about this tomb?"

For the first time in his life, ChenHe corrected WoShi, his master. "It's not a tomb, Master WoShi. It is a shrine! They are all living; we can feel them." A startled WoShi bowed his head to ChenHe, acknowledging his astute observation, while JiaShao wailed outside in religious fervour.

SuWu made the exact observations made by WoShi's scholars. "The immortals are of Han origin, but how is that possible? They are too huge! Look at the size of the armour and the size of the weapons. It's clear that they starved to death, but before that, they were huge men with bulging muscles and massive chests."

JiaShao scolded him from outside, "SuWu, you cannot reason here. You need to have unwavering faith to serve the gods, or else they will not reward you with what you need the most."

ChenHe looked at Qian with concern and said aloud, "We thought if we took Qian away from Changan, he would recover. I wonder what will happen now?"

A tired Qian smiled at his friend ChenHe. "I am relieved! I feel the goddess is pleased. We must help SuJin complete the pyre to release these energies."

HuKui exclaimed in surprise. "What? A pyre in the library?"

Qian said, "It's their resting place, master, not our library."

"Are we going to light a fire here?" asked WoShi in apprehension.

"Not us! Our fire is impure to free the immortals. They are holy men."

"We need to set this place as the immortals described. The gods will free them."

"Will the deities leave us?" asked WoShi

"Yes, master. The bindings that installed a divine spark within the deities will dissipate."

ChenHe said, "Hmm. You sound much better already."

Qian smiled. "Yes. The voices are silent."

SuJin said, "Qian, they are very much here, and I can feel them. They are not fearsome; they are curious about us."

JiaShao commanded them from the door, "Sit down, all of you. Meditate and be one with the spirits. Honour them! Please send the obeisance of your teachers to them." The boys obeyed.

A few minutes later, SuWu sobbed uncontrollably and touched his head to the floor. "Oh, my gods, I feel them. This is bliss! Yes, I will follow SuJin. I will do anything to serve you."

SuJin was silent. He stared into nothing, his eyes vacant but covered in a blue glow. Qian sat smiling while ChenHe giggled. Some unseen force lifted his muscular arm and felt his muscles.

WoShi beckoned to HuKui, and they came out of the shrine. Whatever was happening inside was not meant for them.

SuJin was the first to break the spell, saying, "A violent spark of the goddess remains. She has left it for us. It must be secured before our journey into Tianzhu."

WoShi shouted from outside the door. "It must be the medallion hanging on WangMang's neck!"

JiaShao thundered. "Victory to the Son of Heaven." They could hear the slogan repeated elsewhere in the library as other dwarfs joined in.

SuJin turned to JiaShao and smiled. "The spirits thank you and your people for their perseverance through the generations. The goddess has spoken through the spirits and is pleased with your devotion." JiaShao banged his head on the floor until blood oozed out in happiness at being mentioned. WoShi and HuKui had to restrain him as he laughed and cried intermittently.

SuWu saw the green and black knife with a hilt shaped like two mating frogs from the desiccated corpse and said, "Hey, look at this knife. We have a twin!"

SuJin said, "Not twins! They are Yin and Yang. They can be locked together to form one single dagger. We need them!"

SuJin stood up and told his brothers, "It's time. The immortals are impatient to leave this world."

One by one, the boys followed SuJin as he walked up to each mummy. They sat down, touched their foreheads to the floor before the immortals, and finally kowtowed to the deities, just as they would to the emperor.

Qian was aware of what to do, which baffled WoShi. Why did the spirits speak to him directly if SuJin was the "chosen one"?

Qian responded to WoShi as if he could read his mind. "Don't doubt SuJin one bit, master! He is the one. He will be unstoppable when he gains the inner eye and ears to reach the gods."

Qian looked around and motioned to JiaShao to pay his obeisance by entering the shrine. He refused and kowtowed seven times from afar. He was terrified of the stately mummies, who looked like they would get up at any moment.

SuJin looked around until he found a pile of dust-covered terracotta blocks. Each block had a long brass piece embedded on one side and coal residue stuck to the other. He began interlocking the blocks on the floor, connecting the brass pieces.

WoShi was perplexed about how they would move the brittle mummy to place the terracotta tiles below them when he realised that each mummy was already sitting on a partially assembled terracotta block platform. The immortals had planned this and were instructing the boys.

The young men quietly worked to interlock the tiles to create a giant swastika symbol. WoShi had seen this symbol in the temple, on the palm of the golden man, worshipped by Emperor Wu.

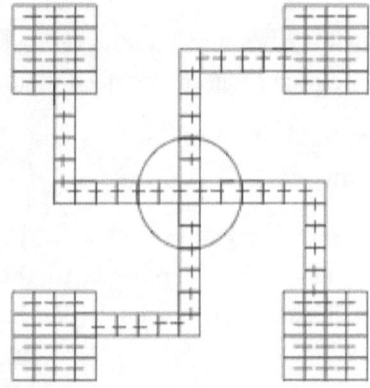

Each of the immortals sat at the edge of a clockwise swastika symbol with the fireplace in the middle.

Removing his hanfu, SuWu reverently collected Zhang Liang's bones and remains with utmost respect and piled them in a circular depression at the centre of the room. SuJin, without looking up, said, "SuWu, there will be a small locket belonging to Zhang Liang in his remains. The immortals say that it's for you!"

The boys had to mix and match the metal edges, especially in the centre, which formed a ring with a deep furrow. They finally completed the assembly with a few blocks to spare.

HuKui spoke aloud, "What does this symbol mean?"

WoShi answered, "It's the symbol of SuJin's birth star, a comet with four tails that turns clockwise. People know it as the swastika, a symbol of purification. You can find it inside Emperor Wu's shrine."

Qian dusted his hanfu and said, "In a vision that I had from the eyes of an eagle flying high, this symbol is alive!" He sat on his haunches. "A white snow-covered mountain is at the centre, and the four legs are rivers of ice emanating from the mountain." Qian added, "I could feel the great life force of Erlang Shen there, the god with the third eye, who sees everything."

WoShi remarked, "The mountain must be part of the cosmic pillar that connects the earth and the heavens. It must be a holy place in the great white mountains."

SuJin respectfully removed the three deities and kept them in the middle of the swastika symbol. ChenHe and Qian dismantled the wooden platform to access the sturdy metal framework beneath the powdering wood. There were thirteen rods and a trident. They fitted the rods into each other, as each rod had slots to hold a matching rod. Soon, the pole became long, and at the upper end, they mounted the trident. The boys broke the wooden roof and pierced the rod through the thatch above.

Debris streamed in, and they ducked and brushed their eyes. A piece of wood hit a mummy, and its hand disintegrated into dust. "Be careful!" screamed SuJin, kicking the falling thatch and wood away from the brittle bodies. A hole opened into the skies above the shrine, letting in daylight. The boys attached a few more rods and raised the trident into the skies.

SuWu and Qian held the rod while ChenHe rummaged within the disassembled platform.

Worried, HuKui told WoShi, "It's a dead giveaway that something is happening here. It won't be long before unwanted visitors pour in. Hopefully, the boys will finish whatever they have set out to do before that. We all have to escape soon after."

JiaShao said, "Don't worry, the tunnels are ready for such an exigency."

ChenHe pulled out a large, blackened metal bowl with a hole in the middle from behind the platform. He grunted with effort as he gingerly carried the heavy bowl and slotted it precisely into the circular depression on the floor, upside down—the metal pieces from the tiles connected all around to the bowl.

The boys slotted the long rod into the middle of the heavy bowl to hold the long pole upright. SuJin placed the idols around the metal pole, locking the deities to each other in preexisting grooves.

WoShi whispered to an equally astonished HuKui. "You are right. Their training is complete. Why do they need mortals like us when they have guidance from the gods and the dead?"

At last, the strange arrangements were complete. The boys respectfully bowed one last time, touching their heads again at the symbol's edge. Qian guided them out of the tomb, saying, "It is too dangerous to remain here. It is now a divine pyre."

Once outside the library, WoShi asked the boys, "What is the danger?"

SuWu answers, "We expect a fire to descend from the skies and consign the wise men to flames. This is their pyre, which will release them from the mortal world and mark the beginning of our journey."

"A fire from the sky? How is that possible?" asked WoShi.

When no one professed an answer, WoShi exclaimed, "This is our library with all our precious manuscripts inside. I cannot let it go up in flames."

SuWu said, "Let us empty it."

JiaShao said, "We need more hands." He took out an ivory whistle and gave a shrill blast. They heard the whistle repeat from far away, and dwarfs poured in.

WoShi thanked JiaShao and was about to enter the outer library to empty scrolls. HuKui stopped him and gestured towards Qian, who was sitting with tears streaming down his face. "Now what?" he exclaimed. The boys held him close.

SuWu left the huddle and approached WoShi and HuKui. "The spirits told Qian they were leaving this realm for good and wouldn't haunt him again. They have blessed us for our journey to Tianzhu!"

"*Battle speed, brothers!* Is what the immortals told us."

JiaShao enthusiastically asked, "Oh, is he joining you three? Is he not going back to the forbidden troops?"

HuKui remarked, "Why is he crying? I thought he wanted to get rid of his recurring dreams."

SuWu said, "Their sacrifice! They remained here for centuries to ensure SuJin took up the Han promise. Their bodies will burn, and they will release their spirits for their final journey to the holy mountain. Their immense sacrifice to Han has overwhelmed Qian."

"How is SuJin taking all this?" asked HuKui

"He's worried! With Qian losing his ability to converse with the spirits, who will guide us?"

They watched as the first dwarf emerged, holding scrolls and manuscripts from the library.

****

WoShi closed the door to his chamber, and an impatient HuKui asked a sniffling Qian, "How can a fire come from the sky? How can a metal rod catch fire without a furnace?" WoShi and JiaShao shared the same concerns.

HuKui wondered. "A fire from the heavens to light the pyre! Bah! Sorry for being a cynic despite all that we witnessed today. You would need a lot of heat to burn metal, like a fire from the comets. Now, that would be a sight!"

SuJin intervened and digressed their talks. "The tomb was the reason for Qian's dreams."

WoShi asked, "Why did the spirits not tell you the location of their resting place if they were conversing with Qian?"

SuJin said, "You are our master, not them. They were waiting for you to declare us ready, which you did today." WoShi was speechless.

SuWu added, "Grandmaster, the spirits believe in all of us, not just SuJin. The immortals' confidence in our abilities weighs heavily on me. Until today, it was all about SuJin. Now, I am not so sure." SuWu placed his palm on his chest and asked WoShi, "Tell me, master, truthfully, are we capable of the deeds that the immortals expect us to achieve? We are no match for their power."

WoShi had no answer. Just then, JiaShao beckoned them outside. The skies had darkened swiftly, and giant thunderclouds rumbled into view, obscuring the sun. Birds filled the air in droves as they returned to their roosts.

The wind picked up to a howl. JiaShao bowed in trepidation to the advancing storm, offering a silent prayer to the heavens.

"Master! Marquis of HanKaoTzu School!" The voice nearby was out of place. WoShi turned to find YangXiong's assistant waving his hand to get his attention.

A surprised WoShi had to shout to be heard above the howling wind. Heavy rain lashed at them under the awning, and WoShi stepped closer. "Speak."

"The high bureaucrats, YangXiong, HuanTan and LuiXiu, have requested that you join them at the library. They want you to come with the boy. They said you would know who," the assistant said.

WoShi was about to follow him when the assistant warned, "They have many soldiers inside and outside the library."

SuJin responded to the assistant instead of WoShi, "I know you are telling our master more than what they asked you to speak, and we thank you for that. I want you to tell them that WoShi is gathering and bringing four boys responsible for raising the trident." The man nodded, and SuJin said, "Run! You should make an excuse to move far away from that place immediately after."

The air crackled strangely, making the hair on their hands and heads float. Lightning sliced through the sky, striking trees and houses that exploded into splinters and flames. Smoke billowed across the city, and winds further stoked the fires, setting huts ablaze.

JiaShao cried, "The gods have unleashed their fury!"

WoShi shouted above the howling wind, "I can't stay here. They will come looking for me and trap all of us. I will go inside the tomb and buy you some time. Make your escape now!"

Qian's hand shot out and stopped WoShi. The boy had an eerie glow in his eyes. Layered with many voices talking simultaneously, he said. "No need for that, teacher. Your service to the avatar is incomplete. We will take care of this small matter."

The strongly accented and guttural voice was a command from the ancient past, stopping WoShi in his tracks. Qian smiled, bowed low to HuKui and JiaShao, and said, "Thank you, masters." Qian made strange gestures into the sky, murmuring in an unknown language.

"Stay," HuKui said and grabbed WoShi's arm. "The spirits want to help us through the possessed boy."

People screamed in terror as hailstones the size of a clenched fist poured from the skies, and everyone ran to find shelter. Ice littered the school, sparkling like fallen stars. The air was thick with a strange, pungent odour that burned their noses and stung their eyes. It seemed as if nature was unleashing its fury for the desecration of the shrine.

Lightning struck the trident, and HuKui yelped in fright as a bright light blinded him. Intense heat singed the hair on his hands.

Lightning struck in continuous bursts, and it seemed that the assaults from the sky wouldn't end. They squatted down, closing their eyes and shielding their ears. Static was everywhere, and the school lit up brighter than a summer day. Thunder crashed and shook the ground so hard that men were thrown to the floor while lightning jagged between the buildings.

Lying on the ground, HuKui saw many lightning bolts connect, all flowing in a continuous stream of energy into the trident. The pole glowed white hot, and the air around it sizzled.

After what seemed an eternity, it became so quiet that they could hear JiaShao's moans. The lightning ceased, and hail no longer fell from the skies. The library roof was burning, and just as they sat up, it rained heavily, wetting everything and quelling the fire.

With the calming sound of rain falling on the roof, Qian said, "Gone, they have gone. The gods accepted the pyre."

They huddled in WoShi's room, and no one came to arrest them that night. By dawn, they ventured out. The sun revealed the carnage caused by the freak storm at the library.

Many buildings in Changan were destroyed, and debris was scattered all around. People were still roaming the streets, too scared to go indoors.

JiaShao returned and reported that the school was minimally affected, and the library had taken hits, but it was salvageable. All that remained of the tomb room were pieces of the wall after it was blown to bits.

Awed, JiaShao reported, "Not a single soldier survived! It looks like the spirits were thorough."

They walked to the tomb to see the carnage. Remnants of charred flesh and black blood covered the walls, and the smell of cooked meat and burnt hair permeated the air.

It was a massacre! Bits of flesh and gore had piled up at the corners, and the floor was slippery with human fat and hair. The mummified bodies had vanished, and pieces of newly cleaved skulls and bones glowed brightly in the morning sun. Mangled swords and spear points were strewn everywhere. Those inside appeared to have cooked in their skin and exploded.

Nauseated by the smell, WoShi rushed out. HuKui seemed unaffected by all the violence. He chirped, "It's about time we had some divine help. Good riddance to those pompous bureaucrats."

WoShi said, "They were learned men, misguided, but my students, nevertheless. Respect them in death."

HuKui looked up to the heavens in mock prayer and said, "Don't be fooled by what they were. This is apt revenge for murdering innocents at the chophouse."

HuKui said, "Come now. I want to show you something." WoShi reluctantly followed HuKui back into the scene of the carnage.

The boys moved back to allow WoShi to see what they were looking at. The brass pole had fallen off, broken where it had touched the deities. The idols had solidified into a giant blob of metal resembling a mountain with a small hood at the top, like a snake.

"This is the mountain I saw in my visions," Qian said in wonder. "SuJin, we must carry this to Tianzhu!"

"Will you join us?" asked SuJin hopefully.

"Stop me if you can," responded Qian with a smile.

SuJin looked at SuWu, who bobbed his head. "We will carry it with us."

On realising SuJin's quandary, SuWu bowed and said, "Of course, Prince, we will accompany you to Tianzhu."

ChenHe said, "*Battle speed, brothers,*" and the other replied earnestly in a single voice, "*Battle speed, brothers.*"

That evening, JiaShao's men performed a peace ritual for the gods. They tore down the remaining walls, levelled the secret room, and moved the metal blob into the underground chamber.

Qian approached WoShi and said, "Master, if the head of the forbidden troops dies before we leave for Tianzhu, send word to me immediately. To protect everyone, I need to become a hunter."

Yad Bhavam, Tad Bhavathi - *Sanskrit* -
"You become what you believe."

PART #2

SUJIN

Generic Descriptions

Mofa	Describes charisma as "Magic"
LaoLi	Strong Chinese beer
Pao	Full body dress worn by men
Nong	Chinese peasant farmer
Hezi	Undergarment worn under the Hanfu
Piyong	School to replace HanKaoTzu, made by WangMang
MingTang	Temple of heaven and earth, the zodiac and the elements worship
ShaoJiu	Strong Chinese wine with high alcohol content
Airag	Fermented horse milk of the Mongols
PaiLou	Chinese archway before you enter a village or town
Chi	Life force energy
Tongyu	The ancient Chinese common language
SwordClaw	The Hun champion SuJin faced at the arena
LianDan	WangMang's champion warrior at the arena
Batu	A Mongolian battle slave of SuJin, sword master Hun, a few years older than SuWu, known as Batu Nachin, the "Loyal Falcon"
CaoShen	Second in command of the Dwarfs at Changan, below JiaShao
Tuhu	The dwarf butcher, a priest and surgeon
WangXun	WangMang's cousin and Imperial minister
LuiRuzi	Infant emperor, succeeding Emperor Pingdi/LuiKan

Ren	Qian's wife at the valley of dwarfs
Wong	Dwarf, who accompanied HuKui to the village, works with Hong
Hong	Dwarf, leader of Wong, Tong and Dong, dwarfs work in pairs.
Tong	Dwarf warrior, reporting to Hong
Dong	Works with Tong as his partner, a warrior
YuanLin	Cannibal bandit leader
YuanYi	Educated brother of YuanLin, manage planning
Pockface	Second in command to YuanLin and the bandit's clever advisor
HeGan	Smart jeweller of YuanLin, loans gold to goldsmiths and knows how to trade.
Zhan	Jeweller friend of HeGan in Changan, holding most of his gold
Sheya	Means, Fang - Tooth of a snake, dagger owned by Qian

#16 SuJin Meets the Emperor

WangMang mobilised the entire bureaucracy in a grand parade to inaugurate the newly constructed MingTang temple. The ceremonies also included opening Piyong, the new civil services school that would replace the imperial HanKaoTzu school.

The parade was divided into civil, military, and imperial contingents. Each contingent comprised hundreds of soldiers on horseback and footmen, accompanied by clanging cymbals, drums, and flutes. Courtiers and palace mandarins, identifiable by colourful rank badges, were carried with much fanfare in sedan chairs. They were followed by hundreds of palace officials and eunuchs holding banners and flags.

The MingTang temple was a massive three-storey structure with twelve grand halls, symbolising the lunar months of the year. It featured gardens with large, interconnected ponds and four wide bridges precisely aligned in the north, south, east, and west directions. The temple's roof contained rooms designated for gold, wood, water, and fire; the earth room was one level below.

Imperial builders had constructed a temporary structure outside the temple as an arena for a much-publicised tournament. The arena featured tiered wooden and bamboo seating on both sides, serving as a gallery for the audience.

WangMang was determined to use the opportunity to assert his dominance over the LuI clan, especially after negotiating peace with the detestable Huns. The unsettling sight of Han soldiers standing alongside a Hun warrior delegation, their traditional foes, was disturbing.

WangMang was confident that the tournament, which featured the fearsome Huns fighting to the death, would further intimidate his rivals and establish himself as the undisputed ruler of Han.

****

The chants of the temple priests reached a crescendo as LuiKan, now Emperor Pingdi, arrived on his litter with his entourage, including ladies from the harem. The dais for the Emperor had to be at the highest level, and his bodyguards used a ramp to carry his litter to the throne, two storeys high, giving him a clear view of the arena below.

The imperial procession paused for WangMang to bow to the emperor. After the Emperor ascended to the top tier, the guards removed the ramp, and WangMang enthusiastically greeted the high officials who joined him to sit one level below the emperor.

Imperial bodyguards spread around the emperor, with two different companies of bowmen watching the crowds. Although both companies were led by men loyal to WangMang, he wanted people to believe that the regent was impartial in protecting the throne.

Twenty grades of nobility were orderly seated on bamboo stands on either side of the imperial stand, and lesser bureaucrats crowded the benches further away from the imperial stand. WangMang, sensing their appreciation for the extravagant event organised, held his interlocked fists high in the air. There was a roar of approval. It amused WangMang that they openly appreciated him under the Emperor's dais.

WangMang's eyes fell on Marquis WoShi, sitting nearby with a student. His disdain was palpable. After the death of his loyal scholars at the school, WangMang had considered removing WoShi many times. However, he hesitated. WoShi was a respected figure in the bureaucracy, and he knew the Empress would interfere, allowing the Lui clan to rally against him.

WangMang felt a strong urge to humiliate WoShi. He recalled the young Emperor demanding that WoShi train students to become his bodyguards. The time was ripe to give the pup a demonstration of how real men fought while he destroyed WoShi. He smirked as he remembered an adage he had learnt at the HanKaoTzu school – *"One arrow, two eagles."*

With a wry smile, WangMang decided to alter the day's programme.

He walked up the heavily guarded steps to the Emperor's dais, where no one could sit. He looked once across the expectant arena and signalled the imperial head priest to begin proceedings.

The heavy-set head priest laboured up the steps to the dais, where the Emperor sat and lay down in reverence before the earthly spark of the divine. The strings of beads covering the Emperor's face rattled, and his bodyguards motioned the priest forward. The imperial chancellor, the bureaucrat executing the Emperor's command, crawled between the boy Emperor and the priest to mediate the ceremony.

Emperor Pingdi went through the motions of the opening rituals, guided by the high priest's chants. He dropped incense into a censer, immediately bellowing a cloud of scented smoke. Guards escorted the priest back, and his relief was evident as he returned to the lower deck, away from the gaze of divinity. His abbots assisted in transferring the lit incense to the other stone pots. The head priest gestured to the chancellor once all the incense pots were lit and was effusing their fragrant smoke.

A drum boomed, and the chatter in the arena died down. The Imperial Chancellor bowed to Emperor Pingdi and, after his nod, declared the opening of Piyong School. Relay criers repeated the message down the gallery aisles, inciting thunderous applause and rhythmic stomping on the wooden deck by the crowd.

The chancellor signalled for silence, and the drums resounded once more. He declared the school's formal opening contingent upon the Emperor's blessed incense permeating every corner of the school. The smoke would also initiate rituals at the central courtyard, the MingTang, for twelve days, after which the temple would be inaugurated with the first rituals and offerings to be made by the Empress Dowager Wang.

A group of high abbots and eunuchs, accompanied by royal bodyguards, marched out with bowls of burning incense to sanctify the temple and the school. Dense, fragrant smoke filled the air as additional priests moved through the seated audience, enveloping the spectators in divine fragrance. Many cried and swooned upon receiving the heavenly scent, while others prayed for intercession for their prayers. Bodyguards covered the upper decks to protect the imperial family and mandarins until the smoke dissipated.

Cheers filled the air, praising the Han dynasty and Emperor Pingdi, followed by cries of "Glory to WangMang" even louder. WangMang expressed shock and bowed his head, feigning humility at being equated with the emperor. Emperor Pingdi, agitated and unusually restless, made wild movements with the beads covering his head, showing his displeasure at his regent receiving high praise.

Senior bureaucrats sitting below the dais frantically gestured to the priests, and the incense was swiftly extinguished. Amid anxious murmurs from the gathering that a miffed Emperor might cancel the inauguration, the chancellor reaffirmed the Emperor's vision for Piyong School. A lone voice shouted, "Glory to Emperor Pingdi," filled with fervour. This sparked a wave of appreciation from the audience, first hesitantly, then rumbling with unified acclamation.

Emperor Pingdi reluctantly nodded, allowing WangMang's felicitation for constructing the temple and the school.

The chancellor said, "Impressed by WangMang's selfless duty to the Han Empire, the Emperor is giving him an entire province as his fiefdom, and the taxes collected there shall go to WangMang for six years." The applause and appreciation for this unprecedented gesture from the Emperor to his regent continued for a long time despite the imperial soldier's repeated drumbeats trying to restore silence. It was as if the drummers had joined the celebration to acknowledge the regent.

WoShi cheered with everybody and whispered to SuJin, "What a farce. All of them are under WangMang's spell, except the young emperor. Sycophancy is at its zenith."

SuJin stared at WangMang, a feeling stirring in his mind that their destinies were intertwined.

As they watched, a bureaucrat in the Empress's colours, flanked by two soldiers, came running, waving a scroll. He screamed as he climbed the open steps, asking for the Imperial Chancellor. "From the Grand Empress Dowager, a message!"

People hastily gave way, scrutinising the chancellor's demeanour. The chancellor's creased brows indicated that it was not a pre-planned interruption. The chancellor knelt, keeping his head bowed, and extended his arms above his head to receive the scroll. With the scroll in hand, he looked at WangMang for guidance, but for some reason, WangMang was busy speaking to a military commander.

The chancellor glanced up at the emperor, whose beads remained still. With trepidation, he bowed his head to the Emperor and carefully scrutinised the seal to confirm its authenticity. He reconfirmed the seal with senior bureaucrats before breaking it open.

Priests and bureaucrats craned their necks as if trying to read the manuscript's contents from afar. After quickly scanning the document, the chancellor hurried up to the Emperor's dais, prostrated himself before the emperor, and conversed in hushed tones.

It was clear that the Emperor was displeased by the message as he motioned to his bodyguard to recheck the broken seal. After confirming that the scroll came from the Empress dowager, he flung himself back into his royal chair in frustration. Intrigued, the spectators leaned forward, eager to catch the chancellor's words first-hand without resorting to second-hand messages for the repeat criers. This was palace intrigue at its juiciest!

WoShi muttered to SuJin, "Another stage-managed event, I am sure. This is getting out of hand, by the gods! I am certain that this boy Emperor can see WangMang for what he is—and will act as soon as he comes of age."

The chancellor began reading in a trembling voice. The pause was enough for the crowd to realise this announcement would be extraordinary.

"The Grand Empress Dowager Wang has bestowed the coveted Nine Endowments on WangMang, elevating him to nobility. A set of imperial ceremonial robes, sceptres, weapons, and privileges for his exceptional loyalty to the Han empire as regent will now be presented."

WangMang stood up in surprise on the lower deck as his supporters cheered loudly, rapping on the bamboo structure. Members of the Lui family wore crestfallen expressions, shaking their heads in dismay at WangMang becoming a formal aristocrat. However, the display of dissent was insignificant against the backdrop of the crowd cheering for him.

The chancellor resumed reading. "WangMang, Duke of AnHan and champion reformer, with your significant policies and ideas, you have restored what had been lacking in the Han these last few years. Your simple and lustrous virtues and humble dedication to duty have made our empire glorious and illuminated the path of all our ancestors. You have carried out meaningful reforms steeped in Confucian principles, the foundation of the Han empire. Your selfless dedication is the highest example of filial piety."

"All within this vast empire agree—including kingdoms, vassal states, and even the Huns—on your ascension with rare Nine Endowments." The chancellor began reading out the names of witnesses from the kingdoms and vassal states who had written to the Empress dowager, praising WangMang's exemplary statesmanship.

When the Mongol names were mentioned in the witness list, the Hun emissary stood up, clasped his hands together, and said something to his delegation. They burst out laughing, creating a stir. The Imperial guards had to make threatening gestures to quieten the Huns.

The chancellor continued, "Let the gods stand witness as your virtues and principles have found great favour with the people of Han. Heavenly lights shine upon you, for many portents have appeared, urging the Han court to elevate and reward you. There are witnesses to over seven hundred auspicious presages of unicorns, phoenixes, and dragons to pious people." He droned on as brightly dressed bureaucrats with servants began handing over the Nine Endowments to an embarrassed WangMang.

SuJin looked on with awe at the opulence of the gifts. It started with a gilded gold wagon drawn by eight snow-white horses. The chancellor bellowed, "A carriage for the duke so that he need not walk." This was followed by servants bearing red silk bales embroidered with the golden imperial seal. A twenty-man highly trained eunuch guard marched out with an oath unto death to protect WangMang and his family because he spoke the truth and would make many enemies. The fourth were sheaves of divinely blessed songs and poems never sung before, written on hemp paper rimmed with gold, which he could use to soothe crowds in times of crisis trouble.

SuJin gasped along with an equally dazed audience as servants wheeled in a ramp decorated in gold and red. Ramps were an exclusive privilege of the Han emperor. The chancellor's voice echoed through the criers in the aisles. "For WangMang to ascend the imperial dais."

Finally, the Chancellor announced the ninth and final reward. His voice had gone hoarse, describing all the gifts: "Rare, aged wine made from grapes and rice cultivated on land that will never be used again for cultivation." The gift was for WangMang to please his ancestors for his selfless service to the Han dynasty.

As soon as the last gift was announced, the courtiers and bureaucratic ministers began fawning over WangMang. They jostled to be heard over one another, raising a loud din in their attempts to be noticed by the great man.

To WoShi, the scene resembled hundreds of ants scrambling towards a drop of watered honey spilt by a careless servant on the floorboard. He smiled at SuJin and said, "This is outstanding politics, and he is winning it, hands down." SuJin looked around at the courtiers, absorbed in gaining WangMang's attention. He had never heard of such an outrageous display of nepotism and sycophancy.

SuJin said, "Master, SuWu told me that since Emperor Wu's reign, the Lui family has produced weak emperors, which has enabled the Wang family to support one another and rise as a clan within the bureaucracy. Most Wangs are content with the power of their positions, but WangMang is different. He aims to replace the emperor." He added, "I can see what he meant by that—this man is evil!"

WoShi sighed and replied, "SuWu is partly correct! I have known WangMang since he was a student, and I can tell you he is ambitious but not this aggressive. He has turned evil after he put on that cursed medallion. Today, he will trample anyone in his path without a second thought." He shrugged and added, "It doesn't matter to us. To fulfil the prophecy, if not WangMang, someone else would have usurped the throne."

SuJin watched as an army of servants cleared WangMang's gifts from the arena. "It's just a question of when he will move to become emperor. Look, the Huns are eating out of his hands, and the threat of war is minimal. Through this demonstration of power, he is preparing both the bureaucrats and the commoners to accept him when he appropriates the throne!"

"Shhh, not so loud." WoShi said, "Irrespective of public opinion, the Empress dowager must ratify his elevation."

SuJin was unconvinced and said, "He has cleared his way to the throne by becoming a noble, with the acknowledgement of the Empress and in the presence of the bureaucrats and commoners. He will be the obvious choice if there is a crisis in the Lui clan for a successor. WangMang is aiming for royalty!"

WoShi grunted with his brows knitted tight. "The Emperor comes of age in a year. Let's hope he proves to be a handful."

They watched as WangMang triumphantly mounted his ramp and boldly strolled onto the dais where the Emperor sat. Since they were now nearly equal in status, WangMang offered the Emperor a slight bow with interlocked hands. Delirious with joy at a commoner attaining royalty, the crowd shouted and cheered WangMang's name. He clasped his hands to acknowledge their appreciation in a generic greeting and sat on the imperial dais.

With a wave of his hand, the drums thundered, signalling silence. Following WangMang's cue, the chancellor issued an open challenge, inviting the nobility to nominate their most skilled warriors to choose four champions. As the message resounded, a military force swiftly cordoned off the arena below the imperial dais. Contestants, including those from the Lui family, entered the arena armed with knives, ready for combat.

It was a free-for-all fight, with a few hundred contestants entering the fray to earn glory. The contest began without much ado as warriors slashed and fought one another. The air was filled with screams from the wounded and the screech of swords grating against each other.

The crowd cheered themselves hoarse, not knowing who was winning, as the challengers fell upon each other, covered in their opponents' blood. The hard-packed earth of the courtyard was soaked in blood and gore as the arena turned into a battlefield. Many of the fighters stumbled over strewn bodies and severed limbs.

Brightly dressed servants ventured into the arena in an attempt to clear the dead, but in their murderous frenzy, contestants blindly hacked at unarmed servants, killing them. Nobody ventured into the bloodied courtyard that had become a killing field.

A few hobbled out, bleeding profusely or leaving their limbs behind, but the soldiers pushed them back with their spears. They couldn't leave the arena unless they formally surrendered to their opponents.

As the fights progressed, contestants of higher ranks were allowed to enter, and the fighting continued unabated. After an eternity, the contestants narrowed down to a few skilled fighters engaging in duels. Many higher-ranked officers had the opportunity to bow out of the arena by yielding to their opponents.

Heavy betting ensued in the gallery, with factions supporting or opposing the Lui clan. Eventually, four undefeated warriors emerged amidst the pile of the dead—each representing the Lui clan. WangMang remained stoic, seemingly unaffected by the contest, even as the Lui emerged victorious.

WoShi was perturbed when four imperial soldiers and their captain made a direct beeline towards him. The soldier gave him a curt bow and said, "Marquis WoShi, Regent WangMang would like to have the pleasure of speaking to you," a statement that was nothing short of a command.

WoShi whispered to SuJin, "If I get detained for any reason, move out of this seat and blend into the crowd."

A man sitting next to them leaned into SuJin and asked, "Young man, do you know what the regent wants with the marquis?"

SuJin shrugged and replied, "Honestly, I don't know. Let's wait for my master to return." Other spectators scoffed at the man, "What can the boy know? He is just a student."

SuJin watched WoShi speak animatedly with the imperial chancellor, and his instincts suggested that something was amiss. The man beside him gestured towards the arena. "Why is the Hun delegate speaking to the tournament's arbitrator? Are they going to join the tournament? Now, that would be a treat!"

****

The chancellor crawled forward, imploring the Emperor to leave the celebrations as it could be unsettling to see more bloodshed. The boy Emperor remained unmoved, flicking his finger to dismiss him. Instead, the Emperor beckoned WoShi forward. His bodyguards shielded him as he was pushed close to the emperor. Thankfully, they did not carry him.

The Emperor asked, "Marquis WoShi, the regent tells me you have introduced weapons training in your school. Is that right?"

WoShi paled instantly but nodded. "True, just some sparring with weapons, celestial."

The beads rattled fiercely. The boy seemed happy to hear this. He enquired, "Some time ago, you promised to provide me with warriors closer to my age. Was this weapons training for that purpose?"

"How can I forget a promise to the celestial emperor? I am preparing a few warriors for your service, but they are still under training," WoShi answered.

The boy Emperor smiled at him. "What an occasion to volunteer, Marquis! WangMang told me to watch how your student will protect me against a probable Hun assassin."

Despite the beads covering the boy's face, WoShi could make out the desperation in his voice when the boy Emperor whispered, "Marquis, give me hope." It was a gentle request but a command, nonetheless, to WoShi. WoShi nodded.

As soon as the Emperor sat back, WangMang turned to the chancellor. "Make the announcements." WoShi closed his eyes in a silent prayer.

The chancellor spoke sombrely. "People of Han, the Marquis WoShi has admitted to the Emperor and regent that he has imparted weapons training at the HanKaoTzu school. The grandmaster has trained a few students to protect the Lui family's honour, as the Emperor demanded in an earlier audience." A stunned silence greeted his statement.

The chancellor continued, "How well these students fare against our enemies has yet to be seen." He paused, horrified by his choice of words, calling the Hun "enemies". He looked with trepidation at the Hun envoy, listening to him a few decks below. The man held his hands to his waist and laughed in delight, throwing his head back at the announcement.

The chancellor cleared his throat and quickly corrected himself: "Former enemies, and now our powerful allies in the north shall be pitted against the HanKaoTzu." A soft groan rose from a few in the audience when they saw how young SuJin was. However, the buzz turned into a chatter of excitement at the prospect of watching their feared enemy, the Hun, in a fight.

The drums resounded again, and the soldiers ensured silence.

"It was through our regent's influence that we have garnered peace with the Huns, and their envoys are here to seal the accord. The Huns are pleased to offer their champion fighter to contest against the four winners of today's tournament." The chancellor paused for the words to be carried across the vast arena. Predictably, the audience cheered as the announcement went through repeat criers.

The Chancellor lifted his hand as the yellow flag waved from afar, indicating that all criers had conveyed the message word for word to the audience. "The HanKaoTzu school shall face either the victorious Hun champion of the upcoming fight or other Hun fighters." To the silent crowd, he cried out, "The victor shall face the empire's fiercest warrior, LianDan, in the final duel."

A buzz broke out on the unequal pitting of a young boy against the Huns when WoShi said, "Terms." With the banter all around, none of the others heard him except the emperor, who had been watching him with uncertainty.

"Speak up, Marquis," the young Emperor ordered. His bodyguard motioned for silence with a single drumbeat from the upper dais.

WangMang turned around, his eyes narrowing. WoShi spoke, "Son of the Sun, heaven's representative on earth, the HanKaoTzu school won't fight an imperial soldier. If we win against the Hun, the school and the students shall be left alone." Emperor Pingdi turned and looked keenly at WangMang. "Isn't that a fair demand, Regent WangMang?"

WangMang grunted and nodded, "Of course, it's agreed. No one will disturb a Han champion."

"... but first, win," he smirked, turning his back dismissively on WoShi.

Emperor Pingdi reiterated WangMang's promise. "If you win, we will grant you amnesty from further challenges and reward you handsomely. On the other hand, if your challenger dies, we shall provide a dignified funeral with all the prescribed rituals for an easy afterlife." The boy Emperor leaned back into his chair, signalling that he was done talking.

****

WangMang had meticulously orchestrated the outcome of the day's fights beforehand. By the end of the day, his champion, LianDan, would emerge victorious over the dreaded Hun champion,

SwordClaw. The Hun would decimate all the pathetic Lui challengers before that to set up a great victory for his man.

WangMang had procured condemned Hun warriors by paying a fortune in blood money. The warriors were renowned for their fighting prowess, and his generals had witnessed their skills before they were brought from the steppes. The Huns were instructed to brutally eliminate all contestants until they faced LianDan and his men, to whom they would concede defeat and die.

SwordClaw had disobeyed the Xiongnu leader, the head of all Hun barbarian tribes, by waging war against a rival tribe and killing many. To send a strong message to the other tribes to stop infighting, the Xiongnu leader commanded his warriors to exterminate the errant tribe. SwordClaw was captured alive, defending his tribe at the western end of the steppes.

SwordClaw willingly offered to forfeit his life to allow the women who could conceive and the male children below the age of three to live. Instead of being executed, they would be merged into the other tribes. It was a good bargain for his forfeited life, an exchange that would save his wives and some of his children.

****

An army of servants worked hurriedly to clear the blood-soaked ground, scattering sawdust and white lime over the blood and gore spilt a short while ago. The expectation of the crowd reached a fever pitch with wild cheers as the last cartload of mutilated limbs and corpses was wheeled away.

Spectators gasped in awe and erupted into shouts of glee when the chained Hun champion was brought into the arena. Very few bureaucrats and members of the nobility had seen a Hun warrior of this size. He was a formidable giant, bare-chested with large limbs and rippling muscles, towering above his captors as they pulled and pushed against him.

WangMang grinned and nodded at the Hun emissary, looking at him for approval. "The Hun is impressive," he told WangYi, his commander in appreciation.

WangYi smiled and said, "Cousin, wait until you see him fight. He's an insolent demon! A killer."

Soldiers escorted the Hun to the centre of the arena, holding their spears to his chest as they unchained him before quickly stepping back. It was clear they had struggled to keep him captive and regarded him as extremely dangerous.

As they retreated to the edge, another soldier, the assistant to the tournament arbitrator, jogged casually beside SwordClaw and thrust a short sword into the ground. In the blink of an eye, the Hun rolled up to the sword and, in one fluid motion that required regaining his feet, beheaded the soldier. It was an incredible display of skill and strength, though not chivalrous.

The horrified audience screamed in outrage as the head tumbled to the ground and rolled to a stop. The brutal strike was so clean and powerful that the headless man walked a few steps, spurting blood, before he fell, convulsing in the throes of death.

The barbarian grinned, revealing his yellow, decayed teeth and showering insults at the soldiers on the periphery. He swung the sword deftly in circles and swayed his body to loosen his joints. By a significant margin, this fierce warrior surpassed the skills of all the warriors in the previous tournament.

LianDan, the Han warrior chosen to face the Hun, was horrified, his face draining of colour. He asked WangYi, "Is he mad, commander? When the time comes, will this Hun adhere to the agreed terms to surrender and die?"

WangYi bluntly told LianDan, "Too late, champion! You must defeat him if he breaks his oath to die."

LianDan looked at WangYi in dismay. "I fear that he will cut me up before he dies."

WangYi nodded in agreement. He consoled LianDan, "Don't worry. We have starved him. Hopefully, his exertions fighting others will make him weak!"

WangMang could not contain his glee and smiled extravagantly at his generals. SwordClaw was a showman, and he would be remembered long after his death at the hands of Lian Dan, his champion. More importantly, this demonstrated to the imperial crowd and the commoners the imposing enemy they faced at the border. Their refuge was only WangMang, whose men could defeat this formidable adversary and, best of all, negotiate peace with them barbarians!

The four reluctant Lui tournament winners were thrust into the arena. It was evident that they had not anticipated this fight after their victory. One contestant surrendered to Hun, expressing his desire to withdraw. SwordClaw ignored the surrender, prompting the spectators to jeer at Hun for disregarding fair play. The terrified man attempted to escape the arena but was thwarted by the imperial soldiers wielding spears. The rule was that no contestant could leave the arena unless the opponent agreed to surrender or was fatally wounded.

The frightened man joined the others, with no choice but to fight. After quickly devising a plan, the tournament winners charged at the Hun from two sides, led by a highborn Lui warrior, the finest swordsman of the four.

Meanwhile, the Hun unhurriedly collected sawdust into two small piles on the ground and waited beside it. He first turned towards his opponent, charging from the left. The leading man screamed a battle cry and ran hard at the Hun with his sword raised. Unlike the other three, he wore a helmet and a leather breastplate as protective gear.

The Hun languidly put his foot on the first sawdust pile, pivoted hard on the balls of his feet, turned a full circle and threw the short sword, impaling the man in the stomach with such force that the blade pierced through the breastplate and stuck out from his back. The man ceased screaming mid-cry and sank to his knees, but the Hun did not pause to observe his handiwork.

SwordClaw stepped diagonally and spun on the balls of his feet on the next sawdust pile, positioning himself beside his opponent, who was hurtling in from the right. The warrior thrust his sword with all his might, and the blade would have impaled the Hun but for his pivot. The sword point flew harmlessly past the Hun, and SwordClaw slammed his elbow into the man's chin wickedly. With a loud crack, his neck snapped, and his head twisted at an odd angle. The Hun snatched the sword from the outstretched hand of the falling man before the corpse hit the ground. The other two contestants halted mid-stride on either side of the Hun. They could see death ahead!

"Screaming in terror, they turned and ran. SwordClaw pursued them with long, swift strides, catching up to one of the warriors. He slashed at the warrior's hamstring, ran past him and abruptly stopped, twisting to position his short sword low behind his back. With his hamstring cut, the warrior's legs gave way, and he fell, impaling himself on SwordClaw's blade. The barbarian's face contorted, and his muscles bulged in effort as he cleaved the sword upward and out, spilling the warrior's intestines and slicing him open from stomach to chest. Demonstrating incredible strength, SwordClaw lifted the dead man on his blade and flung him aside."

He turned to attack the last man. The barbarian bellowed in frustration when the fourth challenger managed to avoid the dazed soldiers at the periphery and escape.

The Hun walked around the arena's perimeter, marked by yellow and red painted bamboo sticks, holding his crotch and gesturing vulgarly at the dazed onlookers. Imperial archers fired arrows into the cordoned area, more in fear than as a warning that he shouldn't overstep the perimeter.

The Hun halted before the captain of the archers, stretching his arm and pounding his chest with closed fists, challenging him to fire directly at him. The captain glared in fury but did not respond. The Hun attempted to provoke the archers into shooting an arrow by gesturing and hurling obscenities at them. Although the captain simmered with rage, he held back his angry men.

An anxious LianDan asked WangYi, "What is he doing? What if the archers fire at him?"

A tense WangYi replied, "The captain did well to restrain his men." When LianDan looked at him curiously, WangYi explained, "The barbarian wants us to break our rules of fair play by shooting him down. What better way to insult Han than by dying unjustly at our hands?"

Flexing his shoulders, SwordClaw walked towards the first man he had attacked by throwing his short sword. The man was still breathing despite the punctured abdomen. Ignoring his groans, the Hun callously placed his leg on the man's chest and yanked out the bronze sword. The sword's edge was cracked, and he discarded it. He removed the warrior's helmet and breastplate and put them on, although they were undersized and picked up his sword.

He grunted in satisfaction, holding two swords in his massive hands. Snagging the swords on loops in the breastplate, he looked down at the warrior, who lay gasping for breath. The Hun undid his breeches and urinated on the warrior, singing loudly.

Angry spectators howled and screamed in disgust, but the Hun was unfazed. He folded his legs and sat down facing the imperial dais, chewing on dried meat hidden in his clothing. He was ready to face the next opponent.

A disturbed LianDan wailed in agony, "Look, he is chewing on meat. He is not starved!"

WangYi had enough of LianDan's whinging and said, "Shut up, LianDan! You are a champion fighter, and he is ready to die. Fight and kill him, and don't embarrass our regent!"

The vast arena that had been a battlefield not long ago now appeared deserted and vacant, with four dead bodies and one giant. No servant or soldier would venture into the arena as long as the Hun remained.

SuJin was captivated by the brutality of the fights and did not realise that WoShi was speaking to him. "A hard man to kill. None of the combatants are a match for him."

SuJin asked WoShi, "What's driving him? Why is he here?" His eyes were glued to the man who killed so efficiently.

"You're next," WoShi nudged a stunned SuJin. "The time has come for the world to see you. We must take him on."

"We?"

"Yes, we!" Holding SuJin by the shoulders, he corrected himself. "You! You will fight before your family and defend their honour. You will fight before your countrymen to show that the Huns can be defeated. This is a command from your emperor."

A bureaucrat approached them and loudly told WoShi, "You must go in, Marquis. We can't keep the Emperor and regent waiting." His eyes conveyed sympathy as he looked at SuJin, an innocent boy about to be executed.

WoShi strode down the gallery with determination. A bewildered SuJin trailed him while every pair of eyes in the gallery was fixed upon them as they made their way towards the arena. People reached out and clutched their cloaks, bidding farewell. Someone lamented, "An old man and a boy to face a barbarian monster? Is this the destiny of Han?"

SuJin glanced up at the dais where vassal kings and the nobility were seated, looking at him in pity. He wondered how many of them were blood relatives.

SuJin looked towards WangMang's vocal supporters and found them quiet, too. After all, he was fighting their common enemy, the dreaded Hun. They watched master and student, old and young, walk down to certain death.

The Lui had come prepared with their fighting men for the occasion. Now, they were utterly demoralised by the barbarian warrior. The Hun champion was a giant. The sheer speed at which he had wielded the sword earlier was frightening. No warrior volunteered for the old man and the young boy.

A clash of metal echoed from the arena. SwordClaw held two swords aloft, slicing and dicing the protesting wind. The swordplay was captivating in its speed and power. Blurring his strikes, the Hun cheekily lunged toward the soldiers guarding the periphery. They recoiled in panic, eliciting laughter from the Hun emissaries hysterically.

WoShi was brusque with SuJin. "Watch how the Hun holds the short swords at different lengths. This is to confuse the opponent with the sword's reach, but his skill with both hands is comparable, although he favours the right. He will switch the lengths in a fight after his opponent has grown accustomed to the reach. The man is a sword master; don't underestimate him."

WangMang was ecstatic, pleased that the audience was terrified by the skill of his Hun warrior. He had paid a fortune in gold, leather, and women to the head of the Hun Xiongnu for purchasing this challenger. Looking at the audience, watching in rapt attention, he realised it was worth it. He had managed a coup of sorts! Once his man, LianDan, brought the Hun down, no one would challenge him. He had not expected the Han champion to terrorise the spectators to this extent.

The death of the Hun at the hands of his imperial warrior would fire the imagination of the commoners and bureaucrats and complete his domination as the true power of the Han. He wondered if he needed the prophecy to take the empire. After all, he had given the Lui clan a chance to show their might before the commoners.

WoShi held SuJin by the arms and said, "Kill him." SuJin remained silent. He had never killed anyone before, and that man down there was larger than life.

The Hun regarded the young boy as his next opponent and was taken aback. Nevertheless, he bellowed a challenge to tear him to shreds, which the criers promptly translated. Intimidated by the towering Hun, SuJin responded timidly, "Master, I am not ready. This isn't our fight." WoShi swung his hand at his face, and SuJin instinctively blocked the blow.

WoShi reprimanded his student by saying, "Keep your hands down." He slapped SuJin hard.

The spectators groaned, "The boy is frightened and rightly so. He will be dead soon."

SuJin asked, "Why did you hit me?"

WoShi told SuJin sternly, "Let the Hun see that you are a reluctant fighter. Let him underestimate you."

WoShi stood straight and declared, "I demand respect for your teacher, blood relatives, and countrymen. Kill him, restore our honour, and fulfil the promise to our emperor. It is your sacred duty."

SuJin slowly released the air trapped in his lungs. "What is the weapon I should use?"

WoShi's reply was surprising, "To demonstrate your skill, nothing but what you wear. Focus, and do not lose the connection between your mind and body. Remember, this is not a sparring session."

WoShi held SuJin by his shoulders and said, "You are ready. The gods have faith in you. Go!"

SuJin ran into the arena toward the tournament arbitrator. WoShi motioned to the repeat crier nearby and shouted, "Say, Han warrior, show the Hun what we are." A few spectators shouted, "Han, Han," but they received a tepid response, and the chant died out quickly.

WoShi clambered back on the imperial deck, and the chancellor approached him. The criers dutifully repeated their conversation. "I thought you would enter the fighting area along with the boy, grandmaster. Why send the boy alone?"

"Fair play, chivalry of the old school." Despite the sombre mood, WoShi's reply was greeted with disbelief and raucous laughter. "A Han boy is more than enough for this challenge. If I entered the arena now, wouldn't two of us face a single man? Now, that be barbaric of the HanKaoTzu school?!" WangMang gritted his teeth in anger while the boy Emperor laughed excitedly.

The arbitrator approached SuJin and asked, "Boy, what is your name?" As he appraised him keenly from head to toe. SuJin was taken aback when the repeat criers asked the same question across the stands, echoing along the length and breadth of the arena.

SuJin wore a simple, faded green hanfu adorned with embroidery of trees and shrubs. He took a deep breath before responding to the question, but it scarcely mattered because the arbitrator had announced before SuJin could reply.

With great animation, the arbitrator pointed to SuJin and screamed aloud, "The Green Hunter, representing the HanKaoTzu school, shall answer the challenge by the Hun, SwordClaw from the steppes! Who will win the mauling, the Bear or the Hunter?" A polite thumping of feet and some clapping greeted his declaration, though many scoffed at the improbable notion that the Green Hunter would prevail.

Most bureaucrats and eunuchs, however, waited eagerly for this round to conclude. They believed the real fight was when the Hun faced

WangMang's champion. It would be absurd and politically damaging if the Hun were the last man standing in the presence of the Han emperor. Therefore, the betting was not on who would win the next challenge but on how long the fight would last.

The arbitrator seemed to assess the mood and looked at the boy accusingly, "Boy, you are not carrying any weapon. Are you planning to outlast the Hun by running around the arena?" He inquired, and the spectators groaned in disgust.

SuJin was annoyed by the suggestion that he would run around the arena to tire the Hun champion and responded, "I am here to prove my filial piety to the Emperor and the Lui family by death or giving death." His response was relayed across the arena.

WoShi smiled as he realised that he might have outplayed WangMang. He spoke to the chancellor, and repeat criers took up his words. "If the boy dies, I may be demoted from a Marquis to a commoner and castrated for bringing shame to my liege." Silence enveloped the arena as the criers repeated it, and the Emperor looked at WangMang for a response.

WangMang narrowed his eyes and touched the burning pendant hanging inside his robe. He ignored the warning from the pendant and said, "An unequal challenge should be rewarded. Should your ward defeat the Hun or outlast the water clock, he will be declared the winner! No more bouts. I shall give you a thousand gold coins." It was a Princely sum. None of the spectators seemed willing to place bets on the boy, except a few dwarfs at the periphery receiving high odds.

On a cue from the emperor, the chancellor lifted his hand and forbade WoShi from replying, ending the verbal dual developing on the imperial dais.

The Hun moved closer to look at SuJin and told him in a raspy voice, "You are a brave one for a Han. I hate everyone in Han, but I promise to kill you swiftly. That is my concession for daring to fight me."

SuJin frowned and told him, "So you knew our language and were acting dumb all along," the Hun grinned and shrugged.

"Know your enemy to kill more," he laughed.

SuJin bowed low to his opponent and ran deep into the arena, making a space between them. The drums boomed, giving the opponents time to warm up. The Hun warrior did not warm up. He was ready. He sat down, crossing the swords in his lap to watch SuJin. The experienced warrior did not want to discount his opponent, however young. He expected his opponent to go through his preparatory moves to warm up so that he could judge his fighting style and ability.

As tradition dictates, a fresh warrior is allowed time to warm up before a fight. Unlike in previous bouts, where the warriors were already warmed up, SuJin was provided the prescribed time to prepare for the fight.

SuJin began swaying and dancing to the beat of the drum in the traditional Han sword dance ritual. His dance moves were exquisite and coordinated, and the audience swayed their heads in tandem with the drum.

An old Lui clansman cried in anguish, "Will a dance extinguish the last challenge of the Lui?"

The drums will stop, and the fight will begin when the water clock is set. The water clock consists of three ceramic pots with narrow spouts stacked one above the other on a wooden rack. The topmost pot is filled with water and tilts to empty its contents into the pot below through the narrow spout. The second pot fills and then tilts into the third pot. The fight concludes when the last pot tilts and runs out of water.

WangMang pulled the medallion from inside his hanfu and let it dangle free against his chest, as it was burning hot.

WangYi approached WangMang and asked, "Cousin, does this bout really require a water clock? The boy will be impaled within moments the fight begins. I have seen this Hun hurl knives to kill opponents back at the steppes."

WangMang laughed, "I have no doubts about an early finish to the bout. I want to ensure that every rule is followed so that when WoShi is castrated into a eunuch, right here in this arena, no one can claim that we did not adhere to the rules."

WangYi nodded in appreciation, "Of course, that makes sense. You have thought ahead, cousin."

The bureaucrat in charge of the drummers watched the servants keenly as they swiftly moved the water clock closer to the imperial gallery because WangMang wanted it prominently displayed.

At a nod from the tournament arbitrator, the stopper was removed from the water clock, and the drums became silent.

SuJin's senses heightened, and everything around him slowed considerably in his mind. The dwarfs had told him this ability was a gift from the gods, and he could hear his breath going in and out. He was ready.

"Run! Keep your distance!" People screamed at him. Nobody expected him to last beyond the time to drain one bowl of the water clock.

Someone else shouted, "Throw him a weapon." Another replied, "There is no point; it'll just weigh him down. Let him run."

The Hun warrior concurred with the audience that the unarmed boy would run, dodge, and weave to evade his sword. Unfortunately for this young one, he was an expert at throwing knives. No one, armed or unarmed, had ever escaped his lethal swords. This contest would conclude quickly.

SwordClaw decided to put on a spectacle and howled his displeasure at the idea of chasing after the boy. He threw down his helmet and discarded his breastplate.

All the dancing had loosened the hair coiled on his head, and SuJin shook his head in irritation as strands of hair fell across his face. He pulled out a pair of filigreed tortoiseshell combs with long brass handles from his hair, letting it drop below his shoulders. He gathered his hair into a bun at the top of his head and secured it firmly with a knot while holding the combs in his mouth.

With his opponent distracted, the Hun warrior charged, weaving from side to side. He wanted the boy to turn and run so that he could throw his sword into his back.

It took a moment for the onlookers to realise that the Green Hunter was charging at the Hun. The barbarian least expected the boy to end his life on his sword. SwordClaw paused mid-stride and adjusted his sword for a simple thrust to the chest, ready to end this foolish fight.

That is when the unthinkable happened: the boy tripped! The Hun saw the boy tangle his foot in his loose leggings as he tumbled and rolled directly towards him.

Everything happened in moments as time slowed down for both warriors...

SwordClaw crouched low, pushing his left leg sideways and his right leg backwards, waiting for the hurtling boy to reach him. He would skewer the boy and hold him above his head in one swift motion.

This was too easy for the skilled fighter, yet the Hun's battle-honed instincts told him something was amiss. He desperately analysed his opponent's moves and identified the anomaly. Despite the fall, the boy still held the combs in his mouth! His eyes were unafraid, and his head was steady as a rock while his body made a flurry of movements – like a kingfisher hovering above the waters, flapping its wings but ready to strike at an unsuspecting fish.

In that instant, SwordClaw realised in shock that his opponent was a skilled warrior. He instinctively pulled the blade in his right hand and lashed out. The swinging sword arc should make contact with the boy somewhere. He bent his body further and adjusted the short sword in his left hand, where the boy's body would careen after hitting the ground. He was sure that the boy would try and glide under his legs.

Instead, the boy soared straight into the air after hitting the ground, rolling out of SwordClaw's line of sight. The Hun bent his neck and angled his eyes upwards, desperate to track his opponent. The boy was upside down directly above him. The boy's coiled hair brushed against his forehead, and loose strands slapped into his eyes. The boy's hands pressed against his ears as he somersaulted and flew across.

From afar, the spectators saw the boy tumble and miraculously fly into the air. He somersaulted over the Hun to land on his feet behind him, barbarian.

A surprised WangMang sprang to his feet, urging the Hun to turn around and kill the boy standing behind him.

Nobody answered the Emperor's question, "What happened? I don't understand." All eyes were glued to the action on the field, which looked too acrobatic to be an attack. The Hun fell to his knees and roared in pain. He discarded his swords and was writhing around, holding his ears.

WoShi smiled smugly while experienced imperial warriors worked out the details. They were all stunned, without exception. The armed Hun had just been attacked!

WoShi explained what had just happened aloud, and excited criers relayed it to the astonished audience. "The Green Hunter of the HanKaoTzu ran in and faked a fall as he gathered momentum for a somersault. Upside down, he landed on the Hun's head to regain orientation and balance. He slapped the two brass handles of the combs precisely into the ears of the Hun, puncturing them before toppling over."

The big Hun roared in pain and pulled out the brass handles. The blood and liquid oozed out, and he lost body balance. Unable to handle the pain, the warrior reached out, found his sword, and slashed his jugular vein. Jets of red blood pumped out of his life rhythmically onto the arena floor, and his body convulsed for a long time before he lay still in the finality of death.

Shocked to silence earlier, the arena erupted into a thunder of joyous screams that refused to die.

SuJin sat beside the fallen man and closed his eyes in prayer. He had just killed someone, and he didn't even know his name. The soldiers had a tough time holding back the enthusiastic Lui clansmen trying to get to SuJin.

Desperate to salvage the situation, WangMang motioned to WangYi. He did not want a hero to emerge for the beleaguered Lui clan on the day he became their equal. He would explain that the water clock was still running.

While the imperial soldiers held back the euphoric Lui clansmen, Hun warriors were subtly allowed into the arena to avenge the death of their champion.

Alerted by the warning screams from the gallery, SuJin jolted upright and moved away. Six Hun warriors had rushed in and surrounded their fallen champion.

Having witnessed how the boy had defeated their champion, they did not rush him but circled him like a pack of wolves, with one Hun facing him. The one in front was their leader, who watched him keenly and spoke to the others, coordinating their attack.

SuJin looked at him intently and noticed that one of his hands was thicker than the other. He was an archer, not a swordsman. Although he was posturing for a frontal attack, SuJin was sure it was a ruse. He took a sideways stance to bring four of them into sight, occasionally turning on the balls of his feet to cover the other side.

Just as they prepared to rush him, arrows struck the Huns, killing two of them, while three others fell, wounded. The leader of the Huns instinctively took evasive action and rolled on the ground, but no arrow was aimed at him. By the time he realised this, SuJin had retrieved a sword from one of the fallen Huns. The fletching of the arrows was golden, indicating that the Emperor's bodyguards shot it.

SuJin heard criers shouting in the aisles, "The Emperor is giving the green hunter the same odds he took for this challenge. It's a one-to-one duel! The other Hun warriors have been brought down at the Emperor's command."

Drums took up their dull thumping, and SuJin and the Hun looked at each other. It was clear that they had to fight. SuJin noticed a resigned expression in the eyes of the Hun as he prepared to fight. The Hun was young, a few years older than SuJin.

The Hun attacked cautiously, but this was more to assess SuJin's sword skills. SuJin moved like a sword master, effortlessly deflecting the blows and casually swatting away counterattacks. The Hun's eyes widened as he acknowledged SuJin's ability to handle a sword. Sweat trickled down the Hun's face.

Although a boy, the Hun realised that his opponent was a superb swordsman and could finish the fight whenever he wanted. He was sparring.

SuJin remained composed in his relentless half-attacks, which revealed his exceptional stamina and endurance. Without a break, they engaged in continuous lunges and parries, and the spectators placed bets on the outcome. The highest number of bets favoured SuJin's victory.

Watching the duel, WoShi exclaimed loudly, "What's he doing? This is not a sparring session. Finish the Hun!" This, too, was picked up by the criers and relayed around the arena.

SuJin mirrored every move of the Hun warrior, showing no intent to kill. The Hun warrior was fatigued, having gone without food for the past few days. Like a leopard cub toying with a trapped fawn, the boy was playing with him, and the Hun realised his end was near. If he surrendered, arrows would take him down.

Before he died, he needed to attempt one last cunning act for old times' sake. Confident that SuJin wasn't fighting to kill, the Hun walked in deliberately close. For a moment, they found themselves within striking distance of one another. The Hun intentionally held back, letting the opportunity slip away. Death had brushed against him. SuJin was shaken from his complacency, recalling his grandmaster's advice: "If you enter a fight, fight to kill or don't fight; there is no third alternative." SuJin battled relief, surprise, and indignation at being outsmarted yet alive.

SuJin locked eyes with the Hun, who gave him a wry smile. The Hun knelt, placed the sword on the ground, and said in passable Tongyu, the Han language, "Boy, you are not destined for death by my hands. I could deceive you because you were sparring, not fighting to kill. Take my life, which is forfeited after you killed our champion. I foolishly believed I was destined for greatness. At least I will pass on to the heavenly green pastures, knowing that I fell to the best warrior in Han."

SuJin heard warning screams, and his eyes caught sight of three arrows flying in from above. It was yet another treat for the spectators as SuJin swung his short sword, expertly deflecting the arrows away from the Hun. The arena erupted in a roar of appreciation as cries of "Green Hunter! Green Hunter!" Whipped the onlookers into a frenzy.

SuJin took a broken arrow shaft, held it high, pointed it at the Hun's nose, and turned the arrowhead back towards him—a clear message that the Hun now belonged to him as a battle slave.

A squad of twenty soldiers arrived. SuJin assumed a defensive posture before the Hun, and the captain said, "Nobody would dream of harming you, Green Hunter. We are not here to escort you to the emperor."

"I don't want the Hun to be hurt. He surrendered to me, and by battle right, he belongs to me," SuJin replied.

The captain grimaced and shrugged indifferently. "The water clock has run out. The Emperor has decreed that anyone who fires an arrow again will die by a thousand cuts, and it will be done right here." Two soldiers led the Hun away, while the others formed two columns to escort SuJin to the waiting Emperor with a reverence reserved for a general.

****

SuJin and WoShi kowtowed. The beads of Emperor Pingdi shook with unrestrained delight. "Oh, what a fight! What a comprehensive victory! Warrior, you have upheld the Lui honour and elevated Han's prestige. I am certain SwordClaw would have thrashed our imperial champion!"

The Emperor turned to WangMang, glaring at SuJin with intense hatred, and said, "What do you say, Regent?" WangMang responded with a forced smile that looked ugly.

WangMang did not like this assertive emperor. It was too early for the boy to realise his absolute power and exercise it. His fears were magnified when he dismissed WangMang callously. "I will call for you, regent. I want to speak to Marquis WoShi."

Emperor Pingdi waited for WangMang to move out of earshot. The Emperor beamed at SuJin. "Allow me to honour you, warrior. What a fight! I am seldom entertained like this," he said, nodding. The beads clinked together, reflecting his excitement.

WoShi cleared his throat to speak, but SuJin interrupted, "Mighty Emperor, the reward we seek is the honour of serving you. As for a gift, perhaps you might consider granting the Hun fighter as my slave, to be set free as I desire."

"Oh, him. You can keep him and the gifts," the boy Emperor said. He asked. "When will your training end?"

WoShi responded, "A couple more years, Your Highness." The Emperor was unhappy to hear that but dismissed them.

They crawled back, and the boy Emperor signalled his chancellor forward. WoShi could not make out his emotions behind the veil of beads, but the Emperor was up to something.

The Chancellor announced, "The hero of Han, the Green Hunter, shall be granted ownership of five villages, with taxes from these villages allocated to him for six years. He shall also receive a house with servants in Changan to be close to the emperor. Following his training, the Green Hunter shall be appointed an imperial bodyguard." Wild cheers erupted in the stands, uniting commoners and bureaucrats in praising the emperor.

A senior imperial bureaucrat interjected at WangMang's prod. "Your Excellency, this gift is far too extravagant for a mere warrior. The Regent and Dowager Empress should be involved in ratifying rewards until you come of age." The chancellor crawled back to the boy emperor, and they spoke briefly.

With a broad smile, the chancellor announced on behalf of the emperor, "The Emperor acknowledges that he is not of an age to bestow gifts upon a hero of Han, who fought to preserve the honour of Han."

The whole arena broke into howls, boos, and angry rants against the bureaucrat. The chancellor waited until the uproar became unmanageable. He motioned for the drums, which beat long and hard to restore order.

The Chancellor turned to the bureaucrat. "For interrupting a royal decree and going against the common propriety of gifting a winner, the Emperor sentences you to forty whiplashes and expulsion from the imperial palace. You may approach the Regent or the Empress

Dowager to ratify this imperial order, as this is the command of an underage emperor."

The gallery burst into laughter, and the cheer for Emperor Pingdi thundered across the aisles and refused to die down.

WangMang saw a brilliant boy on the imperial throne, manipulating palace politics and championing the common man. Although he was his son-in-law, the boy posed a genuine threat to his ambitions. The medallion on his chest radiated heat, and he resolved not to ignore its warning this time.

The chancellor continued, "To appease the bureaucracy, the empire shall withhold the gifts bestowed upon the green Hunter until he joins the imperial guards. The Hun captive shall be handed over to him as his battle slave. Gifts for the champion's victory today and rewards for his trainer will be provided following bureaucratic approval."

The chancellor paused and looked at WoShi before reading the final imperial command. "It is the Emperor's will that the green hunter returns to serve, but not beyond the official coronation next year."

#17 Batu The Hun Becomes Family

Word of the famous fight spread like wildfire through the lands. With each retelling, the exploits of an unarmed Green Hunter and the cunning skill with which he brought down the bloodthirsty SwordClaw were magnified.

Many peasant boys ran away from home, seeking admission to the HanKaoTzu school. WoShi turned them all away, stating that the school was closed. WoShi's rejection did not dampen their enthusiasm, and they camped outside the school premises.

Despite the adulations from the commoners, SuJin was listless and roamed the streets of Changan aimlessly. JiaShao, the dwarf chief, had put his trusted assistant, CaoShen, in charge while he was away, and he reported to WoShi that SuJin was not his usual self.

It did not take long for WoShi and the dwarfs to glean from SuJin that he was disturbed by thoughts of taking the life of a man who willingly sacrificed his life. SuJin had learnt from the Hun he saved at the arena that SwordClaw, a renowned blade master from the steppes, had given his life in exchange for the women and children of his tribe.

A distraught SuJin immediately released the Hun from his bondage as a slave and asked him to leave. The Hun refused to go and told SuJin that it was his destiny to serve him before he returned to the steppes.

CaoShen approached Tuhu, the dwarf's soft-spoken butcher and spiritual leader, to counsel SuJin.

Although SuJin was initially enervated, he slowly opened up to the soft-spoken man. SuJin watched Tuhu masterfully split apart the carcass of a sow with minimal fuss. The large animal broke into manageable chunks of meat under his sharp knife, and it looked as if

Tuhu was severing the strings that held meat blocks together.

Tuhu quartered the meat and neatly arranged the choice pieces on a wooden plank for display. His assistant applied salt and hung the rest of the meat in a blackened enclosure of woven reeds and bamboo rafters to smoke it dry.

Watching SuJin's eyes, Tuhu said, "Smoked dry meat is a staple for sailors. We also have dried fish from the mountain lakes, a delicacy in the royal kitchens."

Sitting forlorn on a woodblock, SuJin absently waved his hands to disperse the smoke. Despite his inner turmoil, SuJin observed that Tuhu was meticulous and did not spill blood on the sawdust-covered floor or the wooden plank. The shop was devoid of flies, and the usual stench of decaying meat that accompanied butcher shops was conspicuously absent.

After inspecting his shop one last time, Tuhu wiped his knives with sawdust and tossed the sawdust into the embers to burn. After washing his knives, he checked the edges while applying vinegar before hanging them up to dry.

He dried his hands, climbed onto a low stool and nodded to SuJin. "You know, letting a bit of smoke in here is intentional. It keeps the flies away. Although the meat might dry on the outside, it locks in the flavour.

SuJin nodded and said, "Your shop and surroundings are immaculate, unlike other butcher shops."

Tuhu nodded. "I am also a surgeon and a priest for the dwarfs. If what's seen outside is unclean, how will they trust me to cleanse the inside of their bodies?" He struck his chest with his clenched fist and gave SuJin a slight nod.

SuJin gazed at him with dull eyes. Tuhu said, "You possess the wisdom of the gods, and all your ancestors have great expectations of you, yet you carry the burden of mortal vulnerabilities."

SuJin blurted out, "Master Tuhu, did I do right? Could I have done anything differently? How can I reconcile the killing of an honourable man in the arena? All my life, I have been told that I need to train hard to kill evil men. However, I ended the life of someone who sacrificed himself to protect his clan."

Tuhu grunted and shook his head. "Telling you that you are right or wrong won't calm your mind; you must figure it out yourself. So, let's reconsider your situation - you worry that you have murdered a man while the man in question wished to sacrifice his life?"

SuJin winced at the word "murdered." Tuhu continued, "The greatest form of sacrifice to the gods is giving up your life for another, while the lowest form of crime before God and man is murder." SuJin cautiously nodded his head.

Tuhu said, "We offer flowers, food, and sacrifice animals to the gods. What tops our offering is a life we willingly offer to save another." Tuhu paused and asked, "Do you agree with me?" SuJin did not respond, so Tuhu continued, "The gods will weigh SwordClaw's crimes against his sacrifice in the netherworld, for he has taken lives too. Did he barter his life on free will?"

Tuhu leaned back his short frame to ease a knot in his back and said, "SwordClaw was meant to die for his crimes against his tribe. The gods will judge his chief for pronouncing his death sentence, not you or anyone else in Han."

SuJin was unconvinced. "I don't want to listen to philosophies that justify the death of a man by my hands."

Tuhu nodded and asked a brooding SuJin, "Why do boars have tusks if they don't hunt other animals for food?" SuJin looked at him curiously, and Tuhu added, "Maybe they use their tusks to fight and defend themselves and their young?"

SuJin reluctantly grunted in agreement. Tuhu grinned. "Let me tell you this. There is no philosophy if one can't protect one's own life. You did well to save yourself from death in the arena and protect your master from castration."

SuJin smiled at that comment. "It's not that I don't understand, Master. I feel responsible."

"Ah. Who is responsible for the execution of a convict? Is it the king or the executioner?"

SuJin mumbled, "The king is responsible, and I agree that the executioner is doing his duty. But my situation is different."

"Is it?" Tuhu's eyes narrowed. "Look at the situation again. Wasn't the convict killed by his actions, especially knowing that his deeds could get him killed if caught? He went against the rule of the land. To live in society, we need rules. The executioner has no sins; he does his duty to his king and land. If he follows written rules, the king is also not responsible."

SuJin remained silent as he pondered on what he just heard. SuJin protested fervently, "I was forced to fight! It was not my desire to fight him."

"Ahh, so that's the issue! You were compelled against your free will to enter the arena. You had to dance to the dictates of WangMang, the Emperor and your tutor, eh?" SuJin flushed and nodded.

Tuhu harrumphed and said, "SuJin, if you want to bend and shape circumstances to your will, you must control the situation. The wider you control the situation, the larger your power."

"SwordClaw knew that his tribe could be attacked if he disobeyed Xiongnu, chief of the Huns. Did he not? His ego led to actions that determined his fate in the arena." Tuhu paused to catch his breath and continued, "SuJin, your problem is a wounded ego, too, because you want to decide who lives and dies in the arena!" SuJin blushed crimson in the face.

Tuhu had SuJin evaluate his beliefs throughout the day. His teaching method involved probing questions that prompted SuJin to think through them.

Later that day, Tuhu said, "I need to wash up and go to the temple. You are welcome to join me." SuJin agreed, and Tuhu asked him to summarise the day's learning.

"Murder is wrong. Failing to protect yourself or your way of life is an act of cowardice. Every person intuitively understands the distinction between right and wrong. Actions come with ownership, while reactions must be endured. To remain guilt-free, your actions must harmonise with your conscience."

"Tell me... in your situation?"

SuJin said, "SwordClaw entering the arena for crimes against his tribe and WangMang pushing WoShi for a fight are actions, whereas killing SwordClaw is a reaction."

Tuhu smiled. "Not bad. Remember, most vile actions stem from words that conceal an inflated ego and misplaced pride. We will explore a few philosophies together."

SuJin bowed low. "Master, thank you for your wisdom. Some of my guilt has been replaced by questions I must contemplate."

****

SuJin regularly accompanied the butcher to the Tao temple to listen to the discourses of holy men. These revered men debated subtle distinctions in philosophy, which fascinated SuJin.

WoShi did not interfere with Tuhu's discussion of religion and philosophy with SuJin. He believed in SuJin's destiny and trusted that the boy would eventually come around. Few heroes could resist the intoxicating allure of fighting for a righteous cause.

WoShi was troubled by the Hun, the battle slave of SuJin, who was now a free man! He was assigned guard duty at the school entrance, which opened into a market street with many shops and chophouses. People were terrified of the Hun and gave him a wide berth after he beat up a few starry-eyed youths hounding SuJin. Commoners at the market tolerated the Hun despite his churlish behaviour because he was the trophy of their hero, the Green Hunter. They called him the "Batu," meaning "the falcon," as he often came swooping out of nowhere to eject trespassers.

After a few weeks, bored with the guard job, the Hun endeared himself to the people of the market by teaching youngsters to make bows and shoot arrows. He would hunt with the youngsters for rat nests for their young pups. Batu bartered the pups to taverns to make wine infused with baby rats, which was much in demand.

The sedate life at the school was occasionally disturbed when the Hun drank too much shaojiu wine. Patrons would fill his wine bowl, expecting him to share stories from the steppes, especially on SwordClaw. The Hun would spin disgusting and blood-curdling tales to the delight of his drinking companions. The problem was that whenever his drinking companions challenged the authenticity of these tales, he would invariably end up in reckless challenges and fist fights, often resulting in damaged furniture and bamboo screens.

The innkeeper tolerated the damages because the grumbling dwarfs would eventually show up and pay for the damages. Moreover, people crowded the tavern to gawk at the famous Mongol battle slave of the hero of Han, ensuring brisk business.

The Grandmaster of the prestigious HanKaoTzu school took offence at the Hun's behaviour and summoned him several times to advise caution. Soon after, the Hun returned to the tavern, imitating the pompous WoShi, much to the amusement of the regular patrons. When WoShi learned of this, he was furious and decided to eliminate the Hun.

When WoShi told the dwarfs he wanted to eliminate the Hun, they were shocked. The dwarfs told him not to underestimate the Hun as he was a bowmaster who was practical and wise to the guiles of the world.

WoShi asked, "How do you know he is a bowmaster? Have you seen him shoot an arrow?" The dwarfs evaded answering him and insisted that the Hun possessed the mind of a strategist, but the grandmaster mocked them. The dwarfs maintained that the man was a God-sent guide destined to lead the boys through the perilous steppes and the frigid Tubote deserts into Tianzhu.

WoShi summoned the Hun and, over wine and dinner, disclosed SuJin's identity as the rightful Han Prince. WoShi did not miss the tremor in the Mongol's eyes - a brief narrowing of his eyes before he concealed it. The Hun was captivated by the forthcoming expedition and asked insightful questions about their travel plans, which annoyed WoShi because he hadn't thought about it.

WoShi stopped drinking and asked the Hun, "Why have you stopped? Let me pour you some more." The Hun declined, much to WoShi's surprise.

The Hun said, "Master, if you drink with me, sip for a sip from the same bowl, I shall willingly finish the jug of shaojiu. I am a little uneasy when we are not sharing the small jug beside you."

WoShi was caught in the act! He thought he could replicate what HuKui did at the monastery, poisoning an unsuspecting SuFei. WoShi grinned, lifted the clay jug, and said, "This one?" The Hun nonchalantly acknowledged. His eyes were sharp and focused on WoShi, unlike a man who had just downed three jugs of shaojiu wine.

WoShi lifted the jug high, but it slipped from his grasp. "Oh, how clumsy...!" WoShi watched in disbelief as Hun's hand darted out to catch the jug before it crashed onto the floor. It was evident to WoShi that he was dealing with a dangerous man and had no idea how to manage the situation. Would he attack? he wondered.

The Hun lifted the jug and dropped it deliberately, shattering the bowl and spilling the wine. "How silly of me! It must be all the drink I had," WoShi was speechless when he realised the Hun had let him off.

A jug brimming with shaojiu was uncharacteristically banged in front of WoShi by CaoShen, spilling some of the wine. They were spying on him and upset with what they had just witnessed.

The Hun said, "I was warned about you, but the Prince needs you." It was the Hun's cryptic answer to why he did not harm WoShi despite his treachery.

WoShi did not bother pouring the wine into the bowl that CaoShen had brought. In a show of trust, he lifted the jug to his lips and drank deeply. "Good wine," he said with a grunt.

The Hun stood up and snatched the jug from WoShi's hand. He looked piercingly into WoShi's eyes. "Master, you had enough wine to poison a night's sleep. Call me when you are ready to talk."

****

WoShi told SuJin the next day, "The Hun reminded me yesterday that destiny will choose your compatriots, not me. I want to ensure he is your choice, not someone lingering about to appease your guilt."

SuJin squinted his eyes as if he could not describe his feelings. "There is something about the Hun that I find reassuring, and I get this sense of blind trust! He claims he has an unfinished duty towards me."

"Do you trust him?" asked WoShi.

"Yes," answered SuJin without any hesitation.

WoShi lifted and dropped his hand in exasperation. "The dwarfs threatened me yesterday and said they would leave Changan if I troubled him. The dwarfs believe he is the perfect foil to the shrewdness you boys don't possess!"

"Really! I haven't seen the dwarfs cosy up to too many people," SuJin said.

WoShi nodded to SuJin, saying, "He is not a meek steppe warrior, what he wants to portray." SuJin's eyes flared in surprise, and WoShi noted, "The dwarfs claim he is a tactician, and I believe them." After a pause, WoShi said, "He trusts you, and I want you to be involved when we question him."

SuJin said, "Let's have dinner with him and probe his background." WoShi refused, embarrassed to face him again over wine, but SuJin insisted it was the best way forward. They apprised CaoShen, and the dwarfs prepared airag, the fermented horse milk the Mongols enjoyed. WoShi asked the dwarfs to add the essence of the night lily to make him speak the truth.

Once the airag was fully fermented, SuJin invited the Hun for dinner with WoShi, Tuhu, and CaoShen to make an announcement. They began by drinking the potent Shaojiu wine. SuJin stood up and bowed to Tuhu, "Master, I enjoy learning philosophy with you, but it's not my destiny."

A smiling Tuhu lifted his wine cup and said, "About time, Prince! I was running out of topics." Everyone laughed heartily.

SuJin turned to WoShi and said, "Master, it's time to call my sworn brothers back to Changan." WoShi asked, "Are you certain? Are you prepared as a warrior to take up arms to defend yourself, your sworn brothers, and your cause?"

SuJin looked at the expectant faces around him and said firmly, "Master Tuhu taught me a philosophy to differentiate good from evil and meditation that helps me focus on deciding which action to take. I hope I am ready!" His declaration was cheered by the dwarfs, but Batu, the Hun, remained silent.

SuJin asked Batu, "What are your plans, Batu?"

Batu said, "I would like to accompany you on your journey to Tianzhu. It is my destiny to serve you, Prince."

Tuhu raised his clenched fists and shook them in appreciation towards Batu and SuJin, exclaiming happily, "Yes!"

Smiling, CaoShen remarked, "We have something for you, Batu, to celebrate our friendship," he presented jars of airag, Mongolian fermented milk.

Initially, Batu shouted joyfully at the rare treat, but then he frowned while looking at WoShi. Ignoring his discomfort, CaoShen poured a cup and handed it to Batu, who leaned back without drinking it.

WoShi said, "An offering of peace." Aware of Batu's mistrust, the dwarfs poured and drank the spiked airag to demonstrate their camaraderie and trust, but Batu hesitated.

SuJin motioned for Batu to drink, and he sipped the airag without hesitation. WoShi was aghast at the trust the Hun had elicited in the dwarfs to drink the spiked airag with him.

WoShi and SuJin refused the airag and sipped mulled rice wine. Piece by piece, they stitched together the Hun's life as the night lily took effect.

Batu was an archer from the Telenggut tribe, led by their clan leader, GurKhan. Unfortunately, he made the blunder of falling in love with the very girl whom the son of GurKhan coveted. In a challenge witnessed by many, he knifed and wounded the GurKhan's son severely. The GurKhan imprisoned him for his insolence but faced stiff disagreement from his tribe because Batu had cut his son in self-defence. GurKhan cleverly transferred Batu as a prisoner to another tribe.

During that time, WangMang's generals brokered peace with the Xiongnu chief, a dear friend of GurKhan. The Han generals bartered for Hun prisoners to fight to the death in the grand tourney. Batu volunteered as a champion fighter to buy time, aware that if he vacillated, he would be eliminated that night before the feast to celebrate the Han friendship.

Batu confessed more because of the effect of the night lily. "When I was born, a powerful shaman told my mother I was blessed by all the ninety-nine deities and spirits who would guide me to a great destiny. The skyfathers wanted me to accomplish something extraordinary."

After a long swig of shaojiu wine, Batu said, "In the tournament, I cursed the skyfathers for deceiving my mother because I was about to die at the hands of a Han pup." With tears streaming down his cheeks, he added, "Strangely, I was not afraid of death. I surrendered to SuJin to die because I had this strong premonition that he needed to live at the cost of my life."

He turned to WoShi and asked, "When you told me about the prophecy and the Prince's destiny, I felt the skyfathers smile. Can you explain why I faced the Prince to be saved?" WoShi squirmed with unease.

CaoShen had passed out! Tuhu struggled to sit up straight and slurred, "There are no coincidences in destiny."

Batu spoke to WoShi in a steady voice, showing no signs of consuming the night lily. "My life's purpose is to ensure SuJin's destiny." WoShi was stunned when he realised that, apart from the first cup SuJin had asked him to drink, the Hun did not touch the airag.

****

The dwarfs invited SuJin and the Hun to join them for the local midsummer festival of Naadam, where WoShi was a distinguished guest.

CaoShen explained, "Naadam means 'the three games of men' - wrestling, horse racing, and archery. We also have dance, wrestling, acrobatics, and various other entertainments, and the food is amazing."

The Hun entered the competition and just about qualified in archery. He was reasonably good at the horse game of hitting the leather ball, although people expected him to outshine his fellow contestants coming from the steppe. However, in freestyle wrestling, he fared better than most. The Hun was quite popular despite his shortcomings with the local people, and they cheered him raucously, chanting, "Falcon, Falcon." In wrestling, Batu lost some rounds, won a few, and made it to round five, albeit with many blows and bruises. His unpredictability ruined the wagers of those who had bet on him and against him, and the gamblers were pleased when he finally withdrew before the main fights.

SuJin remained doubtful about Batu's performance. He told Batu, "That was the most skilled fight I have ever seen... to lose deliberately without anyone noticing!" A grinning Batu nodded at SuJin, who did not realise he had collaborated with the dwarfs to tilt the odds.

A few weeks later, WoShi accepted that the Hun was devoted to SuJin and called him "Batu Nachin," meaning "Loyal Falcon," just as the dwarfs and commoners called him.

****

A couple of weeks later, Batu asked WoShi, "Isn't the training ground for archery in the clearing inside the forest?" WoShi said, "Yes, but it's not a forest; it's the grounds of a nobleman's house."

WoShi puffed out his chest and said proudly, "I gather you are an archer. SuJin is an exceptional archer as well! The others are quite skilled with the crossbow, too. In the event of an enemy attack, they would perform admirably, as every shot they fire hits the straw target."

The Hun smirked and paraphrased WoShi in disdain, "Every shot will hit the straw target!"

WoShi exclaimed, "What's wrong, Batu? Don't you believe me?"

"No, Master WoShi, Han's archery is weak."

WoShi was irritated and said, "What do you mean! Did you not see the imperial soldiers firing in the arena? Our boys are better than that!"

Batu did not argue about that but instead asked, "What about the warriors of Tianzhu? If what I have heard about these people is true, they could be formidable opponents. Archery can't be as poor in Tianzhu as you have today in Han." WoShi's eyebrows went up, and his lips thinned.

"What are you saying, Batu? Han archery is bad?"

"I was apprised of your shots at Naadam, and they're nowhere close to our best." Batu nodded.

The Hun was pensive for some time, and then he spoke, "You spoke of deities with bows. What did the bow look like?"

WoShi said, "It's a double recurve bow. It's longer than the short recurve bow used by you Mongols to shoot from horseback. Perhaps the men from Tianzhu have long arms," and he snorted impudently at his joke. Batu stared at WoShi without seeing.

****

Before starting his Tai Chi routine the next day, WoShi saw CaoShen waiting for him. "Yesterday, I had a strange conversation with Batu. He was all excited about double recurve bows. "It's a cumbersome weapon, and I informed him that the Han imperial warriors had abandoned it generations ago in favour of the simpler crossbow." CaoShen nodded absently, and WoShi enquired, "Did you see him this morning?"

CaoShen said, "Yes, he got up early and entered the market with his bow. He mentioned he would meet you later in the archery practice area."

WoShi frowned and asked, "With his bow? When did he get a bow? A Hun walking through the market with a bow is rather intimidating. Something feels off. I'd better check on him."

CaoShen asked him to wait. WoShi felt annoyed when a dwarf accompanied him carrying a bamboo basket filled with chunks of roasted pork and rice. The dwarfs were sure that WoShi would wish to meet the Hun.

When WoShi reached the clearing, he found Batu stretching to loosen his limbs. He had been at it for a while, and the man was sweating. Batu nodded at WoShi and resumed from where they had left off yesterday, "The deities did indeed use the double recurve bow, but a much longer one." He added, "I checked with CaoShen, who has seen the deities, and the drawings made and kept in the library confirmed it."

"These gods are incredibly muscled and would undoubtedly be excellent archers if they used bows as long as themselves."

WoShi was taken aback and said, "Batu, these deities surely predate the first emperor. No one uses them anymore. Today's crossbow is easier to use, load, and shoot."

Batu harrumphed at WoShi with a serious expression. "Master, I assure you that archery and bows are not your strength. However, they are my speciality." He continued, "Double recurve bows are unwieldy and not a fierce weapon unless paired with an archer trained on them. It takes a great deal of practice and power to wield them."

WoShi looked at Batu's right arm, which was unnaturally larger than his left. Batu nodded, acknowledging WoShi's assessment of his arm. "Yes, I am an archer."

WoShi was condescending. "Big bow, small bow, how does it matter?"

Batu appeared amused. He gestured toward the basket held by the dwarf. "Shall we? Just the thought of pulling bowstrings makes me hungry."

WoShi tried to converse as they ate breakfast, but he gave up when he saw that Batu was preoccupied. After eating, Batu sat back on his knees and gently swung his head from side to side, mumbling a chant.

Batu flexed his shoulders and stretched his body in quick, practised moves. WoShi enquired, "What's with this unusual warm-up? Are you going to fight someone?"

Batu chuckled, "An old war chant, force of practice."

WoShi snorted and asked, "What's all this about?"

"A demonstration. Then probably you will help me. I need to prepare."

"Prepare for what?" WoShi questioned.

"The dwarfs and the good people of the market are hounded for money by unscrupulous informers, although their job is to spy on you and the school."

WoShi looked perplexed, and Batu said, "I ensured they followed me."

WoShi persisted, "Who?"

Batu did not reply. He opened an extended leather-wrapped package to reveal a polished double recurve bow, similar to the ones the deities held but shorter and thinner.

WoShi gasped in surprise, "I didn't notice that here?"

Batu taunted him playfully, "Old man!"

Batu grinned. "This bow is my life!" WoShi was stunned, and Batu continued, "Don't look so surprised! The Han borders are porous, and people can smuggle anything in. Why do you think we succeed in skirmishes? Most of our wealth comes from the Han nobility in the border towns, who pay us to raid their rivals."

He patted the bow and said, "Not everyone in the steppes wants me dead. I had it smuggled through a trader who accompanied the Han generals. Although my friends paid him in leather pelts back at the steppe, he demands more money."

With a grin, he replied to a flummoxed WoShi, "The dwarfs helped me."

"Where did the dwarfs get money to pay this merchant?" WoShi asked, still confounded by what Batu was saying.

"Aw, old Master, don't be so naive. Why would I enter the Naadam contest if not to win or lose, to make money for the gambling dwarfs?" He added sagely, "If you haven't got an ego, everything in life is a trade."

WoShi opened and closed his mouth like a fish out of water. In appreciation, he said, "You have the trust of the little fellows." Batu nodded emphatically without looking up and replied, "They are good people, and they believe in my destiny."

Batu said, "I shall train SuJin and the other boys in the art of double recurve archery, but outside Changan and away from prying eyes. My clan knows of my skills, but they don't care. They have all switched to shorter bows to shoot from horseback." After checking his collection of arrows, he finally chose three arrows and said, "Not in the best condition, but will do for the day!"

He notched the first arrow and let it loose, not taking any real aim, and WoShi innocently watched the arrow take flight. It rose gracefully and flew into the canopy of trees outside the clearing. A shriek pierced the air! The arrow struck someone, and WoShi gasped in horror as a man tumbled from the tree, clutching a loaded crossbow.

WoShi screamed, pointing at the fallen man, "Assassin, assassin!" He wheeled around when he heard the twang of the bow again.

Another arrow was speeding towards a man who had risen from behind a clump of bushes and was sprinting hard. The man was flailing his arms wildly and running for his life, throwing aside a crossbow. Without even a whimper, the man collapsed as the powerful arrow pierced his back and heart, throwing him forward, dead before he hit the ground.

Before WoShi could react, Batu had let loose the third arrow with a grunt, pulling harder on the bow and aiming higher into the sky.

WoShi watched, astounded, as the recurve bow *twanged* and bent forward in the recoil, taking the shape of a trident just after release. The power given to the arrow was so intense that its shaft wriggled and oscillated like a snake before it sped away with a *whoosh*. The arrow's trajectory was spectacular as it climbed higher and higher into the sky. It reached the zenith of its flight and gently curved downwards, gathering speed. WoShi saw an older man labouring up the slope in the distance. The man reached the edge of the trees and paused to look back, safely distanced from any arrow.

The shot was impossible, with the target at a distance greater than anything WoShi had ever seen. The arrow struck the man with such incredible force that he was punched into the ground. Batu had, in a shard of moments, taken out three targets. It was an extraordinary display of archery that the grandmaster of the foremost military school in Han had ever witnessed.

"The Hun was an exceptional master of archery—a bowmaster, as the dwarfs had told him earlier. WoShi grimaced as he realised that, despite his best training, his boy's skills were significantly lacking in comparison."

A trio of dwarfs emerged from the forest and waved at Batu. WoShi was sure that if Batu had missed, the dwarfs would have taken the man down. The Hun dropped his bow and jogged out with a short sword towards the fallen men to retrieve his precious arrows.

WoShi sat in deep contemplation until Batu began repacking his weapons, whistling a tuneless song. He said, "Dead men tell no tales, but dead bodies will raise a stink. Tell me, Batu, how will we get rid of that?"

The Hun assured WoShi. "Leave it to the dwarfs."

****

WoShi was warming himself by a cheerful fire, his back to the door. Batu entered and sat cross-legged next to the fire, adding logs. A servant brought two steaming bowls of quail soup with peppers.

WoShi told Batu, "Thank you for joining me. You did well today." Batu glanced at him sideways and nodded. "I am appointing you as a teacher." Batu's mouth fell open in surprise. WoShi continued, "I want you to teach the boys recurve bow archery."

Batu bowed low to WoShi with his fists clasped in the Han greeting and said, "I will do my best, master of my Prince."

"There is another matter that I need to share. It was unwise of me to think it was irrelevant until today." Batu looked at WoShi with a blank stare. "Zhang Liang has left *you* a scroll on how to make recurve bows. My teacher gave it to me, and now it's yours. You don't know how to read, and between Tuhu and me, we will teach you what it says."

****

WangMang's military commander and cousin WangYi summoned WoShi.

A military captain received WoShi. "Marquis, can you tell us where the Han hero is? I mean, at least where he was seen last? We know you are searching for him too."

WoShi's eyes opened in shock, but he downplayed SuJin's disappearance, saying, "You see intrigue in everything. As you grow older, like I have, everything will have a mundane explanation. SuJin's barbarian slave has run away, and this boy feels it's his responsibility to bring him back."

With a short laugh, the captain said, "Actually, we are interested in the Hun and have sent word across the countryside to locate him."

"Why?" asked WoShi.

"The Hun, it seems, is one of the finest warriors of the steppe. A deadly assassin." WoShi swallowed hard. He was sure of this, even without the detective affirming it.

The captain added, "The Xiongnu now want him back. One of their tribal leaders made a mistake in bartering him to us. Idiots, trading their best warrior to die!"

WangYi entered, and he was curt with the captain, who jumped aside with a bow for his superior and commander. WoShi laboured to his feet to bow to him. WangYi said, "A potential assassin of the Mongols has gone missing in the capital city along with your boy. We need to find them."

WangYi continued briskly, "Marquis, our interest lies in capturing the Hun. We cannot permit a confirmed spy to leave Changan, particularly now that he is aware of the layout of our city. No threat to the imperial throne or the regent can exist as long as I am commander. I want to tell you this directly. Inform us as soon as you obtain any information on the Hun."

WangYi watched WoShi shuffle away, and his captain asked respectfully, "Commander, should we ignore WoShi and his students?"

WangYi hissed, "No, keep a watch on them! Our spies say that their informers around the school have gone missing. They vanished after the Hun. It can't be a coincidence."

Wang Yi commanded. "Find their bodies or locate the Hun. A Mongol can't get far in Han. Use the new hemp paper to send portraits and descriptions across the empire."

With an afterthought, WangYi sneered, saying, "All barbarians can be won over with money, particularly someone with a grudge to settle. We will recruit him and assassinate a few Mongol leaders. That will keep them busy until our regent takes over the empire from the gutless Lui." His captain smiled.

****

The boy, Emperor Pingdi, despised his father-in-law, regent WangMang. His tutors whispered about WangMang's wicked deeds and how he slaughtered anyone who opposed him. He was rapidly approaching the day to become full emperor, and he had decided that his first act would be to demote WangMang to a chancellor with no military powers.

Emperor Pingdi commissioned his trusted bodyguards to gather incriminating evidence against WangMang. He instructed his tutors to organise the Lui clan and their soldiers to stand by while he sought to demote WangMang. He drafted an appeal letter bearing his seal to the Lui.

That very evening, WangXun, WangMang's trusted cousin and minister of the imperial court, requested an audience with the regent. He showed him the letter the Emperor's bodyguard had willingly shared, detailing his plan to demote WangMang.

WangMang said, "I was expecting this; thank you, cousin. For the good of our empire, he will have to go. Our history forgets emperors who have done nothing for the people." Touching the medallion on his chest, he murmured, "My poor daughter, she will become a widow! I shall ensure that she lives a life of comfort, like our dear dowager Empress. We should ensure that the next Lui to occupy the throne is even younger, barely off his mother's teat."

WangXun nodded, "LuiRuzi!"

WangMang said, "I shall keep the tutors away from the emperor; surely a little torture will reveal more of their sinister plans. You tell his bodyguard to report that the Lui families have accepted his command and are busy preparing for my ouster."

A few days later, his tutor sent the emperor a message advising him to leave WangMang alone for the time being. The moon had concealed the red planet of war, which is a bad omen for any military action. The message also recommended that the Emperor consume hot pepper soup to purge evil spirits from his body and counteract the adverse effects of the omens.

Emperor Pingdi asked his trusted bodyguard, "What happened to the tutor? Why isn't he here?"

The bodyguard greeted the Emperor and replied, "Ten thousand years to your life, Your Majesty. Your tutor travels far and wide to meet Lui families and will return soon."

That evening, the palace food taster sampled a small portion of the Emperor's bird's nest soup under the watchful eyes of three different palace officials, including one from the Empress dowager's palace. They had to wait an hour before checking on the food taster for any signs of poisoning.

On that fateful day, the officials were delighted when the bureaucrats in charge of the kitchen invited them to sample exotic wines brought for the Emperor's coronation. They left the food taster under military guard and planned to check and record his health afterwards.

When the officials left, WangMang's men rushed in, forcing the complying food taster to heave out all he had sampled. He was dunked in freezing water and fed an antidote. The man was administered pungent salts to inhale and recover, and quail soup was given to rejuvenate him. After an hour, drunken palace officials returned and recorded the food taster's vital signs as excellent.

When he heard the Emperor was sick, WangMang assembled the best astrologers and doctors. The astrologers cautioned that the red star's influence was considerable, and doctors recommended purging his stomach, suspecting food poisoning. However, they relented when the ailing Emperor insisted on consuming hot peppers instead, as his tutors had prescribed. Physicians of the dowager Empress also checked the boy and declared that the illness was mild.

WangMang was upset by the doctor's allegation of food poisoning and commanded every bureaucrat to taste the hot pepper preparation. The palace officials tasted the fiery peppers amidst much cheerful banter. They burnt their tongues and screamed their miseries, with tears streaming down their faces. Indeed, these peppers were potent enough to drive evil spirits away.

In an extraordinary show of filial piety, WangMang and his daughter, Empress HuangHuang, sampled the hot pepper soup, demonstrating their deep concern for the ailing emperor. After all, they were family.

The Emperor suffered severe stomach aches and chills, and his health deteriorated. After days of excruciating cramps and dehydration, he died. The untimely death was analysed, and astrologers attributed it to the powerful evil spirits that had possessed the Emperor when the moon swallowed the red star.

WangMang couldn't control the uproar unleashed by the Lui clan, who suspected an assassination, during the ensuing weeks of turmoil. The unrest ceased when the empire was engulfed in severe drought and famine, and the Yellow River turned south for the second time.

#18 Valley of The Dwarfs

SuJin enjoyed the wind blowing through his hair and the scents and sights of vast open vistas. They lived off the land, trapping rabbits, marmots, and other small animals. Batu led him into the mountains, guided by a leather map provided by CaoShen.

SuJin asked Batu, "Why are we meeting my brothers by the lake in the mountains? Wouldn't it have been easier to meet them at Changan or somewhere else closer? We sent word to them long ago, if I am right."

Batu replied, "Before they set out for the valley to go fishing, they must make some wooden contraptions."

"What?" SuJin asked. "Fishing? I thought you hated water!"

"Now, did I agree to go fishing?" Batu shot back. "You will. It's your challenge. I'll be occupied with other tasks."

SuJin furrowed his brow. Surely, catching a fish can't be too difficult!

Batu added, "The dwarfs trust you, Prince. They have permitted us to enter their ancient fishing grounds."

SuJin said happily, "My sworn brothers will be there! I wonder how much they have changed since I last saw them."

After a pause, Batu said grimly, "Now, don't expect me to hug Han pups as if I'm greeting lost brothers. I am here for you."

SuJin laughed and shifted in his saddle. "They are also coming to Tianzhu; we have only each other to rely on in a foreign land. One day, you will come to trust my brothers."

Batu was uninterested. "You keep whatever Tuhu said and the discourses you heard at the temple to yourself, Prince. I have seen too many men die because of misplaced trust." With a faraway look in his eyes, he mumbled in pain, "Keep trust to yourself."

Batu examined the markings on the map, feeling pleased whenever he could identify them. He cursed the dwarfs when he couldn't locate any landmarks. SuJin recognised the issue and dismounted to search for markers from a lower perspective, understanding that the dwarfs were short in stature and travelled on foot. Despite travelling on a horse, they spent many weeks in the open, evading people and habitation before reaching a snowy mountain range.

They followed a narrow path that wound back and forth up the mountain. A valley with a few dilapidated huts perched high on its slope came into view. Somewhere, a stream cascaded down the hill, and they could see the silver water reflecting from the plains below. The mountainside was rocky and showed abandoned efforts at step-farming. It appeared that the people here lived in dire poverty; no self-serving tax collector would undertake the long journey to those huts.

SuJin and Batu climbed the dirt track to the huts and discovered that the short street ended in a dead end, where the mountain towered above them. The mud and reed houses were smaller than usual, and the thatched reed doors were set low—like dwarfs! They had arrived at their destination, but where was the lake?

The roar of cascading water was deafening, and the wind carried the spray from the rapids beyond. The rocks were wet and slimy, and the place was bitterly cold. SuJin shivered.

Batu seemed unfazed by the cold and very much present in the moment. He remarked, "Great! With that sound drowning out everything, we are like straw targets for a novice archer. I hope your friends ask before they shoot arrows at us." SuJin frowned in annoyance at that comment.

As they approached the huts, the air exuded an overpowering stench of fish, snapping SuJin's wandering mind into focus. Two men sat on a wooden platform at the end of the lane, dangling their legs. They were not dwarfs.

Batu simpered, glancing at the old men. "Now, that is an obvious decoy. Where are your friends?" He wrinkled his nose in disgust at the smell of fish and muttered, "... but then, we are in the right place."

They cautiously trotted forward, and a stoic SuJin scanned back and forth, searching for the slightest anomaly or movement. Batu looked at him and grunted in appreciation. "Finally, looking about with the eye of a warrior."

"This could be a trap! Why don't the dwarfs show up?" Batu said, fidgeting with the reins.

SuJin reached out and firmly grasped the bridle of Batu's horse. "Relax! I don't sense any danger."

Batu looked at SuJin incredulously. "Sense danger! What do you mean?" SuJin's assessment did not impress Batu, "What are you? A shaman? At least let us confirm that whoever is hiding here is friendly! Shouldn't your friends come out to hail you?"

SuJin looked Batu in the eye and said calmly, "Trust me!" Batu watched SuJin trot ahead, undeterred, with a string of foul curses that would shame a veteran tavern keeper.

Batu caught up to SuJin and screamed, "Oh, sky gods, here we come!" Turning to SuJin, he angrily said, "What a way to go! Walking into an obvious trap with the words... I don't sense any danger!"

They trotted their horse right up to the platform, and the old men grinned. Sensing movement, Batu turned around. Three young men and several dwarfs were assessing them from behind stacks of straw. They held crossbows. More dwarfs clambered down from the rooftops. They assessed Batu with open curiosity, largely ignoring SuJin.

SuJin smiled at Batu, who spat on the ground in disgust at walking into a trap blind. Thankfully, this one was a mock drill by SuJin's friends.

SuJin dismounted and grinned in genuine pleasure at his friends ChenHe, Qian, and SuWu. Unlike the messy tangles of adolescent boys, his friends looked older, better groomed, sprouting moustaches and clean braided hair.

They rushed forward and hugged him with hoots of glee. "Prince! We missed you."

Qian pushed ChenHe and SuWu aside and apprised SuJin by walking around him. "You have grown into a seriously handsome man. I would never have recognised you but for your sloppy, uncombed hair. Does the comb still fall off?" They laughed and slapped SuJin's back, clearly aware of his combat with SwordClaw.

SuWu turned to Batu and said, "Sorry. We knew it must be you coming this way. I used the opportunity to assess the positioning and readiness of our defence."

Batu shrugged, showing indifference, and packed his throwing knives into his bundle. "Yes, we could *sense* that," he said to a confused SuWu.

An infant cried. SuJin looked to see two young girls walking towards them. The one holding the bawling infant handed the baby to one of the men perched on the platform. The girls came and stood beside ChenHe and Qian, giving SuJin a shy smile and a bow. Their familiarity with his friends flummoxed him until realisation dawned on him, causing his jaw to fall open in disbelief.

ChenHe patted the girl standing next to him and, with a sheepish smile, said. "My wife."

He gestured towards the man holding the infant and said, "My son and father-in-law."

Qian placed his hand over his wife's stomach and patted it. "Ren, my wife. She is pregnant."

HuKui, JiaShao, and their wives joined them, leading mules with small packs on their backs. They hailed SuJin with wide grins and scrutinised Batu openly.

SuJin looked around and exclaimed, "Are all of you married? It's unbelievable!"

Batu whispered under his breath to SuJin, "Obviously, your *sense* didn't tell you that they were married."

SuJin looked at Batu and laughed. Batu said, "I *sense* a valley behind this mountain. It must be the one with fish."

"Lake with fish? How do you know that?" SuJin enquired innocently.

Batu looked at him and thundered, "Because I can smell the fish drying here!" He pointed to his wrinkled nose. Then he pointed to his ears and said, "I can hear water falling behind the mountain." SuJin smiled and nodded, least offended.

Batu's curt response to their exalted Prince did not go well with the boys. "Barbarian! Hun," said ChenHe with distaste. His tone implied they expected Batu, a battle slave, to be subservient to their Prince.

Boisterous talk by his friends swamped SuJin, and he introduced Batu as an equal, surprising his friends.

Ignored by the men, Batu and the women reluctantly introduced themselves. His peculiar mannerisms and accent quickly had the women smiling and laughing. Batu joined the women in preparing fish and rice.

****

"This is the last leg of our journey," Batu remarked to SuJin as they stepped onto a trail that curved around the steep mountain. The temperature dropped sharply as they turned to the opposite side of the hill, and the roar of the rushing water made conversation difficult.

Cold spray soaked them, and soon, they were shivering.

Walking their mounts in a single file beside a steep gorge, they had to cross the stream before climbing up to the valley beyond. SuJin could see dwarfs with bows on the other side of the gully, effectively covering the narrow path. JiaShao gestured to the armed dwarfs and shouted above the din to SuJin, "Improvements made for your security."

SuJin shouted back, "Really, am I under attack?"

JiaShao laughed, saying, "My brothers have taken your protection seriously. Once you leave, we will abandon these mountains for some time."

The path descended to a broad stream below, and the narrow ravine gushed freezing winds from the mountains, throwing tiny shards of ice at their faces. SuJin shuddered, "It's so cold down here! I can't bear it!"

JiaShao said, "The valley is covered in mist, and the lake waters are freezing with glaciers. We will do our best to keep you warm, Prince."

Batu turned around and said, "It's nice to know that our god's emissary can feel the cold like us mortals." Everyone laughed except ChenHe. He had taken an instant dislike to the Hun for patronising SuJin, his Prince. He stiffened at Batu's flippant remark about his Prince, his hero.

ChenHe grumbled to Qian and SuWu, "Our Prince is not raised in the palace; else he wouldn't stand for such liberty from a Hun. A barbarian slave! Look at how he talks, like a lord from the palace."

Qian shrugged his shoulders in indifference. "It's not just SuJin; Grandmaster WoShi and CaoShen hold him in the highest regard. There must be something about him that impressed them, and it can't be his rough Hun looks." ChenHe scoffed in disdain.

SuWu cautioned them, "We have practically assembled here on this man's instructions to catch a fish. Something will come of this, I am sure." He looked at Batu, who skipped over the wet rocks and said, "If this barbarian is not destined to be with us, he will drop off somewhere." ChenHe jeered at SuWu for suggesting that the Hun would accompany them to Tianzhu.

****

They ascended the rocky rim of the gorge into a misty valley. Hills surrounded the valley and had a towering snow-covered massif to one side, the highest peak in the range. Below the snow-capped mountain, a glacier met the lake, serving as a perennial water source. Through the mist, forests of dense green foliage blanketed the mountain slopes with no visible gaps. SuJin could see a cluster of huts nestled beneath pine trees by the lake. A well-worn path led directly to the settlement.

HuKui took it upon himself to inform Batu, "You are fortunate today; the mists are thin, and you can see the valley. Beyond our huts lies a path that winds up to the edge of this valley and down into a village, where we get our supplies. The cart track is flanked by thick, nearly impenetrable green foliage, a tangle of shrubs and vines. This valley is mist-covered throughout the year, nourishing these plants. The constant sound of dripping water can be unsettling, but we've grown accustomed to it."

"CaoShen provided directions to enter the valley via a lesser-known path; it's longer but more discreet. Nosy villagers watch everyone coming and going if you take the main cart path." He gestured across the lake and said, "See those tree-lined slopes. A narrow horse trail leads down to the plains and is the shortest route to Changan. That road connects to the village road at the valley's edge."

JiaShao joined them and said, "That road's a thoroughfare for bandits, and few men venture there." Batu's brows creased upon hearing bandits. Looking at Batu, JiaShao clarified, "They leave us alone. The bandits have fervently spread rumours of fierce dwarf cannibals inhabiting these valleys. They claim that vile creatures and spirits roam about shrieking for blood when the valley is misted out." Batu still looked concerned.

"What's your worry?" HuKui probed.

Batu replied, "Bandits in Han don't operate alone. They survive on the patronage of some high official or bureaucrat." HuKui looked at Batu in disbelief, and Batu said with a grimace, "I should know. We often deal with bandits and corrupt officials at the border. Know one evil, and the other can't be far behind."

HuKui consoled Batu. "Don't worry. No one could be bothered about ragtag dwarfs and a few fugitives."

Batu glanced at SuJin, who was strolling with his arms folded against his chest to ward off the cold. "I hope that's true. We must defend this place until he retrieves his mofa. I mean, he doesn't have his magic yet." Batu nodded to HuKui, mounted his horse, leaned back, stretched his hands out with palms facing upwards, and prayed to the sky fathers. The horse trotted away, grazing on tufts of grass.

SuWu approached HuKui, observing Batu's antics, and asked, "Who is this man? I mean, really... What is a barbarian doing here?"

HuKui said, "From what little I have gathered from the dwarfs, despite SuJin defeating him at the arena, if this man is against us, we are dead."

SuWu was shocked and said, "Really! Come, let's talk to the Prince."

They approached SuJin, and SuWu asked, "Prince, can we trust him, the Hun?"

SuJin responded straightaway. "Who? Batu, of course!" Realising their predicament about trusting a Hun, the traditional enemy of the Han, he declared firmly, "WoShi took his time but trusts him now, and the dwarfs at Changan adore him, especially Tuhu."

After a few moments of contemplation, SuWu said, "Very well! He is worthy of our trust, too."

HuKui sighed and said, "You leave us little choice, Prince. If he is good for you, he shall be a brother to us."

SuJin smiled in gratitude and said, "I am sorry. I should have been here earlier, but first, I had to clear my mind. Thankfully, Tuhu helped me."

HuKui looked up into the skies, opened his arms, imitating the Hun, and said, "Aren't we all at the beck and call of the gods? Death is final, my Prince and none will escape its clutches." HuKui changed the subject, saying, "So, you have come here to catch the monster dragonfish."

SuJin's eyes widened in surprise. "Monster dragonfish? What's that!"

HuKui looked at him blankly and said, "I haven't seen this fish in all my time here, nor have anyone, including the dwarf fishermen. The older dwarfs, however, swear that dragonfish haunt the depths of this icy lake."

JiaShao joined the conversation. "It comes up on full moon nights when the lake is shrouded in mist or during heavy rain when its surface is obscured. The dragonfish is the spirit of the forest."

HuKui rolled his eyes in disbelief and said, "If you say so, master JiaShao. It would be no less a feat to hunt an animal no one has seen!"

A morose JiaShao said, "To capture a spirit of nature, it should first allow itself to be captured, and we must suffer repercussions. That is the law of nature!"

HuKui was sceptical about what JiaShao said and asked, "Are you sure a dragonfish is in there? What if it's just someone's imagination?"

Furious, JiaShao verbally lashed out at HuKui. "You never believed there was a shrine in HanKaoTzu until you saw it for yourself. My elders always tell the truth."

HuKui flinched and said, "Don't get flustered, JiaShao. I believed WoShi when he described the green-black knife because I had seen the cursed blade. Similarly, we need a sign!"

SuJin picked up a flat, smooth stone and tossed it parallel to the tranquil surface. It skimmed across the surface, skipping many times before finally sliding into the depths. HuKui asked SuJin, "Why do the Hun want this fish?"

JiaShao interjected and said, "A foolish dream of the Hun! The sacred dragonfish cannot be seen, let alone caught! These creatures are ancient spirits and keep to the depths." SuJin shrugged, expressing his ignorance, and tossed another stone to skim across the surface water.

After watching for a while, JiaShao and HuKui whispered together while looking at the Prince furtively. HuKui hesitantly approached SuJin and asked, "Prince, we have been talking amongst ourselves, including our wives, and we all feel you need some love and care that a family can provide. SuJin was dumbfounded, and HuKui quickly added, "We have many beautiful girls here, sisters of our wives. Maybe you can choose a wife or two for yourself? After all, you have come of age like your brothers, and they are married. We are all married."

HuKui squirmed as SuJin shook his head repeatedly in disbelief. "Master! In the midst of all this?"

JiaShao hastily added, "The Yellow River has turned twice and can, at best, turn again after the next snow melt. That is next summer, or it may take one more year. Who knows! You should live with a woman and enjoy life before..."

Whatever he wanted to say remained unsaid as SuJin frowned at them. Shaking his head, SuJin said, "No. We leave when ready, and we are not taking families."

"Who knows..." HuKui stopped when SuJin lifted his hand to stall him.

SuJin declared, "Leave me be. My life has been dedicated to honouring our ancestors. You heard the immortals speak and know of their faith in us. I will journey to Tianzhu, and I cannot allow thoughts of a wife and child to weigh upon me."

JiaShao added awkwardly, "The woman wanted me to check in with you. CaoShen believes you have become a monk and might not pick up a weapon again." HuKui looked away, embarrassed.

SuJin was saddened by what he heard, and his eyes brimmed with tears. He gestured towards Batu, who was trotting on his horse along the shores of the lake some distance away, and said, "The Hun, a stranger until recently, believes in my destiny."

Then, in a smaller voice, he said, "He believes in me, even though I am not myself..." He added in determination, "Yet!"

JiaShao did not want to give up easily and said, "SuJin, all your decisions will change when you meet the right woman; trust me, the right one will come along soon enough."

SuJin scoffed at them, "Let's not bring up this topic again."

JiaShao responded fiercely, "Wasn't one deity a woman?" SuJin's ears turned red, and he turned towards the serene lake and flicked a stone. In the awkward silence, their eyes followed the stone as it skipped across the lake.

A giant blue-black fish rose from the depths, breached the surface, and fell back with a massive splash that set off waves around the lake. SuJin baulked in surprise and turned towards HuKui. "Did you see that... did you see that ...?" He repeated, his eyes agog. HuKui was frozen still, not having ever seen a fish that size.

The dwarf chief fell heavily to his knees with his mouth half-open. "Impossible! The fish shouldn't come up!"

HuKui countered, "That's no fish! That's a monster!"

JiaShao looked at SuJin in wonder and exclaimed, "In all my life, I haven't seen that fish! You throw a stone, and it comes up like a pet dog! What are you?"

Loud shouts rang out across the lakeside as people gathered to witness the strange sight of the massive fish breaching the surface.

HuKui whispered, "Is it running around in ecstasy at the arrival of our Prince?"

"I don't know what to say. This is too much for me to handle," said JiaShao.

Uninterested in the excitement of the fish surfacing, a few ladies approached them and waited a little away, giving SuJin bashful smiles. It looked like they had something to discuss. HuKui and JiaShao unenthusiastically excused themselves and walked over to them.

They had come to check on SuJin's preferred criteria for choosing a wife. Their animated conversation reached SuJin. Every family seemed to have a daughter of the right age to offer him a wife.

SuJin gazed at the choppy surface of the lake in mortification. He could hear the ladies' discontent as JiaShao told them the Prince was not interested in a wife because he was on religious abstinence.

****

Over dinner, JiaShao reminded the new entrants to dispose of their food waste in a hole they had dug to keep the camp safe from black bears. Nodding in comprehension, Batu picked up and dumped SuJin's reed bowl of fish bones into the pit while the others watched in shocked silence. No one had ever cleared SuJin's eating bowl; he was their equal and did his chores himself.

A lot had changed since they left Changan. The boys looked at each other, realising that they had a Prince in their midst, and he had privileges.

SuJin yawned and retired to his allotted hut, the largest. He was tired, and after weeks of sleeping on uneven surfaces, the double straw mattress on a flat mud floor appealed to him.

ChenHe got up and declared, "That's our Prince. I shall watch over him during the night." SuWu gestured towards the Hun, chatting with the ladies and washing bowls by the lakeside. ChenHe's face twisted with anger, and he said, "A Hun to guard a Han Prince while we are still around. Shame!" ChenHe went home, retrieved his staff, and moved towards the hut occupied by SuJin. He surveyed the surroundings carefully and lounged by the door.

A little later, a young girl crept up to him and shyly demanded to speak to SuJin. ChenHe was outraged to find that it was his younger sister-in-law, and he hissed, "What are you doing here? Shouldn't you be with your parents?"

She replied firmly, "My sister sent me to check on the cute Prince."

"What?" ChenHe growled at her.

She was not cowed down and unabashedly told him, "My sister asked me if I aspired to be a Princess, and I said yes. I would do anything to become a Princess."

ChenHe was outraged and asked, "What do you want to do with the Prince?"

"My sister said the Prince would need his bed warmed in this cold. Women do it in palaces. She said if I worked diligently for his happiness, I could become his consort, and all my friends would bow before me."

ChenHe snarled at her, "I will tear the skin off both your backs if I see you anywhere near my Prince. That is a royal Prince, not some village mutt! We are here to submit to his slightest whims and fancies. He will decide who will keep him warm at night. Now off with you, and don't come back." After many arguments and appeals, ChenHe spanked the girl. She stomped her foot and ran away weeping.

ChenHe snorted loudly, smiled, and leaned back, unaware that he would be turning away girls from numerous families that night. As the night progressed and no more girls turned up, ChenHe finally relaxed and drifted off to sleep.

Someone touched him lightly on the shoulder, and he woke up with a start. "How many times do I..." He stopped. "What are you doing here?" he blurted out, realising too late that Batu had come out of the hut.

Batu flashed him an impish grin lit by the moonlight. "I couldn't sleep with all those romantic talks between you and the village girls. Why couldn't you go elsewhere and do the talking, perhaps by the lakeside or under a tree, with the full moon and all?"

Enraged, ChenHe roared and pulled out his dagger, "Get lost before I skewer you like the Hun pig you are. How dare you sleep in the presence of our Prince? I am protecting him."

"Protecting him!" retorted Batu, who was quick to anger. "I was inside the hut all this while, and you didn't know that, you dimwit! Shouldn't you check inside once before resting your ample backside like an ugly pailou in front of a village?"

No one had ever insulted ChenHe like this before, and in the moonlight, Batu could see the vein throbbing in his neck. ChenHe replied softly but with deadly intent, "Do I look like an immobile village archway to you, a pailou? I am going to kill you!" Flexing his broad shoulder, ChenHe moved forward menacingly, and Batu drew a dagger. They circled each other, ready to fight.

SuWu rushed in with a drawn sword, followed by others alerted by the loud voices in the still mountain air. He pushed against ChenHe with his shoulders to no effect. The heavyset and muscular ChenHe was a wrestler who shrugged off the shoulder push. SuWu pivoted and attempted to trip him, but ChenHe countered by tripping him instead.

By this time, Batu had backed away to relative safety. It took the combined efforts of HuKui, SuWu, and Qian to subdue ChenHe and bring him to the ground, but thankfully, the fight had left him.

SuWu turned to Batu and snarled, "Not a day has passed since you arrived, and we are already at loggerheads!"

HuKui shouted at SuWu, "He is a barbarian! Get a hold of yourself!"

SuWu rushed into the hut to check on SuJin and found him listening to their arguments with eyes wide open. Frustrated, SuWu came out and stood with his hands on his waist. He stared at Batu and asked, "What happened here?"

Batu shrugged his shoulders and walked past deliberately close to ChenHe. He violently connected his shoulder with SuWu, pushing him aside as he entered the hut and shut the door. SuWu bounced off the bamboo wall. He took a few deep breaths to calm himself and purposefully walked into the hut to confront Batu. In a brazen display of contempt, Batu lay snoring, clearly avoiding any attempt to talk.

SuWu came away in disgust. ChenHe could make out his resentment and asked, "Do I need to explain?"

SuWu shook his head and said, "We don't need to guard the Prince. He has his protection."

"But-", began ChenHe,

"Leave it." SuWu cut him short, "We weren't with SuJin all these days, and the Hun has developed a routine of protecting him."

Qian voiced the question they all had in mind. "Tell me, SuWu, was SuJin awake when the Hun insulted ChenHe?"

SuWu looked unhappy to reply. "I can't be sure about that. It was dark inside. He is tired from the journey?" He shrugged, but his friends weren't fooled.

#19 Batu Is Accepted by The Boys

Through generations, dwarfs made offerings to the giant fish, believing it to be a dragon spirit that guarded the lake and forest. Hunting them was not just sacrilege; the repercussions would be disastrous for the clan.

JiaShao expressed his fears. "I feel a deep sense of unease about hunting sacred spirits. SuJin will need to bear the burden of any curses from the spirits. He is responsible, irrespective of what the Hun or WoShi wants. The dwarfs will ensure a ceremony of death befitting a pious soul once we catch the fish."

Qian looked around and said, "SuJin is not here, Master JiaShao, to receive your curses. What's the big deal in hunting a fish? We eat them all the time, and your men are fishermen. How many have they caught over the years!"

JiaShao was angry. "Did you see the fish surface while you were here? It came out to a call from SuJin."

Qian said, "Aw, come on, Master. SuJin threw the stone that attracted the fish. We didn't do that before."

SuWu said, "I am baffled by the need to hunt this fish. Why not any other fish?"

JiaShao replied, "I assure you, SuWu, that these fish are spirits, and they know SuJin. The dragonfish is moving about restlessly and breaching the surface. I haven't seen such behaviour, nor have the dwarf elders in their lifetimes. This is beyond us."

JiaShao frowned at his men laughing boisterously at the lake's edge and bellowed at them, "Be warned! Forfeiting a life is the bare minimum you can expect when dealing with powerful spirits."

To hunt the giant fish, the dwarfs cut long bamboo from the forests and assembled a raft under the supervision of Tong and Wong.

Long lines of braided silk were laid out on the sandy bank, ending with brass hooks thicker than a grown man's thumb, with the other end looped and fastened to metal loops on the raft. The plan was to row the raft around and tire the animal once it snagged on the hook. It would make it easier for the men to drag the animal to the shallow end.

SuWu watched Batu rummaging within a cart and grimaced in distaste. "No one wants to ask the Hun about his intentions."

JiaShao patted SuWu on the arm and said, "Now, you boys, stay away from the barbarian. He is quite a handful. Let me handle him. He seems friendlier to us dwarfs."

Batu looked up, gave a high-pitched whistle, and waved at JiaShao. "What does he want, now?" grumbled JiaShao. "Hope he doesn't want to hang one of us dwarfs as bait!" SuWu guffawed.

JiaShao approached Batu, and they spoke animatedly. Tuhu had sent carpenters to the dwarf village with instructions on making the wooden presses to shape the recurve bow, and WoShi had paid for them. Together, they took stock of the presses and other tools while unloading the cart.

SuWu heard the bleating of sheep and saw dwarfs slaughter them for bait. The offal, mixed with blood, was poured into bamboo baskets lined with pine sap to make them watertight. Choice chunks of meat were distributed to the cookfires. All the huts stood empty as the entire community gathered to witness the hunt, creating a festive atmosphere!

Wong hailed JiaShao, "Chief! The raft is ready, and we had better go now. The water's too cold, and our feet are freezing."

JiaShao left Batu to his intrigues and rushed to the raft, folding his breeches to his thighs. SuWu and Qian did the same and clambered onto the raft. They shrieked together when freezing water splashed through the gaps in the bamboo raft and wet their feet.

The cold numbed their feet, and they had to take turns manning the raft. Qian pierced goat meat onto the hooks with shivering hands. Dwarfs in two fishing boats towed the big raft to the middle of the lake.

JiaShao gestured with his thick arms while dwarfs on the boats tipped buckets of blood and offal into the crystal-clear water. After a brief pause, the water around the raft churned silver as fish of all sizes fell into a feeding frenzy. Despite the chaos, tightly packed fish swirled with a noticeable gap in the middle, turning and roiling but avoiding something beneath.

SuWu called out to no one in particular, "The dragonfish is beneath us!" Qian cast two lines with hooks overboard into the throng of fish. They felt many tugs on the lines as fish followed the bait, but the smaller fish tore it apart before the hooks reached the lakebed.

Unable to handle the cold for long, they exchanged places with the fishermen from the smaller boats. This time, they pulled in two large bighead carp fish. They tried again and caught more carp but did not hook the dragonfish.

The dwarf fishermen engaged in animated discussions, concluding that the line was not reaching the lake bottom where the giant sturgeons resided despite the heavy hooks. The smaller fish were stripping the bait apart. JiaShao commanded, "Let's return to the shore and think this through. My bottom is frozen stiff, and my toes are blue." They decided to try again after lunch.

The fishermen were greeted heartily with their haul of carp piled on the raft. Women quickly rubbed their wet bodies dry, and the men sat near the cookfires to warm their wrinkled hands and feet. Despite their failure to snare the dragonfish, the mood was upbeat because they expected to hook it shortly. Lunch was lavish, and hot mutton soups, grilled mutton, carp, and snow trout steaks were served.

When they returned to catch the dragonfish, they did not throw offal to attract smaller fish. Instead, they dropped the heavy hooks, and the bait quickly sank into the depths. They did not have to wait long before one of the lines tugged and became taut. The bamboo raft swung hard and tilted at one end.

The dwarfs on the boat screamed out instructions, "This is it! Move backwards! Balance the pull! Let the fish tire out!" SuWu, JiaShao, and others moved back while Qian lay down to test the silk rope and found it stiff as a bronze rod. The men were euphoric at snagging the massive fish when the second line stretched taut! Another one! The fish yanked the lines hard from below, causing the large raft to tilt precariously and, to the horror of the men watching, be dragged into the lake.

The men on the raft fell unceremoniously into the icy water. Amid shouts from the boats, those overboard swam desperately towards the smaller vessels, screaming in terror. After witnessing the sheer power of the creature from the depths, they feared an attack.

Suddenly, the raft righted itself with a loud splash and floated serenely on the surface.

Ignoring the biting cold and displaying no fear, Qian climbed onto the raft and pulled the fishing lines. They came away quickly into his hands. He held up the frayed ends of the thick line and shouted in dismay, "Cut! The hooks are gone."

Drenched and shivering from the cold, the men quietly rowed back, realising that the hunt was dangerous – Had the monster fish made its escape, or had they escaped its crushing jaws? Despite all the anxious faces and hushed whispers, Qian was euphoric! He was confident they would catch the fish soon and was thrilled by the exciting hunt.

As they gathered by the fireside for lunch, he danced naked with an impromptu song, much to the dismay of those present.

He severed our lines and shattered our raft, but victory will be mine,
Mark my words, O' dragonfish, in coals, you'll make your bed.
Your bones shall weave a woollen pair, Yima shall have needles spare,
Mark my words, O' dragonfish, in coals, you'll make your bed.
Your fat will light our wicks so bright, A torch against the night,
Mark my words, O' dragonfish, in coals, you'll make your bed.
Content we'll burp, my wife and I, hum'in lullabies,
Mark my words, O' dragonfish, in coals, you'll make your bed.

The dwarfs, led by Tong, Dong, and Wong, joined the dance, swaying around the fire, whistling in unison to Qian's verses and singing the chorus together.

HuKui tapped a baffled JiaShao on his shoulder and said, "Qian has gone mad! It must be something he picked up with the forbidden troops. Singing a song to insult his enemy."

JiaShao muttered gruffly, "No enemies here! The swim in the freezing water has addled his brain!" After a pause, he added, "We dwarfs are considered odd because of our short stature! Look around at all these boys in their prime! Each one crazier than the next!"

HuKui chuckled. "Can't deny that! The gods do seem to have a sense of humour!" Looking at the dwarfs dancing, he asked, "What about your boys? They are dancing too. Aren't they crazy?"

JiaShao frowned and said, "Nah, they're just shaking their limbs to keep warm."

****

As daylight faded, they lost more hooks and had to stop fishing when the raft upended again. Dinner was a sombre affair, with plenty of hot tea and fish. SuJin joined them for dinner and listened to all that happened but remained aloof.

SuWu enquired, "Where were you, Prince?"

SuJin trained his finger at the tall peak behind them and said, "On that! I was meditating."

Batu yawned loudly and interjected, "Sorry to state the obvious, but we have loads of fish, but not the fish."

A livid JiaShao blurted, "What is the need to catch the dragonfish? We have caught so many different ones. Why can't you go for the paddlefish, carp, or choose any other?"

HuKui took the opportunity to reinforce the question. "Yes, Batu! Why do we need to catch the monster fish?"

Batu contemplated seriously for a while, grunted, and nodded his head. "I shall confide everything, provided the right motivation is given." HuKui's eyebrows cinched together.

Chuckling, JiaShao lifted his short arm and stood up. "Batu, my friendly Hun, we shall serve you wine. I apologise for not treating you like the true barbarian you are!" Batu's eyes lit up.

"JiaShao, my dear friend, by far, you are the tallest man in this valley!" He said and bowed low.

JiaShao tutted with a smile. "Ah, Batu! To a dwarf, you have just given the highest of compliments. I hope our wine takes you beyond the realms of barbarians to the hallowed pastures." Batu grinned.

"Today, my friend, I will go so high that I shall converse with the spirits roaming above the clouds and sniff the flowers growing in the heavens."

ChenHe sarcastically remarked, "For all you know, he could descend into hell, meet his clan and come away with a splitting headache." Batu glanced at him and grinned wickedly. The dwarfs erupted in laughter; nothing more entertaining than watching two men build up the tension and posturing for an explosive ego clash.

A fat wineskin was sent around the fire to cheer up the disheartened men. Women sat in the outer circle, listening to the men, whispering to each other. Batu moved closer to the fire, and everybody crowded in to listen.

Batu took a long and appreciative swig of the rice wine. He reluctantly passed the wineskin to HuKui, seated beside him, and lifted a fish steak off the smouldering fire. Batu bit into the steaming meat and said something appreciatively in his native tongue. He translated, "This is the good life! Sharing tall stories while we drink with the sky fathers." The women giggled; they were his devoted admirers.

He looked at the women and asked, "Beautiful women, listening to the heroic tales of their men explaining how that one massive fish..." He paused in suspense and said, "...escaped, with hook, line and raft!" The women squealed with laughter, much to the men's discomfort.

JiaShao stood up, placed his hands on his hips, and regarded Batu disapprovingly. "If it's so easy to catch the dragonfish, why don't *you* go into the lake!"

Batu shrugged his shoulders indifferently, "Not my job!"

Uncharacteristically, SuJin intervened. "He is afraid of water."

A resentful HuKui asked, "What's his interest in the fish then?"

Batu frowned at the morsel of fish in his hand and said, "This fish needs more salt." It took a few more swigs of wine before JiaShao and HuKui could loosen Batu's tongue.

"The Bow, the double recurve bow, is a legend," Batu said, standing up and enacting the pose of the deity. SuWu understood and quickly explained to the assembled men that Batu was referring to the idols they saw at the school holding recurve bows.

"Very much the same," Batu frowned at the interruption.

SuWu continued disregarding Batu's slow narration. "That bow is a composite double recurve bow, a formidable weapon of war." SuWu paused and added, "Unlike crossbows, these bows need incredible strength and stability of hand to strike a target. You can decimate a small army by firing arrows over a long distance, arrows that go whistling to punch through shields and armour."

Qian asked, "How far can the arrow travel?" SuWu looked at Batu for an answer.

Batu took another swig. "A little less than a Li," he said, and the men gasped.

"Impossible!" scoffed ChenHe, "that is more than two thousand steps."

Batu ignored ChenHe and said, "The archer would need great arm strength, like lifting two hundred Jin of weight." He cheekily added, "A little less than the weight of this man," gesturing at ChenHe, but no one laughed.

"How do you know this? You weren't there with us to see the deities, and it's all melted now," said ChenHe.

"True, I wasn't there. So, what?" Batu retorted.

JiaShao raised his hand. "CaoShen would have shown Batu the deities." SuWu looked at JiaShao in surprise. The dwarf chief nodded and said, "Days after WangMang's visit, we made a cast of the deities in clay. We constructed a replica of the shrine in the cavern below." The boys glared at JiaShao for not disclosing this earlier.

A shocked SuWu said, "Let me guess, WoShi isn't aware!"

With a twinkle in his eye, JiaShao replied, "We haven't had the opportunity to discuss this matter with him."

SuWu asked, "Why? Why not tell WoShi?"

JiaShao pointed his finger at SuJin and SuWu, saying heatedly, "For you! WoShi did not show any urgency in locating you. What if WangMang desecrated or destroyed the place? At that time, we didn't even know that you existed! All of you arrived years later, and that too as boys."

SuWu nodded and bowed in humility, "Of course."

Batu beckoned for the wineskin that Qian was holding, who was listening intently. "Ahh, all this tongue-wagging makes a warrior thirsty." Qian extended his arm just as ChenHe lunged for it. Batu was a shade quicker in snatching it.

SuWu missed the unfolding drama between his burly sworn brother and the Hun. As the grinning audience watched a brawl develop, SuWu explained, "If we are going to Tianzhu and the warriors there use these weapons, we shouldn't be left wanting. We ought to be able to wield them, too."

Batu happily exclaimed, "Yes, yes," as he patted his wineskin. SuWu was uncertain whether he was admiring the wine or his assessment.

"We don't have the strength to pull such a bow," lamented Qian.

"Nor the stamina to sustain three to four hours of intense archery with that bow," Batu added.

Qian's wife, Ren, asked, "Why have we carried the wooden presses?" SuWu stared at her.

Batu turned to her and whistled appreciatively. "You're not just beautiful; you're intelligent as well. Taken?" Laughing, she patted her pregnant belly. HuKui looked surreptitiously at SuWu, who had stiffened at the exchange. Batu did not miss either of their reactions.

Batu showed Ren an exaggerated face of disappointment. Holding his chest, he grimaced as if he were dying. The ladies and the dwarfs laughed at his antics.

ChenHe snatched the wineskin from Batu's hand, and he frowned.

SuJin cleared his throat, and the fireside quietened down. "What has all this got to do with the dragonfish?"

Batu bowed to SuJin and immediately responded, "It's all for the glue preparation, my Prince." Batu was met with frowns and a flurry of questions. He explained, "These bows are composite, made of bamboo, wood, and metal strips. It's an ingenious combination of all three! All of these materials are bound together to create the bow. Each layer is cured before the next one is added on top, and the special ingredient here is the magical glue that holds it all together."

SuWu asked excitedly, "So, this glue will you get from the fish?" Batu clawed at his throat exaggeratedly as if he were dying of thirst. HuKui reached across, pulled the wineskin from a furious ChenHe, and handed it back to Batu. Batu grinned in appreciation.

HuKui apologised, "ChenHe, we can't let him stop now. We need to know the purpose."

Thrilled, SuWu repeated in wonder, oblivious to the tension building beside him, "This fish provides the glue."

Batu took a long swig, wiped his mouth on his sleeve, and swayed on his feet. "The large ones must be several hundred years old and emit a thick substance from their insides. Sometimes, they are as hard as stones. We powder it, melt it in a pot, and it becomes glue. It sets hard once applied."

"Like pearls?" voiced JiaShao.

With a creased forehead, Batu asked, "What's a pearl?"

HuKui immediately interjected, saying, "Never mind that!" He did not want the discussion to meander again.

SuWu leaned closer to Batu and asked, "Won't it rot?"

Batu shook his head and said, "No, but we must keep it in oilskins and away from moisture. With some care, it should serve us well for many years. We can wet the bow, but not with vinegar, as it will melt the glue."

Ren said, "SuWu, the wooden presses are to shape the bow."

Batu bowed low and said, "That's right, lady."

Qian turned towards the lake, threw his arms wide, and said, "Hear me, giant monsters, spawn of the river dragons. I will melt you into glue."

JiaShao screamed, mortified, "What are you doing, Qian? They will hear you! Do not mock the spirits."

Qian scoffed, saying, "You just heard the barbarian, Master. They are just fish! Massive sturgeons from the river. Not spirits!"

Batu cautioned Qian, "Tuhu told me that they are intelligent beings."

In disbelief, Qian looked at Batu and said, "Intelligent? A fish!"

"Tuhu told me that we would meet dragons here."

JiaShao threw his stunted arms wide and lamented, "What made that pious man disclose this ancient secret to you, a barbarian!"

Batu chuckled and said, "Not for me. He did it for SuJin." He paused before continuing, "Tuhu also said that the spirit would consider melding into a worthy being upon its host's death."

SuJin asked, "What about the making of a recurve bow?"

SuWu leaned in to listen to Batu, having realised he always provided a straightforward answer to the Prince.

Batu said, "WoShi shared a scroll with Tuhu that contained instructions on how to make this bow. He mentioned it had been passed down through grandmasters since the time of the first emperor. Tuhu said we would find the beings here that could give us the glue, and CaoShen gave me a map."

HuKui groaned, "Isn't this too much?"

JiaShao said, "We are all sacrificing our lives for SuJin. Now, nature itself will die for him! God, help him leave Han soon!" Just then, a dwarf whispered into JiaShao's ear, and he followed him.

ChenHe approached Batu and snatched the wineskin from his grasp. He drank deeply, gulp after gulp, finishing it all. With a loud belch, he thrust the empty wineskin into the chest of a belligerent Batu. ChenHe said, "Han rice wine is far too intoxicating for you, barbarian. Don't drink too much of it."

Batu burst into Hun expletives and said, "Ah, finally a Han, challenging a Hun after a few swigs of wine! I swear that a lactating pup from the steppe could piss more on a night like this than you can drink."

Batu threw his arms wide and told the grinning dwarfs, "Why don't you use him as the raft? He is broad and has enough foul air to render the fish unconscious." An outraged ChenHe blustered and retorted with profanities, leading to a heated argument between them.

In a drunken stupor, they shoved one another, preparing for a brawl. ChenHe's wife came wailing and pulled him away.

A disgusted SuWu saw SuJin watching the scuffle with a smile. He angrily yelled at SuJin, "Why are you smiling at the behaviour of this foul-mouthed drunkard? A Hun is insulting our brother!"

SuJin continued to smile and said, "Ask me about Batu's drunken behaviour sometime later, SuWu. When you get to know him better."

It was a cryptic response, but SuWu huffed at him. "Then, it will be sometime soon." They looked at the two drunks standing apart, trading insults about their country, family lineage, and culture. In the end, Batu staggered away, whistling a nimble tune. ChenHe consoled his weeping wife and returned to the fire.

Frustrated, SuWu remarked, "If we have to keep giving him a drink to get some information out, we will be here for a long time."

SuJin laughed loudly and said, "Oh, SuWu, that's what he thinks of your fishing. We shall be here for quite a while." His sworn brothers glared at the Prince.

ChenHe turned to SuJin and yelled, his words slurred by wine. "How can you tolerate that grass-eating mongrel...?"

JiaShao returned and said, "Enough! That is our Prince." ChenHe stopped spewing swearwords, but he thumped his chest repeatedly in frustration.

JiaShao said, "WoShi has sent word through our men. Many have arrived today. They left Changan because CaoShen was worried about an imminent search of the school premises. He has sealed the entrances to the underground tunnels, and the dwarfs who could be spared have come here. This means we'll be here through winter."

HuKui stood up and told everyone grimly, "We can't be complacent with the Prince in our midst. Trouble accompanies him."

Qian retorted, "Yes! We know that, Master HuKui. He is accompanied by trouble in the form of Batu, the incorrigible Hun." The dwarfs laughed, and some of the pent-up tension dissipated.

SuJin stood up, looking tense after listening to JiaShao. HuKui and JiaShao followed him as he walked to the lake's edge. SuJin fell to his knees and pressed his forehead to the sandy bank in obeisance. They heard him say, "Hear me, dragon spirit, protector of the lake and forests. Let God's will manifest through me to appease our ancestors. Become a part of us if you find us honest in our pursuit!"

JiaShao teared up at SuJin's reverence for the spirits and hugged him with his stunted arms. "You are a good man, humble and pious. The spirits will surely answer your prayers." A big splash in the lake made them look up. Waves rolled over the place where SuJin had touched his head.

"The spirit has heard you," JiaShao said fervently. Scooping up the water, he threw it over his head in devotion. He asked SuJin to return to the camp fireside.

JiaShao told the boys about SuJin's prayer and how the spirits acknowledged him by splashing in the lake. Qian rolled his eyes and declared, "It's a fish, not a spirit, master. Our Prince has gone overboard with Tuhu's influence."

JiaShao scoffed at Qian and said, "Be quiet! Don't you dare insult the spirits?" He kept his hand on SuJin and continued, "I am not finished speaking. WoShi has commanded that once the bows are ready, all of you must undergo archery training. HuKui and I will teach you how to survive in the forest world."

Qian looked confused at this suggestion and reminded JiaShao, "Master, if I recall correctly, we are trained in archery."

JiaShao said, "I was referring to the Tianzhu bow."

ChenHe ridiculed JiaShao. "A bow is a bow, however fancy it looks! Pull the string, point at the target; leave the string, and the arrow goes forward."

JiaShao admonished ChenHe, "Is a long sword, a short sword, and a dagger all the same to you?" ChenHe gave a sheepish grin, and the boys chuckled.

Qian asked, "Who did you say would train us on these new bows?"

JiaShao smiled in unrestrained delight, and Qian and ChenHe looked at each other in horror.

ChenHe asked JiaShao hoarsely, "Come again. Who did you say would train us? That barbarian?" JiaShao stared back at him without answering, but his broad smile said it all.

Qian was furious. "What?! What can we possibly learn from that arrogant drunkard? Has Master WoShi lost his senses to make our mortal enemy a trainer? Savage? Slave! We are the finest archers in Han and do not need a barbarian mother-in-law to instruct us!"

ChenHe added, "Unless we are shooting at him!"

SuJin interjected fiercely, "Enough! Batu shall decide your training." That halted all arguments, and he continued, "We begin once the bow is ready. Batu wants us to unlearn the crossbow and strengthen our arms." SuJin glanced at the hostile faces surrounding him and said, "Later, he will teach us to shoot from the saddle, the Hun way, using smaller bows."

Qian leaned over to ChenHe and whispered, "You can bet the good days are over. Arduous work begins, but before that, let's teach that mongrel of a Hun a few archery lessons." ChenHe grinned.

SuJin excused himself, and SuWu accompanied him. Qian waited until SuJin was beyond earshot and told JiaShao, "Little master, we will show you how to shoot arrows. No barbarian can match our abilities."

JiaShao frowned and said, "But the Prince specifically asked you not to use crossbows."

"Don't worry, little master. This is just a small demonstration to the Hun to crush his arrogance. A slave can't become a master just because our Prince is humble and falls for all these rubbish talks from Tuhu. We won't take things lying down!"

ChenHe added, "I want to see that condescending smirk wiped off his face."

JiaShao grinned, never one to back down from a chance to wager. "So, we can bet on who is better at archery – the haughty Han lads or the mannerless Hun! No decent dwarf worth his salted fish will pass up such a mouthwatering challenge." JiaShao hailed his fellow dwarfs, alerting them to the opportunity to wager.

Dwarfs love gambling, and eventually, everything Qian and ChenHe owned, including their hanfu, knives, sandals, combs, and precious earrings, was pledged for the wager. Qian and ChenHe left happily for their huts, slapping each other on the back. They had just made a fortune at the expense of the gullible dwarfs.

Tong told a grinning JiaShao, "You look mighty pleased. It will be a valuable lesson for them not to underestimate their opponent, particularly Batu."

JiaShao laughed. "Childish ego drives these boys. This will be a hard lesson in humility!"

Wong said, "Master, we run a risk on the wager! We haven't seen the Hun use a bow?"

"Did I not tell the boys!" He grinned, adding, "Oh, it must have slipped my mind! You will find Batu to be an exceptional archer. The dwarf boys who have come in from Changan swear that Batu's skills are extraordinary."

Wong grinned with his chief, "So, there is no risk!"

JiaShao said, "Most of you will train alongside the boys. I shall convince Batu."

****

As the days passed, they caught numerous fish but lost even more hooks to the elusive dragonfish. The boys, especially Qian, became increasingly desperate.

In the meantime, Batu, with the help of the dwarfs, had built a large hut with sloping roofs. He set up wooden frames, metal links, horns, feathers, and carpentry tools in specific arrangements to make the bow. The children followed him, curious and asking questions about the various contraptions, and a fortunate few began to work for him.

Batu and the dwarfs hunted deer and killed a few old horses to extract fibres from their tendons, and the venison was sent to the cookfires. The misty valley was unsuitable for sun drying, so they cured the skin and tendons along with the fish in the sunny valley beyond the gorge. The skins of the animals were stretched to create oilskins for storing the bows, and Batu instructed the dwarfs to beat the dried tendons to extract the stiff muscle fibres for weaving bowstrings.

A couple of days later, JiaShao announced to the boys that Batu had gathered all the components and was ready to assemble the composite recurve bow. He needed the fish glue.

They were running low on wine, and Batu complained boisterously about the rationing, ensuring everyone knew of the unfortunate situation.

JiaShao sent his men to the village to purchase provisions from the farmers, including wine. They were also instructed to bring larger hooks made by the blacksmith.

****

A week later, JiaShao summoned the boys. "Traders have been informed about a dangerous outlaw, a Hun, and possibly a boy travelling together. Their portraits and horses are described on hemp paper, pasted at all waystations. One horse is black with white hooves, while the other has a diamond patch on its head. Gold coins are offered as a reward for their information or capture."

SuJin was shocked and asked Batu. "How did they get the description of the horses?"

"We bought these horses from a trader known to the Hun," Batu said, adding, "Good to know that we can't return to him. Surely, he is now compromised."

When they sat down for dinner that evening, Batu said, "This is horse meat. Did we butcher any today?" He paused dramatically and continued, "Unless... one of them died of boredom?"

JiaShao laughed heartily and said, "We haven't killed any horses. This is the meat from the horse you butchered earlier."

Batu screwed up his face in disgust. "*Ptui!*" He spat the meat out. "That was many days ago—putrefied, cold meat. You dirty Han eat carrion, *ugh*! What will your ancestors say to this? How dare you call *me* a barbarian!"

Qian's face flushed with irritation. "The meat was stored beneath the glacial ice; it hasn't spoiled!"

In annoyance, Batu said, "I am willing to exchange my share of long-dead, putrefied horse flesh for your wine."

HuKui snorted and said, "Batu, I suggest you keep your hands away from everything purified, especially the rice wine. It's putrefied rice! What about your precious airag— putrefied horse milk? Have you tainted the graves of your ancestors by pouring wine?" There were nods and smiles all around at the apt rejoinder from a scholar.

Batu grinned but changed his line of attack. "Boys! It seems we will be here a little longer while we wait for the fish to die of old age." The dwarfs and the ladies laughed as Batu told stories about how the old dragonfish would surrender to the frustrated men by clinging to their long beards that fell into the lake.

Batu's crass comments hit Qian hard as he watched his wife, Ren, wiping tears of laughter from her eyes. He signalled to SuWu and ChenHe, and they left the fireplace in a huff.

****

Early the next day, hearing voices, Batu came out of his hut and found ChenHe holding a crossbow, aiming at a target some distance away. Batu swore loudly, "What the... that's my leather cap."

The target was a travesty drawn with wet charcoal on a board made with bamboo slats. Batu's cap, folded to resemble a wineskin, was pouring wine into his mouth. Bulging fish scales were his eyes, and dry pine leaves were used for his hair. The entire camp had turned up, and people giggled and laughed from either side of the target. Mothers held on to screaming toddlers, not allowing them to cross the target area.

Upon seeing Batu, the crowd erupted in a cheerful welcome. Hearing the commotion, SuJin stepped outside. After a quick appraisal, he settled on a rocky outcrop, a barely suppressed smile playing on his lips.

The board was mounted on a three-legged bamboo support. Qian examined the bracing pole, which provided stability to the target board. He waved his hands, signalling that it was secure. Qian stretched and paced, loudly counting twenty long steps to the chant of the boisterous audience.

Batu walked over to the bamboo bucket of water beside their hut and angrily punched through the thin ice. He splashed water on his face, gargled exaggeratedly, and spat it at ChenHe's feet. ChenHe shrieked in disgust, provoking roars of laughter.

Batu shouted his challenge, "So, you white-bellied Han…" He included everyone gathered in an arc, finally stopping at ChenHe. "And this barrel of lard wants to challenge me, the greatest archer from the steppes."

"Ha, let me see that…," he shouted, delighting the dwarfs who had placed their bets on him earlier. They hooted with a series of owl calls, showing their support to the annoyance of the womenfolk, who backed their men.

Batu said, "Go on, you pompous Han brats, show me what you got."

ChenHe grinned at Batu and said softly, "This is it, dung-smeared nomad! We won't tolerate any more of your insults. We shall show you what true archery is. Double recurve bow! My stinking foot in dung!" ChenHe pulled the drawstring back and locked the crossbow into the firing position. He walked to the distance marker that Qian had drawn and stood behind it.

ChenHe aimed, relaxed, licked his finger, adjusted the height and angle, and fired the first arrow. It zipped out, hitting the top edge of the target board. The crowd erupted in cheers and applause. He took his time with the second arrow, which struck the board, drawing more cheers. The third arrow found its mark, striking Batu's cap, fastened on the board as a wineskin. The onlookers erupted into wild excitement as his wife ran to hug him.

ChenHe's wife screamed out at Batu, "If it were a real Hun enemy, he would be lying dead on the grass by now." The lively audience whooped in delight, and Batu spat on the ground.

Next was Qian. He came and stood behind the target line, and pregnant Ren screamed, "Qian, your son is dancing inside me! My eyes are his eyes, and he is watching his father." The ladies hooted and laughed as she added, "Make him proud of his father."

Qian used a different crossbow, which was probably used by the forbidden troops. The bow fired smaller darts and had a lever to pull the bowstring and load the darts quickly. The distance for firing darts was considerable, and as he aimed, there was palpable tension in the watching crowd because the bow looked puny. Whispers died, and silence reigned.

Qian fired six darts, drawing, aiming, and firing the darts in one continuous motion. All the darts hit the caricature drawn, and with screams of joy, the crowd rushed in to smother a grinning Qian.

Batu smiled stiffly and said harshly to SuWu, "Now, let's see what you have."

Although he was prepared, SuWu hesitated and glanced at SuJin, but the Prince remained non-committal. ChenHe moved the crowd back for SuWu's demonstration as he fired arrows from a longer distance, further from their mark. Qian counted thirty strides from the target board, and the crowd whooped!

SuWu held a regular bamboo bow used by hunters and pushed five long arrows into the sandy soil, keeping one in his hand. He aimed and let loose the first missile. Unlike the shot by ChenHe or Qian, this arrow was released with power and thudded into the wooden board with a solid thwack! The target would have toppled over but for the bracing support behind. Whooping loudly, Qian ran to the target and checked the bracing support, ensuring it was set wider to withstand further impact.

SuWu punched three more arrows on the cap into a broad square. Qian ran to the target and drew a square box with a piece of charcoal around the arrows. He squealed and danced around the target before he broke away. Onlookers went berserk as men and women clapped and shouted, "SuWu, SuWu," having witnessed one of the best archery demonstrations of their lives.

SuWu notched the final arrow, and taking careful aim, he paused his breathing and gently let loose the barb. The shaft leapt out of the bow and flew across the open space in an arc. *Thwack!* After a silence in anticipation, the crowd erupted into wild cheers. The arrow was embedded right in the centre of the square Qian had drawn around the four arrows. The last shot had the finality of a skill that couldn't be bettered. Dwarfs moved close to the target board to marvel at the phenomenal shot.

ChenHe tapped a rhythm with bamboo batons while Qian hooted in sync with the beat. Qian started an impromptu dance around Batu, soon joined by the younger men and women, laughing and shouting in carefree delight. The dwarfs picked up the rhythm, tapping batons against trees and logs. ChenHe, leaving his batons behind, joined the dance with his wife.

Batu watched them stoically and walked over to SuWu. He had to shout above the noise. "That was impressive. The shots will shatter the board once you work more on your wrist strength." SuWu listened with half a mind; his eyes were on beautiful Ren. She danced with Qian, hopping from one foot to the other with her swollen belly.

ChenHe laughed raucously at Batu's comment, and to the crowd's utter delight, he fell on his back and cycled his arms and legs, mimicking an infant. Qian hooted and said, "SuWu almost toppled the target with the power of his arrows, and this barbarian says he needs to strengthen his wrist."

Qian danced towards the dwarfs, holding his hand out and closing his fists alternately, demanding payment against the wager. JiaShao, dancing with him, motioned that they had to see Batu's archery skills to finalise the wager. Qian danced towards Batu and goaded him to take up the challenge. The Hun stood resolute, ignoring his plea.

JiaShao pleaded, "Batu. Show us why WoShi holds you in high esteem for archery."

Batu waved his hands with a grunt, declining the challenge. "I am not a street performer."

SuJin stood up, and the dancing stopped. He thundered, "It's time, Batu! Show them archery! I will catch the fish."

Batu stared at SuJin for some time and bowed. "As you command, Prince. I was planning my revenge to slog them in training. On second thoughts, let me humiliate them now." Batu entered their hut and returned with a double-curve bow and a quiver full of arrows.

The curious onlookers noted that the arrows were different. They were longer and had a metal tip, while the other end was fletched with more feathers than usual. The chattering in the audience quietened to a persistent buzz when Batu notched an arrow. He walked further back from where SuWu had stood to hit the target.

Qian ridiculed his bravado. "What's he trying to do?" ChenHe did not answer. He glowered at Batu.

Without aim, the first few arrows left the bow, one after the other. The arrows whizzed and struck the bamboo tripod below the target board, an equal spacing on either side, from top to bottom, in a perfect line with a series of audible *thwacks*. It looked as if he was testing the range.

Batu took two more arrows, bit off the fletching of one of the arrows, and fired it to the right, away from the straw target, followed immediately by another that flew straight. The first arrow flew outward, curved in an arc, smashing into the bracing support behind the target, knocking it out askew.

The second arrow struck the target a split second later, uprooting it and sending it cartwheeling into the forest. The sheer disdain with which Batu dismissed the Han archery demonstration was mind-numbing.

In the silence that followed, SuWu fell to his knees and bowed his head in defeat.

"He is using magic! He is using magic!" Screamed one of the onlookers.

"He has charmed the arrows. They are listening to him," said another.

"How is this possible?"

JiaShao turned to Qian and asked with a smug face, "Do you accept defeat?"

Qian looked at JiaShao and sputtered, "He hasn't shot at the target-"

"Enough!!" shouted SuWu uncharacteristically loud, and ChenHe and Qian cowed down.

"I shall join in to repay your debts, but don't insult a bowmaster."

Upset at losing his cool on his brothers, SuWu explained in a milder tone to Qian and ChenHe. "Our chi is strong and bonded with the bow." He choked, paused, and said, "... but for Batu, the chi, his life force is bonded to the arrow."

Batu whistled to someone and entered the hut. Two small boys broke away from the crowd to fetch his arrows. A mother shouted among the onlookers, "So, this is what you do, learning from the Hun. You should have told me; I would have gladly let you go." The crowd quietly dispersed.

A thoroughly chastened SuWu approached SuJin and said, "I don't know if we can master such archery skills through training. He is an army in himself," SuWu remarked humbly, and SuJin responded with that knowing smile he had acquired from Tuhu.

SuWu said, "Honestly, you don't need us for Tianzhu. This one man is enough."

SuJin's smile widened. "Time, my sworn brother will show you what each of us is capable of."

The Prince held SuWu's shoulder and said, "Batu is a skilled archer, a warrior! He is someone reliable to have beside you in a battle, but you, SuWu, have the skills to avoid the battle itself! You are a strategist!"

"Your grasp of a situation to plan a siege or a long, drawn-out war is unmatched. WoShi considers you far superior to anyone he knows. I will fail in Tianzhu if you don't accompany me. Each of us has a role, and our destinies are entwined."

In an afterthought, SuWu said, "You have changed, SuJin! You have become a saint!"

20 Making of The Recurve Bow

Whenever Batu spoke, he was listened to with rapt attention, and all his requests were followed without question. Batu always had a wineskin in his hand as hidden stocks were opened for him.

As he walked around, accompanied by a group of admiring young boys, HuKui commented, "What a character! I can't believe that the Hun horde sent him to die. If they have a few more like him, we would be hard-pressed to defend the wall."

SuWu spoke to Qian and ChenHe, convincing them of Batu's worth despite their humiliation. They reluctantly agreed to suspend hostilities until they got to know him better.

Qian said, "We must catch that fish to regain our prestige. Ren keeps saying that she can't face the other women in the village after the barbarian's bashing."

ChenHe said, "Yes, capturing the fish will bring back the honour we lost!"

SuWu responded harshly, "ChenHe, we haven't lost any honour. We have merely lost to a better, more talented man. He is part of the golden glow, a big brother."

****

That evening, around the fire, SuWu asked SuJin, "You told Batu that you would catch the dragonfish."

SuJin nodded, "I am pleading with the spirits for that."

SuWu said, "I must confess that I have had dreams since we decided to catch the dragonfish. I always end up with the fish facing you underwater. It was as if the fish was waiting for you."

Qian chuckled, "Now, you are having dreams too, not just me!"

JiaShao looked at SuJin and said, "How can that be? Our Prince hasn't been on the lake, not once. Moreover, the water is too cold to dive below, and that option is ruled out." Polite smiles were exchanged all around. Frankly, no one expected the Prince to dirty his hands with the work of the lowly fishermen.

With piercing eyebrows, SuJin asked, "How long have you had this dream? I mean, how many times?" The serious tone in which SuJin asked the question made the boys pause.

SuWu gave a flippant reply, "All the time. I even daydream on the raft these days." Sensing something unusual, the boys waited expectantly. "It's the same dream always, with slight variations. Maybe the position that I watch changes in the dream."

Qian said, "Look, all of us are trying to catch the fish! We dream about it, so what? I, too, dream about fish, but I cannot touch any of them in my dreams. They go around me in circles!"

SuJin said, "I might be having the same dream as you. I see the monster fish and something behind it speak, but I can't hear them."

HuKui exclaimed, "Oh! Isn't it strange that all of you dream of fish?"

SuJin said, "I am going in there tomorrow." He gestured to the lake.

"No problem. We have plenty of space on the raft; it's just that your feet will get wet and go numb."

JiaShao jumped, spilling his bowl of soup. "What! You are so susceptible to cold, and you can fall ill. Moreover, lowly fishing is not the job for a Prince."

SuWu added, "That's right, Prince. We have lost all our hooks, and I don't see any difference with you coming onboard the raft."

SuJin looked SuWu in the eye and said, "I didn't mean going out on a raft. I want to go underwater!" Shocked silence greeted him, and

JiaShao could have been knocked over with a feather.

HuKui joked, "Don't tell me you can breathe in water."

"No, I can't, but I can hold my breath longer. We practised holding our breath with WoShi to achieve stillness in the head. I have further practised calming my breath with Tuhu. I mean, holding my breath and chanting to keep my mind and body still, ignoring the elements."

HuKui was not swayed by this grand statement and ridiculed SuJin. "Prince, we have seen that you can't handle the cold. How do you intend to endure the extreme cold of the water?" He reminded SuJin, "We wipe your body with hot water. You sit by the fireside and sleep under a pile of blankets with your mattress heated by rocks. Perish this insane thought!"

SuWu recognised that look of defiance in SuJin, and he nodded ever so slightly.

JiaShao intervened. "No one, not even the experienced dwarf fishermen, knows how deep this lake is. Who knows what monsters and dark spirits reside in the murky depths?"

Realising that SuJin was indeed serious about going underwater, HuKui became angry. "Why? We can't stay on the raft for long with just our feet wet, and you want to immerse yourself in that freezing water? It's sheer madness—a death wish!"

SuJin gave that all-knowing smile that SuWu was now wary of and addressed HuKui and JiaShao, "Masters, the cold affects me; believe me on that. To meet the dragonfish, I must go underwater. I climb these mountains to chant prayers in the biting winds. I hold my breath to become one with this extreme weather."

HuKui opened his mouth to protest, but SuJin stopped him. "I've made my decision. Please accept it. Moreover, it seems you have exhausted all your options for catching the fish with hooks."

JiaShao looked hurt by SuJin's words. "So be it. Prince of Destiny.

These are no ordinary times, nor are you an ordinary man. Why should you listen to insignificant men like us."

SuJin leaned over, took hold of JiaShao's hands, and said sincerely, "Let me try, master. We are not getting anywhere." JiaShao stiffened when SuJin grasped his hands, but after a moment, he relented.

JiaShao announced, "Let's pray and give offerings to Mazu, the sea goddess and daughter of the celestial dragon."

Qian reminded him, "Don't forget that I, too, dreamt of fish."

Still bristling with anger, HuKui mocked Qian. "You dreamt of small fish, not the big one." Qian grinned at HuKui.

Now that SuJin was determined to go underwater, Qian delved into its intricacies. "We must assess how long the Prince can hold his breath underwater. He must reach the lakebed swiftly, kill the fish, and emerge from the depths before he runs out of breath. We must dry him quickly and wrap him in warm blankets."

Qian added, "We must braid multiple lines to reinforce an arrow or a spear. Fasten some ropes around SuJin, and let's have several men pull him out quickly."

SuWu added, "He should hold a large stone to reach the lakebed faster."

JiaShao and HuKui's faces reflected their worry while the dwarfs murmured among themselves, with many cynics shaking their heads in disbelief. A concerned HuKui told JiaShao, "I am going home; I simply can't cope with this." He walked a short distance before stopping, saying, "Call me for the prayer to Goddess Mazu. I will ask my wife to prepare special food to appease the goddess with our offerings."

****

Early the next day, SuWu went to SuJin's hut to escort him to the lake.

Batu was packing grain and leftovers from the camp. SuWu was curious and asked, "I hear that you ride out to the rim of the valley most days. Are you scouting? Isn't this valley too misty to see anything?"

Batu mounted his horse. "My friend, I am alive this long not because of chance or faith. I am alive because I don't believe calm and peace can last long." He patted the two reed baskets tied on either side of the horse and said, "I spread grain and food in and around the paths for birds and small creatures. Animals, like humans, follow patterns. In time, birds will recognise and treat us as one of them. They will alert us to intruders just as they warn their own, with or without a mist. They are our first perimeter of security."

When Batu left, Qian caught up with SuWu and asked, "Is he on his way for Hun-specific morning ablution? Crazy Huns must ride a horse to start their day!"

SuWu chuckled and said, "No, he is protecting us." Qian looked at SuWu questioningly, and he explained.

Qian expressed his admiration. "The man is overpowering, true, but as we come closer, he grows on you!"

****

Naked, SuJin chanted his prayers and flexed his limbs, but he could not control his body from shuddering in the extreme cold. JiaShao said, "Shouldn't we do this in the afternoon?" SuJin refused, although they could see puffs of his breath in the frigid air as he breathed hard. The dwarfs tied a leather belt around his waist and looped a thick rope to haul him up. SuJin sat with his legs crossed over one another, and when he motioned, they lowered him into the lake near the shore, where it was shallow.

He did not sink but bobbed in the water and fell over, slamming his head on the raft's side. He cried out in pain, bleeding from a bruise. They pulled him in, and SuWu attended to his bruise while ChenHe rubbed him dry with blankets.

SuJin shuddered uncontrollably, his teeth chattering from his brief exposure to the freezing water. Despair was evident everywhere, as the first attempt had failed.

JiaShao urged them to give up, but after warming up a bit, a shivering SuJin insisted they should continue. Surprisingly, JiaShao's trusted men, Wong and Tong, encouraged SuJin to try again and asked JiaShao to leave.

An hour later, they tried again but placed a rock on his crossed legs, and this time, he sank quickly. The men on the raft held their breath to time SuJin underwater. They watched him sit serenely on the sandy lakebed with hardly any air bubbles escaping him. Despite all of them letting out their breaths in gasps, SuJin remained motionless, and SuWu panicked.

They pulled SuJin out, and he surfaced, shivering yet elated. He smiled and signalled that he could have stayed underwater longer while SuWu rubbed him dry. His ability to hold his breath was phenomenal, but he had bruised his leg where the rock had scraped him when they dragged him up, and his head throbbed from the knock he had sustained earlier.

It took them more than three days to perfect the drop. SuJin raised his hand to indicate that he wanted to surface, and the dwarfs sang and repeatedly recited a short verse praising goddess Mazu to measure his time spent underwater.

SuWu and the dwarfs perfected their routine. They would wipe SuJin dry, wrap him in woollen blankets, and carry him to the fire ashore to warm him. He would lie down on a bamboo pallet with heated stones underneath until he sweated.

SuWu said, "Although we are prepared regarding SuJin going

underwater, we still have a few problems to solve. How do we catch the fish? How do we bring it up?"

With his teeth chattering, SuJin added, "How can I see underwater?"

Qian recalled, "The people of the Mai kingdom use transparent shells over their eyes to hunt fish with barbed spears made from bamboo."

HuKui asked, "Really? Is that even possible?"

"I heard this from a master of the forbidden troops while discussing poison dart craftsmanship using sea snakes and cone snails."

HuKui flopped beside SuWu and said, "We need to honour and appease Oshun and NuWa, the goddess of this river. A solution will emerge."

Sitting beside the fire, SuJin was reasonably warmed and asked, "Does she have dragons?"

HuKui hesitantly replied, "LongMu, the goddess of the Yangtze River, has dragons. Have you seen her in your dreams?"

SuJin shrugged and said, "Not the goddess, but I saw three sets of bright red eyes behind the fish, and their movement was snakelike. They were very distant yet still watching me." JiaShao covered his mouth to suppress a scream, trembling in fear.

That evening, JiaShao, HuKui, and SuJin offered incense to the goddess LongMu at the lakeside after praying to Mazu, the goddess of the sea. At the same time, the dragonfish breached the surface numerous times.

SuWu was consumed by the problem of how to hunt underwater. A few days later, he idly watched kids holding sticks run towards their target with a whooshing sound, knocking them down and imitating Batu's arrows. With an idea flickering in his mind, he walked closer to watch them play when he saw little children run to the lake to dip something shiny that became transparent as it touched the water. It was a large fish scale.

Quickly catching on, he went to the water's edge and dipped his head underwater, holding a large fish scale over his eyes. He could see, but the scale was too small and brittle. It broke! Batu refined his idea by polishing the cartilage of the giant paddlefish, which became transparent underwater and didn't break easily. He devised a glue made from the dissolved cartilage of the carp fish to secure the eyepiece in place.

The downside was that the glue holding the polished cartilage did not adhere to the eye for long once it was soaked in water, and the polished eyepiece rotted within a day. Qian observed that this did not matter, as SuJin had to be quick in the hunt before he ran out of breath. The dwarf fishermen were assigned to catch a giant paddlefish and store it beneath the glacier ice a few days before the hunt.

During their discussions, Wong said, "We don't need to snag the fish on ropes. Once dead, the carcass will float up." The other dwarfs nodded.

SuWu disagreed, saying, "What if our Prince hurt the animal but didn't kill it? We won't be able to find it in the large lake. We need to tie the fish and drag it up." After deliberations, everyone agreed that, considering the size of the fish, it would be better to pierce its sides with barbs and pull it up.

They tested the crossbow underwater, but the arrow moved slowly and barely advanced. It was unsuitable for spearing large prey. To spear the fish, SuJin had to approach the creature up close. Qian and the dwarfs crafted metal spears with barbs to thrust into the fish's side. They created an eye hole at the back of the spear to attach a rope for retrieving the speared fish animal.

SuJin stated what the others wouldn't. "Somehow, I have to become the bait. That will bring the fish close enough to strike." The dwarfs gazed at SuJin with unrestrained awe. He was going to depths unknown in freezing water and now planned to become the bait to face the fearsome dragonfish in its realm!

After a long silence, SuWu bowed his head to SuJin and said, "Prince, we had better keep dropping meat into the depths without the hook to feed the dragonfish. We need to ensure the fish comes to you quickly."

JiaShao protested vehemently, "I can't stand this foolishness. I forbid it!"

SuJin told him softly, "I must do it, master! There is no other way." JiaShao crossed his arms and turned away. Tears welled in his eyes, and HuKui consoled him.

Looking at SuWu, the Prince confirmed, "Yes, it makes sense to attract them to come closer to bite the bait as soon as I touch the lakebed."

Qian advised SuJin. "The head of the fish is all bone. You must strike the underbelly, and all animals instinctively protect that." SuJin exclaimed, "Then gods help me! How do I get beneath the animal?"

****

A few days later, SuJin said, "It is time."

SuWu asked SuJin, "How do you know this?"

"I sense someone urging me to go down to face the fish."

"What?"

"Yes, and fish will fight to kill." He exhaled hard and said, "Let's not tell the others until after."

SuWu asked with genuine concern, "Prince, can we win against dragons?"

"You mean the eyes? They won't attack! It's between the fish and me." SuJin emphatically closed the discussion. "I'm going in tomorrow. I've been told the dwarfs have kept a paddlefish under the ice."

****

After offering prayers to the river and sea gods, Batu fixed the smooth cartilage cups with glue around SuJin's eyes, and a sombre team rowed into the misty lake. SuJin wore the belt that secured him to the raft and had three barbed spears with removable bamboo handles strapped to his back.

Qian wore a spare belt with a hook in case he needed to dive in and drag SuJin up. He whistled to the dwarfs on a boat a short distance away, and they dumped day-old blood and offal into the lake to keep the smaller fish at bay.

Large chunks of meat were strapped to SuJin's chest, and he was drenched in blood and stinking offal as bait to attract the dragonfish. He scrunched his face and said, "I better go in now. I can't take in this stench."

ChenHe hooked a large rock, strapped in leather, to SuJin's belt to remain anchored to the lakebed for as long as he wished. SuJin slipped off the raft and disappeared into the depths without a splash. SuWu shouted weakly as the lines rolled out, "*Battle speed, brother!*"

****

SuJin held onto the eyepieces as he was dragged swiftly down. His ears popped painfully, and he opened his eyes when his feet touched the sandy lakebed. A cloud of silt bloomed around him, and he peered through it to look around. Having never tested this depth before, the men on the surface let down a great deal of rope, causing an excess of coils to descend around him.

SuJin was in a world of colour, one of absolute silence. He realised that this was the state of mind he needed to reach in meditation and tried to slow his heartbeat, as Tuhu had taught him. Perhaps it was the hours of practice going underwater; anyway, it worked! Time stopped, a sense of calm descended, and all movements slowed. Strangely, he was immune to time slowing down around him because he could think and move normally.

He looked around, stunned by the beauty around him. Rocks were grey, and the lakebed glowed a bright translucent yellow. He could see plants with thin, long leaves swaying gently in the current. The aquatic forest had an abundance of silverfish, their shimmering bodies creating a mesmerising spectacle as they dodged through the leaves. Fish zipped past him in streaks of silver while others swam gracefully above his head; he could see the gleam of light on the surface far above.

A massive fish swished toward him, attracted by the blood. SuJin readied his spear. However, the fish turned and fled into the darkness. He knew that whatever scared the fish was not him but something behind him.

Before SuJin could turn, an enormous shadow passed beside him that seemed to go on and on before a colossal tail flicked his head and made him tumble over. He would have been thrown away but for the hook that held him fast to the heavy stone. It took him some time to regain his balance through the current created by the gigantic fish. Though he was anchored to the stone by a leather strip, he had to paddle his legs to regain his balance. The beast turned around lazily to assess the trespasser in its world, and he saw rows and rows of razor-sharp teeth in its mouth. Far out, he saw three sets of glowing red eyes watching him.

Up close, the creature was enormous! Its round eyes did not blink, and they were larger than his clenched fist. They had seriously underestimated the size of their quarry. At that moment, he realised that neither their braided lines could hold the fish nor could his spears harm it, let alone kill it.

A shiver went down his spine when he thought about the meat strapped to his chest. He frantically yanked out the chunks of meat and pushed them away. The meat floated away, leaving dark trails of blood that looked like smoke in this alien world.

Despite having three spears tied to his back, he couldn't help but feel ridiculous, considering how undersized they were for a fish of this size. SuJin remained undeterred and swiftly retrieved a spear for each hand. He was ready to attack, aiming to injure and scare the fish away.

More ropes dropped around him from the raft above.

The attack was sudden.

With a swish of its tail, the dragonfish surged toward him, opening its massive jaws to deliver a bite that would snap him in two. As the creature raced at him, ropes tangled in its enormous maw. He thrust the spears forward, but his arms felt heavy, like lead in water, and they moved slowly.

SuJin was done for and said a silent prayer, "Ancestors, I have done my best. Forgive me if I have displeased you!"

The lines of silk and hemp stuck in the mouth of the fish pulled taut, just beyond a waiting SuJin. Its mouth was yanked up, and the animal's colossal underbelly hurtled towards him, and he slammed the spears into the fish's underbelly. The lines snagged tightly in a loop around the fins, and the animal panicked, twisting and spinning about to escape, inadvertently wrapping more of the lines around it.

SuJin held tightly to the spears he had lodged into the animal, and despite the anchoring rock, he found himself wrapped firmly against the animal's side. He was squeezed and bound tightly, along with the rock, to the side of the fish. If it weren't for the initial set of silk ropes that snagged and supported the weight of the fish, he would have been sliced through.

He was drowning. He heard someone speak in a rasping voice as if the owner had not used the human tongue for a long time.

"You, bidden lifeforce, faithful to the Lord invoked with sacred names three times, four times, nine times - we accept your prayers and honour your ancestors. Prince of Destiny, we give you one of ourselves - a life for lives."

Just before SuJin passed out, he felt something push the massive beast upwards with tremendous force, and a bright light beckoned him into its warmth.

****

The sun cut through the mist, bathing the valley in bright light. It had been a while since the dwarfs had ceased their chant, expecting SuJin to surface or the lines to go taut. Indecision was etched on their faces, and there was a palpable tension as they gazed into the depths. Should we give him a few more moments or pull him out?

One of the bamboo handles that held the spear bobbed to the surface. A dwarf screamed, galvanising the people at the surface into action. SuWu and the dwarfs pulled on the ropes frantically, but it stretched tight suddenly. All of them screamed as the ropes were whipped out of their hands, giving them severe rope burns, and they were thrown into the icy water.

JiaShao's eyes bulged in shock as the raft was completely yanked a few feet below the surface.

They watched the submerged raft shake violently from side to side, like a rag in a storm. Abruptly, the raft shot out of the water and crashed into a boat. With a cracking sound, the fishing boat shattered into bits. A dwarf screamed in agony as the jagged edge of the fragmented bamboo raft pierced his thigh.

JiaShao screamed instructions as all the boats converged towards the wrecked raft bobbing on the choppy lake. "All of you, pull! Tie up the slack!" Turning, he shouted to a boat near the injured man, "Take him ashore!"

Qian swam to the raft, shouting, "Get back on the raft this instant! Pull, pull, the ropes have slackened," and men scrambled onto the raft. There was no tension on the ropes as they pulled up all the slack.

A gigantic fish shot up from the deep waters, soaring high, before crashing down in a splash that set waves, pushing the boats away and drenching everyone. "Pull in the slack, tie it up!" JiaShao screamed at the top of his voice, and the dazed men obeyed his authoritative command.

The dwarfs pulled in the loose rope and spooled it around two iron spikes as their eyes ogled at the size of the fish, which was more than double the length of the raft as it thrashed about.

HuKui saw a motionless SuJin tangled in the ropes and screamed, "The Prince is tangled on the side of the fish. Someone, cut him loose!"

SuWu, frozen in shock at seeing the monstrous fish up close, galvanised into action. He shouted to ChenHe, "You kill the monster. I will free the Prince," and he jumped into the water.

Tong expertly threw ropes in a spiral and snagged the beast's thrashing tail. The fish desperately tried to dive and escape but was strangely floating. Though the silk ropes were wrapped tightly, it was evident that something unnatural was holding up the massive mountain of fish from below.

ChenHe, screaming war cries, thrust his knife repeatedly into the head of the fish. Its sharp teeth raked his hand, but he did not give in as he ripped its head. The enraged fish floundered from side to side, churning up spray and foam, but clearly, it was tiring.

A vexed SuWu, howling in dread at the sight of the motionless Prince, frantically cut the lines holding him. Qian screamed at SuWu to stop, but in his distress, he did not heed his warning. Qian looped a rope to his belt, gestured to Wong, and leapt off the raft towards a hysterical SuWu.

Everything happened in moments. Qian managed to hook himself to SuJin's belt just as SuWu cut through the last silk rope that held SuJin. SuWu turned towards Qian, who was screaming at him about a stone.

To SuWu's surprise, both SuJin and Qian sank from his sight despite the carcass of the fish floating on the surface. He shrieked when he realised that SuJin was still locked to the heavy anchor stone, and he had just cut him loose.

SuWu looked around helplessly at the ropes lying about and shouted, "Forget the fish! Pull up all the ropes! SuJin and Qian are underwater!" "No one heard him in the commotion except Wong.

Laments and screams could be heard from the lake shore. Despite his misery, SuWu wondered if trouble had erupted ubiquitously everywhere for killing a spirit!

****

Qian tried desperately to unhook the heavy stone as they plummeted underwater. The crook of the hook nestled securely in SuJin's belt, and it wouldn't budge.

Unexpectedly, their descent slowed, and Qian thought they had reached the bottom. He made another attempt to free the heavy rock from SuJin, and it came off effortlessly, as light as a feather. Sensing something unusual, Qian looked around and found they were suspended in a weightless sphere. He looked around to see big and small fish swimming slowly around him, just as he had dreamt.

He was amidst something supernatural. He could feel an unworldly chill deep in his bones. Were the spirits real, after all? He wondered.

He froze when he saw red eyes and a large black snout. A dragon! A guttural voice flooded his ears, "You are insolent, arrogant and reckless, yet worthy – no hesitation in protecting the Prince of Destiny. We give you one of our own.

A life for lives."

Qian involuntarily screamed, "No!" as an image of his blood-covered wife holding his son flashed before him. The bubble collapsed, and water gushed into his mouth.

Wong, SuWu and HuKui pulled them to the surface. Both boys were unconscious, and they turned them over and pressed on their backs until Qian vomited water and coughed awake.

Wong held SuJin by his legs up and head sloping downwards onto HuKui's lap while SuJin massaged and repeatedly pressed SuJin's stomach with open palms. After many agonising moments, SuJin retched and groaned. He coughed out blood and water from his nose and mouth.

SuJin moaned in pain and said hoarsely, "My chest, it hurts."

Their relief was short-lived. Qian was hysterical after he regained consciousness. "Take me ashore! I want to see Ren! Something is wrong. I will not allow the dragons to take her." SuWu panicked and galvanised into action, leaving SuJin in the care of Wong and HuKui. He frantically rowed an exhausted Qian ashore.

The entire village milled about quietly. Something was indeed wrong, and the mood was sombre and mournful. Before the boat reached the shore, SuWu screamed at the men, "What's wrong? Tell us, now!"

Somebody answered, "Ren went into labour and died in childbirth. The midwives couldn't save the baby." SuWu's legs buckled, and he collapsed onto a howling Qian in a dead faint.

Dwarfs came rushing to care for the boys. After reviving SuWu, one of the older dwarfs said, "Don't take the loss of a woman too hard. Childbirth is a risk all women go through; many die."

With their arms wrapped around each other, Qian and SuWu sobbed, unable to contain their grief. While SuWu wept wretchedly, Qian kept repeating with vacant eyes, "*Life for Lives.*"

Warming up beside them, SuJin asked hoarsely, "The Lord with three times, four times, nine times names saved us. Which god has one hundred and eight names?"

HuKui stared at SuJin, and JiaShao exclaimed, "Leave them be! Their minds are addled! They were underwater and unconscious for far too long to be sane."

****

The women hurried to prepare fires, and all the blankets in the huts were taken out to cover the brave men. They rubbed the shivering men with hands warmed by the fires, and after the elders confirmed their recovery, dwarfs carried each man to his hut.

SuJin was exhausted and frequently coughed up blood. HuKui and ChenHe led a team of men, each carrying heated stones to keep the Prince warm in his hut. They applied hot poultices and massaged him while medicinal incense was wafted into his hut. The men tended tirelessly to their hero throughout the night without a moment's rest.

The dwarfs extracted every tooth from the fish, and JiaShao thanked the spirits with prayers and blessed them. At his instruction, the women made lockets from the smaller teeth for all the warriors who ventured into the lake.

****

Batu supervised the cutting of the fish. He, too, was staggered by its size, and HuKui found him shaking his head in disbelief. "That boy is truly a god!"

HuKui solemnly concurred. "Nothing else can explain this."

Batu set up many clay cauldrons and cut out the considerable swim bladder unique to the species, the spleen, and other organs, including the soft cartilage and bones. The meat was distributed to the cooking fires.

The thin membranes that made up the swim bladders dissolved in hot water, along with the soft cartilages, with continuous stirring. The liquid thickened, producing a fishy smell. The glue preparation required constant stirring over low heat, and Batu did it without stopping through the night. The glue could become brittle and weak if the broth solidified into lumps and burned. They kept the glue stew, as Batu called it, light and watery and constantly on low heat because they needed the glue to last the entire bow-making process, which would take weeks.

The excess glue was kept under the ice to solidify by the dwarfs, much to Batu's discomfort. They consoled him that the glue could be used to make smaller bows.

With Batu busy in the workshop, a triumphant ChenHe with a bandaged arm sat guard for SuJin.

****

JiaShao and HuKui offered prayers to Mazu and Long Mu, thanking them for their bounty and for protecting SuJin. To their surprise, a heartbroken and chastened Qian joined them. He had buried his wife and child while the village women ululated for the passing of their souls. Death during childbirth was a common occurrence, and the women prayed for deliverance from death when it was their turn.

SuWu was grief-stricken and refused to eat for several days; it took considerable persuasion from HuKui and JiaShao before he relented and had some soup.

HuKui confided in Batu, "SuWu and Ren loved each other, but fate is cruel. Qian proposed to her father before him."

"I noticed," Batu said. "She was a fine woman."

****

Unlike a regular bow, the recurve bow has a unique design. The two ends curve away from the main body.

Batu had collected long hardwood, metal fillers, horn strips, and resins to make the bows. Each strip was heated over coal and steam to bend it into shape. Under his guidance, dwarf carpenters used wooden presses to adjust the shape of each piece so that it fit together.

The bow took shape piece by piece. Batu made grooves that were pulled and pressed into precise slots. After that, the composite bow was assembled and checked for balance and power. The bow was reassembled with other matching pieces if the balance and performance were poor. It was a painstakingly slow job, and Batu was a discerning craftsman who judged the merits of the bows by testing them.

Once he was satisfied, the composite bow was taken apart and reassembled with generous amounts of fish glue, and each joint was securely bound with hemp thread. Once dry, the individual components were assembled and glued again. The finished composite bow was firmly wrapped tightly in silk strips and held over embers to dry on the outside. Finally, it was placed in wooden presses to ensure the shape did not distort while drying.

SuWu strolled into the workshop and, looking at the many bows stashed around, exclaimed, "How many bows do we need? We are but a few men?"

Tong, who was assisting Batu, smiled and said, "It looks like a lot! Doesn't it? What you see are all discards."

"We are preparing three sets of bows: one for you boys and another as standby or gifts for a few warriors in Tianzhu, and they are in individual wooden presses to retain shape." He showed a set of smaller recurve bows and said, "Those are for us!"

SuWu was taken aback by the effort put in by Batu and his men, and he said, "I hadn't realised it before, but this requires a great deal of skill and hard work." Work!"

Tong smiled and said, "Backbreaking, but satisfying."

SuWu was impressed and asked, "What's next?"

"Batu said he would employ the womenfolk to make the arrows. Food shall be prepared for the community by the men until the arrows are made."

SuWu was uncertain and said, "We have short arms?"

Tong laughed, "We have even shorter arms, brother!"

On a serious note, he confirmed, "I thought so too until I tested the bows during assembly. The recurve bow action is very different from that of normal bows. The bow bends significantly inward at the edges when pulling the bowstring back. The middle of the bow compresses, while the extreme ends experience pulling tension. On release, they work together to provide immense power to the arrow. The feel is different with these bows; they behave differently from the Hun recurve bows as well! These are special bows."

SuWu bowed, thanking Tong, and just then, Batu walked into the workshop. He asked, "Are you here to see me?"

"Yes," SuWu said, and Batu motioned for him to speak.

"Why fish glue? We sacrificed lives for it! Qian said he heard a voice saying, *Life for lives*." He added after a pause, "He still laments the loss of his wife. All this for a fish! Was it a worthy exchange?" SuWu was close to tears.

Batu said, "Qian got it wrong!"

SuWu looked at Batu and said, "You mean they are unrelated?"

Batu began working on a bow, and without looking up, he said, "It was two lives that were exchanged underwater. SuJin and Qian's life in exchange for his wife and child. It is better to believe that Ren sacrificed her life for all of you."

"Two, not one!" repeated SuWu in deep pain.

"I will be candid with you, SuWu. Many more will die around us, and perhaps some of us, too, before all this ends! So, stop grieving! Think of the many lives we are destined to save, not the few who die; life for lives means sacrifice! The spirits have sacrificed for us! Let's make it worthwhile!"

****

Batu engaged the entire village in crafting arrows. He tasked the dwarfs with crushing the dried tendons until they yielded loose fibres. The fibres were intricately woven into bowstrings. After applying grease, the bowstrings were stretched in the sun until they stiffened.

The women made arrows, and Batu taught them how to judge balance and optimal weight. He promised to spend a couple of hours with them every day, but at other times, he would be with their husbands, training them in archery.

Arrows were made of straight shafts of reed and birch. Children were given the job of dropping the bare shafts vertically from a height with a small stone tied to their tip. The ones that landed within the target circle were selected to be made into arrows.

Diverse arrow tips were crafted from various materials, including bone, bronze, and hardwood. The fletching directing the arrows required bird tail feathers, particularly those from ducks. Batu sent the dwarfs to hunt for birds outside the valley.

Each of the arrows with fletching was hung on a string horizontally and marked for the balance point. Many had to be weight-corrected using glue to make the lighter side heavier for balance.

Batu Nachin, the "loyal falcon," checked each bow every two days, adjusted the weights to prevent warping, and returned them to the wooden frames filled with dry rock salt to avoid moisture.

The last step was to apply the pine tree's protective resins to lock in the fish glue from moisture and extend its lifespan. The women made intricate spiritual designs, engraved symbols of power, and embedded their hair and that of their young ones on the bow grip to bring luck to their men.

When the bows were finally finished, they looked like they were made from one piece of exotic material. Each bow was placed in dedicated wooden frames and wrapped in oilskin for storage. Batu packed the bows onto a wagon, covered them in straw, and stored them away from sight.

That evening, the village celebrated with songs and dances, paying homage to the dead and the spirits of the lake. A smaller dragonfish frequently breached the surface, and all the men and women gathered to bow to it.

Batu praised the women for their exceptional work, and the ladies gifted him a leather cap with an eagle in flight embroidered on it.

HuKui asked Batu, "Why did you store the bows on a cart instead of in the workshop? We can move them to the cart when we need to travel. Now we don't have a cart."

Batu replied, "My friend if we have to move quickly, we can't sit down to pack."

HuKui snorted and said, "If we need to move quickly, we won't be dragging the cart along."

Batu grinned and whispered, "I have thought about that. There is a small cave a little away that we can use to hide the cart if we don't have time to escape with our belongings." HuKui nodded.

Batu announced that the men would begin archery training on the double recurve bow, which garnered loud cheers.

21 Batu Teaches Archery

Batu's training was unconventional, which left the boys feeling frustrated. The dwarfs selected by JiaShao for archery also complained, stating that the training seemed illogical and resembled more of a scouting exercise.

Batu began his day by sending the warriors individually in different directions into the forest, where they were tasked with hiding a broken arrow. They returned when he shot a whistling arrow into the sky. He asked the boys to describe the path and location where they had hidden the arrow. After listening to everyone, he randomly assigned boys to retrace the route described by another to retrieve the arrow. The boys failed miserably in this task, day after day, but Batu remained indifferent.

HuKui confronted Batu, "I am a master as well. I cannot grasp your method of teaching. What sort of training is this? ChenHe doesn't even know which direction the sun rises to describe to someone else where he hid his arrowhead!"

Batu was unconcerned and said, "It is required, HuKui. They will figure it out." Then he added, "If you are interested, you can help the boys."

"You mean I can disclose the locations?"

"Don't be silly, HuKui. I mean, how to remember waypoints."

Batu reaffirmed his requirement, "Without mastering the technique of 'seeing and memorising,' we don't touch the bow." HuKui remained adamant, and Batu continued, "I am interested in the arrow striking the target in their *mental picture*. It requires practice!"

"Mental picture? What's that?" HuKui enquired with a frown.

"A picture of the target accurately painted in the mind." Batu elaborated, "Reality changes every moment, and so should their mental picture. In a battle with fast-moving targets, their mind should create a mental picture where the target sticks out like a sore thumb on a five-year-old."

Realising HuKui was confused, Batu explained, "Conventional archery advocates firing at stationary targets, hoping that the speeding arrow strikes the target. In a battle, striking to immobilise enemy leaders would lead to their rout faster. Picking them out and shooting without thinking could be the split-second difference between success and defeat!"

Before HuKui could ask more questions, Batu said, "Ask them to use their heads instead of the muscles in their backsides. Maybe they will succeed. Now, don't disturb me. We are running out of wine frequently, and I am brewing airag from goat's milk!"

Batu did not care to communicate further, so HuKui took it upon himself to convey the essence of the training to the boys. "You need to retrace the path by taking a series of mental pictures of each turn or path in sequence and describe it to your brothers."

Qian was cross and said, "Why can't he tell this directly? We could have saved time."

SuWu snorted, "As if he cares. Let's be happy he shared what he is looking for with Master HuKui."

A distraught ChenHe cried in anguish, "Do you know how many places look identical out there? Every place has rocks, trees, paths and whatnot. So, what mental picture are you talking about?"

SuWu said, "Let's try it. We have seen Batu use the bow. He doesn't aim, so let's try and make this mental picture."

SuWu and Qian took the initiative to solve the problem. Walking to the lakeside, they urged each other to describe what they saw. To their dismay, each explained what they saw in their unique way.

They sat together, removed irrelevant information, and concentrated on a few features such as direction from the lake, rock formations, and any other unique features. They memorised the sequence to recall and practised together a few times. After that, their success in locating a place by mere descriptions increased considerably. The dwarfs, too, picked up the technique quickly.

However, their success was short-lived, as Batu sent them on horseback further away. The boys struggled to identify locations, and frustration grew within them. At SuWu's insistence, they kept practising, but their interest waned.

A few days later, SuJin consistently started to bring back broken arrowheads. HuKui asked, "SuJin, how are you getting it right?"

SuJin laughed and modestly said, "I was fortunate to receive descriptions from SuWu and Qian these past few days. I believe Batu has intentionally provided me with their descriptions. I am not great at memorising, so I focus on and remember the exceptions in their descriptions."

HuKui asked, "Exceptions, like what?"

SuJin said, "Well, it could be a broken tree, a split rock, the sound of a stream, or the smell of something rotting. I remember these. Otherwise, my mind is blank." SuJin reiterated, "I remember just one or two unique features and nothing more. I ignore the rest of the descriptions."

HuKui added, "So, no gods involved?"

SuJin laughed and said, "Oh no, not this time."

Qian was fascinated and said, "Interesting... so you don't strive to remember the forest, just what strikes your mind, and your mental picture is more empty than full." SuJin nodded enthusiastically. They adopted the technique, and SuWu and Qian quickly mastered it.

ChenHe and a few dwarfs failed, and Batu gave up on them but promised basic archery training. The rest were pushed hard to ride out, retrieve the arrowhead, and return quickly.

Some days were given to JiaShao and HuKui to break up the intensity of Batu's training.

The first lesson that HuKui imparted was to teach each of them a unique call to identify themselves.

HuKui taught the boys how to track animals and explained the predatory skills wolves use. He described how they hunt alone in stealth or as a pack, using cunning to bring down bigger prey. He made the boys check the wind direction frequently to remain downwind. HuKui also taught them to recognise unique smells on their forest forays and read subtle signs left on the forest floor.

Qian taught the boys how to camouflage effectively, using light and shadow and hiding in sparse undergrowth.

On his part, JiaShao imparted skills to ambush and flee, covering their tracks. The dwarf master's teaching was unique because he always prepared multiple escape paths before planning an attack.

Although most of these lessons were familiar to the boys, their success in tracking and evading was phenomenal when they combined their learning with the recently acquired 'mental picture' skills to track each other.

HuKui and Qian discussed their knowledge of estimating the size of a scouting party by examining empty camps and the time the enemy had left their camp. Batu imparted vastly different knowledge, such as distinguishing professional scouts from bandits, forestalling an ambush, and feigning retreats.

The pick of the students in all these lessons was Qian. He took to the lessons like a wolf cub, and within days, he was ahead of anything

HuKui had to offer. He could disappear into the undergrowth, and none of them could find him.

When HuKui appreciated his extraordinary skills, he played it down, saying, "I have a distinct advantage over all of you because of my forbidden troop's training."

HuKui remarked, "Truly, you are Black Death, and I pity your enemies."

Qian cautiously said, "There is one forbidden troop warrior who is better than me. That was before meeting the dragons in the lake!" All of them looked at him curiously.

After a few moments of indecision, Qian said, "I have a confession to make. I have a presence within me, helping me when I am frustrated or focused. It began the day we caught the monster fish!" SuJin smiled at him in sympathy while the others looked at Qian in disbelief.

JiaShao blurted out, "You have a spirit within you?"

HuKui asked, "Do they trouble you with dreams?"

Qian said, "No! No dreams, but try to manifest what I want." Seeing the incredulous faces around him, Quan laughed and added, "When I try not to make a noise in the forests as I move stealthily from one tree cover to another, the dry leaves beneath my feet don't crackle. I instinctively know where my target is looking, which shadow to move to, and when to stand still. I cannot explain all this, but having been with the forbidden troops, I know I have help!"

JiaShao stared at him incredulously, and Qian shrugged before saying, "I don't know if I will continue to receive this help once we leave this valley!" He looked at SuJin and added, "The spirit is within me because I helped SuJin. They call him the - Prince of Destiny."

JiaShao responded, "It's a spirit, *a living force*. You need to continue your prayers and offer sacrifices. I think the dragon spirit has merged with you, Qian."

SuWu frowned and asked, "You mean a spirit has left the lake and taken refuge in Qian? Is that possible?"

JiaShao said, "My ancestors have encountered such individuals. These spirits are not gods but can extend their influence over their hosts and immediate surroundings."

Qian stood up, bowed low to JiaShao, and implored him, "Master, teach me the sacred prayers. I believe the spirits want to help us."

JiaShao regarded SuJin with a questioning expression, pondering if he possessed a spirit within him.

SuJin smiled and said, "Life for lives! Qian saved me from death."

That evening, JiaShao and HuKui declared that they were done with their training. JiaShao said, "You are an army now!" The dwarfs cheered loudly.

SuWu asked, "Why do you say that master? It's just SuJin and Qian who have excelled."

HuKui laughed and replied, "What else? 'Brick,' the ferocious pit fighter! SuWu, the 'Strategist!' 'Batu,' the Hun archer! 'Black Death,' with a spirit! Finally, the 'Green Hunter' with the power of the gods to lead."

He looked at JiaShao and asked, "Am I wrong to call them an army?"

JiaShao and the dwarfs emphatically replied, "No!"

****

Batu called the boys to his workshop and said, "We shall begin archery training."

Batu showed a heap of damaged, misshapen bows and said, "Take one."

SuWu quipped, "Aren't those discards?"

"What do you suggest we do with my misshapen bows?" He frowned and asked, "Do you expect me to give away the painstakingly crafted recurve bows to novices for strength training?"

SuWu asked incredulously, "Are we still novices to you?"

Batu nodded. "Very much, still pissing on your mother's lap." The boys glanced at each other and shook their heads in disbelief!

JiaShao asked, "What's the purpose of a weapon if it's kept under wraps?"

Batu said, "Little master, I have deliberated with WoShi, who agrees that the bows are for our journey. We can't use them in Han without raising eyebrows."

Batu told JiaShao, "You or CaoShen once mentioned that dwarf merchants could transport anything anywhere in Han. Can you transport the bows to the steppes?"

JiaShao confidently said, "Of course. They will be available outside the wall when you leave. We need to be in Changan to organise that."

HuKui looked at JiaShao incredulously and asked, "You can do that? Deliver the bows to the steppes?"

JiaShao laughed and said, "We dwarfs have friends in high places. Don't you worry?"

HuKui grumbled, "Probably deep pockets."

JiaShao paused for a moment before making his decision. He raised his hand and whistled sharply, catching the dwarfs' attention. He announced, "It's time. Our work here is done. We are leaving for Changan!" The boys were speechless at this unexpected decision from JiaShao. The dwarfs received the command joyfully and cheered loudly.

JiaShao turned to the astonished boys and said, "The bows will be delivered beyond the Han borders or wherever you prefer. Don't worry about that. Perhaps we shall commence trade with the Huns for dried fish and salt."

With a sarcastic smile, Batu said, "Dried fish and the Khan. Now that's a sight I would love to see."

JiaShao turned towards SuJin and bowed low.

"No," said SuJin. Batu looked mystified, and JiaShao felt confused.

"Oh, you wish for me to remain behind? Prince, is that your desire?" JiaShao bowed deeply and said, "As you wish, Prince. We shall remain here." SuJin smiled warmly at the man who had risked so much for him. He walked over and embraced JiaShao tightly.

SuJin said, "I don't want you to go to Changan. Make plans to return to your village. Be a farmer, hunter, or trader; till the land for crops and fish when it pleases you. Take our womenfolk with you. You are free!"

JiaShao did not entertain any arguments. He nodded and said, "Prince, it shall be done as you command."

HuKui was taken aback by JiaShao's sudden decisions. Curious, he asked, "JiaShao, will you do as he says?" He emphasised by throwing his hands up, "Just like that!"

JiaShao replied to HuKui, "If a mute fish obeys him, who am I to dishonour his request?" He walked over to inform the dwarfs while a bemused HuKui looked on. The boys felt a profound sense of unease. JiaShao was a constant presence and a reliable father figure, and they felt empty inside at the thought of him leaving.

Sensing their disquiet, SuJin told the boys, "Changan is volatile. Until we return from Tianzhu, we should be content that our friends and family are safe." ChenHe was distraught and kept looking at his wife, who was happily chatting with the other women, unaware of the recent developments.

Batu said, "Let's begin training, but wait." He ran to his hut and returned with the Hun bows, saying, "You can use these bows once you are ready. The bows belong to men who died in the arena, and they will be honoured if you boys use their bows."

Batu's training began with strength exercises for their wrists. The warriors had to stretch their hands out and wind a string around a bamboo stick with a heavy stone hanging below. He made them perform finger exercises to strengthen their grip. After that, lessons came on how to string a recurve bow and where to notch an arrow using their thumbs. Finally, the boys had to describe the mental picture before lifting the bow to fire.

****

The warriors had to train their arms to pull the bow at will and release them until they were out of arrows. Always in lots of twenty! SuJin and the others ended the first few days unable to hold up their hands in pain, sometimes bleeding after the intense practice of pulling the stiff bowstrings. Batu gave them leather finger guards, but despite this, hard callouses developed on their draw fingers that regularly broke open. The boys lost count of the number of bowstrings they broke.

HuKui organised women to massage the hands of the men after four sessions of twenty arrows with fish oil and hot fomentation. Batu changed from lifting rocks to holding heated stones to warm and heal their hands at intervals to speed up the development of calluses.

Notch the arrow, pull, hold your breath, align the target with your mental picture, and gently release it without firing. Drop the arrow and pick up another until you complete a quiver of twenty, then begin again. They had to turn from left to right and centre in large arcs each time, keeping their heads steady and always describing their mental image of what they were targeting before releasing the arrow.

Batu made the boys balance on bamboo. Like riding a horse, the poles were shaken up, down, and sideways. Despite the movements, they had to keep their heads and hands steady. Muscular ChenHe suffered from headaches and sickness when rocked up and down on the bamboo, but he was not excused from training. No warrior was given any concession as they practised together.

Batu did not spare the dwarf archers; they were also fully engaged. JiaShao was pleased that his men performed strongly alongside the boys, particularly Tong and Wong.

JiaShao asked Batu, "Why is the mental picture so important? The arrow travels quickly. When will the training be complete?"

Batu nodded. "Imagine throwing a spear at a fast-running deer. Will you throw it when the animal is now or just a little ahead?"

JiaShao said, "Ahead!"

Batu nodded, "Ahead - is the mental picture! The arrow - is the spear! The distance the arrow has to travel is considerable for a recurve bow. These boys are not hunters; they are warriors. Their training will be complete when they consistently strike a moving target with the arrow fired in their mental picture while on the move, themselves."

Batu's explanation remained vivid in their minds as the training intensified: "The arrow is the weapon, and it must strike your target in your mental picture. Thus, the arrow hitting the target is an extension of your mind. The bow doesn't determine where the arrow goes; your mind does!"

****

The boys soon improved their archery skills considerably, and Batu was pleased.

SuJin insisted that the boys spar with one another using swords and daggers, not just bows. They carried their knowledge of keeping their heads still and using the mental picture technique to strike with swords and knives during stick fights. It was no surprise that their attacks were deadly, and the boys had to be careful not to injure each other.

In all of these fights, SuJin was invincible! Watching him spar against multiple opponents was a treat. He used minimal moves at unimaginable speeds to disable and defeat his opponents.

HuKui and JiaShao watched him incapacitate a fully armed SuWu, ChenHe, Qian, and Batu together, although they used feints and coordinated attacks.

JiaShao proudly asked HuKui, "Isn't he something? Do you have any doubts that he is the one?"

HuKui responded cautiously, "I pray he is not compassionate towards his enemies when the time comes. That is likely to be his single failing. He doesn't kill."

Batu shifted the archery lessons to include horseback fighting. He ensured the training was varied and continually challenging to keep the men motivated over long practice stints. He had one group of mounted men ride out and pick up arrows fired by others into the sandy lake bank. They had to swing down on either side of the horse to retrieve the shafts.

By sundown each day, they were exhausted. Batu let them sleep for a few hours before training them again in the darkness or early morning. He made them practice regardless of the weather conditions: windy, rainy, or snowy.

He made them train on horseback in dense foliage, uphill and downhill, firing arrows while sitting backwards on a horse, like the Huns. The boys devised acrobatic manoeuvres from the back of a galloping horse that impressed Batu, the Hun from the steppes.

Batu did not interfere in their improvisations but never allowed the boys to aim at their targets. Instead, they had to fire arrows based on their mental picture.

****

JiaShao led the dwarfs, weeping women, and children back through the ravine with cartloads of dried fish and bows. He planned to reach their village before winter set in.

The camp was silent that evening, and there was no laughter. Qian strummed soulful music on a discarded bow, which reminded them more of their loneliness.

With the onset of winter, food became scarce, and black bears ventured into their camps to search for food; Batu fed them.

****

Winter brought snow to the valley, intensifying the cold. HuKui asked Batu to give the boys a break. Batu proposed that they go hunting instead, and the boys readily agreed, grateful for a respite from their usual routine.

It was windy, and light snow swirled, reducing visibility in the forest. They found a herd of deer, but the snow was deep and treacherous on either side of the forest paths. The fleet-footed animals jumped over the snow, crossed a stream, and paused on the mountain slope across the valley, looking back at them.

Batu asked, "Any suggestions on how to acquire our lunch?"

SuWu told Batu, "Our arrow can reach the deer because we are uphill. The stag keeps us in its sight to bolt to safety at the slightest provocation."

Batu took out four arrows. The first was fitted with a bone head, with holes and ridges carved into it. It was a whistle, and he turned it, fixing the whistle inwards. The other arrows had a metal pin as their arrowhead.

He shot the whistling arrow high into the air by pulling back the bowstring so much that ChenHe thought for a moment that the bow would crack. The arrow soared high without a sound, and after reaching its zenith, it arced down, whistling, ahead of the deer. The confused animals stopped, searching for the source ahead. Batu shot three arrows in quick succession behind the first.

As the arrows left his bow, SuJin quietly said, "You will drop two, not three. The stag will escape with the herd."

The whistling arrow dropped ahead of the herd, and the leading buck backed hard, stopping the herd in its tracks. The arrow hit the last deer in the file, and Batu's second arrow struck down another deer. The third arrow skimmed off the wide antlers of the prancing stag.

The boys turned to congratulate Batu on his incredible shots, but he was staring at SuJin in disbelief. "Your mental picture indicated that the arrow would miss the stag?"

SuJin shrugged, "That is how it felt to me."

As the men relished venison that evening, Batu said, "An arrow is not a defensive weapon, unlike a sword or a shield, which are meant to strike and parry repeatedly. Once fired, it is forfeit; make it count or don't use a bow."

The boys practised with Batu throughout winter.

With the arrival of spring, the snow melted, and the valley burst into green. Creepers grew with a vengeance around the trees. HuKui was restless that WoShi had not sent word yet, and they had no information on the political situation in Changan.

When the dwarfs went down to the village to buy essentials, HuKui joined them to gather information.

****

HuKui was shocked to hear that the imperial army had not abandoned its search for the fugitives, who matched the descriptions of SuJin and Batu.

HuKui didn't want to stay in the village any longer. He had to advise SuJin and the boys to leave directly for the wall and wait on the other side.

They bought provisions for the journey back. The village shopkeeper spent good money that evening in the local tavern and boasted about the visit of his wealthy customers, the dwarfs. The information was relayed to the notorious bandit Yuan Lin, who decided to investigate.

#22 WoShi Meets Ailing Empress Wang

Since the death of the young Emperor Pingdi, the imperial throne had remained vacant, and the nobility was growing increasingly restless. To exacerbate matters, WangMang mandated that the wealthy voluntarily relinquish their riches to the poor.

Bureaucrats unleashed imperial soldiers to confiscate the wealth of the rich. However, the nobility and wealthy merchants united and repelled the imperial forces with mercenaries. With the older bureaucrats siding with the nobility, WangMang was hard-pressed to contain the rebellion.

WangMang negotiated a truce with the Lui clans and proclaimed two-year-old LuiRuzi as the new Emperor.

****

LiPing, the fearless general of the fast-foot regiment responsible for palace security, was above reproach and one of the longest-serving bureaucrats. Perhaps his reputation as the Butcher of Han made people hesitate to remove him from his position. Sworn to protect the imperial family, he possessed the authority to eliminate threats and assassins without explanation.

High-ranking officers favoured him because he avoided palace politics and aligned himself with the bureaucratic hierarchy. Using his spy network, he prevented numerous assassinations of mandarins, earning him respect and favour in the palace.

LiPing had one failing. He was scared of WoShi, the grand master of the HanKaoTzu school and erstwhile adviser to the emperors before the time of Emperor Yuan. WoShi had asked him to meet him, and he was anxious. He knew of a cunning and ruthless WoShi from his younger days, far from the meek grandmaster he portrayed today.

WoShi's non-interference in palace affairs in recent years surprised LiPing. Nevertheless, he suspected that WoShi was planning to remove WangMang from power, and that was something he wouldn't do. His solemn oath to protect all palace members was a trust he wouldn't break, regardless of the political situation.

LiPing did not want to meet WoShi without protection because he intended to refuse WoShi's call for WangMang's assassination. He brought along two killers from a notorious gang that his men employed to eliminate threats in the city.

LiPing's mind drifted back decades to when a corrupt prime minister and his eunuchs held influential positions in the bureaucracy. They exploited the common man by demanding bribes to lower taxes and defraud the imperial treasury. The situation reached a tipping point when greedy officials began extorting bribes from farmers and merchants entering the city by road or boat. When the farmers protested in the streets of Changan, the prime minister unleashed the imperial army, killing them all. No one came to trade in Changan for weeks, and the city starved.

The matter reached the Emperor's ears despite the prime minister's best efforts to filter all information. The Emperor was also informed that revolts by peasants across the Han Empire were picking up against the royal family for its corrupt rule.

Vexed at the extent of corruption within the palace walls, the Emperor summoned WoShi, the grandmaster of the HanKaoTzu school.

WoShi consoled the Emperor by assuring him he would restore the common man's confidence through a purge. "I shall clear this dung from the palace courtyards!" He declared in court.

WoShi gathered Lui warriors and mercenaries using the Emperor's seal and launched a coordinated attack on the corrupt prime minister and his men from the lowest levels. The ensuing bloodbath was no less than that of a battlefield. LiPing was part of the cleansing and was indebted to WoShi for his elevation to an officer. WoShi instructed LiPing to employ extreme violence to deter senior Mandarins from engaging in corruption ever again.

During those times, *lingchi* came into existence, better known as "*death by a thousand and one slicing cuts*," the goriest of all public executions! Hundreds of commoners and bureaucrats cheered and watched as the prime minister and corrupt eunuchs begged for a quick death in the city square. On LiPing's command, the executioner skilfully cut away fingers, nose, and ears, opened their stomachs, nicked their liver and organs with minimum blood loss and had the victim scream and watch themselves being butchered alive. The sheer horror of lingchi silenced the crowd, and there was a general sigh of relief when the executioner finally cut the tongue and gouged out the eyes of the lawbreakers.

LiPing's brutality stunned both bureaucrats and commoners, and he became famous as the "*Butcher of Han.*" To this day, a mere mention of Lingchi frightened convicts to confess in his presence.

****

The HanKaoTzu school was near the temple of Illumination, and he planned to visit the temple before moving to WoShi's residence. The evening mist was thick enough to hide his identity.

He reached the school courtyard, and a house servant ran inside to announce the presence of LiPing, the thousand-cut butcher. A dwarf introduced himself as CaoShen and asked LiPing's guards to stay in the kitchen while he took their master to meet WoShi.

CaoShen guided LiPing away from the house through a sprawling garden that lay unattended. They reached an impenetrable bamboo grove, or so he thought until the dwarf disappeared to the other side. He followed into a short green tunnel that opened into a large clearing.

A wooden hut with a steep roof stood in the middle of the clearing. To reach it, they had to walk over round white pebbles. The ground beneath was levelled, and hard-beaten, and the rounded pebbles crunched loudly under their feet. LiPing noted with interest that it was difficult to approach the house unannounced.

He entered a spacious, well-lit wooden room where the subtle scent of lemongrass and incense wafted from a metal platter. He could discern the aroma of freshly sawn pinewood—indeed, the hut was newly built.

In the middle of the room, a steaming teapot sat on a small bed of coals. Pebbles crunched outside as CaoShen walked back without informing him. LiPing sat down to wait for WoShi.

He heard pebbles crunching under the feet of running men and seized the hilt of his sword. The bodyguards he had hired burst into the room with their swords drawn. They halted upon seeing LiPing and sheathed their swords. One of the guards said, "We were led here by a mutual friend," and LiPing grunted. Their spy in WoShi's household was not useless after all.

WoShi walked in from somewhere inside with a dwarf. LiPing stood up and bowed crisply, bringing his hands together in front of him. "Marquis, greetings. We meet after a long time."

WoShi acknowledged the bow with a quick clasp of his fists and sat down in one seamless move that hardly ruffled his dress. He extended his hand and said, "Tea!" The dwarf servant seated himself and poured two steaming teacups between them on the low table.

LiPing politely refused. "I don't drink tea unless I prepare it. Old habits that ensure the security of the imperial family," he laughed fretfully.

WoShi nodded and said, "It's wise to be careful." He slurped the hot tea and grunted in appreciation. The floor creaked as the dwarf walked around the room. It had to be hollow, LiPing deduced, and he wondered why this place had been chosen as a meeting place.

After a couple of sips, WoShi said, "Leave us." The dwarf gestured to LiPing's guards to leave.

One of them told LiPing, "Chief, this is a trap."

The dwarf commanded, "Did you not hear the Marquis? Leave!"

The city killers regarded the short dwarf with contempt. "How do you intend to make us leave half-man?"

LiPing weakly gestured to them to leave the room. The two guards reluctantly approached the door and stopped.

WoShi commanded again, "I said, leave!"

The city thugs unsheathed their swords and said, "We will stay."

LiPing shrugged and told WoShi, "These men are used to violence, Marquis. Let them remain."

At the sound of many feet on the pebbles, the killers shouted in alarm and rushed outside. There was a clash of swords, and someone fell. LiPing was startled when one of his bodyguards staggered into the room and collapsed in a violent seizure, struggling to remove the tiny darts lodged all over his body.

LiPing drew his sword but hesitated when two dwarfs entered and knelt, pointing fist-length blowpipes at him. Six more dwarfs followed, all carrying a variety of blowpipes secured in their belts and wielding swords. One dwarf approached the fallen man and struck him on the temple with the butt of his sword's hilt. The sound of the skull cracking was loud, and LiPing grimaced.

WoShi said, "I will not have the likes of them listening in."

A grim LiPing glanced at his unconscious guard and said, "They are the killers of the city, and their sworn brothers won't take this lying down." WoShi tilted his head toward the unconscious man and replied, "You mean they will come here for vengeance?" The dwarfs unceremoniously dragged the unconscious man by his feet out of the hut.

"Haven't we lost quite several prominent citizens to this gang? I agree that with their imperial patronage, they wouldn't hesitate to take revenge." He stared into Li Ping's eyes and said, "I assure you that Changan will be rid of this gang before daybreak. Of course, credit will go to WangMang's vigilantes."

LiPing exclaimed, "Dwarfs! Can they beat seasoned thugs?"

WoShi smiled and said, "Don't be fooled by their diminutive sizes. Each man is a better warrior than the best of your elite soldiers, and they fight in pairs in a fighting style long forgotten."

Li Ping insisted, "The darts made the difference in the fight. They slowed down my men."

"Irrelevant. I asked the dwarfs to try it out for future exigencies. It works!" WoShi smiled at LiPing.

LiPing said, "These darts work fast!"

WoShi said, "The darts of the sea people, Sumpit of Palawan, can't kill. We can pull out the darts before the poison freezes the heart. However, if these men have many darts in them and are unconscious..."

The dwarf who had stayed beside WoShi interjected, "A merciful death in their sleep. Far better death than what they meted out to their innocent victims in the market. It will be a pleasure to eliminate them tonight." LiPing looked up to see the cold eyes of the dwarf determining his response.

WoShi was caught up in the details of dart preparation. In a neutral tone, he explained, "The poison on the darts is made from the toxic latex of a palm tree found in Palawan. They prepare the poison by thickening the watery latex into a paste, using a green leaf to hold it over a small flame. If it gets too hot, the leaf dries, and the poison weakens!"

LiPing commented, "These darts do not have latex in them. The poison darts you used have acted much faster."

WoShi arched his eyebrows and smiled at LiPing, a smile a teacher reserves for his astute student. "A dear friend of mine prepared the poison recipe to kill me. I was curious about its effects. It works well, doesn't it?"

LiPing realised he was being threatened and confided in— a typical technique used by forbidden troops to recruit spies who could not be swayed by money. LiPing boldly sheathed his sword and sat back to face WoShi. He was convinced that this man was as deadly as when he first met him, even though he displayed a mild demeanour to the world.

The dwarf set a fresh cup of tea before him. WoShi said, "Perhaps we can start anew?" The situation was non-negotiable. If he accepted the tea, the discussion would continue. Would they allow him to leave? Alive!

LiPing exhaled loudly and accepted the tea. The tea had a light mint flavour and was surprisingly good. He grunted in appreciation. WoShi knocked off an invisible speck on his hanfu coat, a nervous reflex, relieved that LiPing would listen.

WoShi said, "I have something important, but before that, I want you to know that your bodyguards are WangYi's spies. They would have reported on you meeting me if that is any consolation for their death."

LiPing argued in disbelief, "I don't believe you. Why would WangYi, of all people, spy on me? WangMang trusts me."

WoShi laughed and said, "You should know better; after all, you spy on your spies." LiPing's face turned ashen.

"I am sorry, Marquis. I shall face death at your hands but will not engage in anything against the imperial palace." He leaned back in defiance.

WoShi gave a slight nod. "Fair enough. I wouldn't accept anything less from the security head of the imperial palace. But if I were to propose raising the glory of our empire without directly involving the people under your protection, would you help?"

LiPing pondered and replied, "I will gladly collaborate if the regent or the royal family agree."

WoShi acknowledged him, "Frankly, I wouldn't need your help if I had the blessings of the imperial family."

WoShi stretched his legs, removed a kink, and folded them back. "I am getting old and can't handle too much intrigue. I shall be direct with you, General. I must tell you a story before that. Say it I must, if anything is to be accomplished through you." LiPing copied WoShi and made himself comfortable. He needed time and an opportunity to escape this place.

WoShi said, "Our empire possesses abundant military knowledge regarding weapons or strategy. We are militarily far superior to our nomadic neighbours, the Huns. However, when our explorers ventured beyond the steppe during Emperor Wu's reign, they encountered culturally and militarily formidable civilisations."

"Did you know we defeated the Huns because of larger horses? We bought them from the kingdoms out west and bred more horses for the army. Imagine an invasion from across the steppe, and I am not talking about the Huns. Do we know anything about our enemies beyond the steppe?" He scoffed at himself. "Sure, we have the wall, but is that enough?"

WoShi shrugged exaggeratedly and said, "We spy on our people instead of gathering intelligence from powerful military nations. Do we know what weapons they use, their military strategies, the size of their armies, and whether they possess any technological military advantages?"

LiPing cringed at these observations. WoShi was right. They focused on internal squabbles, resulting in a corrupt bureaucracy and a weak military.

LiPing probed, "What do we need from beyond, Marquis? You need to speak to WangMang, not me. What am I doing here?"

WoShi grunted and said, "Let me get to that. We have ample iron ore in Han. We produce cast iron, which is heavy and brittle. What we need is the recipe to create rustproof and flexible iron."

LiPing was not impressed and replied, "Our bronze swords can cut flesh, the same as a sword made of a different metal. We do not need flexible iron, and to my knowledge, such a metal is not available anywhere."

WoShi could not contain his irritation. His response was caustic, "Spoken like a true frog, threatening a snake entering its pond."

WoShi pulled a box from beneath the low table where the tea was served and retrieved a knife. He wedged the thin blade into the wooden floor and pulled hard—it snapped with a tinny sound! He drew a green-black knife with a double frog mating as a handle from his waistband, and LiPing squirmed in his seat. He recognised this knife! WoShi wedged the knife in the floorboard, pulled it back, and let it go. The blade oscillated wildly with a whirring sound but did not break. LiPing was intrigued. This was not about WangMang.

WoShi said, "Qin Shi Huangdi, the first Qin Emperor, wanted the immortality elixir, which was said to be found not at one, but at four places in Tianzhu. We sent out a large army with the best of our men to confiscate the elixir of life, crossing the perpetually white mountains. No one returned from that expedition, and soon they were forgotten.

Eighteen years later, six to eight of the original twenty-five hundred returned. They remained in the mountains and were known as the "golden glow." They are the immortals we revere to this day.

After a pause, WoShi added, "The immortals helped Zhang Liang and LuiBang to defeat the Qin, and the Han empire came into being."

LiPing nodded, "A true tale merged with myth."

WoShi cocked his eyebrow and asked, "Which part?"

LiPing clarified, "The part of the immortals is a myth."

WoShi did not nod. "I thought so, too, until I saw the mummified bodies of the immortals." LiPing was shaken!

"It must be someone else. If they were indeed immortals, how could they die?"

WoShi said, "WangMang has seen them too, and the medallion of the immortals hangs around his neck." LiPing was astounded! His men had already informed him that WangMang was wearing something beneath his hanfu.

LiPing enquired, "And what's this got to do with light, flexible iron that does not rust?"

"This knife and medallion are from Tianzhu. We need to send someone they expect to acquire the recipe. I believe that this medallion is his identification."

LiPing could not hide his disbelief. "You want something that the regent wears?" he added sarcastically. How about the Emperor's seal or the necklace worn by the Empress?"

WoShi sighed heavily and said, "I may be an old man now, but I remain the strategist that the Emperor or Empress will summon in a crisis. We need iron to triumph in a war in the future. We can use iron to make ploughs, carriages, and spades. We have many uses for this light, sturdy metal that does not rust." WoShi pleaded with LiPing, "Shouldn't securing the iron recipe be our foremost concern for a greater Han?"

WoShi revealed information about SuJin and his sworn brothers from their time at the chophouse to LiPing. He said, "While their destiny is certain to unravel, we can seize the opportunity to acquire the recipe for rust-free iron."

LiPing did not disclose that he knew SuJin. He asked, "Will the boys return to Han with the recipe? What if they stay back in Tianzhu or die?"

WoShi said, "I am sending my man CaoShen along with them. He will return as soon as he acquires the recipe. The prophecy is not his concern."

LiPing doubted, "If the Yellow River turns thrice, it has not happened in a lifetime before!"

WoShi smiled and said, "The river has already turned twice and is full of silt. We can expect a third one shortly. The prophecy is unfolding as foretold."

LiPing persisted in expressing his concerns. "Tianzhu must be a large kingdom or many kingdoms. How will they find their way? Who will the boys meet?"

WoShi grunted and was candid about what he thought. "Monks from distant kingdoms are visiting our lands through the port of Malaka. We have learned from these monks about an elusive Aryan race in Tianzhu. A massive river changed course after an earthquake, and they had to abandon their lands. I believe that our boys need to find these Aryans, and a part of the prophecy we are unaware of will come to fruition."

LiPing harrumphed and said, "I don't know about the significance of the medallion, but I do know that WangMang won't take it off his chest. He keeps it on while he is washed, too."

WoShi exclaimed in shock, "Oh, that means we need the Empress to take it from him."

LiPing laughed. "The Empress? Forget it!" He added, "The Empress is ill and confined to her private chamber. She doesn't attend court anymore for nobles and bureaucrats to reach her. It's just her maids and doctors who attend to her needs. People going in and out of her palace are managed by men loyal to WangMang. They are there to prevent any petition to remove him from reaching her."

WoShi was concerned. "We don't have time! Once the Empress dies, WangMang will have no one to stop him from usurping the throne. We need to reach out to her. Now!"

LiPing was unimpressed and remarked, "I must warn you that if someone manages to sneak past all defences and reach the Empress, she won't listen. Surely, asking the Empress to tell the regent to give up his medallion is preposterous."

"That is why I am volunteering myself!" WoShi declared.

LiPing looked at WoShi, speechless. "You're desperate!" He finally muttered, adding, "I'm not sure how you can convince the ailing Empress to accept your crazy "prophecy" and "flexible iron better than brass' for Han and then make her persuade the regent to relinquish a medallion he treasures."

LiPing advised WoShi, "It seems a far-fetched proposition."

WoShi was resolute. "If anyone can, she might listen to me. She is our last hope!"

LiPing was sceptical that the Empress would listen to WoShi. He said, "She isn't going to listen to anything you say against WangMang, even though I've been told she is not pleased with his role as regent."

"I have to try. I need to appeal to the Empress." WoShi was firm.

LiPing remembered his promise to ShiDan to help SuJin. Perhaps this was it. Since WoShi was only interested in speaking to the Empress, LiPing agreed to help, but nothing more.

As LiPing crossed the bamboo grove, CaoShen hailed him by swinging a burning torch and handed him a cylinder—two pieces of cork held together by a brass band.

As LiPing examined it, CaoShen said, "Be careful with that! Inside is a hollow brass needle filled with numbing poison and sealed with beeswax." When LiPing looked at him, perplexed, CaoShen added, "For you! It will freeze your body and numb your pain."

LiPing stared at the dwarf in disbelief and replied, "I won't need this. I'm not doing anything illegal!"

CaoShen shrugged his shoulders. With a resigned sigh, he took the slim cylinder and said, "If I end up using it, let history remember that the butcher of Han looked at death in the face and laughed."

****

Two weeks later, on a cue from LiPing, WoShi left for the "temple of healing," where three medicinal deities—BaoDaDi, the god of medicine; ShenDaDi, the divine farmer of medicinal herbs; and HuaTuo, the heavenly physician—were revered and worshipped. Doctors and astrologers had gathered here to give medical advice and offer prayers for the ailing Empress.

WoShi joined the group as a physician specialising in dreams and portent explanations. The group warmly welcomed the old man as one of their own. They were to reconfirm the medication that the palace physicians prescribed to the Empress and report to the bureaucracy.

A day later, there was a commotion, and the imperial guards demanded that the doctors identify themselves with their invitation scrolls. A bureaucrat checked the invitation scrolls, and he caught a fake invite and apprehended a doctor despite the latter's screams of innocence. Alarmed by the intrusion, LiPing commanded the physicians to board carriages and arranged accommodation within the Empress Dowager's palace.

Unfortunately, they could not visit the Empress directly. Imperial physicians attended to the Empress and dismissed the external team's medicinal recommendations to the bureaucracy. Undeterred, LiPing pressed the palace physicians to consult the invited doctors and astrologers to discuss the Empress's illness, threatening to replace them if her health deteriorated.

After many arguments, ridicule, and raised voices, the doctors could not agree on the treatment to be given to the Empress. WoShi stood up and addressed the group: "Old age can't be reversed. It must be endured." The boldness of WoShi's address shocked the palace physicians, who demanded his removal, but the palace bureaucrats were interested in hearing him out.

WoShi continued, "I recommend bringing the Empress out of the dark room twice daily to expose her to the morning and evening sun and gently massage her body. She should be given hot soups made from watercress and broth from bird's meat."

Palace bureaucrats were impressed with WoShi's commonsense assessment. Despite the cold, they moved the Empress out of her chamber in the mornings and evenings, considerably improving her health.

LiPing told the bureaucrats, "This old physician has proven very competent. I shall personally take him to assess the Empress while she is lounging in the garden."

****

LiPing escorted WoShi and said, "We are on our way to wake a bear in hibernation. I can't predict how the Empress will react when she recognises you. You are not meant to be here."

With a stony expression, WoShi grimly declared, "It's quite likely that she will become angry when she finds us unannounced in her private chamber, but we have no other options."

LiPing decided to cut down WoShi if things went awry. WangMang would be pleased to see WoShi dead. The regent might believe him if he claimed he recognised and killed WoShi as an imposter. How he would convince bureaucrats that he did not recognise WoShi, despite the grandmaster wearing a common Hanfu, was a problem he would have to face.

They arrived at a spacious foyer overlooking a garden filled with snow-covered pine trees, a frozen pond, and bridges adorned with a light dusting of snow on their guardrails. The sight was breathtaking, and WoShi stood and took a deep breath, savouring the moment.

LiPing asked, "What is the matter, Marquis?"

WoShi said, "I want this scene to be etched in my mind if I die today." LiPing grunted in assent.

The silk curtains were pulled back, allowing waning sunlight to stream into a red-coloured pavilion. The Empress was napping on a couch with raised cushions, and incense was lit in the arbour. She was surrounded by her maids and physicians, who softly whispered to one another.

WoShi and LiPing were stopped by a eunuch some distance away, and they bowed formally to the sleeping Empress. The senior physician sent his assistant to whisper about her discomforts and diet. WoShi patiently listened to him, nodding frequently, and said aloud, "Ahh. Is she sleeping well? Without dreams?"

The attending maidens looked up in horror as a senior attendant waved her hand, shooing them away. The damage was done, and the Empress awoke.

She said, "I wasn't aware that it was visiting time. Who is that man? Am I dressed appropriately, girls?" She inquired.

There was a confused silence, and WoShi bowed low and said, "As the Han mother wishes, I shall leave."

He turned to leave, but LiPing blocked his path. "The Empress did not ask you to leave. She commanded that you announce yourself, physician." WoShi looked at LiPing in confusion as the maids assisted the frail dowager Empress into a seated position.

The Empress said, "You must be the dream doctor who advised me to get fresh air. Tell me, what did I dream about?"

WoShi said, "Celestial majesty, you dreamt that your grandson was upon the dragon throne and the empire was peaceful and prosperous. All the Han ancestors and your son in heaven are pleased with his just rule."

A smile spread across the Empress dowager's face, and she said, "Outrageous!"

"Come closer, old man."

Li Ping prodded WoShi to move forward. The Empress Dowager squinted at him and chuckled, recognising WoShi. "Oh, I thought I was done with intrigues for a lifetime."

"I could have sworn that my voice is familiar, but now I don't need to swear. I know. Are you speaking to me in the afterlife, WoShi?"

WoShi chuckled and bowed low to the Empress. Realising that WoShi was there to convey something significant, she asked, "Should I send away the maids and physicians now that I am in your caring hands, dream catcher?"

WoShi said, "Empress, that would make it easier for you to decide on your next course of action." She waved her hands, hurrying the maids and physicians away.

WoShi sat down on a step leading into the pavilion, some distance from the Empress. The Empress dowager giggled, "WoShi, you cunning old fox, you got through without WangMang's knowledge. I am impressed. So, to what do I owe this visit? Something my nephew did, I suppose." She laughed, adding, "Ah, palace intrigue is stale without your flavouring. There is no charm left in the impotent Lui.

I am a failure to the Han bloodline and remain alive because I dread facing the illustrious Han ancestors."

WoShi replied, "I wouldn't be here if I couldn't change that, Empress."

The Empress snorted in disdain. "You expect WangMang to usurp the throne, and the Han line will end. You want to avert that. Why else would you be here?"

"No, not at all," WoShi said, and the Empress's eyes opened wide.

"Great Empress, could you give me time to explain?"

The Empress yawned deliberately. "Go ahead; forgive me if I nod off to sleep. You aren't the first one to advise me against WangMang."

"Empress, I hope you will strive to be healthy and accomplish what must be done once I am finished speaking," WoShi added. "Allow me to keep your pompous physicians busy until we are done here." Empress Wang chuckled at WoShi's audacity and watched him beckon the senior physician forward.

WoShi commanded the doctor like a servant. "Bring the Empress crushed apple juice mixed with the essence of recently picked Reishi mushrooms – in juice extract. Four portions of apple juice mixed with one part of water, crushed and strained with two Reishi mushrooms."

WoShi turned around, dismissing the astonished doctor, and spoke to the Empress. "Do you remember your wedding, Empress?"

The Empress replied, "Don't dabble in meaningless talk. No woman forgets her wedding. How is it related to WangMang?"

WoShi said, "Empress, I am not here to talk about WangMang's rule or misrule. Frankly, it's the least of my concerns." The Empress furrowed her brow in surprise.

WoShi said, "You were chosen for your birth under a particular star alignment to enhance the prosperity of Han. The time has come for you to make far-reaching decisions to set the course for Han."

The Empress's face became solemn. "It has not worked out as the astrologer predicted. My progeny could not give birth to a male offspring, and look at where the empire is heading. Lui will give way to a Wang or civil unrest, maybe." She showed discomfort but held back her emotions. WoShi waited until the Empress regained her composure. No one interrupted the most powerful person in the empire when she wanted time to gather herself.

After a long pause, she said, "I have hurt the sentiments of the gods, and these days, I have stopped pleading for their forgiveness. WangMang is obsessed with transforming the peasantry, but I doubt the people will eagerly embrace these reforms. We seem to have lost the mandate to rule," she sniffed.

She looked at WoShi to confirm her assessment, but the man was smiling. "Did I say something humorous, old man? I thought I was describing tragedy," she said, annoyed.

WoShi chuckled and said, "Great Empress, you have done your job as the gods decreed, and nobody will fault you, surely not in the afterlife. This, I promise. Let me explain."

He told her about SuJin. Her face changed, and she clenched her fists, displaying all emotions, from curiosity to sadness to murderous rage, as WoShi described SuJin's life from a student to a warrior.

She frequently interrupted WoShi to confirm with evidence and events. When the physician returned with her drink, she asked him to pour it into two bowls. Then, completely departing from tradition, she motioned WoShi to share the drink.

The pompous imperial physician felt embarrassed and hesitated to pour for the lowly country physician standing before him. The delay infuriated the Empress, and she said, "I shall send you to the Huns as their doctor for disobedience." He quickly poured the mixture into another cup, and with trembling hands, he bowed and offered it to

WoShi, who callously shooed him away.

The Empress took a sip and smacked her lips in appreciation. She dripped with sarcasm when she said, "So you want me to give up on my grandson? In your words, the finest of the Han lineage ever to be born, the greatest Han warrior, and a true gentleman. A Prince endorsed by the gods and most suitable man to rule this empire by birth and quality."

WoShi said, "Yes! Han ancestors demand it."

She laughed and mocked WoShi. "I don't believe a word of what you say. You are a paranoid old man! Surely, this is your convoluted plan to overthrow the regent?"

WoShi was ready for this outburst and said, "The Yellow River has turned twice and is poised for the third, with silt piling up. WangMang is a witness to the tomb of the immortals, and he has a pendant taken from there. Surely you agree that two emperors have died without a progeny, not counting your son." Empress Wang was irritated.

WoShi continued earnestly, "I have no authority to convince you and don't want to say anything more, Empress. Why don't you make an evaluation yourself? Recheck the evidence. A Lui gem of imperial origin is like a diamond and will shine through."

Empress Wang leaned forward and snapped at WoShi. "XuPing was heavy with child, and I had her executed. With no witnesses to the conception and birth, how can you stand in front of me?" She coughed, and her maid approached her, but she curtly waved her away. Despite her vehemence, she was interested in hearing WoShi out.

WoShi handed over an old scroll. "What is this?"

WoShi said, "It is a transcript of what the palace astrologer discussed with Crown Prince LuiAo. He predicted that XuPing would die, and her son would be lost." The Empress read it twice and checked the scroll for its age.

She said, "He told me! My son told me what the palace astrologer said but did not mention XuPing or the child. I executed XuPing hastily, unnecessarily doubting her character!"

She pondered for a while and remarked, "Yes, Emperor Cheng was adamant that his son from XuPing wasn't dead. I wish he had a better hold on his harem. Isn't it ironic that, ultimately, it was his lack of control over the women in his life and their machinations that got him killed!"

Empress Wang sat up to conclude the meeting and said, "WoShi, prove the boy's lineage, and perhaps I shall consider the evidence."

"There is a witness to his conception and birth," said WoShi.

Empress Wang sat up. "What! Both? Who?"

"Three, in fact!" The Empress fixed her gaze on WoShi as he continued, "Fang the witch, ShiDan, and your palace security head, LiPing, a confidant of Emperor Cheng." LiPing looked at WoShi in surprise, shaken that the Marquis was aware of his role in SuJin's birth.

WoShi continued as a stoic Empress Wang listened. "XuPing did not leave the harem, and after the fertility rituals, she was placed under house arrest. She was a chaste woman, and Emperor Cheng was aware of this. ShiDan, the eunuch, and LiPing, as bodyguards, stood guard when Emperor Cheng impregnated XuPing on the first day of her house arrest. "They were present again when the witch cut out your grandson from XuPing's womb." The Empress dowager winced; a tear fell from her moist eyes as she clenched her pillows tightly with her frail hands.

She looked at her trusted head of security with cold eyes. WoShi told her, "LiPing and ShiDan were under oath to Emperor Cheng not to disclose anything until his son was born, fearing that he might be kidnapped. Unfortunately, the outcome was different, but as prophesied."

Empress Wang shivered with unbridled rage and told WoShi, "Old man, if any detail, any single detail, turns out to be untrue, you will die the foulest death possible, and I shall watch it done. My son tried to convince me that I had a grandson, but I did not believe him."

The Empress looked at WoShi with piercing eyes and said bitterly, "I let my son down! I let him down because I trusted people like you in doubting faithful XuPing."

"Why didn't any of you speak up then?" the Empress wept, her fragile frame shaking. Her maids hurried forward, only to be scolded. "Stay back! Let me be."

WoShi waited until the Empress dowager regained her composure. She sniffed and said, "So, my grandson wishes to ascend the throne?"

"No!" WoShi insisted, "The prophecy cannot be altered. As the grand Empress of Han, you must have faith in his destiny. Of all people, you should ensure that he departs for Tianzhu. The Prince will release all Han ancestors from their celestial oath."

"Is WangMang aware of this?"

"I don't know, and he wouldn't be too bothered about this," WoShi said.

"Bring the boy to me. A mother can identify her progeny. If he is true, the bigger task is to persuade the palace courtiers and the bureaucracy to see it my way."

WoShi pleaded with her, "Let him go! SuJin is a Prince of destiny!"

The Empress sneered at WoShi. "You still want me to listen to the advice of your kind after all this! I am a grandmother, and I need my grandson beside me if that is the last duty to my dead husband and son. I will tear this empire apart to get to him and annihilate anyone in my way."

She glowered with resolve but added a severe warning, "Pray, WoShi, that he is my blood, or else you will witness a mother's wrath for giving her hope!"

WoShi was alarmed. This discussion was not going the way he wanted.

"Can my grandson and WangMang reconcile?" She inquired.

WoShi said, "No... Not if the prophecy is to play out. WangMang's fate is to bring chaos to Han, while SuJin's fate is to fulfil the promise of his ancestors in Tianzhu. It is as foretold."

The Empress raged. "All you want is the medallion hanging around the neck of my nephew. I suppose that if it weren't for this minor detail, I could have died without knowing that I had a grandson."

WoShi kept quiet. "Isn't it?" She demanded passionately, and WoShi remained silent.

She gazed at WoShi for a moment and said, "Get out!"

She curtly told him behind his back, "You might have done what you feel is right, although I doubt you had the best interests of the Lui clan." WoShi paused, turned around, and bowed.

She asked, "You swear you did not know about my grandson until he joined the school?" WoShi nodded.

Empress Dowager Wang said, "Wait until I mull over this vexing, bittersweet problem."

She clapped her hands and said, "I am hungry!"

****

The Empress summoned WoShi a day later to the courtroom. She was dressed in all the regal finery that befitted the position of an Empress dowager. The entire court, including WangMang, was in attendance.

The court administrator called WoShi forward and said, "Marquis, the Empress commands you to bring SuJin, the green hunter and your apprentice, to this court. He is to be entrusted with an imperial assignment."

WoShi bowed low and said, "As you command, celestial Empress." She beckoned the eunuch responsible for making announcements.

WangMang stalled the eunuch and addressed the court, "Great Empress, all your wishes are my commands. Please don't vex yourself any further. I shall set up the entire military and bureaucratic machinery to locate him."

The Empress smiled sweetly at WangMang and told him, "I assure you, nephew, this is not your priority. I want the Marquis to be responsible." She gave WoShi a stern look and added, "... but you will punish him if he fails."

The Empress legalised a scroll by imprinting it with her seal above the Han seal. This scroll allowed SuJin to travel freely through any province or county, collect horses and grain from the local governor, and receive all the privileges of an esteemed guest of the Empress.

Palace mandarins wondered whether the Empress had become senile, but the presence of the wily WoShi, the cunning strategist, dispelled that thought.

****

WoShi entered the dungeons and looked at LiPing's rotting body. His face showed signs of swelling, with his nose, ears, and lips torn apart. Dark blood clotted on the stumps of his fingers, and the rank smell of decay was pervasive.

Trembling with rage, he turned to CaoShen and said, "WangMang has gone too far this time. Prophecy or no prophecy, I will kill him."

He touched LiPing's stiff body and said, "The gods won't forget your sacrifice, Commander. We will avenge you." He turned to the dwarfs and asked, "Where and how did you find him?"

"We purchased this corpse from a scavenger paid to dismember and dispose of the body discreetly. The scavenger said that the palace guards mentioned it was the work of a murderous gang in Changan."

WoShi arched his eyebrow in disbelief. The dwarf said, "The palace guards did not acknowledge that the body belonged to LiPing, but the scavenger recognised the butcher of Han."

WoShi said, "Prepare the body and ensure a proper burial with all rituals. Their torture would have made him reveal everything."

CaoShen said, "No need to panic." He pulled aside LiPing's cheek and showed many purple puncture wounds inside. He said, "LiPing needs our respect. The man bit into the dart tip before being captured and was frozen stiff with poison. They mutilated his body, but he wouldn't have felt anything. They wouldn't have found the dart until it was too late. Indeed, the butcher of Han laughed in the face of death!"

WoShi said, "We must warn SuJin."

CaoShen said, "I will set out immediately to bring the boys back." He looked at LiPing's body and added, "Just one other thing, Master."

WoShi asked, "What?"

"This is not the handiwork of WangMang. He couldn't have had time for this. The rot on the body suggests LiPing was dead before you met WangMang at court." WoShi looked at CaoShen with wide eyes and mouth agape, and he continued, "Someone else high in the imperial hierarchy! No alarm was raised when the celebrated butcher of Han went missing."

"Who?" Asked WoShi with a growl.

"This is the handiwork of the Empress Dowager." WoShi looked at CaoShen, wide-eyed in shock.

"What!" He exclaimed and, after a while, nodded in comprehension. "Of course, it makes sense." He bitterly added, "This is an execution. Revenge! I wonder if she watched LiPing's torture!

He exclaimed after deep thought, "She did not punish LiPing for keeping the inception and birth of her grandson a secret. She punished him for not informing Emperor Cheng that his son was alive. That was the betrayal!"

23 HuKui Is Captured

The dwarfs usually bartered salt, fish, and pelts with the village for horseshoes, nails, and millet. With almost a complete village occupying the valley this year, purchases were unusually high.

HuKui paid the village head with a gold coin for their purchases. In these remote villages, gold coins were seldom seen, and the dwarfs' single coin quickly became the hottest topic of conversation.

Over wine, the village head boasted about how the villagers thrived that year due to an unusually high trade with the dwarfs. He subtly suggested that the dwarfs might be allied with bandits. How else could they possess a gold coin, require many provisions, and buy all the wine they brewed?

Elsewhere, HuKui and the dwarfs realised too late that they had drawn too much attention by paying in gold and were eager to leave. Villagers came from their homesteads to gape at the dwarfs when they heard they paid in gold.

One of the wooden axles on their cart cracked as they descended the rough mountain path. The fix would take two more days, as the village carpenter needed to cut the log to size, and metal bands had to be wrapped around the axle for reinforcement before they could depart.

****

YuanLin, the bandit chief, was itching for some action. He pondered, raiding the village out of boredom, flexing his enormous arms and easing a kink in his thick neck, but he quickly dismissed the thought. None of the villagers had money, and some of his men had families here. Moreover, it did not fit into his dear brother YuanYi's plans to make them respectful city dwellers.

He was forced to idle away his days before the merchant convoy he planned to attack arrived beyond the mountains. After the raid, they would return and disperse into the settlements on this side as farmers.

It troubled him that the dwarfs had regular people with them who were not from these parts. Could they be harbouring fugitives? His brother's sources reported a reward for capturing two fugitives linked to the dwarfs.

Alas, his brother, YuanYi, was superstitious about dwarfs and avoided them like the plague. He was insistent that they should leave them alone, stating, "Brother, they are unfortunate, and if you kill them, their misfortune might befall us!"

YuanYi was away, gathering intelligence on the movement of the heavily guarded merchant convoy. Attacking the heavily guarded convoy would result in a high death toll, and they had hired many villagers as arrow fodder. After the Yellow River had turned, the countryside sprouted many settlements, and the starving families provided him with plenty of recruits.

YuanLin understood greed, and his method of securing his men's loyalty was a stroke of genius. He would share their attack plan upfront, allowing his men to negotiate their price based on the risks involved. Invariably, inexperienced recruits jumped at the chance to man the vanguard to earn more money but faced the battle's brunt. None of the survivors complained as they chose the position themselves.

Knowing that imperial captains tracked bandits through the loot they sold or pawned, Yuan Lin did not share any gold with his men. Instead, he compensated his men in smaller coins through credits for purchasing grain and meat from shops. The majority of their pay was withheld as security to ensure loyalty.

His jeweller, HeGan, melted down gold recovered from the raid to create imperial coins. HeGan and his brother, YuanYi, arranged to loan gold coins to city jewellers, who primarily lent them to traders. Precious stones were set into new jewellery and traded to unsuspecting goldsmiths. YuanLin laughed at this arrangement, as he did not need to hoard his treasure and appreciated his brother's brilliant mind. No one, including YuanLin, could count, but they knew a considerable amount of gold had been amassed.

His counter was to pay out any man who wished to leave his gang, but hardly anyone accepted this offer. The allure of easy money held them back. It was another matter that no one could trace the few who had quit.

YuanLin had a troubling tendency to take the lives of his captives without any sense of restraint. He justified the killings by claiming he could not leave any witnesses. YuanLin loved the power he wielded over hapless men—to see their fear and defecation as he tortured them. It helped that his men feared him for his brutality and avoided getting on his wrong side.

****

They planned to attack the heavily armed caravan from all sides on the open plains, where the caravan guards least expected it. YuanLin was eager to test the discipline of his recruits. Would the vanguard baulk and falter under a heavy fire of arrows?

What better way to prepare the men than to attack the hapless dwarfs? Wiping out a band of nomadic dwarfs in a remote valley would hardly catch anyone's attention. Exposing the recruits to the heady rush of violence would ensure discipline in the subsequent raid.

YuanLin regarded dwarfs as imperfect men and craved their extermination. Unfortunately, his men were reluctant, fearing the dwarf's association with vengeful spirits. Shamans had warned that these spirits would claim their young of similar stature and plague their villages.

His brother mentioned that in Changan, the fugitives fled from a school with many dwarfs. Could they be hiding here? It wounded his pride that the imperial army offered a higher bounty for the Han boy and a Hun than his head.

YuanLin had sent his scouts to spy on the dwarfs in the valley. They reported a few carts, including the one that came to the village, an empty pigpen, mules, and a few horses—nothing more. However, they also reported that a few boys and dwarfs trained with weapons. So, who were these people? They had to be fugitives, but were they the ones he was interested in?

****

YuanLin lost his family in a brutal famine, and he and a few other boys survived by resorting to cannibalism. Finally, the local magistrate arrived with soldiers to eradicate the abominations. They tried to hide and flee, but the search was thorough. His younger brother convinced him of the futility of fighting against the imperial guards. They locked themselves in a cage and persuaded the soldiers that they were victims and survived.

A well-meaning bureaucrat took them in, but YuanLin ran away. His brother stayed behind, learned to read and count, and became a minor officer in the county. YuanLin became a bandit and ruthless killer with a taste for human blood. Much later, his brother, YuanYi, saved him from an imperial ambush, and they have been together since then. YuanYi became the link between the bandits and the county officials.

YuanLin listened to a scout recount their reconnaissance of the dwarfs. "The rebels are young boys, and some horses are the shorter Hun breed. The black horse is a good steal. Tan would be interested in that horse!"

The other scout confirmed, "Yeah, the black one with the white hooves. It's a beauty."

YuanLin snapped his head forward. He was grinning, no more waiting!

****

HuKui broke camp early, and they were high on the mountain trail by first light. They had lost sight of the village behind them in the morning mist and were nearing the pass that led into the minor valley. They needed to traverse this valley, ascend the higher slopes of the next mountain, and descend into the dwarfs' valley.

They had only a few hours to reach the ridge, beyond which they would be under the watchful eyes of the Hun. HuKui realised he had a newfound respect for the barbarian and his constant vigil.

HuKui told Wong, the dwarf leading the horse cart, "The Hun will give us an earful on how slow we are, coming in late by a few days. His tongue is sharper than a knife." The dwarf laughed. They all idolised the fun-loving Hun. He had helped the dwarf warriors improve their archery and horse riding by leaps and bounds.

With his longer stride, HuKui soon outpaced the slow-moving cart. On hearing excited chatter, he turned around. Wong had unloaded a few bamboo stems packed tightly with black powder - a mix of saltpetre extracted from the sediments of the mountain caves, yellow sulphur, and charcoal. Batu had asked them to bring back the smoky black powder used by Shamans to create a diversion to sneak into Changan.

HuKui ran back to stop Wong, but he was too late. He watched in fascination as Wong fired the powder with a flint. The powder sputtered and *whooshed*, throwing up black smoke in a cloud. Without waiting, Wong ran to the other side of the road to light another stem of black powder.

An explosive CRACK resounded and echoed through the valley, accompanied by a heavy belching of black smoke. HuKui grimaced and rubbed his ears, which rang with a high-pitched sound—the aftereffect of the explosion. Pungent-smelling smoke billowed into the sky, and bits of bamboo scattered everywhere.

Wong desperately tried to ignite the second black-powder bamboo stem, but it refused to catch fire. "Come on, come on, please catch fire!" He pleaded.

HuKui screamed at him, "What are you doing, Wong, you idiot!" He walked over and slapped the flint from Wong's hands. The dwarf looked up in dismay when two arrows struck down near them.

A voice cut through the mist, "Listen to your bigger friend, small man! Stop lighting the noisy black powder; it gives me a headache."

Another voice said, "Ahh, the pungent smell. They have just burnt the exploding bamboo stems used by shamans for chasing spirits away!"

Someone else exclaimed, "The cursed valley is the abode of spirits."

The first man's voice said, "All the spirits will remain here. You can add to it, but none escapes."

Wong's shoulders slumped in defeat! He looked at HuKui and said, "Too late, anyway!" HuKui peered into the morning mist to see the silhouettes of men on horses. Bandits?

The voice laughed and said, "Don't bother! It's a valiant attempt, but your friends can't hear the noise. The valley of the dwarfs is further up."

"Not from this distance, for sure," another voice said.

"Shut up!" Said the first man. "No one told me they had bought black powder from the village!" He continued, "It's fortunate we planned to ambush them here instead of further up. That noise would have ruined my surprise for the others."

The man trotted his horse forward and looked down at Wong. "I love people who take the initiative. They have *a delicate flavour*. Although small as you are, we might still make a meal out of you. A soup, maybe." He laughed, and more voices joined in.

HuKui watched in despondency as mounted men trotted towards them from the road above while many on foot approached from below. They were surrounded.

About twenty-odd men had them covered. The men were heavily armed, and four had drawn crossbows aimed at them. One man, his face disfigured by smallpox, acknowledged Wong with regret, "Good try! Nobody can hear the thunder from this distance. The crosswinds that slice through the valley will disperse the black smoke. Look, there's none of it left!"

The man with pockmarks looked back at the mountain peaks faintly outlined in the morning light and scratched his chin. "You might see the smoke if you're up on the mountaintop, but who's crazy enough to be up there in this cold."

Someone chipped in with a laugh, "Pockface, don't worry! Even though you joined us late, we have arranged to cover the paths from the valley to the plains. If anyone dares to come investigating, our men will waylay them."

Their leader, a big man with broad shoulders, said in appreciation, "Good!"

The large man asked Wong, "So, why are you carrying black powder? You're no shaman! Do you wish to frighten the fish in the lake into spawning tiny ones your size?" His cronies erupted into laughter, and the leader looked around and grinned.

Wong grinned back at him and said, "There are dragons in there. I'm sure you'll meet a dragon spawn soon and regret waylaying us." Some of the men stared at Wong in fear.

The big man glared at Wong. "You shall soon tell me everything going on there. Unfortunately, it will need to wait until tonight. Some interesting people, including a small man like you with an imperial scroll, are waiting to spill their guts to me. Who knows, by evening, your friends might join our intimate discussions within a bowl of soup." He flapped and slurped his tongue suggestively, and Wong couldn't suppress a shiver at what that meant.

A puzzled HuKui asked the man who seemed to be in charge, "Who are you, people? We have nothing valuable. So please, allow us to go in peace."

The leader acted surprised at not being recognised. "I am YuanLin, a respectable bandit. I steal from people," he smiled, waiting for recognition. His men hooted and slapped their thighs in laughter when they realised HuKui did not recognise their leader.

A smiling YuanLin's face fell in mock defeat. He held up his hand, and the group stopped laughing, except for a few sniggers that continued. "Ah. Too many people from the plains are flooding the mountains these days!" He turned to HuKui and said, "You don't recognise me by sight; that's fine! Not many have seen me! At least, you would have heard my name, YuanLin… " He batted his eyes with false sincerity.

HuKui pleaded, "I am sorry; I do not recognise you. YuanLin, we are peaceful men who catch fish and shall leave soon. Wong, isn't that true?" With a smile, he glanced at the dwarf, seeking reassurance.

Wong sharply warned HuKui, "This is not a chance meeting; it's an ambush. They know what we do in the valley. I have seen these men in the village."

A recent bandit recruit holding a mace remarked in alarm, "No! We cannot let them go. They can identify us."

In irritation, YuanLin turned to the man. "If they try to escape or give you trouble, you have my permission to soften them with your mace."

YuanLin hailed Pockface, saying, "What has this quaint countryside become? Look at this man. He hasn't heard of the famous YuanLin! Do they at least know that a crafty bureaucrat, not a Han emperor, rules them?" He smirked in disdain, and Pockface shrugged.

Pockface gestured to Wong and remarked to YuanLin, "We could use him. Quick thinking on his feet! He was smart to use the black powder! In a different circumstance, it would have created trouble for us."

After appraising him, YuanLin told Wong, "We have a Wong in our midst, too. Join us now and live! We can call you Tall Wong or Big Wong, whatever you prefer. I could use intelligent, proactive men. Tell me, my friend, how did you deduce we were waiting for you?"

Wong cleared his throat and spat on the ground. Then, with rank contempt, he replied, "I am not your friend and never will be. I could smell your foul breath downwind, almost a Li away. I thought an animal was rotting."

Pockface interjected angrily, "Enough, small man, you are flirting with death! Your mare would have whinnied and alerted you to our horses, which is how you guessed. Nobody else would use this road so early in the morning!" Pockface's interjection was an attempt to protect Wong.

A bandit told YuanLin, "He is taunting you, making you angry to earn a quick death." The muscles on YuanLin's unshaven face twitched, and he scowled at Wong, "I have changed my mind. I will kill you last, small man. You will be cut down to size for your impudence." He displayed a false smile that promised plenty of nastiness.

Realising their predicament, HuKui said, "We are fugitives like you. Let us go; we have nothing of value on us."

YuanLin grudgingly agreed at first, and his face brightened. "Whatever made you think we're on the wrong side of imperial law? I'm here to claim the reward on your friend's heads." He watched in satisfaction as HuKui's face turned pale. He continued, "I can't believe that lousy imperial rebels like you have a higher bounty on your heads than what the miserly magistrate of Zhou set on mine. How can this empire stoop so low? I mean, rebels have higher prices on their heads than bandits and murderers!" His cronies burst into peals of laughter.

Upon hearing the mention of the "magistrate of Zhou," the dwarfs realised who the bandit leader was, and their shoulders drooped. YuanLin grinned and moistened his lips, moving his tongue like a snake. The dwarfs had positively confirmed YuanLin's identity. No one had ever escaped from the clutches of the dreaded *cannibal of Zhou*!

Unaware, HuKui said, "Look here, I am a scholar and have two bits of gold in our camp. I shall part with them. You can be on your way after that."

"What if I keep your bits of gold and sell your fugitive friends?" YuanLin laughed and pushed his horse close to HuKui, nudging him towards the mountainside.

HuKui angrily said, "Your life is what you'll get if you leave us alone! This is my word, or the boys will track you down, no matter which hole you hide in." HuKui proudly realised the undeniable truth: the boys would hunt these men down.

YuanLin feigned a yawn at HuKui. "Boys, eh...! Boys usually scamper off with their tails tucked firmly between their legs when they see me." YuanLin's insolence baffled HuKui. Why weren't they negotiating? Weren't they thieves? After money?

YuanLin said, "At least we can prosper from your death! Did I forget to mention that I am here for the Hun? I shall hand him over, perhaps dine with the magistrate, and tickle his wife. Now, that would be a laugh." He chuckled and pushed back the long locks of hair covering his face, exposing yellow teeth filed into incisors like those of a wild animal. The teeth repulsed and alarmed HuKui. He was missing something odious about this man.

YuanLin addressed his men. "Let's make a move. I am hungry! I hate tame surrenders. If the valley is cold, I shall return to the village and wait for my brother while you close things here." Pockface grunted in agreement.

The bandit chief pulled on his horse and trotted up the path. The bandits prodded their prisoners to walk up the trail, pushing them to the mountainside to prevent their escape.

The bandit with a mace walked alongside the dwarf, driving the cart. Wong cautioned HuKui. "Master, it is futile to negotiate with these monsters. That is the dreaded cannibal of Zhou. He eats his prisoners, and no one has made it out alive from his clutches."

"Don't talk unless spoken to," said the bandit, and he swung his club hard at Wong without warning. With all the training from Batu, Wong ducked dexterously out of harm's way. The blow glanced off the back of the horse, and the mare bolted forward with the cart.

Riders ahead scattered as the horse-cart charged through them. In that moment of confusion, Wong launched himself over the mountainside, sliding down a scree-covered slope and disappearing into the mist.

Bandits galloped back and enquired, "What happened?" The man who had swung the club held the mace up and said with an embarrassed expression, "He ducked."

"Where is he?" Asked Pockface. The bandit cautiously gestured to the steep side of the path.

YuanLin was furious. "Why would you try to damage my merchandise?"

The bandit responded, "He was talking too much, Chief. I wanted to soften him for you."

YuanLin said, "Capture him alive! Chop one of his feet for impudence and cauterise the wound. We don't want him to bleed and cheat us with a hasty death. Don't forget to bring back the feet that ran away from me."

HuKui gagged on hearing this and pleaded with YuanLin, "Please, I shall bring him back. There is no need for drastic measures."

YuanLin said, "Shut his mouth, I've heard enough." A bandit punched HuKui's midriff, and he collapsed with a groan, clutching his stomach.

YuanLin asked for the mace from the bandit responsible for Wong's escape. He frowned and said, "Good balance! Why would you miss a strike?" He held the mace up and suddenly smashed it on the head of the offending bandit, splitting his head like a ripe watermelon. The man would have dropped like a stone hadn't another bandit caught him. The man held up the body as YuanLin continued to smash the head to a pulp, screaming in fury, "This is the price you pay for letting the half-man escape. How do I trust you with holding a full man captive?"

With his fury abated, he was back to smiles and acknowledged the bandit holding up the dead body, covered in blood and bits of gore. The man callously dropped the headless body over the side of the road and mounted his skittish horse.

YuanLin sniffed the bloodied mace and sighed in pleasure. He licked bits of brain on the mace. "Fresh, warm meat, but too early for me! I have a delicate stomach."

YuanLin looked up to see the recent recruits looking on in horror and said, "What are you waiting for? Go, get him. I will make an exception and feast on his brains tonight. No one escapes YuanLin, and you can tell him that." HuKui retched violently.

YuanLin addressed his men sternly. "No more surprises for me unless it's a gift!"

Utterly chastened, two bandits tied up HuKui. They tied his hands and his feet together behind his back, stretching him out like a bow. One of the bandits said coldly, "Someone has to pay for the blood of our man." They tied him behind the cart while the dwarfs were tied to the side of the cart.

HuKui was dragged over the rough terrain behind the cart while the dwarfs sullenly walked behind. HuKui screamed as the sharp scree stones cut into his clothes and flesh, shredding him into a mass of red meat. His body was battered, and one of his eyes was swollen shut. Blood from his face was flowing into his mouth and nostrils, choking him. HuKui passed out.

Pockface stopped the cart after seeing HuKui's condition. He warned the bandits, "Now, be careful with that one. We don't want him to die and upset YuanLin. Put him on the cart. He isn't going anywhere." The bandits cut the loop and hung HuKui on the new axle the dwarfs had bought in the village.

They left the mountain path near a stream and walked deep into a clearing among the trees to their camp. YuanLin waved at the large contingent of his men waiting there. He told his cooks, "Serve me your morning rubbish."

He motioned to a pair of expert archers, "We have a half-man on the loose, a smart one. Let's see how the recruits capture him. Go leisurely after breakfast when the mist has thinned."

****

SuJin was practising Taichi high above the misty valley. Taichi had become a meditation in motion for him, coordinating his mind and body with the cold breath and elevating his consciousness. Since waking up from facing the dragons underwater, he was experiencing a heightened awareness. This created a sense of unease that drove him to scale the mountain before the first rays of light.

SuJin sensed a disturbance in the air—a faint rumble, like distant thunder! Hundreds of birds soared into the skies, their frantic flight visible above the mist. He thought he saw smoke in the distance, but it dissipated quickly.

Something within him quivered, and he sensed his friends were in trouble. He clambered down the cliff in double time and rode hard into camp. He slipped his horse with a slipknot to the hitching post and chirped like a squirrel when it spotted a bird of prey, his distress signal.

Batu was the first to reach SuJin. He was holding a bow notched with an arrow, and a quiver full of arrows hung from his waist. He looked calm, but his eyes were alert. He asked SuJin, "Do we make a dash for it or fight it out?"

SuJin said, "Wait! I don't know what it is. It could be a false alarm." Batu relaxed a bit and asked, "What happened?"

"I was up in the mountains, above the low clouds of mist, when I heard a clap of thunder and saw smoke. Hundreds of birds took off from the valley, leading to the village."

Batu stared at him and asked, "Did this thunder reverberate?" SuJin nodded. "That means the thunder was within the valley; it must be the black powder of the shamans."

By then, the others had gathered. Batu said, "We must presume this is a warning of an attack from our men coming in from the village." The boys nodded.

Qian asked, "Who could it be? Imperial forces, villagers, or bandits."

"SuWu, what do you think?" Asked SuJin

SuWu said, "Attacking our men away from the village makes sense only to gather intelligence. We are poor and of no consequence unless someone is after the bounty on Batu and SuJin."

SuWu continued, "JiaShao told me that most villagers here have bandits living with them, and they have informers at all the way stations to forewarn them. Our men would have come away if such an attack was imminent. No, it's not the imperial soldiers."

Qian asked, "How about villagers?"

SuWu puffed out his cheeks and said, "A morning ambush to gather intelligence suggests someone knowledgeable in combat, without witnesses. Not villagers! At most, they would imprison our men and wait for us to come down.

Qian persisted, "That leaves the bandits. Perhaps someone has informed the bandits about the bounty for capturing SuJin and Batu."

SuWu nodded, "It's feasible, which implies they are working with imperial bureaucrats."

SuWu looked at Qian and called him by his forbidden troop's name. "Black Death, You are our best tracker. Report your preliminary observations and avoid engaging with the enemy. We need information to prepare a counterattack."

SuWu motioned, "Batu, ride out to the stream, warn the dwarfs there, and get back."

SuWu turned to ChenHe and said, "Move the cart with our stock of dried fish, food, saddles and all valuables into the cave we made for storing the bows. Cover up all traces leading to the hiding place." ChenHe ran to hide their possessions.

SuJin told SuWu. "I shall go with Qian."

SuWu firmly refused. "Prince, let's wait for Qian to return before we do anything. We are blind to many aspects, whether we are targeted for an attack or if this is a false alarm. If so, what is the size of our enemy, and where and how are they deployed?"

Batu agreed with SuWu and said, "Qian! He will tell us whether we should fight or run."

SuJin calmly said, "No running! *We stick together and protect each other, always.*"

They watched as enthusiastic dwarfs rowed Qian out. SuWu whispered, "*Battle speed, brother.*"

Qian dipped his hand into the lake, anointing his hair with the water and offered prayers to the spirits. The mist swallowed him, and the tendrils in the boat's wake moved and closed like a jackal's tongue, smacking before a meal.

****

The dwarfs began arming themselves with throwing knives, arrows, swords, and cudgels. Hong, the warrior leader, told his team, Tong and Dong, "Normally, I would discount anyone saying that the dwarfs were under attack. Unfortunately, we have seen too much of the Prince to ignore his forewarning."

Tong grinned, "This is war, brothers, and with him on our side, the gods are with us."

Dong dramatically declared, going down on one knee and looking to the skies, "In a battle between evil men and the dwarfs, may the gods withhold their thunder and lightning. Instead, let them grant us a river of blood for our voracious knives and accept the demise of our enemies as an offering."

Tong snorted and scoffed at Dong. "Just because you trained under Batu and HuKui doesn't make you an undefeatable warrior, but don't worry. I am here to protect you!"

Hong ignored the bloodthirsty prayer and the bragging. "What happened out there? Until today, the villagers and the bandits have tolerated us."

Batu advised them. "If this turns into a battle, make it count. Kill anyone who has touched your brothers. Word spreads. It's the simplest way to ensure you aren't troubled again." The dwarfs nodded in agreement, their sparse beards bobbing up and down.

Although shrouded in mist, they could hear wings flapping as numerous birds flew from the valley periphery towards the lakeside. SuJin looked at Batu, and he shook his head. Strangers were entering the forest, and by the looks of it, there were many of them! Batu excused himself and rode out to check the streamside.

Restless, SuJin fiddled with his toy—a small but heavy brass ball tethered to a long leather strip. He flicked his wrist to throw the ball, striking a tree trunk and pulling it back into his hands just as it touched the target. He threw the ball repeatedly, hitting the same spot and weathering the wood under his assault. Batu had crafted a toy for children to hurl at one another, using a woven reed ball and a silk thread. The toy fascinated SuJin, and he had one made for himself with a brass ball used by the dwarfs to weigh fish.

Tong motioned to Dong with his eyes. SuJin wasn't looking at the tree trunk, but it struck true each time at the exact spot he had hit before. The dwarfs watched while they sharpened their knives, organising and selecting arrows from their pack.

An hour later, Batu returned with information that the streamside was calm, and the dwarf archers were on their way to fortify the defences at the lakeside.

ChenHe was gobbling up the meat and fish prepared for breakfast. SuWu couldn't hold back his annoyance and said, "Worried about your next meal, ChenHe?"

ChenHe grinned and let out a belch. "This is my way of preparing."

Tong and Dong giggled, and an irate ChenHe retorted, "What's there to laugh about? Aren't you tiny guys worried about fighting big boys?" He flexed his thumb and index finger to ridicule them.

Tong timidly responded with humility and an exaggerated bow, "Warrior of immense size, I mean…"

Dong interrupted Tong and earnestly rephrased to ChenHe. "The silly man means to say you have an immense presence."

Tong swiftly caught on and continued, "We are wondering if your burp will give away our position, like the black powder!"

"The man means to say that your dynamic presence and manly fragrance... would make the enemy tremble..." Dong couldn't continue with a straight face and burst out laughing.

Bending over with laughter, Tong asked, "Can an explosion from your ample presence make the birds of the valley fly away? Perhaps the Prince is mistaken. The explosion must have occurred closer home."

Dong added, "We need to keep the path upwind clear for our enemies to escape!" The dwarfs held on to each other and laughed.

ChenHe frowned for an instant before he smiled, "Let the pile of bodies speak, my tiny comrades. My two to your one." The dwarfs cried out in unison, "Accepted!"

Hong heard the exchange and screamed at the dwarfs, "Enough of your idle bluster. Save your strength to blood your knives. We could be under attack at any moment! Remember to strike without giving away your position. The mist won't hide sounds!"

ChenHe trained his finger at Tong and Dong and spoke with his mouth full, "You... I will crush the heads of our enemies with my bare hands, and I shall think of them as your empty heads. So, keep your ugly faces away from me in battle. I could make a mistake and slam your heads instead."

Tong bowed and said, in all seriousness, "No offence, big man. I'm just getting your blood boiling for the many kills ahead." He paused and added to a grinning ChenHe, "In your dreams! Don't curl up, sleep somewhere with all that food inside, and miss the action." Dong hooted with laughter.

An infuriated Hong chased the dwarfs away and apologised to

ChenHe for their rude behaviour.

ChenHe underplayed their verbal exchange as friendly banter. "Aw, let them talk. It could be their way of priming up for battle. Who knows what fate awaits us? Let's pray that our lamentations are minimal once the battle is done."

****

Near mid-morning, SuJin observed movement by the lakeside, and he chirped like a squirrel, gathering everyone. The dwarf fishermen paddled their boats, dragging the raft across the lake, and they heard a horse neigh. Qian was returning with a magnificent horse on the raft. One of the dwarfs led the horse into their makeshift corral, and Qian ran towards them.

"Let's gather in Batu's workshop." Qian sat cross-legged to share his reconnaissance as the men gathered around him. "Bandits, and they plan to attack us. They will overwhelm us, running in from the forest in one big wave."

"How do you find that out?" Asked ChenHe.

Qian gave his friend a lopsided smile and motioned towards the corral. "I was bringing in the rider, but I left him in the lake as fish food when he said he would torture and kill my wife and child. He is my first sacrifice to the spirit of the lake!"

Hong said, "And so it begins."

"HuKui is a prisoner, and he's been hurt badly," looking at the grim faces around him, Qian added, "The man I captured was confident that he would not survive the day."

Hong tentatively asked, "What about my brothers?"

"Prisoners, although one dwarf is on the run. The bandits are searching for him."

"Couldn't you try to rescue HuKui?" Asked ChenHe. His life might be ebbing away as we speak."

Qian's face showed concern. "I am blind to what's happening beyond the valley. I could have tried, but it would have alerted the bandits. They have prepared an ambush somewhere on the road."

SuWu asked, "How do you know this? I mean, how can you possibly know what's happening down in the valley, far away from here?"

Qian nodded. "The scout told me. These bandits are quite organised! Scouts frequently travel from one end to the other, updating their leaders. We should break that first."

Qian proposed, "Ideally, we should rescue HuKui after eliminating the bandits here. We have thick mist cover and know this forest like the back of our hands. Thanks to Batu!"

SuJin interjected, "Let's do both: counterattack here and there!"

SuWu disagreed, "We don't have enough warriors for that?"

Qian added, "There could be over fifty bandits to attack us here, maybe more."

SuWu looked at SuJin and said, "That's too many, and we are too few. We can't split up."

SuJin said, "I can understand, so spare just one!" SuWu looked at SuJin incredulously, and the Prince said, "I will rescue HuKui."

Batu sidestepped the discussion and asked Qian. "Don't you think they would miss a man and a horse?"

Qian grinned at Batu. "These bandits are clever. The scouts are split into two groups, one behind the other, with a messenger in the second group whose job is to run back to inform someone called Pockface that they were attacked." He smiled and said, "I took out their man guarding the horses of the second group and sneaked past the first group."

"Impossible," said Hong. "The switchback path is too narrow, just wide enough for a horse or a man, and the cliff is too steep." Qian smiled at him.

Batu whistled in appreciation. "That's a tremendous feat! Like a Hun! How did you pull a man and a horse out from between them with the cliff in the way?" Hong nodded vigorously in agreement with the question.

"Not like a Hun! More like a forbidden troop scout!" He added modestly. "The mist cloaked me, and I had help. Spirits directed me along an animal trail to avoid the road, and I walked past an ambush party with archers on the road."

Batu gazed at him incredulously, and Qian remarked, "The bandits were distracted by an aggressive bear and her cub. Surely, the spirits were at work." Batu exhaled noisily with a whistle, and an astonished Hong stared at Qian.

SuWu asked Qian, "Did your captive mention their motive for attacking us?"

Qian gestured towards SuJin and Batu. "Them! It seems they want them but also use the opportunity to blood their recruits and give them some experience before some major raid."

Hong asked, "Who are these people?"

Qian looked around before answering. "YuanLin, the infamous bandit, and his men! The dreaded cannibal of Zhou."

Hong gasped and said, "Oh, this is severe! Brutal stories of that loathsome bandit haunt every village! They take no prisoners. Cannibals!"

Dong climbed onto a workbench and announced grimly, "Today, we put an end to the dreaded cannibal of Zhou. Many innocents have prayed to the gods for his destruction. Good people have died horribly, and their prayers have brought him here." Dong flung his hand at SuJin, stamped his foot, and shouted dramatically, "To die at the hands of a god!"

SuJin was annoyed. "Dong, we fight them together. All of us."

SuWu ignored the easily excitable Dong and told Qian, "Many recruits, you say! We can use that to our advantage by creating confusion in their ranks. You and ChenHe should use the cover of the mist to take out their leaders from the rear. We shall handle their main attack."

SuWu told Hong. "There are too many for a frontal attack. You should attack and retreat into the mist, terrorising the fresh recruits. Fight in pairs, one to scare, the other to kill. Batu and I shall concentrate on taking out anyone regrouping the bandits with the bow."

SuWu stood and addressed everyone, "The bandits will come and set fire to the huts. Do not panic; do not resist them. Let's pour lard and fish oil on the hut to create a large blaze that will silhouette the enemy in the mist. Dwarf archers will man the raft and shoot from the lake. All of you must be clear about identifying who is a friend or foe in the mist." SuWu warned everyone, "Remember, this is not a duel for engaging in one-on-one fights that may exhaust you. Be fierce and evasive. Strike to kill, vanish, and strike elsewhere. They should feel that we are many."

Batu cleared his throat, capturing their attention. "Apply ash from the fires to your faces and swords," he instructed, "and strap a small branch with leaves behind your backs to avoid being identified as a person in silhouette."

The dwarfs bowed to Batu with gratitude for his wise words, and he became embarrassed. "The sky gods will punish me for revealing all the secrets of the Huns to the Han." Everybody laughed, easing some of the tension and patted each other on the back, wishing luck. With the golden glow on their side, no one appeared overawed by the large host.

SuWu asked SuJin, "What about you, Prince? How and where do you wish to fight?"

SuJin replied, "I will attack the bandit camp where HuKui is being held."

SuWu became anxious. "Can't we wait to eliminate the bandits in the forest before pursuing them?"

SuJin disagreed, "It may be too late for our foster father."

SuWu tried to dissuade SuJin and said, "YuanLin is an infamous bandit but experienced. He is a bloodthirsty cannibal who cuts and eats his captives alive. He will have no dearth of men protecting him, and they won't be fresh recruits but battle-hardened criminals."

SuJin stood up. "That is enough information for me."

SuWu began to dissuade SuJin from going out alone once more, but he stalled him "Enough!"

No one opposed the Prince, and Batu advised him. "SuJin, you won't be supported by backup if you venture into their camp alone. If you leave them alive, they will deceive you with pleas for mercy and sorrowful tales, then strike when you least expect it. Valour is not a virtue among the unscrupulous men."

SuJin asked Batu, "What do you mean?"

Batu replied sharply, "Don't take prisoners. Trust dead bandits and no one else."

SuJin looked at the heavy mist rising steadily over the lake like smoke from a large fire and could feel something stirring within him. "I shall not heed cunning words."

In the absence of JiaShao, Hong blessed SuJin. "Let the gods within you unleash their fury on these flesh-eating worms from hell."

Tong added, "Let your blade swing freely like a bamboo leaf in a hurricane and cleanse the earth of evil."

Dong and the other dwarfs clapped their hands, clenched their fists, lifted their stubby hands in blessing, and shouted, "Likewise."

SuWu asked Hong to depute two of his best warriors with SuJin. Hong motioned to an ecstatic Tong and Dong. SuJin stood up to leave, but SuWu held him back. "Wait! You should cross the lake and go by the bandit's road. Qian and ChenHe shall join you."

SuJin said, "I need a horse."

Qian responded confidently, "You will have your horse, my Prince."

SuWu bowed low to the departing boys, *"Battle speed, brothers."*

****

Tong remarked to Dong as they crossed the lake, "Isn't the mist unusually thick today? This will surely help."

Dong peered into the thick white mass, saw fog tendrils spinning in spirals, and said, "Hmm... actually, the mist is alive. It must be Qian's dragon spirit."

ChenHe told the dwarfs accompanying him, "I pity the bandits who come up against Qian. Their mouths wouldn't have time to form a scream before they tumble into the netherworld."

Tong agreed, "I just hope he leaves some for us."

ChenHe snickered without a trace of joy. "You shall have that in abundance. We are attending an imperial dinner at the palace where bandits are served on a platter, course after course."

****

The smell of wood smoke wafted down, and a horse whinnied. Qian motioned to SuJin, putting his palm out flat and closing his fingers deliberately, except for two. A signal instructing him to wait for twenty breaths before following. He strapped his bow into the leather harness on his back and pulled out two throwing daggers with a brass ball as the hilt edge. He pushed the blade into a loop in his hanfu sleeve and wrapped his fingers around the brass ball. To a casual observer, it looked as if his hands were empty!

SuJin pointed his index finger straight up the sheer slope, indicating that he would skip the first set of bandits and climb the steep slope to attack the second group stationed further up.

SuJin whispered, "*Battle speed, brother,*" Qian mouthed silently, "Likewise."

Qian raced up the path, swinging and pumping his arms hard and glancing back occasionally as if to outrun someone following him. A man came out unhurriedly onto the road, holding a crossbow and said, "Stop! We have you covered." Four armed men moved in behind him.

Qian did not slow down, and the bandit raised his crossbow, but his casual stance was more in preparation to strike the running man with a blow to his head. Qian sprinted forward and effortlessly dodged the blow, slamming his elbow into the bandit's chest. The bandit dropped his crossbow, fell to his knees, and grimaced in pain, "Ah... my ribs!"

In the same instant, Qian hurled his knives at a pair of bandits. The surprised men clawed at their throats, now sprouting daggers. Before they stumbled to the ground, Qian retrieved the loaded crossbow from the first bandit, shot a man through the chest at close range, and swung the crossbow at the face of the last bandit standing, who still had not recovered from the shock of the attack.

Qian paused just enough to retrieve his knives and ran up the road. He had to reach anyone waiting beyond the second set of bandits guarding their horses.

Hearing the commotion, six bandits burst onto the road with drawn swords, but Qian had already run past them. Swiftly coming to terms with the ferocity of the attack on their colleagues, they turned to see Qian running up the slope.

ChenHe, still some way down the path, burst into a run with a wild cry, swinging his mace. Four bandits turned to face ChenHe, coming up the path. One of the bandits aimed a crossbow at Qian. SuJin walked in beside the bandits from the same path they had just come out on and wafted into them like a summer breeze. They did not realise an enemy was in their midst until too late.

SuJin flicked the brass ball, which smashed into the back of the head of the bandit, aiming his crossbow at Qian. The man dropped the crossbow and fell limp. The others turned around in surprise, and SuJin cut down all five bandits in a flurry of sword moves.

ChenHe found the situation on the trail contained by SuJin and lumbered off into the trees from where the bandits had emerged. SuJin heard loud cries for mercy followed by silence. The dwarfs emerged from the bandits' first camp with bloodied knives and silenced the bandit, who had sat up groaning from the blow to his head from the crossbow.

The first bandit, elbowed by Qian, had dashed forward with a sword. Upon witnessing the sheer skill with which SuJin dispatched his comrades, he threw himself to the ground and cried out for mercy.

Qian sauntered down the slope, flicking his bloodied sword. He said, "Can you believe a messenger scout mounted his horse to ride away, but I reached him before he could gather his wits to dash off?" He looked at SuJin, who stood motionless, staring at the man who had surrendered to him.

Qian rolled his eyes in disgust. "What are you waiting for, Prince? Batu will skin you alive for acting stupid. You need to kill these vermin in the rush of battle. No prisoners!" SuJin stood frozen.

Qian was angry and curt. "We need to go."

SuJin turned to Qian and shrugged helplessly, "He isn't holding a weapon."

Qian was high on battle rage, and he growled. "He was holding one, wasn't he? You continue to be a mule, SuJin. So, what is he here for, if not to kill us? Braiding hair?" He pointed to the discarded sword and said, "There lies his weapon!"

SuJin looked about helplessly, and Qian ominously said, "If you fall to treachery because of your misplaced honour and foolishness, it's all over for us. After devoting a life to training as a warrior, do you want to lose your life to a cowardly strike on your back?"

"You stupid imperial brat!" Qian screamed in frustration. SuJin looked at Qian in shock! No one had ever spoken to him like that before. SuJin's face flushed, and it seemed like he would strike Qian.

Qian was not done speaking, "I can't let you go on, SuJin. HuKui and the dwarfs are lost. You broke the oath to your brothers by putting us in peril. I shall proceed with ChenHe and attack the bandits from the rear. We will take on the bandit leader later."

SuJin's face flushed with anger, and he said, "I won't let HuKui die."

Qian shouted back at him, spraying spittle, "Go back to the valley and remain behind the protection of SuWu and Batu."

SuJin snarled at Qian. He was dangerously close to striking his brother in rage. "Go back? What do you mean by that?"

Qian calmed his breath and, controlling his emotions, said, "I cannot allow your sloppiness to impede our battle. I fear your benevolence towards these murderers more than their swords or arrows. Shamelessly, you will lament and mourn our dead, and no one will tell you that it's your disregard for duty that killed one of us. You are, after all, the bloody Prince!"

A vein was throbbing fast in SuJin's neck, and something snapped inside. With an angry snarl, he attacked Qian and hit him repeatedly.

ChenHe rushed forward and held SuJin in a bear hug. He went limp in ChenHe's arms and wept uncontrollably.

SuJin's blows had bruised Qian. He wiped his bloodied nose and, ignoring SuJin, kicked the man, prostrated at their feet, and asked, "Speak. How many?"

"Seventy-six, including YuanLin," the man replied without hesitation. The bandit tried to convince Qian, "The young man is right. You can't win against us! There are too many of us! I can take you to our chief. Join us to become rich. All you need to do is give up one boy and the Hun!"

Qian turned to SuJin and laughed hysterically, his split lips oozing blood-red spittle down his chin. "Listen to the bandit speak. He wants us to sell you and Batu; we can all walk away from this battle! What a laugh!" SuJin was sniffling, but his eyes were set hard. Qian's accusations infuriated and hurt him. His face turned red with indignation.

SuJin shrugged off ChenHe's hold and screamed, "Enough! I have difficulty in striking someone who is begging at my feet. I can't do it!"

Qian turned his back on SuJin and slashed the strap securing the waterskin tied to the man at their feet. He washed the blood from his bruised nose and drank in deep gulps.

SuJin asked the baffled bandit who had crawled closer to him, "If you are loyal to your cause, why did you surrender to me?" The bandit moistened his lips and said, "To save my life!"

SuJin mulled over what he had heard. "You do not value the lives of others, but once overpowered, you appeal to the decency of your opponent, the very person you set out to kill moments before."

The man was candid in his response, "We are bandits. What do you expect? Honour from us. We are in it for the money!"

Qian gestured to ChenHe.

SuJin said, "You should die, else the death of the people you murder, henceforth, will stain my hands."

The bandit looked up at SuJin and said, "I am Tan..." The brass cudgel from ChenHe smashed down, smattering SuJin and Qian in blood.

ChenHe passionately said, "No prisoners—that is what we decided. I thought the Prince was questioning him. Sorry about that." SuJin's hanfu was splattered in blood.

Tong sat on one knee and screamed to the sky, "The Prince is anointed in the enemy's blood! The bonfire that will burn the evildoers to ash is now lit!"

Dong beat his chest, screwing up his face in sorrow. "Woe to the enemy! The mothers and sisters of our enemies have already begun their lamentations!"

Qian rolled his eyes at the belief the dwarfs had in the Prince and almost missed hearing SuJin say, "You are right. I have behaved like a pompous ass, Qian."

SuJin gave Qian a solemn nod and said, "I finally understand some of what Tuhu taught me. Death holds honour if the cause justifies the sacrifice! Removing evil and restoring order is a warrior's sacred duty, and I have faltered. I did not recognise the evil in this man. I heard him with my ears; I did not see his evil heart."

He gave Qian a bow and said, "Your sharp tongue has cut me deep, but it has alleviated my apprehensions. Tuhu said that inaction by a warrior is as good as death for the people and the cause he defends."

SuJin declared to Qian solemnly, "I shall not waver again."

Qian started, "How do I believe...." SuJin stopped him with a raised hand.

Qian vacillated, not knowing what to do, and walked away. He motioned to the dwarfs to get the horses tethered in the shrubs. The dwarfs were stunned to see the rare and large Ferghana breed of horses tethered to the low branches of a tree.

Dong said, "These bandits are fabulously rich!"

When they came out leading the horses, ChenHe exclaimed, "Where did these wretched thieves come across such fine horses? These beasts will command a fortune in any market. Why do they have to steal from others?"

Tong harrumphed in disgust, "Surely the bare bones of an honest trader, bleaching in the desert sun, can't answer that!" SuJin selected a spirited grey horse.

Qian called the dwarfs and whispered to them, and they surreptitiously glanced at SuJin. After drinking water from the waterskins, the boys moved out. The dwarfs remained behind to move the captured horses into the forest. They would return for them later.

ChenHe held the reins of SuJin's horse as they walked up the path. He said, "It's a shame we can't ride these magnificent horses into battle."

As they walked higher and neared the pass, the tree line ended. Ahead were ragged scrubs, scanty grass, and scree. The barren mountaintops offered no hiding place. It was windy, and the mist was thin at the heights.

The warriors paused where the path forked, one path leading up to the rim of the ridge and the other down into the valley of the dwarfs. They had to part ways.

ChenHe handed the reins to SuJin and said, "Take care, Prince. Save HuKui! He dedicated his life to us. Remember, you answer the prayers for justice. None of these cannibals deserve to live and torment innocents.

With an unholy fire burning in his eyes, Qian said, "I can feel the dragon writhing in me to destroy this evil. Destruction leads to creation!" For SuJin's benefit, Qian added, "The dragon says that removing forces that torment creation is more pleasing to the gods than sitting in meditation and burning incense."

SuJin smiled, "If you know how, let loose the dragon."

Qian nodded and said, "Battle *speed, brother!*"

SuJin responded, "Likewise," he trotted his horse up to the ridge.

Qian folded his fists, bowed low, and whispered, "Prince, make us believe!" He brandished his knives and purposefully strode down the path into the valley. ChenHe quickly bowed to the back of a departing SuJin and hastened after Qian. The mist in the valley roiled over, welcoming "Black Death" and the "Brick" into their midst.

SuJin's keen ears picked up the sound of two horses following behind at an unobtrusive distance. SuJin said aloud to the horse, "Qian! He has set the dwarfs to follow me to ensure I don't leave anyone alive!"

#24 Bandit Attack

SuJin looked at the rutted cart path twisting in switchbacks from the ridge top. He could see the plains on the horizon, shimmering in the heat. The smaller valley below was covered in a thin mist and appeared deceptively peaceful. However, the serene view did not distract SuJin, as a wave of irrational anger crept over him. He wanted his quarry to mark him before he attacked them. He patted his horse and took a few deep breaths, outlining himself against the skyline for anyone waiting below.

SuJin trotted downhill, made a few switchbacks, and stopped. Two archers stood on either side of the path, holding traditional bows instead of crossbows. Their arrows were notched but held down; they only needed to raise the bows to shoot. Three other men wearing leather armour waited further down with drawn swords. Their stance and mannerisms indicated to him that these were experienced killers.

If he turned to run, the archers would feather him down. SuJin raised his hand and called out to the men ahead, ignoring the archers. "Hello there! I have a message from your brothers on the trail."

One of the archers instructed him, "Keep your hands visible on the reins and keep moving until we tell you to stop." SuJin looked at them and said, "Are you the leader? Can you take a message?" Then, he got closer to the archers.

The bandits planned to place him between the archers and the men with the swords before disarming him.

As he approached, the archer standing on the left side of the road with blackened, rotten teeth asked, "Is that blood on your hanfu?"

The archer on the right studied SuJin's horse and shrieked, "I know that horse; it belongs to Tan. He would never part with it." SuJin yanked on the reins, causing the horse to rear up on its hind legs, dangerously tottering near the edge of the road. SuJin struggled to calm the horse, bending backwards and off balance while pulling on the reins. It seemed as if he was inexperienced with horse riding.

SuJin's left hand dropped, his wrist flicked, and his hand was back on the reins. The archer on the left dropped his bow as he slid to his knees, a knife in his throat. The archer on the right had moved to cover the rider on the rearing horse; his eyes were locked on SuJin. The men standing down the road shouted a warning, and the archer instinctively glanced at them. At the same instant, the horse landed on its forelegs, and SuJin slid forward across the horse's back, flailing his hands to cushion a nasty fall. Just as his torso cleared the neck of the horse, he flipped a dagger with hardly any change in his tumble.

The knife plunged into the archer's midriff, and the man screamed. The arrow flew harmlessly over the cliffside. SuJin whipped around the neck of the horse and straddled back in a stunning acrobatic move. It was a surreal experience for seasoned fighters to find themselves on the receiving end of a counterattack.

With a blood-curdling scream, two of the bandits ran towards SuJin, keeping pace with each other despite running uphill, one on either side of the road. He couldn't fight on both sides of the horse simultaneously. Whichever side he attacked, the bandit would feint an attack and duck out of the way, while the man on the other side would slash at the rider. The third bandit ran a little behind, holding his sword lower to strike at the leg of the horse to cripple it.

SuJin crouched low on the horse and galloped hard at them. Moments before he came into the swinging arc of the swords, SuJin turned the horse to the side of the cliff. The horse climbed up the vertical cliff a few strides before skidding back onto the path beyond the pair of bandits. The running men turned together as one when a metal ball snaked out from SuJin's hand and smashed into the temple of a bandit. He stumbled into his colleague, and they went down in a heap.

SuJin slid off the galloping horse and lunged with his sword at the bandit. He allowed the bandit to deflect his blade outwards. The bandit grunted in victory! All he had to do was bring up his sword to cut SuJin. He hadn't noticed the boy tossing a metal ball across his neck from inside his sword strike. A thin leather strap curled around his neck as a metal ball spiralled tightly into loops around his neck. The other end of the leather strip was knotted to the horse's saddle. Before the bandit could bring up his sword, the man was yanked off his feet, and, with a snap, his neck broke. The prancing horse dragged the body forward.

SuJin sidestepped and stabbed his sword in and out of the gaping mouth of the bandit, who had recovered from his collision and attacked him from behind, and the man fell on his face, spewing blood.

He heard horses approaching and whirred back but relaxed when he saw that it was the dwarfs who were following him. Tong slid to a halt next to him while Dong galloped ahead to catch the runaway horse that was trying hard to dislodge the dead weight of the corpse hanging from its saddle.

Tong bowed to SuJin and bashfully said, "Master Qian instructed us to help clean up."

SuJin grinned, "Yeah, I'm sure! He would have asked you not to leave anyone alive."

Tong grinned and said, "Yes, but I wish we had one alive to know what lies ahead." SuJin gestured to a bandit he had knocked down with the brass ball.

Tong handed SuJin a water skin and waited until he had had his fill. Then, he splashed water on the bandit, and after a few moments, the man came to his senses. He began to babble incoherently as he sat up, massaging the side of his head.

SuJin exclaimed, "Oh, a mute!"

Tong walked over to the bandit and thrust his short sword into his shoulder. The man screamed and rolled from side to side, crying out in agony. He sat up and unleashed a torrent of obscenities at Tong.

Surprised, SuJin asked Tong, "How did you know he was faking?"

Tong replied nonchalantly, "I didn't."

The dwarf looked at his sword and asked, "How many?" The man started speaking immediately. He did not want to antagonise Tong.

"Seventy-odd under YuanLin. Three cooks, one goldsmith, and prisoners, including a half-man like you," he grimaced in pain, holding his bleeding shoulder and occasionally feeling the bump on his head.

They heard horses coming up the slope, and the bandit screamed, "Help! Shoot them first." It was Dong, returning with SuJin's horse. The panic in the bandit's eyes looked genuine this time, realising that all his colleagues were dead.

"How many in your camp?" SuJin asked, and the man blurted out, "Ten to twelve, besides the cooks and prisoners from the cart."

Tong prompted, "And..."

The bandit said, "Not counting the men pursuing an escaped half-man!"

Tong aimed an arrow at the bandit's stomach and said, "Do you know that stomach wounds are the worst? It can take a long time to die, especially when the intestines are punctured."

The bandit added hastily, "Of course, two exceptionally skilled archers are with the men hunting the half-man."

SuJin thanked Tong for obtaining the information and patted his horse. Dong handed him the brass ball and said, "Prince, double the count of bandits ahead, given by the man."

Tong urged SuJin to leave, "Prince, don't bother with this scum. Leave him to us; he has a full confession to make on how many he killed."

The bandit was alarmed. "Can't you understand? I am helping you here! What can one man do against the horde down below? Run away! Escape! YuanLin and his brother have tentacles in every city, and they will track you down. Stay away from cities, and maybe you'll have a chance to stay alive for a few years!"

Tong told the bandit, "Oh, don't worry yourself sick about the health of our Prince. I don't need to be an astrologer to predict that there won't be a YuanLin beyond today."

Dong handed SuJin his throwing knives after cleaning them. Tong told Dong, "Water the Prince's horse, brother." SuJin checked the edges of his knives and the balance one last time while Dong watered his thirsty horse from a water skin. SuJin mounted up and, with a nod to the dwarfs, dashed down the trail.

Tong told the fallen bandit, "Although our Prince is an army by himself, he has a flaw! Unlike your coward, YuanLin, he cannot kill people grovelling at his feet, even though they are lying murderers like you. That's why we follow him. My brother and I grew up clearing our fields of weeds and vermin." He gave the bandit an unpleasant smile.

Tong told the fallen bandit, "It's time. Now, you need to go your own way. Hell is waiting!"

The frightened bandit said, "Now, look here. We can work out something beneficial. I can give you gold, lots of it! The goldsmith tied up by YuanLin is part of our gang and knows where all our gold is kept." Tong listened impassively and shrugged his shoulders. "Who cares!"

Realising that he was not making any impact in enticing the dwarfs with gold, he tried to scare them. "YuanLin will eat the raw liver of that young warrior tonight while the boy is alive! I can help you escape his wrath. The butcher will hunt you down, you know. He is pure evil, a demon-spawn monster! Nobody can defeat him."

Tong remained nonchalant and said, "You didn't listen the first time we said this. Our Prince will kill him. Dead men can't follow up on threats."

Realising that he was about to be executed, the fallen bandit said in spite, "Do you know that one of your kind escaped YuanLin? I spotted him and informed our men where to find him. It will be a sport to see him cut open while he screams to welcome death."

The bandit was successful in making Tong respond in anger. "Let me thank you for that," he said, swatting his open palm below the bandit's lower jawbone. The bandit had a surprised look on his face as blood bloomed in spurts from his severed jugular vein. Tong dispassionately wiped a thin brass blade on the tunic of the bandit and pushed it back into the oversized sleeve of his tunic. Tong grasped the high saddle and effortlessly hoisted himself onto his horse while his friend Dong passed him the reins.

Tong turned to the bandit who was desperately trying to stem the flow of blood and said, "If I did wrong, see you in hell. Don't be afraid to die alone. A crowd will join you soon."

The dwarfs galloped down the road after SuJin.

****

SuJin heard the distant sound of hooting and laughter. He dismounted from his horse, walked to the path's edge, and looked over the cliff. The mountain opposite jutted into the valley so much that a narrow gap separated the two peaks.

He found the runaway dwarf pinned on the other mountain!

The dwarf lay flat in a slight depression above a crumbling scree fall, just where the cart trail swung around the protruding cliff. He was precariously perched behind a small rocky outcrop, barely covering his body with some part of his torso visible between two boulders. The bandits aimed at that gap to shoot arrows, but their attempts had, so far, been in vain, hindered by a strong breeze blowing across the valley.

Many arrows lay scattered on the slope, and it appeared that some wager had been placed to make a strike. Laughter erupted as another arrow narrowly missed the dwarf, harmlessly bouncing off the rock. SuJin realised that the sport had been going on for some time, and it was only a matter of time before the bandits lost interest and took him down by climbing up.

SuJin looked at two men standing apart, watching the proceedings dispassionately. They had to be the dreaded archers of YuanLin. Wong was living on borrowed time!

SuJin galvanised into action. He brought his horse forward, hailed the bandits across the wide-open space, and screamed, "I am coming for you!" The bandits stopped and stared, not perturbed by a lone man. Realising that help was at hand, Wong yelled insults at the bandits, mocking their aim and hurling abuse at them to provoke them.

The two archers urged the bandits to climb the screefall and bring down the dwarf. They looked at the man across the hill, notching an arrow in disbelief. Shooting across the open valley in the heavy wind was silly.

SuJin made a silent prayer to the dragons of the lake and fired three arrows in quick succession, compensating for the wind, aiming for the crowd of bandits clawing their way up the mountainside. He galloped hard towards the bandits, not waiting to see where his arrows landed.

The wind swept the arrows across, and one struck a large man who had nearly reached the hapless dwarf, skewering him from behind. Another arrow pierced a bandit's leg, shattering his bone, and he tumbled off the slope. He fell onto others, scrambling behind, bringing them tumbling down. The third arrow narrowly missed a bandit and rebounded with a broken shaft that tore open his face, causing him to scream and fall. The remaining bandit recruits scrambled down the slope in panic.

The accuracy and power of the shot rattled the experienced archers—

one shot from that distance striking a target could be luck, but not all three in quick time! Anxious, they took positions to shoot the horseman and commanded the others to eliminate this formidable threat. They could see the puffs of dust as SuJin sped across the narrow path and realised he would turn blind into them.

In their panic, they forgot about the dwarf. Wong clambered down the slope to the dead bandit and armed himself with a crossbow and a quiver full of bolts. Hiding behind the dead man and using the advantage of higher ground, he launched barb after barb at his attackers in a ferocious counterattack that would have made his archery master, Batu, proud.

The two bow masters of YuanLin steadied their bows, waiting for SuJin to come into range. They could hear the horse galloping hard and readied their bows. The rider would come into striking range as soon as he turned the corner. He would need both hands on the reins to make the turn, which was the vulnerable moment to strike.

As the horse swung around the corner, the archers released their arrows, aiming for their adversary's torsos. The horse was riderless! Had he fallen off? No! The boy acrobatically leapt off the horse and ran down the slope! Before they could react, a searing pain coursed through their chests, forcing them to drop their bows. Together, the bow masters believed they were invincible and were shocked that both had been struck! They collapsed to the ground, an arrow protruding from their chests.

SuJin had planted his feet on the saddle and steered the horse by yanking a single rein with his teeth at the last moment. He held his bow in his left hand, with a short arrow wedged between each finger of his right hand. He launched onto the mountainside and dashed a few steps before sliding down to the road, having already let loose the arrows at the mental image he locked in his mind after turning the corner.

SuJin dropped the bow and rolled onto the path in a low crouch, coming up with his knives. Not a single arrow or bandit came at him. Many bandits lay on the ground, screaming in agony and terror, while many others were motionless, dead! He recognised Wong as he slid down the scree slope, holding a crossbow.

Tong and Dong careened around the corner and reined in their horses. Tong shouted, "Wong, it's us!" Wong held his arm up, urging them to stay put.

Wong went about slitting the throats of each bandit, ignoring their pleas for mercy, and cutting the jugular of the dead ones. Blood drenched the entire body of the dwarf, except for his white eyes and snarling teeth. He looked like an apparition from hell when he smiled and slit their throats.

The dwarf's fury was finally sated after he accounted for every bandit. Wong retrieved a water bag and poured the water over his head and face, washing away some of the blood. He sat down and wept in relief.

Tong and Dong rushed forward to hold him. Wong wailed, "I am sorry I left HuKui and our brothers to warn you. I am not afraid to die but to be cut and eaten alive! I couldn't bear that thought." He was inconsolable.

At the mention of HuKui, SuJin asked Wong, "HuKui...?"

Wong snivelled and, between sobs, said, "Monsters! They said if I surrender, they will plead with YuanLin for a quick death for me, as he doesn't like half-men. One of my feet would be cut off for running away, and I would have to carry it. They said that they dragged HuKui on the path to make him tender and skinless to be cut and eaten like a fish without scales! I don't know if he will survive. All he did was talk nicely and try to reason with these fiends."

He screamed at SuJin, spraying spittle, "These are not men, and none deserves a clean death."

SuJin contemplated for a while and said, "I should get going."

Wong said, "Prince, turn at the stream crossing. They are in a clearing, deep into the trees." SuJin nodded.

Dong led SuJin's horse to him and, kneeling, offered him a waterskin, treating him like a Prince. SuJin drank greedily and poured the remaining water over his head, mimicking Wong's actions. He checked his weapons, filled his quiver with arrows from the fallen bow masters and mounted his horse.

He was ready.

Wong sniffled, wiped his runny nose on his tunic, and said, "Wait! Give us time to flank their camp." SuJin looked at the dwarfs and said, "Are you sure? You look tired!"

Wong added, "I will rest after these abominations reach the netherworld."

Wong fell to his knees, and SuJin looked at him with curiosity. "Prince, I want you to promise me something."

SuJin said, "If it's in my hands, Wong!"

Wong said, "Prince, I implore you to maim YuanLin and his men, but do not kill anyone. They are cannibals, and their execution should be in the hands of a butcher like me who slaughters pigs. None of them deserves the honour of a warrior's death from a Han Prince.

SuJin blanched at his vicious demand and asked, "Wong, we can't be like them. Give me a reason not to kill YuanLin outright other than to appease your rage?"

Wong stood up and said, "I was an apprentice to Tuhu, just as you are. I must set an example for all men to heed the anger of decent men against monstrosities that pretend to be human."

SuJin was indecisive, and Wong declared, "Let me become them, Prince! I will hold up a polished brass mirror to their deeds when I open the doors of hell!" Tong and Dong looked on in trepidation at the violence emanating from the gentle Wong.

SuJin ignored Wong and trotted his horse down the path, and all three dwarfs bowed to him, but Wong was weeping. SuJin stopped and said, "Alright, you go first."

****

YuanLin had never lost a raid and took pride in remaining anonymous, as he left no witnesses. His brother invested heavily in spies and meticulously planned all his raids, and along with Pockface, he always emerged victorious. No one outside his team had seen his face, and what little people heard about him were accounts planted by his men. He relished hearing about his exaggerated deeds, which were whispered with horror in taverns and chophouses.

This raid on the dwarfs was different. YuanLin undertook this raid without consulting his brother or Pockface, but the odds were overwhelmingly in his favour. He intended to capture the fugitives and present them to his brother.

In anticipation of his rise as the local governor's military confidant, he had brought his entire gang of outlaws to blood the recruits. The timing was perfect for separating the chaff from the grain, and he had commanded his men to remain passive while the recruits were blooded. Discipline was crucial for the upcoming raid on the heavily armed caravan, and YuanLin intended to use this opportunity to weed out the weaklings.

He relaxed against a tree, dreaming of his celebration with the governor for the capture of the Hun and his return to civilised society. It would be some time before he could indulge in his favourite pleasure of carving live flesh. He intended to make this outing memorable and suppress his cravings for a long time.

YuanLin whistled cheerfully and unrolled the exquisitely crafted leather pouch that held his torture tools. He had taken it from a portly imperial magistrate and his entourage, who were returning with tax money and beautiful slaves. He shuddered with delight, and a joyful smile spread across his face as he recalled the thrill of using the tools on the magistrate and his favourite concubine.

He scowled and asked Pockface, "What's keeping our men from bringing in the dwarf? He can't have run far on his stunted legs."

Pockface shrugged. "Left to our men, he would have been captured long ago. We have sent fresh recruits! I hope they bring him alive, as you instructed."

YuanLin snapped, "They will do so. He will be alive until I say otherwise."

Pockface told YuanLin, "I wish you had sent me to the Valley of the Dwarfs. Something feels off! It's unusual for anyone to buy the black powder of the shamans."

YuanLin laughed. "I am sure you would want to supervise this minor scuffle, which is precisely why I asked you to stay back. Let me see how the boys manage this raid. We have nothing to lose."

The bandit chief said, "I have commanded our men not to attack the dwarf's camp until the evening. Waiting in the cold is a test of their discipline," he added as an afterthought. "If they are discovered before time and are forced to attack, there will be hell to pay."

Pockface snorted in disdain, "I bet five gold coins that our hidden men will be discovered before evening."

YuanLin chuckled heartily and said, "That's a lot of money, eh?" He nodded and added, "Sure, I shall take you on that wager because if I lose, I will deduct this payment from the men who have failed me."

They heard a horse sauntering towards the camp. "About time," muttered YuanLin.

He heard his guard on the perimeter say, "You are not Tan! Who are you? Why are you alone?" YuanLin raised an eyebrow at the surprised grunts and moans. Pockface picked up his sword and covered YuanLin.

YuanLin wasn't perturbed, not by a single man entering his den. "Pockface, it's just one man. Let him enter! We probably missed counting one of them back at the village." They heard repeated thumps of the bows around the camp! The camp was under attack, and they could hear screams of pain from their men.

Pockface turned around in confusion but couldn't determine how many armed men surrounded them and rasped, "We need to stall them for time. Our men will return any moment." YuanLin swiftly packed away his precious torture tools and set them aside. He picked up his mace and sword.

It was unusual for YuanLin not to be in control of a situation. It was a rarity, but he always prevailed with his cunning.

His three cooks had already dropped flat on the ground, offering no resistance. YuanLin spat at them in disgust as they held their faces in the mud and outstretched their hands in complete surrender. "Cowards!"

They heard bird calls followed by the chatter of a squirrel. The hidden men exchanging signals!

A boy stepped out from behind the trees. He held a short double-recurve bow used by the Huns.

Pockface realised they were not attacked outright, which could mean that the boy wanted to negotiate the release of their captives. He said, "Look here, boy." The boy shot him twice in quick succession, each arrow piercing his shoulders, and Pockface fell back, shrieking.

YuanLin narrowed his eyes when he realised that the boy had not killed Pockface but had merely wounded him. He could hear whimpers from his guards all around. None of his men were killed outright, just incapacitated. Why?

The young man strolled into camp, and he locked eyes with YuanLin for an instant before dismissing him entirely. There was something about those piercing eyes that made him think of hell. He decided to eat those eyes raw before the evening was done!

The boy freed the man they had dragged behind the cart, carefully cutting the ropes that bound him. A murderous rage surged within YuanLin. No one, nobody, had shown him disdain like this young man. It was an affront to the dreaded cannibal of Zhou.

Did he not know who he was? Unlikely! He wouldn't be so casual around him otherwise.

YuanLin remained convinced that SuJin and his men had been overlooked by the overzealous bandits in the village. He remarked, "Someone who can't count is to blame for missing you in the village."

He turned to Pockface and said, "You wouldn't have missed them." He laughed, adding, "It seems you're indispensable, even for a scuffle."

The boy turned to him and commanded sternly, "Don't talk! I will get to you in a while. My master needs attention." YuanLin blanched in shock at being told what to do! The boy released one of the captive dwarfs they had captured in the morning. He quickly untied the others, and they armed themselves and spread out.

HuKui was bleeding badly. One of his eyes was swollen shut, and he could barely open the other. SuJin brought a water bag to wet his chafed lips. HuKui twitched open his good eye and smiled.

HuKui mumbled, "I knew you would come." He grimaced in pain and said, "Let him know what pain is before he dies!" He whispered something, and SuJin bent down to listen. He repeated, "I want to watch."

SuJin acknowledged hearing his master by tapping HuKui's unbruised inner arm. He cradled HuKui and leaned his back against a tree trunk. HuKui groaned.

YuanLin stood still and giggled at himself for obeying a boy. He could see an aura around the boy that frightened him and demanded obedience. He tried to shake away the feeling, and with a deep growl, he acted like a wild beast on the offensive. He flexed his sizable muscles and bellowed in unrestrained rage. No sword could block the powerful strike of his club. All he needed was one swing to connect and deliver a debilitating blow that would crush skull and bone. Before the day was out, he would teach this impudent pup what pain is. He would encounter darkness in the netherworld because his piercing eyes would be in his stomach! He burst into uncontrollable giggles.

YuanLin stepped towards SuJin, and an arrow smacked into the earth before him from the edge of the clearing. "Don't! The Prince asked you to wait and wait, you will." YuanLin stepped back and waited.

YuanLin saw a dwarf emerge from the forest, covered in dried blood. Something about him seemed familiar, and YuanLin looked again. It was the same dwarf who had escaped! Did this mean all his men, including his bow masters, were dead? Impossible! There had to be some other explanation!

It was as his brother said: Dwarfs bring bad luck! How he wished he had heeded his advice. Too late for regrets!

On seeing Wong, Pockface, despite grimacing in pain, begged YuanLin, "We need to surrender! Negotiate! Let them go."

YuanLin snarled at him and said, "It's the incompetence of your men that has put us in this position. We left behind a boy and a few dwarfs in the village who had sneaked up on us."

Pockface retorted with a bitter laugh despite his agony. "No! You just lost your bet! The boy has come from the valley of the Dwarfs." Yuan was stunned. That would mean he had come through his best men stationed on the cart trail. Impossible! One boy and a few dwarfs!

SuJin jogged to his horse, tethered at the edge of the clearing, and returned with his swords. He armed himself with a long sword in one hand and a short sword in the other. He swirled the swords around his wrists and adjusted his grip towards the hilt to achieve the correct balance.

YuanLin threatened SuJin, "Before this day runs out, you will tell me all your secrets from the time you crawled out of your mother's womb. But I am curious. Are you one of the fugitives that the imperial palace is looking for? Why?"

SuJin considered the question and answered, "I am your Prince and lord."

YuanLin mocked him, "Huh, a Prince, eh! You are a long way from Changan and in the den of YuanLin. The last I heard, WangMang was making Lui infants into emperors. They seem to die out faster than the change of seasons." He missed his men's usual sniggers and added, "I had planned to capture you, but I have changed my mind. I will kill you."

SuJin retorted, "All I see is a bully who got his way because of corrupt imperial rule." YuanLin laughed and flexed his arms as a series of knots were released. He was prepared for a duel.

YuanLin skilfully swished the long broadsword in his right hand, flexing his thick wrist. The long blade began to hum, vroom, vroom, vroom. The giant mace, loosely held in his left hand, served as the counterweight as he swayed back and forth like a court dancer. He grinned, watching SuJin gauge him for any weakness.

As SuJin walked closer, YuanLin began to sidestep and move in a circle around him. He disoriented SuJin, making many movements while going around.

SuJin focused on the massive sword, creating mesmerising patterns in the air, and his head spun. He breathed heavily and forced his mind to slow, and the sword's speed decreased, as did all the movements before him.

He studied his adversary from head to toe. Although his forearms were muscular and equally proportioned, the man's left wrist was slightly more developed than the right. The sword served as a distraction despite the skill on display. The mace in his left hand was the primary weapon! His instincts compelled him to check every aspect of his opponent, and he observed that YuanLin wore sturdy shoes with wooden soles and leather straps. Unusual! The tip of the boot on the right leg was cracked and had a slit.

SuJin held his sword near the hilt, even though the extended handle could enhance the reach of his strike. This was something he had learned from SwordClaw. He lunged at YuanLin's right to gauge the arc of his sword hand. YuanLin held back his strike and smiled, revealing his serrated yellow teeth. He had a measure of how this boy would attack and knew what to do. The boy might be skilled, but he was no match for his guiles.

YuanLin planned his attack. He would make a few sparring moves, bringing the club higher while lowering his sword as a counterweight. At the last moment, he would swing the club hard across his opponent's skull. Of course, the boy's sword would instinctively rise to block, but the sheer weight of the metal mace would come crashing down, shattering both bones and the sword.

YuanLin anticipated that SuJin would duel conventionally, lunging high for his neck, slashing, blocking, and then lunging low for his stomach! YuanLin moved faster, circling SuJin and urging him to commit to a strike.

SuJin turned on the balls of his feet, always keeping YuanLin abreast and watching him. Drops of sweat fell from YuanLin's face while he moved around, but he did not slacken his pace. It would be over soon.

SuJin faked a lunge, watched YuanLin deflect his strike with his sword, and noted the grip on his mace tightening.

One or two more feigned moves, and YuanLin was confident that SuJin would commit to a strike, evading the sword's arc. He would step to the side and swing the mace.

He was relishing this duel. He suddenly changed direction, moving counterclockwise. To test his attack plan, he drew closer to bring SuJin into the arc of the mace while swinging his sword to distract the boy. As YuanLin anticipated, SuJin lunged and pushed back.

SuJin, however, had taken half a step back and bent his body, creating the impression that he had retreated. As he leaned forward, SuJin relaxed his grip on the sword, allowing the hilt to slide forward and increasing his reach. Maintaining the mental image, SuJin drove the tip of his sword directly into YuanLin's wrist, severing his tendon without any noticeable change in his sword movement.

YuanLin dropped the sword from his lifeless hand in disbelief and stepped back to safety with a roar of pain. He realised too late that the boy had planned to strike his wrist, not his chest.

Although YuanLin moved back, SuJin followed him and came up beside YuanLin's face. For a moment, their faces were a fingerbreadth apart, and SuJin could smell the rotten breath of his foe and the rank stench of an unwashed body. Alarmed, YuanLin staggered back. He needed space to swing his mace, but SuJin kept pace with his movements, always right next to his face.

Unable to find his footing on the uneven ground, YuanLin fell back. In a desperate attempt to strike his enemy, he swung his mace fiercely while kicking out with his right leg. Rather than evading, SuJin pushed the falling YuanLin and leapt high, slamming down onto the bandit chief's feet. With a loud crack, both of YuanLin's ankles gave way, and he shrieked!

The mace rose, albeit more slowly, and SuJin snatched it from

YuanLin's hand as his body toppled over. YuanLin screamed, unable to endure the excruciating pain. He held up his knees with one arm, and both feet dangled like wet cloths, and he cried pitifully.

Wong gestured to the knife protruding from YuanLin's lifeless boot and said, "Treachery!"

HuKui smiled and whimpered despite his wounds. Wong was ecstatic and bowed low to SuJin.

SuJin told Wong, "He is not going anywhere. Help Master HuKui."

"Of course. Immediately." Wong said.

The dwarfs were preparing a bamboo stretcher when the bandits' cooks, a family, implored them. "Little masters, we are captives too. Please believe us. We shall take care of your friend. We know how to treat wounds."

Tong and Dong hesitated, but one of YuanLin's older captives seconded them. "They speak the truth. They are not bandits." It was CaoShen from Changan, and he had bruises all over.

Tong was surprised and asked, "Why didn't you speak up earlier?"

A bemused CaoShen said, "I could see you were all busy, and what could I do but watch?" The dwarfs grinned in happiness and relief as they quickly released and updated him on the fight in the valley. He was next in the hierarchy to JiaShao and would take over.

Tong and Dong set about releasing all the other captives of YuanLin. Tong asked CaoShen who the goldsmith was and told him what he had heard from the bandit on their way in. CaoShen gestured to one man who had extended his hand to be freed and said, "Not that one! Let him remain bound."

The three cooks did not delay in attending to HuKui. They opened bags strapped to a mule and removed fresh linen and medicinal plants. They washed HuKui in warm water, bound his wounds, and fed him medicinal soup, and he fell asleep.

Tong asked the cook, "How is he?"

The cook said, "One of his eyes is scraped. The man will have scars but should recover with care in a few weeks."

An astonished SuJin approached CaoShen and asked, "What are you doing here?"

CaoShen smiled warmly upon seeing his Prince and patted him. "That was an incredible duel against a man full of treachery. WoShi will be proud of you when I recount this duel. However, first, my duty. The Marquis expects you to return to Changan immediately. An imperial summons awaits you."

CaoShen said, "I foolishly tried to save a few days by taking the bandit road, thinking nobody would care about a dwarf, but their scouts captured me." He added grimly, "YuanLin would have tortured me, but for you."

CaoShen picked up the leather pouch that YuanLin had set aside and gave it to Wong. "We will need this!"

Wong opened the package and whistled. He held the leather-wrapped torture toolkit towards a whimpering YuanLin and grinned; the man's face drained of colour.

CaoShen said, "I want to be there to interrogate YuanLin, but we should take him to the valley. If the fight is still ongoing, we can make his men surrender. Let his men see the Cannibal of Zhao begging for mercy!"

Wong and most imprisoned dwarfs remained at the campsite to dispose of YuanLin's wounded bandits. Tong and Dong accompanied SuJin back to camp. They prepared a wooden stretcher to carry HuKui, and just as they were moving him onto the stretcher, he woke up and asked for Wong.

HuKui instructed Wong, "Don't spare anyone, but make sure to give Pockface a quick death."

Wong acknowledged him grimly, "I will spare no one, Master."

HuKui held his arm and said, "Be strong. I wish I could be there with you. Remember everything. I will listen to you many times about how each one of them died, asking forgiveness for every innocent they killed."

The cooks—mother, father, and son—carried HuKui to the road. They wrapped him in a reed mattress and hung him from a bamboo pole in the cart. The dwarfs tied a whimpering YuanLin's hands to his broken feet and dumped him in the cart. Following CaoShen's instructions, they bound YuanLin's goldsmith to the cart.

SuJin asked CaoShen, "Who is he?"

CaoShen answered, "He is HeGan, the elusive treasurer of YuanLin and his brother. He is just a nobody for WoShi to interrogate."

"Why is he a captive if he is part of the gang?"

"We need to find out. I suspect it has something to do with stashed gold."

Wong waited and watched the party of SuJin move out of earshot before they tortured and killed YuanLin's men. They left the bodies to rot in the open.

When they eventually departed from the clearing, it was already late evening. The dwarfs were pleased to confiscate many pack horses, weapons, and food.

****

In the fading light above the mist, thick smoke billowed from the camp. Descending into the valley, they saw the carnage. Corpses and dismembered limbs littered the path.

SuJin stopped to watch a bear devouring a corpse and carrion birds making a meal of the dead in the waning light. He saw hundreds of carrion birds circling in the sky and wondered how nature learned of death so quickly!

Batu rode up to meet SuJin and asked, "Is everything alright?"

SuJin smiled at Batu. "I should ask you that. You had a larger host."

"We lost eight warrior dwarfs and our huts. Many have nicks, scrapes, and burn injuries, but we have prevailed despite heavy odds. The casualties would have been higher, but something in this valley helped us. I can't explain it!"

"Was it the mists?"

"Not only the mist, the shrubs, the trees; everything. Despite the mist, animals and carrion birds are already here to clean the valley. Isn't it strange?" SuJin grunted.

SuWu dashed to SuJin and exclaimed, "Thank the gods, you are safe! Qian was concerned about you, and we were setting out to find you." SuWu quickly narrated what had happened in the valley. He told the Prince that before the attack began, a bandit scout rushed down the slope, screaming for the men to retreat.

SuJin was surprised. "How did that one escape Wong?"

SuWu shrugged and said, "Doesn't matter! Batu took him out with an arrow right in the middle of the forehead, and all hell broke loose. The bandits started fleeing instead of fighting. The experienced bandits set fire to the huts and tried to rally their men, but the blaze exposed them like deer caught in swamps, and Batu decimated them. He ran out of arrows and used crossbow bolts. Don't ask him how he managed that! To top it all off, they faced an ambush from Qian and ChenHe. It took time, but we routed them."

Hong gazed at SuJin, his smile smug. He asked, "It was truly bizarre. Did you have a role to play in this, Prince?"

"What?" Asked SuJin.

"I mean, the mist seemed almost alive with forms resembling apparitions moving. We saw dragons and the spirits of men gliding through the forest. The bandits were terrified."

"I can see what you mean, Hong." He watched as Qian strode through the shrubs, and mist swirled around him like bodyguards.

SuJin told Hong, "I wasn't here! It's because of him that the mist is alive! The dragon spirit is within him."

Bloodied as he was, Qian appeared fresh, as if he had just begun fighting. He looked at SuJin. "You delivered," SuJin nodded.

Hong stared at Qian as two pillars of mist swirled around him like a spinning top. He said, "Prince, you weren't joking! He is indeed the reason."

SuJin looked at Hong, puzzled. "Now, why would I joke about something like that?"

CaoShen asked, "Did we kill them all?"

SuWu said, "Not all of them fought. Some gave up, while a lucky few escaped. We have gathered the wounded, mostly fresh recruits. They are all stripped of their clothes and made to sit by the lake. The cold teaches a man the value of life more than anything."

SuWu said, "The carrion birds in large numbers will eventually bring the villagers to investigate. Let them see what has happened here. Many were harbouring bandits,"

CaoShen said, "We should leave."

On the Prince's nod, SuWu declared, "We leave the valley tomorrow."

****

Wong and CaoShen tortured YuanLin in front of his men and killed every bandit. The newly recruited bandits, pleading for mercy, were let off after one of their thumbs was cut.

CaoShen told Hong, "I can't imagine anyone troubling the dwarfs ever again."

Early the following day, the golden glow rode out with CaoShen and their captive, HeGan, the late YuanLin's goldsmith. They crossed the lake on the raft and followed the bandits' trail.

A few hours later, the dwarfs abandoned the valley and left for their village. They moved downstream, laden with spoils from packed horses, weapons, and plenty of spare mounts. The cooks, concerned about being targeted for working with YuanLin, joined the dwarfs to care for HuKui.

25 Ride into Changan

SuWu asked CaoShen as they trotted into a sizable sandy depression in the desert, "Shouldn't we be coming up to the border city of Guyuan? I hope the war gate is open."

CaoShen replied, "Yes, we will restock our supplies there and continue to ride into Changan, avoiding the main thoroughfares."

HeGan, the jeweller who worked for YuanLin, looked startled. HeGan was bound at night and allowed to ride free with them at other times. He scrambled his horse up the sandy depression and glanced back, shading his eyes against the direction they had come. Curious, Batu asked, "Why are you looking back? Do you expect someone to follow us?"

CaoShen dashed up behind HeGan and struck him hard with the horsewhip, making him shriek. "Speak up, captive! You have seen what we do to those who offend us!" HeGan looked at CaoShen with repugnance. He had witnessed the man's brutality while torturing YuanLin and his men.

HeGan looked at CaoShen with disdain and said, "I am not Pockface to anticipate the moves of YuanLin's brother. If I were to speculate, I would expect him to follow us."

Batu was intrigued and asked, "Pockface, the bandit? What's going on here, CaoShen?"

CaoShen answered, "Don't bother, barbarian."

Batu frowned and said, "That will not do, CaoShen. I want to hear all of it. The man is hinting at a possible threat!"

SuWu rode up and said, "CaoShen, we are transporting a prisoner of the bandit, who should be free. Remember, you, too, were his prisoner a short while ago. He deserves his freedom, but instead, you often hurt him."

Batu agreed with SuWu, vigorously nodding. He asked, "What's significant about taking this man to WoShi?" HeGan bowed to Batu while rubbing his arm where the whip had struck him.

CaoShen told SuWu, "Look, all his facial hair has burned off. He's their goldsmith!"

A smarting HeGan said, "YuanLin, the bandit, tortured and killed people to steal their gold. You, CaoShen, tortured and killed YuanLin for his gold. How are you different from the bandit?" He stared at a glowering CaoShen and continued, "Dwarf, am I saying something wrong?"

A miffed CaoShen told SuWu and Batu, "When we tortured YuanLin, he commanded HeGan to disclose all their gold holdings to SuJin in exchange for a quick death."

CaoShen continued, "HeGan and YuanYi, the bandit's educated younger brother, managed the distribution of gold across Changan and other cities. Scared of his brother's fickle temperament, YuanYi entrusted HeGan with keeping tabs on the gold they loaned to merchants and city goldsmiths. YuanYi spied for the bandits, paid local goons, and bribed bureaucrats for information."

He pointed his finger at the goldsmith and said, "HeGan melted the gold ornaments the bandits looted, added copper, and minted them into Han gold coins. The coins were loaned to traders and jewellers. This way, they didn't have to hoard and guard gold."

Batu smiled and said, "Brilliant."

SuWu asked HeGan, "Why were you imprisoned if you were a close confidant?" HeGan grinned and did not answer.

SuWu sided with Batu, saying, "Someone wants him for the

information he holds or wants him dead. It must be this YuanYi. The goldsmith is subtly informing us that we are being followed."

"You think so?" Asked Batu, and SuWu nodded.

Batu said, "I check our camp perimeter as a habit every day, and frankly, I haven't seen any tracks or evidence to suggest that someone is following us. I shall be on the lookout."

When they dismounted for a break to cook food, HeGan prostrated in front of SuJin. He said, "Prince, I need to speak to you."

A surprised SuJin asked, "Me! Are you sure?"

CaoShen ran to HeGan and said, "You shall not address the Prince. I forbid it."

SuWu quickly intervened and told CaoShen, "We need to break for food. Let us hear the goldsmith."

HeGan told SuWu, "Let me make it clear to you. I will listen to the Prince and no one else."

SuWu shrugged, unconcerned. "We all listen to him. He is the Prince."

ChenHe whistled cheerfully as he prepared a fire. He said, "I was tired of eating dried, salty fish and rice. Today, we have some meat to stew." He pointed at SuWu and added, "If we reach a city or village, I am going in for a proper meal."

Batu exclaimed while wetting his lips, "Hmm... I am parched, like this desert. The nights are unbearably cold, and sobriety is killing me!" They grinned at each other, forgetting their long animosity.

SuWu muttered, "The stomach is where they have found lost love."

SuJin motioned to CaoShen, who was still badgering HeGan. "I am curious now. Let him speak." CaoShen glared at HeGan for precipitating matters and turned away in frustration.

HeGan folded his legs, sat down, and waited for the boys to gather. ChenHe wasn't interested. He was busy skinning a giant lizard speared by Qian.

HeGan said, "Everyone in my village is related to me in one way or another; we are goldsmiths, but I also knew how to count and read words. YuanYi recruited me with lies, and later, YuanLin warned me that if I ran away or died of natural causes, the entire village would be burned, but only after he had his way with my immediate family and parents." SuJin nodded in understanding, and HeGan added, "He doesn't joke about his threats."

"Liar, you intended to escape! Is that why they bound you like a prisoner?" CaoShen quipped

"Hmm... but it was destiny for me! Imagine if I were let free in YuanLin's camp!" He levelled his finger accusingly at CaoShen and said, "You and your bloodthirsty, half-mad half-men would have tortured and killed me despite my screams claiming that I am not a bandit. Isn't it?"

Batu exclaimed, "Phew! It's a good thing you were tied up! You were lucky to escape certain death! Wong's battle rage was something to behold."

HeGan gave a grim smile and nodded. "I thought of it as providence until I overheard you speak about the expedition. That got me thinking. Am I alive because of luck or destiny? Maybe it's destiny, but let the Prince confirm it."

SuWu asked, "Tell us why YuanLin tied you up in the first place."

HeGan said, "I blundered! I was overzealous in explaining to YuanYi that we could earn more money by funding moneylenders for trade with many foreign ships arriving at Panyu."

SuWu said, "YuanLin will not buy that! He's a bandit, not a trader." HeGan nodded in agreement.

"I did not mean to fund trade on the seas – far too risky! I told YuanYi, his brother, that we should fund and capture trade on the Yellow River. From the seaport to Changan! All the wealthy, from imperial to bureaucratic, want exotic cotton cloth, spices, and jewellery. The foreigners desire our silk and ceramic pots. We have plenty of gold and the muscle."

HeGan added, "Bribing bureaucrats in Changan for trade is safer than raiding caravans. To gain political immunity and the muscle needed to manage the business, YuanYi planned for his brother to function as a henchman for the county governor. This would provide him with enough victims to satiate his hunger for torture as well."

SuWu gasped when he realised, "Of course, you were bound not because of YuanLin but because of his brother YuanYi. He wants to secure the gold before they abandon their thieving lives."

Batu said, "Once the gold is retrieved, you will become redundant. They will kill you." HeGan dipped his head dourly in agreement.

HeGan coughed and cleared his dry throat, and Qian handed him a waterskin. He drank deeply from it and smiled at Qian in gratitude. Qian asked, "What do you want to tell us? You can rest assured that you are safe with us."

"It's not my safety that I want to speak about," HeGan turned to SuJin, "I'm not sure why you must go to Tianzhu, and I do not question that. However, expeditions are not the same as climbing on a horse and riding to the next city!"

CaoShen angrily interrupted, "Stick to what you want to confess, bandit! Don't ridicule our Prince," SuJin lifted his hand in irritation and stalled CaoShen.

He gestured to HeGan and said, "Speak, man. I believe you have something to say. Destinies bring people together for a reason." Batu chuckled at that.

HeGan said, "Frankly, I aimed to negotiate my freedom with your master in Changan. I would have given him an obscene amount of gold and walked away. Few can resist the allure of the yellow metal." HeGan leaned towards SuJin and said, "It's just that I am convinced that my destiny lies in helping you. No, you need me! You do not realise how much you need me, but in the coming days, everything will become clear."

CaoShen derisively said, "That you will do. Once you gain the trust of these boys, you will give us the slip." The boys ignored his comment.

Qian moved closer to HeGan and asked, "How do you plan to help us?"

"It's not just money that you need for your expedition. What about a reliable guide, supplies and transport for your journey there and back." The boys looked at each other and nodded.

HeGan said, "I can organise the expedition to Tianzhu."

CaoShen interrupted their discussion. "No need for your help, bandit! We will squeeze the gold out of you. The Prince can travel with that money. Perhaps capturing you was our destiny to obtain the gold for the expedition."

HeGan laughed scornfully at CaoShen. "You know nothing! Your brain is as stunted as you are." CaoShen roared and rushed at him, but Qian intervened and stopped him before the dwarf could land a blow.

Qian said, "Oh, stop it, CaoShen. Why don't you walk away for some time?" He turned to HeGan and sternly said, "You, stop inciting him."

HeGan persisted, "Let me explain to the foolish dwarf!" CaoShen growled fiercely and swung his meaty hand in a mighty swipe, but Qian deftly blocked it.

"Let's assume you carry enough and more gold for your travels. Who can you trust to help you reliably? Wouldn't you alarm people in a foreign land, unable to speak their language yet going around brandishing gold?" SuWu felt very uneasy hearing this, and HeGan added, "Unscrupulous men are everywhere, and you could end up being cheated or robbed. Most likely killed."

Everyone had gloomy faces except for CaoShen. "Shut him up; let's take him to WoShi. Our master will have a plan." SuJin glared at CaoShen, and he cowered down.

Batu was uncertain and said, "Gold, it will ease our travels, won't it?"

SuWu reminded Batu, "HeGan is right! HuKui and the dwarfs used a single gold coin in the village store. See what it has led to? Death and destruction!"

SuJin asked, "What's your proposal, HeGan?"

"To get to Tianzhu in the shortest possible time, you must use a trade route. We barter goods at various trade points along our route as merchants for supplies and guides." They waited, holding their breath, for HeGan was about to say something portentous.

"We go by sea!" There was a stunned silence.

"What!" Qian and SuWu exclaimed together.

"No, no water," insisted Batu.

HeGan continued unabashedly, "I make it my business to know trade and traders because goldsmiths finance trade. Transactions with other countries are in gold, better than bartering."

SuWu asked, "Can you take us to Tianzhu, then?" HeGan vigorously nodded.

Batu asked, "Why not go by horse overland? Through the steppes."

HeGan said, "Traders naturally align towards the safest route, and we have established trade with many kingdoms up to Tianzhu, such as Champa and Siam!" He looked at the pessimistic faces around him and said, "I am surprised you don't know that we have ships coming into Panyu from Tianzhu!"

SuWu asked, "We have much to discuss. Tell us, why are you offering all this? In exchange for what, HeGan? Do you want to negotiate a share of the gold?"

HeGan puffed out his chest and said, "I want to accompany you to Tianzhu." SuWu became speechless, and he looked at SuJin. No one expected that.

SuJin said, "We shall reserve our decision until after we meet WoShi, our master."

Batu asked, "What about the gold?"

HeGan said, "I don't care about gold! It's an evil metal, and the smell of death surrounds it. I make gold work for me and nothing more. It's trade that excites me!"

Batu laughed and said, "YuanYi is not worried about gold. He is worried about you! You are a dangerous opponent! Someone adept at handling people, with the same deadly intent as warriors with weapons."

HeGan smiled. "That is what I keep saying! You can buy any swordsmen if the price is right."

Batu nodded and said, "Except SuJin!"

HeGan seconded him. "Yes, except him! His disregard for gold is the reason I spoke up."

****

Batu wrapped his horse's hooves in leather to minimise tracks and surveyed a wider area, bringing all his tracking experience to the fore. Before long, he came across horse tracks! The tracks were not behind their trail but in parallel, wide and away, alongside their direction of travel! Detecting their pursuers would have been impossible but for HeGan's warning.

They were nearing the small town of Guyuan, and the Great Wall built by the Qin was visible, winding off into the horizon. SuWu told HeGan, "This is probably the last stop before our ride into Changan."

Shuddering in the icy wind, HeGan drew his coat tighter around his body and confidently said, "You will find YuanYi here. He is a negotiator, like me, and will approach you."

Qian asked, "How do we identify him?"

"No need for that. YuanYi will find you to expedite matters. He will negotiate after assessing your vices. He will likely isolate and capture one of you. Trade me for an exchange."

Batu laughed, "That's a challenge I want to take on. Let them capture me with free booze."

"No," said SuWu emphatically. "You will stay here with SuJin. A Hun may not be a rarity in this border town, but the imperial soldiers may still be on the lookout. Why complicate matters?"

CaoShen disagreed, saying, "The lookout notice is removed after the Empress Dowager's decree."

SuWu said, "Maybe! Let's not risk it! We cannot expect soldiers to understand a transition from foe to friend overnight or WangMang to remain quiet."

Qian asked, "HeGan, why would YuanYi contact us? Won't he be scared of us, especially after we killed his brother and their gang?"

HeGan said, "YuanYi has a fallacy. He believes that everyone has a price and can be bought. He will discover your weakness." HeGan added bitterly, "Moreover, you should know that YuanYi will be confident that I won't utter a word about gold. We have learnt from experience that the prospect of securing easy gold drives people mad. So, he will approach you expecting you to know nothing about gold."

SuWu said, "Somehow, I believe this is sound advice."

Batu said, "They have a Hun tracker, and he is good but won't be effective within the town. If you don't want them to tail you, lose them within the town, not outside. Our advantage is that they don't know we know. Keep it that way."

Batu found a sheltered area amidst sparse vegetation and dunes to camp, offering some protection from the freezing desert winds.

****

SuWu, Qian, and ChenHe rode into Guyuan to replenish supplies.

After making purchases, they stopped at a bustling chophouse serving skewered meat, steamed rice, stir-fried soybeans and cucumber. The constant chatter and laughter were soothing after the silence of the wilderness and their long sojourn in the dwarf valley. The boys regaled each other with stories about their experiences working in a chophouse.

A smartly dressed man caught their attention as he weaved through the crowded space, effortlessly striking up conversations and exchanging familiar banter with the patrons before approaching them. He smiled disarmingly and introduced himself. "Best of greetings to you, young strangers. You look travel-weary. Do you have something to trade?" He whispered conspiratorially with a charming smile. "Or someone," he laughed aloud.

SuWu smiled at him warmly and asked, "Why do you say that?"

The man gestured to SuWu's sweat-stained, dust-caked hanfu neck and armpits that accompanied long rides. He laughed delightfully. "I make it my business to meet strangers. I am a trader interested in procuring and providing whatever is needed between a buyer and a seller. Most times, I am happy with a small fee."

Qian said, "Interesting! Would you like to join us?" The man looked surprised; the offer genuinely delighted him.

He waved to the head cook and sat down. "Can I interest you in some freshly brewed LaoLi? It's mild and the finest drink in these parts."

SuWu asked the man, "So, what do we call you?"

"My friends call me Yi." He looked at SuWu intently, but he held a blank expression. "You boys must be travelling from Changan, I suppose. I hope you can share something about what's happening in the capital."

SuWu smiled and said, "Actually, we are travelling towards Changan. Our home is in a village beyond."

"Ohh! I see," Yi said.

"I heard that imperial soldiers are on the lookout for an escaped Hun and a murderer. However, I'm more interested in capturing a runaway goldsmith who swindled a wealthy and influential bureaucrat out of his gold. He was last seen with bandits and is a dangerous man." Seeing the boys' interest, he added, "Mercenaries are searching for him, and death will befall anyone found with him."

"What does he look like?" Qian asked to confirm whether he was speaking about HeGan.

"The man has no hair on his face, all burnt away from tending the fire to melt gold, not even eyebrows, and he wears a blue hanfu." Yi hesitated and asked, "Have you seen anyone fitting that description? The bureaucrat is ready to pay good coin for his capture, and I assure you that I can negotiate a high price for you."

Qian narrowed his eyes slightly and said hesitantly, as if he were confiding a secret, "Yes, we too have heard about the escaped Hun, but it seems the Empress has pardoned him or something. Anyway, it doesn't bother us. We have come as far as possible and will return to our village." His answer confused Yi. It neither confirmed nor refuted the presence of HeGan with them.

"Oh, interesting! Are you travelling with others?" Yi looked around and asked, "Where are they?"

SuWu and Qian exchanged embarrassed glances. SuWu

conspiratorially admitted, "We are travelling with a few others, but it's of no concern. We will be going our separate ways. We have been riding for many days and need a break from the severe cold. We came here for hot food and to curl up somewhere warm!"

"At least for one night!" Qian said firmly.

"You may share my fire; my home is nearby," Yi offered graciously.

ChenHe joined the conversation, steam escaping his mouth as he munched hot buns filled with pork. "Tell me, Yi, are you from this place?"

Yi smiled tolerantly, "My new wife is from this place."

ChenHe slurped on LaoLi noisily and said, "Really, so you are home, not on business?"

"My dear brother is dead, and I must marry his wife. You know we practise levirate marriages. If one of us dies, we marry the wife to keep the children and family provided for."

Yi added, "She is still mourning. Be my guest here for the day, at least. Who knows when we shall meet again? Perhaps I can come up with some interesting proposals." Yi smiled and excused himself to meet other guests but signalled to the innkeeper to keep the wine flowing.

Qian cautioned, "This wine is very potent, yet he said it's mild!" SuWu harrumphed. They continued eating and drinking and saw Yi slip out of the chophouse. It was time for them to leave, too. He would return with reinforcements.

ChenHe stood up and, with slurred speech, asked for more pork, toppling back and breaking a bench. Soup and wine splashed onto patrons, who screamed in disgust. Matters escalated quickly as SuWu and Qian, taking cues from ChenHe, became boisterous and quarrelled with the patrons, throwing food at them.

The chophouse owner pounced on them and demanded that they

leave immediately. When ChenHe grew unruly, he informed them that the garrison commander and his men were expected soon, and they would be thrown into a dungeon for their misbehaviour.

Not getting any response from ChenHe, the innkeeper promptly called his kitchen hands, and together, they carried ChenHe out, accompanied by wild cheers and jeers. Since they were guests of YuanYi, the innkeeper instructed his boys to help SuWu and Qian onto their horses. After considerable effort, they hoisted ChenHe onto his horse and tied his feet beneath the saddle to prevent him from sliding off. SuWu and Qian laughed hysterically at the sight and nearly fell off their saddles when the kitchen staff slapped the rumps of their horses, sending them galloping down the road.

After passing the main crossroads, SuWu told Qian, "That was a good show, and we didn't pay for the food!" He laughed. "I thought you'd be thrown off the horse when the kitchen hands slapped your horse."

Qian chuckled and remarked, "I had some strong wine, but not enough to get drunk. Fortunately, Brick gave us a timely hint to leave with that drunken show before YuanYi returned."

Qian patted ChenHe, sprawled flat on his horse, and said, "That was a good one, brother Brick. Falling back and breaking that bench—it looked so realistic. It's good that you emptied our wine under the table." They laughed and prodded ChenHe, eliciting no response but a deep snore!

Qian and SuWu looked at each other in surprise and muttered curses.

****

The boys were gone when YuanYi returned to the chophouse with his men! Instead, the angry owner confronted him and told him about his guest's rowdy behaviour. His men rushed outside to check the streets. It was too late; the boys had disappeared.

YuanYi was seething with anger. He wanted to apprehend the boys. If that attempt failed, he planned to create a ruckus and throw them into a dungeon for the night. That would have given him the night to deal with HeGan in the desert.

YuanYi asked the chophouse owner, "Are you sure the boys are drunk? They could pretend, you know!"

The owner mocked him and said, "Hah! You can't fool a man who serves wine for a living. It is our job to identify drunks and throw them out." He showed his stained hanfu and said, "Look, I still have the drool of the fat man on my tunic!"

****

The sky was clear, the moon was about three-quarters full, and the horses made no sound as their hooves sank into the sand. The night was so cold that water froze in open pots. Sleeping in the open would be difficult without cocooning themselves from head to toe in woollen blankets. They wouldn't hear an assassin in their midst.

A bandit hooted like a night owl, signalling their scouts.

From the edge of the wide gully where the camp was set up, the scouts scrambled back to confirm that only two men and a dwarf were present with the goldsmith. HeGan was tied up, and the others were sleeping, wrapped in blankets.

YuanYi whispered to the scouts, "Do you think it is safe to go in and take out the goldsmith? They are warriors, you know."

Their scout replied, "I have been watching them all day, and the cold and tiredness from the long ride have caught up with them. They have gathered enough twigs to burn for three days." In admiration, the man added, "Their Hun has bound twigs into rolls and arranged them cleverly so that a bundle rolls into the embers of the preceding roll for a continuous fire. No one is stirring from their blankets, not tonight!"

The second scout confirmed, "Same routine as previous nights. No guards."

The men decided to rescue the goldsmith. "No," said YuanYi emphatically, "we will not rescue the goldsmith. We will smother him to death, and if that is not possible, we will shoot arrows at him and make our escape." The bandits were displeased, for that would leave YuanYi alone in knowing where to collect their gold. Much of the gold belonged to the men under YuanLin and was held back as surety. Now that most of their colleagues were dead, the bandits wished to claim it all.

The stealthy Mongol tracker was assigned to smother the goldsmith. With the goldsmith securely bound, the task would be effortless. Bandits waiting at the periphery would shoot at anyone who moved in their blankets. This was the perfect plan, for it was impossible to emerge from a blanket, arm oneself, and discover the positions of hidden archers in the dark.

YuanYi waited out of harm's way while the others moved in. As they neared the camp, a bandit hissed to the tracker, "Change of plan. Rescue HeGan! The share of our fallen brothers now belongs to us."

The Hun used his arms and legs like a desert lizard, hugging the terrain as he moved towards the goldsmith. He found HeGan covered up to his chest in twigs, and a blanket was spread loosely over him. The bandit paused, trying to make sense of it. He locked eyes with the wide-awake goldsmith and motioned for him to keep quiet.

The man crawled closer, and to his surprise, the goldsmith disappeared under the twigs. Too late, the Hun realised that he had crawled into a trap. The twigs piled over the goldsmith formed a protective barrier to shield him from incoming arrows, and someone had pulled the goldsmith under the twigs to safety.

He snagged his feet on a silk thread in his panic to escape, sending rolls of leaves and twigs sliding into the fire pit. Sparks flew, and flames crackled, transforming the sedate campfire into a bonfire. The Mongol froze in horror before dropping all pretence of stealth to sprint away. He grunted and fell, struck by a knife thrown into his back.

The bandits, crouching low at the periphery, sprayed arrows at the sleeping men. Yuan Yi did not wait. He mounted his horse to escape, but the silence made him pause. He waited and watched as his men gingerly stood up.

YuanYi paused and looked back anxiously. He felt foolish about his anxiety! Of course, his men had killed the sleeping men before they could react, and he trotted his horse to the periphery of the gully.

The bandits spread out, taking their time to check the silent campsite. The blaze had blinded them, obfuscating the mounds in shadow.

Suddenly, a volley of arrows struck them from outside the camp. The bandits panicked and fled towards their horses, but the archer mowed them down.

YuanYi swore bitterly, turned his horse, and dashed away.

SuJin rushed into the camp, and Batu shouted, "Flaming firepits! One of them has escaped." They climbed to the gully's edge and watched the man galloping away in the moonlight. The short bows they carried were not suitable for shooting at that distance. Suddenly, they saw him jerk and tumble off the horse.

"What in the heavens!" Exclaimed Batu.

"Our boys have him," SuJin said.

A little later, SuWu trotted into camp. Qian followed with two horses, one laden with a snoring ChenHe and the other dragging YuanYi's body.

Batu looked at a slumped ChenHe and grinned. "We saw you kill the bandit, Qian. There was no need to drag the sand dune here to prove your archery skills." He was referring to a knocked-out ChenHe, who was snoring in a deep sleep.

SuWu laughed, "ChenHe is full of bandit hospitality. He has both our shares of LaoLi inside him."

Batu winced in exaggerated pain. "Ah! All that booze to himself!"

CaoShen searched YuanYi's body and found gold coins and jade pieces sewn into the seams of his jacket. They checked his saddlebags but found nothing of value.

HeGan approached them and asked Qian to tear the saddle apart at the seams. They discovered a leather scroll sewn in with a list of names, cities, and gold loaned that YuanYi had set aside for himself.

HeGan glanced at the list and remarked, "This is a list of loans that I am unaware of. Devious, despite his proclaimed fear of his brother, he has diverted considerable gold."

Looking down at YuanYi's lifeless body, HeGan said, "He could have simply walked away, glad to be free of his monstrous brother!" He glanced at the boys and remarked ominously, "Gold and greed are inseparable. It is a cursed glitter that lusts for death; hardly a few escape its clutches."

Their journey to Changan was uneventful, except for the lively banter with ChenHe, who had woken up with a splitting headache.

26 Boar Attack on HeGan

Jin gold coins served as the currency for exchange as trade flourished across borders. The exchange rate between the humble copper coin used by peasants and the high-value gold coin was steep, and most people struggled to count such large numbers. Traders exchanged copper coins by stacking or weighing them, utilising the square hole in the centre to tie them into bundles. Many bundles were required to be exchanged for just one Jin gold coin.

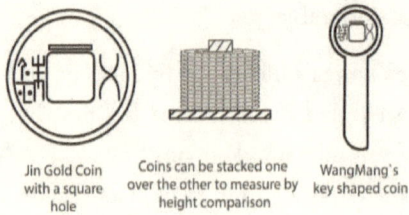

Jin Gold Coin with a square hole

Coins can be stacked one over the other to measure by height comparison

WangMang's key shaped coin

In a surprising move, WangMang banned the Jin coins and introduced his own "knife-shaped" coins, throwing trade into chaos. The objective was to prevent the Lui clan from hiring mercenaries with their hoarded Jin gold.

Despite being illegal, traders reverted to older coins for large transactions to match the weight of gold, as WangMang's "knife money" was known to be lighter. WangMang covertly decided to buy back all the Jin gold coins through jewellers and use them to mint knife money. With the ensuing Jin coin shortage, he was confident that the traders would switch to knife money.

****

Unable to make sense of the gold crisis, WoShi summoned the boys. CaoShen was the first to speak. "Master, we should exchange all the bandit's gold immediately before it becomes worthless." WoShi remained pensive, and CaoShen continued, "Let's redeem all the Jin coins for the official knife money. What difference does it make to us? It's all ill-gotten gold."

WoShi asked SuWu, "Do you have anything to say?"

SuWu gestured to HeGan. "Let's hear him out."

CaoShen reacted instantly before HeGan could speak. "What's your opinion, goldsmith? Weren't you an adviser and treasurer to the flesh-eating bandits?" He gestured towards SuWu and said despondently, "Some people value your opinion."

Qian bristled in indignation and appealed to SuJin. "Prince, HeGan is our friend! CaoShen takes pleasure in insulting him at every opportunity. I don't know why Master WoShi tolerates his behaviour. It is time that we left this place."

ChenHe supported his friend and said, "Yes, the mofa has left this place." He repeated, "The magic is gone."

SuJin was bemused and said, "Qian! ChenHe! This is our home. Where could we possibly go?"

"No, this isn't our home! We should leave for Tianzhu," Qian insisted. WoShi furiously stroked his beard, glancing from one boy to the other.

SuJin said, "HeGan is our friend, true. However, he needs to earn the trust of others, and we can't do that for him." He looked at SuWu and asked, "What do you think, brother?"

WoShi cleared his throat loudly. "Enough! HeGan, what do you suggest we do with the gold? Shall we exchange it for WangMang's new coin or hold on to the Jin coins?"

HeGan said, "I suggest we invest the gold in trade. The Yellow River is bustling with shiploads of silk, porcelain, tea, and paper leaving for the coast. We are currently trading with lands beyond Tianzhu." He glanced at a scowling CaoShen and added, "If you wish to hoard money, hold Jin coins, not that ridiculous knife money." WoShi grunted in agreement.

WoShi said, "If we invest the gold, we could lose some, but then we can take back our money either in Jin coin or knife money, whichever is popular."

CaoShen protested vehemently, saying, "No! We should exchange it for knife money and hoard it." WoShi looked at the boys, clearly expressing their resentment towards CaoShen to each other.

HeGan ignored CaoShen and asked WoShi, "Master, how will you explain all this gold to the imperial treasury when you exchange it for knife money? We have a lot of gold with us, rivalling the richest."

WoShi harrumphed, realising that HeGan was right; the HanKaoTzu school couldn't be seen handling large sums of gold. He waved his hand at HeGan and said, "Go ahead, invest the gold. The boys believe in you. Let me see how you repay their trust." He gestured to CaoShen. "Come with me." CaoShen ran after WoShi, gesticulating and protesting his decision to give HeGan access to the gold.

All of them heard WoShi say, "It's time, CaoShen. If HeGan is a skiver or a cheat, let the lads recognise their mistake in Changan. You should be with him to ensure he doesn't skimp on the gold."

****

CaoShen insisted on accompanying HeGan to redeem the gold and tally it. Qian joined them to see what trade was all about. They visited goldsmiths to redeem the gold; however, no one was willing to part with the Jin gold coins as they sold them to the imperial treasury at a higher rate. Undeterred, HeGan redrafted the promissory notes on leather bearing the goldsmith's name, addressed to CaoShen for the equivalent in gold.

After exiting the goldsmith's shops, HeGan negotiated and bought gold ingots from traders by surrendering the promissory notes. Qian asked HeGan, "How are we making money? I can't understand."

HeGan chuckled. "We are selling gold to buy more gold."

"What! That is preposterous!"

HeGan confided in Qian when CaoShen was out of earshot. "We have moulds to die-cast Jin coins and possess the original Wu recipe to make them from ingots. We add silver, copper, and tin to produce authentic coins of the correct weight, width, and height. No one can spot the difference.

Qian was puzzled. "To what end? Where is the profit? What's your plan, you crafty bandit?"

HeGan giggled. "The ingots we buy are pure gold, but Jin coins aren't pure gold; they are a mixture of gold and other metals. Not many know this! Mixing other metals into the molten gold creates more Jin coins! The extra coins we get from adding other metals are our profit."

A thoughtful Qian said, "However absurd this feels, you are selling copper and tin at the price of gold."

HeGan grinned unabashedly, "It's called trade."

"Who performs the ingot-to-coin transformation for you?" Asked a curious Qian.

HeGan said, "I come from a jeweller's family and have trusted relatives in Changan. Not once has YuanYi suspected this, and now you keep it to yourself. These are trade secrets!"

CaoShen was baffled by the purchase of gold ingots, but he did not intervene because HeGan always gave him equivalent Jin coins a few days later.

HeGan and CaoShen negotiated with bureaucrats, traders, and shipowners to fund trade. They also hired a few apprentices to manage their burgeoning business.

****

On one of their many visits to meet Zhan, a renowned jeweller and friend of HeGan, Qian saw an imperial general examining the knives on display, which a thin, sharp-featured foreign man sold.

The general sat astride a horse while one of his assistants picked up the knives to which he gestured. Qian saw the blacksmith vendor drop something to the ground and use his feet to conceal it while openly displaying his other wares, including leather scabbards. He overheard people whispering that the general was none other than WangYi, the regent's cousin. The general bought a few knives and moved down the street.

His curiosity was piqued. Qian asked the foreign blacksmith, "How much for the knife?"

"Which one?" The man asked with a foreign twang and a charming smile, pointing to his wares in a wide arc.

"The knife under your foot," said Qian.

The man whistled in wonder. "I can't believe this! I was told that someone would ask for the silver knife without putting it up for sale, and here you are."

Qian laughed, "Now, don't con me with an exaggerated tale. I am with the city's finest traders and hear incredible stories all day." With his eyebrows knitted, he asked, "Who said someone would ask for the knife without seeing it? That's unreasonable!"

The blacksmith chuckled. "You just did, didn't you? You asked for the knife without seeing it!" Qian smiled sheepishly, and the man added, "An old woman! A woman of God from our city told me I could demand any price from the man who asked for the silver knife, and he would pay." After giving Qian a thorough look-over, he continued, "She said he had better pay because the knife will save him and his friends many times!"

Qian smiled back and said, "Ah! This is undoubtedly the best story I have heard about making a sale in the last few days! Let me look at this famous knife that only the two of us seem to know about?" The blacksmith grinned and retrieved the knife. He lovingly wiped it clean and applied oil to the blade before handing it to Qian.

The blacksmith said, "The old lady asked me to call the blade Sheya."

Qian arched his eyebrows, "Sheya, meaning fangs of a snake."

The man nodded. "The tooth."

Qian whistled in awe at the workmanship of the simple knife, which was incredibly thin and slightly curved at the tip. Unusually, the knife blade was a shining silver, not the usual bronze colour. The knife had a sharp edge on one side and a serrated edge on the other. Its hilt was oversized and leather-braided, offering an excellent grip. The handle nestled snugly in his palm. It was simply the perfect weapon for Qian, and he wanted it badly.

"How much for this small knife?" Qian asked.

"Twenty old Jin gold coins and no negotiation. Exclusive price, just for you."

Qian's jaw fell open in shock, and he exclaimed, "That is beyond expensive! Why? All the knives in this market won't cost that much!"

The blacksmith shrugged and said, "That's the price! I'm sure you will consider your life and that of your friends more than all the knives in this market! It's a knife from the gods, and you are its master once you pay me." The blacksmith seemed sincere as he explained, "The hard silver metal of the blade is rarer than gold and harder than anything we know of, and the edge doesn't wear off easily. Yet, it's flexible and small enough to be hung inside your waistband."

Qian became critical once he heard the exorbitant price. "The dagger's hilt is too large to hide in a waistband." Realising that the man was a foreigner, Qian exclaimed, "What is it made of? Who made it? Which kingdom?"

"I come from a beautiful kingdom down south called Champa. The ore for this blade came from a burning rock that tumbled down from the sky. The metal is tough, and we used rock coal to melt it with a new furnace to handle the heat. However, there was so little of it after days of toil that we had to settle for a knife."

Qian returned the knife reluctantly. "I don't have twenty Jin coins. I haven't seen that kind of money in my entire life."

The blacksmith muttered, "What are twenty Jin coins to someone who walks with the richest man in Changan?"

Qian couldn't hide his shock. "Sure, HeGan deals in gold, but that doesn't make him the richest."

The blacksmith gave a noncommittal nod, and Qian asked curiously, "Do you think he is that rich?"

The blacksmith said, "I will be here until I sell this knife to you. Next time, it will cost you thirty Jin coins. I shall go back to my kingdom after this sale."

Qian asked, "Why me?"

The man said, "I tried selling it to the king of Champa, but the god-woman at court intervened and declared it was intended for a man in Changan. She has blessed it with her blood on the hilt after using this knife to execute convicts for the seven different crimes that are punishable by death. It is a holy knife!"

A customer came to inspect his wares, and the blacksmith turned away from Qian. The display of bronze knives, short swords, and scabbards was impressive, but an astounded Qian now had eyes only for the silver knife.

****

A tired CaoShen was relaxing with his foot soaked in hot, scented salt water when a young apprentice they had hired to help keep track of business approached him. "What is it, boy? Aren't the numbers adding up?"

"Master, it's not that. We apprentices had a discussion amongst ourselves about the stock."

CaoShen bobbed his head at the boy to continue. "Master, we can see that purchases of our goods are in effect for trade with the port cities. The problem is the space required to store all this material in the next two months of rain."

CaoShen's brow creased, and he asked, "What do you mean?"

"We will need over twenty-five shiploads of space below deck to transport the material to the coastal cities. The boy continued to explain, unaware that CaoShen was astonished. "With the rain expected soon, the imperial guards won't allow carts to muddy the roads leading to the city docks."

The boy smiled sincerely, proposing a solution. "We should shift our loading and unloading to the docks outside the city and ask our traders to deliver their goods there instead of coming into the city, where priority is always given to the military ships."

A shiver went down CaoShen's spine, and he croaked, "Thank you for the information. I shall reward you with higher pay for this insight. Let me consult the Grand Master WoShi."

CaoShen sagged onto his chair, bewildered, and murmured, "HeGan! Are we dealing with all the trade of the empire?"

****

"What's this I hear, HeGan?" WoShi asked sternly. "Are we dealing in so much gold that we can buy all of Changan?" The boys gasped, but HeGan remained unfazed.

HeGan replied, "Substantial is a better description."

CaoShen was bitter, but his anger showed through. "I should have doubted you when you asked for the city to be divided into five parts to manage business. I lost track of the overall total. Thankfully, the apprentices were smarter than you imagined."

"Ahh, that explains it," remarked HeGan. "We should have kept the apprentices separate in five places as well. I forget that boys from your city are well-versed in counting."

"Enough!" WoShi exclaimed in anger. "We are in dangerous territory. WangMang's port master will soon learn about us funding large trades, and he won't need any excuse to raid the school."

HeGan wasn't cowed by WoShi's outburst. "Master, you said that meeting the Empress could happen at any time now that her health has improved, and we should be prepared to leave soon after." WoShi reluctantly nodded, and HeGan continued, "What do you want me to do?? Relationships of trust in trade take decades, but I am securing that goodwill by paying a premium to established merchants. Some of our consignments will be lost, but we will have a functioning network of trade developed up to and beyond Tianzhu by the time you decide to travel."

WoShi hissed at HeGan. "This is not a small wealth, HeGan. We are talking about purchases in gold, rivalling the imperial treasury."

HeGan locked eyes with WoShi. "I won't lie to you. The port master is one of our own, and we have invested in existing businesses using the names of nobles to avoid raising suspicions. For now, I need all your trust. I worked for a bandit, and I know what I'm doing. I need time to redistribute the wealth to reliable traders and jewellers along the Yellow River."

SuWu interjected, "HeGan. That means all the gold is lost if you disappear!" HeGan nodded.

SuWu said, "Hmmm. More like a wager! Win or lose everything."

WoShi looked grim, and HeGan shrugged. "When the Prince is ready, I will take him to Tianzhu. I apologise if I don't have answers to all your questions."

HeGan bowed to SuJin, "Prince, I am sincere. Please trust me."

HeGan dramatically swore an oath to show his sincerity. "Let me split into a thousand pieces; my stomach burst with ten thousand worms, my limbs fall off, and my teeth rot if I am not truthful."

"Silly oath of fealty!" Said SuWu in disgust.

SuJin smiled, "Reminds me of the overzealous dwarf oaths."

CaoShen scoffed, "Words from a bandit?"

HeGan turned to SuWu and said, "If my words are not sincere, call a priest and ask me to swear on the gods!" He pointed his finger at SuJin and said, "Just don't make the Prince doubt my sincerity."

CaoShen told WoShi, "HeGan is cunning and a known accomplice of the most dreaded bandits. If things go wrong, he will disappear. Do I need to explain our fate at the hands of the merciless imperial soldiers?"

HeGan turned to WoShi and stated, "I have spoken and am done! You can decide my fate here and now, but I will not tolerate any further disrespect from SuWu and CaoShen."

When no one said anything, Qian proposed, "Let HeGan fortify his allegiance by entering the warriors' brotherhood."

Horrified, CaoShen yelled at Qian, "That's extreme, even for you, Qian! Did he cast any forbidden magic on you? You have championed him since we took him in as a prisoner."

HeGan bowed low to Qian. "Heaven willing, I shall repay you one day, Brother Qian. At the moment, I have little to give, warrior!"

WoShi looked at HeGan with a frown. He was uncertain.

Surprising everyone, Batu interjected. "I, too, must take a brotherhood oath." He glanced around with a sheepish expression.

SuWu was unhappy and exclaimed, "I think we were discussing HeGan here, not you, Batu!"

Batu said, "Come on, SuWu! All of us trust HeGan!" Looking at his startled face, he added, "At least Qian and I do." CaoShen jeered at this declaration of faith.

Batu gestured to HeGan and reminded SuWu, "This crafty fox could have got us killed at any moment! Remember our time in the desert when he saved us from the bandits? He could have killed us then and kept the gold, couldn't he?" SuWu nodded at HeGan and took a step back.

WoShi laughed contemptuously and motioned to SuJin. "A barbarian and a bandit want to swear allegiance to you, Prince of Han. Do you accept such low forms of life as your sworn brothers?"

"It's not just SuJin, Master!" Qian interrupted hotly. "I shall proudly call them my brothers."

WoShi laughed contemptuously. "Oh! Let me look at the illustrious people surrounding the Prince of Han," WoShi mocked, adding, "Qian, a scholar, quick with a knife and even quicker to make rash decisions. Your impulsive decisions can endanger the entire team." Qian gnashed his teeth in anger at WoShi.

WoShi turned to SuWu. "A strategist who implicitly trusts those around him, making the team weak from within." SuWu was distraught upon hearing this caustic remark from his master, and WoShi added sternly, "You do not cross-check every shred of evidence as part of your service to the Prince. If you had investigated HeGan, we wouldn't be in this situation." SuWu remained silent, but his face had crumpled in distress.

WoShi gestured towards ChenHe, who paused while chewing on dried meat. "Who? Me! Now, what did I do?"

WoShi said scornfully, "A pit fighter who is more pork than human!" ChenHe grinned, not one bit affected by his master's barb.

He gestured to Batu, "A drunken and quarrelsome barbarian whom people avoid like a fisherman trying to sell yesterday's fish." Batu bowed low to WoShi. He, too, did not take offence at WoShi's rant.

SuJin interrupted WoShi before he could continue. "Led by a vagabond who has the trust of fine men, despite his numerous failings." WoShi paused, and SuJin added, "All to fulfil an oath made by his ancestors to dead men and unknown gods." SuJin grinned, realising that WoShi was testing their resolve as a team – the golden glow!

SuJin softly declared, "Master, if anyone present is unworthy because of their flaws, it's me! I wouldn't trade any of these men for an army of skilled warriors or shiploads of riches."

SuJin's response pleased WoShi, who toned his voice down. "Sworn brotherhood is sacred. It is not a prayer but a divine ceremony to seal a bond between all of you and the gods."

SuJin bowed low to each of his brothers and HeGan, saying, "I wouldn't accept anything less than a sworn brotherhood sealed in blood."

WoShi said, "The first Emperor began life as a commoner, Lui Bang. He was an outlaw in the Qin Empire! Zhang Liang, a disgruntled strategist, and Ha Xin, a discarded warrior from that era, assisted Lui Bang in overthrowing the powerful Qin Empire."

WoShi continued, "The gods who helped these men in founding the Han dynasty have gathered you for a purpose. Allow me to assure you, I have long ceased passing judgment on the men chosen by destiny."

WoShi continued, "I had hoped to conduct the ritual of filial piety and brotherhood after meeting the Empress, but it seems we won't have time later. Thanks to HeGan." He added, "First things first. Respect CaoShen's misgivings; all of you appear to accept everything without question."

WoShi asked, "Why do you have so much faith in HeGan? A bandit and embezzler!" The boys exchanged glances. WoShi raised his hand to stop any response from a livid HeGan.

Batu responded first. "Although we did not treat HeGan as a prisoner during our journey through the desert, he left markers for the bandits to follow. He was setting us up for an ambush!"

The boys looked shocked, and CaoShen screamed, "Why did you not tell us this during the journey, Batu? We wouldn't be discussing him today. After all that, how can you declare now that you trust him?"

HeGan looked at Batu, astounded. "How! How did you figure this out?"

Batu nodded to HeGan and continued. "We could have crossed the wide-open desert landscape in many ways towards Changan. Despite this, the bandits found us and kept pace with us."

Batu grinned at HeGan and added, "We wouldn't have figured anything out if you hadn't given us a veiled warning. We were focused on looking back for pursuit, not ahead or beside our tracks." He added, "I deliberately left the ropes untied the night we were attacked. You could have walked away, and I would have let you go! After all, your warning saved us from an ambush."

Qian said, "He stayed!"

Batu continued, "Whatever happened that night was as he planned. It was his well-placed hints and tactics that made us win!" SuWu looked dumbfounded at HeGan, who was shaking his head at Batu.

Qian remarked, "He suggested that we travel by sea as traders instead of travelling on a caravan as warriors."

SuWu added, "Thinking back, he asked us to break YuanYi's saddle, where we got the promissory notes for gold. He could have asked for the horse, and we would have given it to him."

ChenHe added, "He warned us that YuanYi would meet us in the eatery at Guyuan and what he would say."

WoShi threw his hands up in mock exasperation and asked, "Anyone else?" The boys smiled at HeGan.

"It's settled. Call Tuhu," said WoShi to a chastened CaoShen. "Let's get these boys to swear the brotherhood oath to each other," WoShi added good-naturedly, "If they break the oath to the gods and their ancestors, let demons break their backs, and vultures feast upon their eyes."

SuWu grinned at WoShi and said, "Master, don't exaggerate! We are still smarting from the beating you gave each of us."

CaoShen remained unconvinced about HeGan and cautioned him, "Our ancestors, all the ancestors of Han, will rain misery upon anyone who breaks the brotherhood bond."

SuJin said, "CaoShen, that is not enough. We need you to acknowledge HeGan as a brother!"

Nobody disobeyed the Prince. A fuming CaoShen removed the dragon fish tooth necklace he wore and gave it to HeGan. "You keep this. I shall take it off your dead body when you show your true colours."

WoShi said, "That will do, CaoShen."

****

On the next full moon night, Tuhu invoked Yueshen, the moon goddess, with offerings to mediate their plea to the three patrons and five deities for the solemnisation of the warrior's brotherhood. To propitiate Yin and Yang, they began with offerings to Fuxi, the patron of heaven, followed by Nuwa, the patron of Earth. Finally, they propitiated the flame deity and the god of humanity.

WoShi asked SuJin and SuWu to perform propitiation rituals for Huangdi, the yellow god, the first ancestor of the Han, who had four faces and was worshipped by the imperial household. This request to join SuJin astonished SuWu, who demanded an explanation. WoShi was brusque and dismissed his question. "Not now, just do it."

The following day, the boys, accompanied by Batu and HeGan, swore mutual consent to formalise the brotherhood of the golden glow in front of Tuhu and the other temple priests. The oath promised assistance, loyalty, and protection to each other; they lit and wafted incense to the gods as divine witnesses. Using a ceremonial knife, Tuhu nicked the insides of their palms and inscribed their names in blood on a silk cloth. He collected a drop of blood from each of them into a cup of rice wine. Using the embers from the ritual fire, Tuhu employed the ceremonial knife to cauterise and seal their wounds.

Tuhu solidified their eternal brotherhood by burning the blood-stained silk cloth bearing their names while chanting prayers. He added more kindling and incense to the embers and poured a few drops of blood wine, creating a cloud of steam. Tuhu wafted the sweet-smelling smoke over the assembled people, declaring their bond as witnessed by man and God.

"The ritual of the brotherhood is now complete," he declared.

The boys, priests, and guests had food and wine amidst much laughter and cheerfulness. Tuhu continued with his prayers and meditations, pleading for the success of the golden glow and their safe return to Han.

Tuhu was concluding the prayers when HeGan approached him and offered money to conduct prayers for twelve moons to appease Jinshen, the god of gold.

Tuhu asked him, "Are you sure you want to do this? Jinshen is a formidable deity who demands blood for gold. Don't take any offerings to him lightly. He is a trickster. Someone you care about could get hurt or killed."

HeGan said, "I am his greatest devotee!"

Tuhu said, "Alright. What blood sacrifice are you offering?"

HeGan thought for some time and said, "Cut the small toe of my foot as a blood sacrifice."

Tuhu grunted his approval. "Umm, that will appease Jinshen for certain! I need to get your blood brothers to witness the sacrifice."

"Why are they required?"

"We priests do not take sides between a god and a devotee regarding blood sacrifices. I must remain neutral. However, we need witnesses in case Jinshen misinterprets the premise of the sacrifice. His sense of humour is not palatable to many."

HeGan resented Tuhu's suggestion and said, "I have sacrificed to Jinshen before, offering him deer, foxes, rabbits, and birds, and he hasn't rejected my offerings." HeGan was visibly uneasy about involving his new brothers. "I am insignificant, a bandit. Let's not involve others."

Tuhu did not relent. "Who knows! As part of the golden glow, you are now part of deific scrutiny. Why do you consider your adversaries to be human? In the coming days, you may battle errant gods and demons." HeGan's shock was evident as he swallowed hard.

HeGan retorted, not believing the priest. "Gods don't interfere directly in human lives, priest!"

Tuhu ignored him and sent his assistant to summon SuJin and SuWu. "Qian and others are too excitable. I don't want a mischievous God to twist the facts." He gave HeGan a piercing stare and said, "Potent forces are at play when SuJin is involved. You will soon understand what I mean by saying the gods will be involved."

Tuhu was washing HeGan's feet when SuJin and SuWu walked in and overheard the priest commenting, "HeGan, this toe is damaged. It's just a small dead stump! How can you offer this as a blood sacrifice to Jinshen? Mind you, he is a proud god!"

HeGan said, "Priest, that stump is a living part of me, and I will feel pain when you amputate it. The god of gold will see my pain more than my smelly stump."

Tuhu looked unconvinced, and HeGan said, "Just make the offering, priest. You have been paid."

Tuhu hesitated and said, "Don't negotiate with me! Jinshen, the god of gold, explicitly requires blood, which isn't this. As a priest, I shall proceed with the sacrifice on one condition."

"What's that?"

"You should stay away from your sworn brothers for twelve moons while I complete the monthly sacrifices. Otherwise, you might bring the evil eye upon them with your recklessness!"

HeGan smirked, "Ridiculous! We would have reached Tianzhu by then, and I shall be with them. I'd rather get this ceremony done elsewhere."

Tuhu stood up and bowed to HeGan. "So be it; take your money back. I shall be on my way."

SuJin intervened, "No, HeGan. Whatever it is, Tuhu should do it. You need to meet his conditions."

HeGan frowned at SuJin and bowed to Tuhu. "Priest, I am sorry. I shall meet your conditions once we leave Changan before your first sacrifice." Tuhu agreed sombrely and reminded him that there would be thirteen sacrifices, including today.

Tuhu asked SuJin and SuWu to hold HeGan while he cut the toe and offered it to Jinshen in the ritual fire. The priest and butcher sliced through the toe before HeGan could realise what was happening, and he screamed.

Despite HeGan squirming in pain, Tuhu held up the mangled toe and exclaimed, "This sacrifice hasn't yielded much blood, HeGan! Do I need to cauterise the wound?"

"You've cut my bone!" Screamed HeGan, beating his hands on the floor in pain.

SuJin and SuWu stepped back in unison, dragging HeGan with them. Bewildered, they looked at each other, and Tuhu asked, "What has happened?"

SuJin said, "I saw the medallion!"

SuWu added, "I saw it too. How can this be?"

HeGan, squirming with pain, exclaimed, "Did it have bright stones studded that shine like stars?" Looking at SuWu's surprise, he said, "I saw it, too!"

SuJin and SuWu waited until Tuhu offered the toe to the ceremonial fire. After cauterising the wound, they helped a hobbling HeGan back to his sleeping mat.

HeGan said, "I shall make that gold medallion for you. I shall put quartz stones of water jade as stars."

****

The Empress Dowager informed her palace administrator, CaoTeng, that she was ready to meet WoShi and SuJin. CaoTeng sent soldiers to guard SuJin and placed an imperial banner at the school to signify imperial protection.

****

Qian was chatting animatedly with the foreign blacksmith when HeGan hobbled over. "I see you here most days. What do you keep buying? Don't you have enough swords and knives, warrior?" The blacksmith quietly withdrew Sheya, the fang knife.

Qian told the blacksmith, "It's all right. He is my brother. Can you show him, Sheya?" The man shrugged nonchalantly and displayed the silver knife with its oversized leather hilt.

The blacksmith chastised Qian, "It's supposed to be your secret weapon. Be careful to whom you disclose what weapons you carry."

Qian grinned and said, "It's not my knife for sure. I can't afford thirty Jīn gold coins. It costs as much as ten to twelve farms. You can buy a village with that kind of money!"

HeGan whistled, and his eyes narrowed as he examined the knife. "Although it shines, it's not silver or any metal I know."

The blacksmith said, "It is iron, flexible, and can cut through brass like butter. Tell your friend here to buy it. He is destined to save lives with it!"

CaoShen walked up to them and scolded Qian. "Don't chat with foreign vendors! They are glib talkers who can sell you the hezi you are wearing. Let's meet Zhan before he leaves for wherever he goes."

HeGan handed the knife to Qian. "See you around. Sometime later, we need to talk about business in Champa."

As they walked away, HeGan asked CaoShen, "What's a hezi?"

CaoShen grinned at HeGan, "I keep forgetting you are not from the city. A hezi is underwear. You wear it under the hanfu."

HeGan was puzzled and asked, "Why do you need to wear something under your clothes? You are already covered, aren't you? What if you want to relieve yourself in a hurry?"

CaoShen sighed loudly and said, "Never mind! We will talk about it some other time."

HeGan followed CaoShen as Qian critically examined the exquisitely crafted knife scabbard. It concealed a cleverly hidden splinter resembling a small metal pin, with serrations capable of severing through hemp rope.

There was a commotion, and Qian looked up. HeGan was wiping his stained hanfu. Qian chuckled, saying, "He recently lost a toe and is hobbling about. Now, look, he has slipped and fallen in the mud!"

"It's not mud; it's blood!" Observed the knife blacksmith, adding, "Someone threw it on him."

Amidst warning shouts, a giant boar with long tusks charged down the street, scattering shoppers and vendors. The creature's tusks were fitted with bronze barbs; it was a killer boar trained to kill in the fighting pits.

"Look out!" Qian screamed, and he sprinted towards HeGan.

CaoShen saw the charging boar and managed to get out of its way. "Mad swine!" He shouted. HeGan hit his bandaged foot on a cobblestone and howled in pain. He hopped about on one foot.

The boar slashed with its tusks, throwing HeGan up like a leaf in a storm. Infuriated by the blood on HeGan's cloak, the crazed animal turned to attack again.

Qian covered the distance in a few long strides, screamed at the boar, and lunged. The animal pulled back, holding its hard head out to ram him while stamping its hoofs. Qian realised he was going to hit the head of the boar with the small knife in his hand.

Qian fixed the mental picture of his foe and slammed the knife into the boar's eye. The boar squealed and slashed upwards. Qian slid under the raised head of the animal, pushing his legs wide on either side of the animal. He tripped it, as ChenHe did in pit fights. He held the boar upside down and ripped the knife across the other eye and, holding onto its flailing head, deftly stabbed the animal many times. He rolled away quickly but could not avoid its thrashing head. The sharp tusk pierced his arm, and he cried in pain.

The blinded animal stood up and thrashed its head, attempting to hook its tusks onto its attacker, but it remained standing with its legs splayed, waiting. A soldier rushed in and thrust his spear into the animal, but it held its ground, swinging its muscular head. It took a long time for the animal to fall over and die.

Someone tapped a bleeding Qian on the shoulder. It was the blacksmith who demanded the knife back. Qian reluctantly relinquished the absurdly powerful blade with regret. He told the blacksmith, "The large hilt is essential! It provides an extraordinary grip for the blade."

CaoShen attended to HeGan. Helpful people guided Qian to a nearby apothecary to treat his deep bruise and called for a litter to carry the injured HeGan. Despite his severe injury and significant blood loss, HeGan insisted that they take him to Tuhu.

****

HeGan was writhing in pain as Tuhu swiftly cleared his worktable where pork had been chopped earlier, and CaoShen and a few others laid him down.

Tuhu pressed his hands to the sides of HeGan's neck, feeling for his carotid arteries and blocking them while he murmured a throat chant. HeGan passed out! Tuhu washed his hands with rice wine and poured the potent rice wine over the long gash on his thigh. Thankfully, none of his major arteries were severed despite the deep wound.

Tuhu sutured the wound with sinew made from pork intestines cured in vinegar and salt. The priest then boiled medicinal leaves, roots, and spices. After cooling, the sweet-smelling paste was packed and bound over the wound.

Tuhu wiped his hands clean of HeGan's blood, looked down at the sleeping man, and said, "Why am I not surprised by your condition,

HeGan?" He scraped the blood from the table into a bowl and set it aside.

Tuhu told CaoShen, "I need his blood to appease an infuriated Jinshen." He gazed at HeGan and said, "I warned him! He may be a clever trader, but you can't short-change a god!"

CaoShen said, "This is something HeGan wouldn't have expected."

Tuhu said, "Perhaps Jinshen will acknowledge HeGan's blood sacrifice now!"

"Will he live?"

"Yes, he will. I am sure of that," Tuhu responded. "He is returned for a purpose."

"Miraculous escape, saved by Qian. That wound is vicious."

CaoShen asked, "Aren't you going to cauterise the wound?"

"No, the wound is deep. Hopefully, we won't need to open it again to clean it. If the wound festers inside and we cauterise it outside, the man will die."

CaoShen asked, "How long before he wakes?"

Tuhu said, "I will give him a brew to keep him drugged for a few days until the wound mends. We need to flex his legs afterwards for him to walk, and that's when the pain will hit HeGan."

CaoShen said, "No, not yet, priest! Don't give him any draught to sleep yet. On our way here, he asked me to bring SuJin. He wants to tell him something. Something significant, he said."

Tuhu did not like that but agreed. "We have already drugged him to some extent, and we will continue administering medication. I know that SuJin is set to meet the Empress, and perhaps it's significant. Anyhow, he will be delirious and in a great deal of pain."

****

SuJin and SuWu rushed over as soon as they learned that HeGan had been attacked. Imperial guards, assigned as their bodyguards, cordoned off the shop against curious onlookers who had gathered. The crowd soon realised that Han's hero was visiting Tuhu and began screaming, "Hero of Han, Green Hunter, save us! Long live Tuhu, the butcher! Long live Tuhu, the doctor."

Tuhu kept his stout hands on his waist and greeted SuJin with a smile. "How did this happen? I was living a quiet life as a butcher, and now you have made me a celebrated doctor in my street?" SuJin grinned, and Tuhu's eyes twinkled. "Good to see you so soon, apprentice!" Tuhu chuckled and said, "I don't know what has made me famous. Is it my butchering skills or my surgical skills? Time will decide, as both have commonalities."

SuJin tenderly said, "Actually, in time, it's your spiritual strength that will make you sought after."

Tuhu frowned and said, "Hmm. You have touched an empathetic point on spirituality." He exhaled heavily and continued, "Do you realise dwarfs struggle with inadequacy? Short stature and physical limitations make us inferior to the frailest of men. Society looks down on us. Our mothers beat their chests in despair when they see us. Despite all this unfairness we face, we believe the gods treat us as equals to other men."

Tuhu smiled and told SuJin, "Doubts plague me most days, especially when I advise my brethren to be brave and face life. I fear the gods we pray to have given up on us because of our imperfections! Maybe we have stunted souls as well!"

Tuhu smiled radiantly and said, "I can finally rest these gloomy thoughts. The gods surely accept our prayers and sacrifices." He gestured happily to a supine HeGan and said, "Look, Jinshen, the finicky god of gold, has responded to my sacrifice."

"As a priest, I gathered Jinshen needed a proper blood offering from

HeGan. So, I demanded blood to complete my sacrifice, but he negotiated." Tuhu laughed. "Jinshen has ensured I have enough of his blood with no bickering to complete my offering."

HeGan gained consciousness after Tuhu applied honey locust fruits and crinum leaf powder to HeGan's nostrils. He woke up to the pungent smell, but the sleep concoction he had earlier left him delirious. Tuhu fed him a broth of ultramafic tuff, a rare volcanic rock, and cloves boiled in a light pork fat soup to spruce him up. They burned incense around him to prevent evil spirits from infecting his wounds.

HeGan gave SuJin a tired smile and whispered into his ear. SuWu and Tuhu watched as an incredulous look crossed SuJin's face. A little later, HeGan grimaced in pain and asked for CaoShen, despite Tuhu fretting over him to rest.

SuWu enquired of SuJin, "Is everything all right?"

SuJin shook his head and said, "I don't know what to make of what he said. HeGan is delirious and is talking about the power of the medallion. He says that there is a maleficent spirit within it! What's incredible is that he asked me to draw the spirit into myself when I touch the medallion."

SuWu found it amusing and burst into laughter. "Ugh! Truly, a man can get messed up in his thoughts from a loss of blood and a whiff of the dream smoke."

"I can't believe that he summoned you to tell this!" SuWu shook his head in incredulity.

Tuhu gave HeGan the sleeping draft that lulled him back to sleep. CaoShen did not speak to the boys, but for some reason, he left weeping after he talked to HeGan.

****

WoShi was briefing SuJin and SuWu on the etiquette for meeting the Empress. A solemn CaoShen walked in and gave SuJin a curt bow.

SuJin asked him, "What's wrong, CaoShen? You look vexed! You seem to have had a change of heart after HeGan got hurt." CaoShen gave him a watery smile.

SuWu shook his head in disbelief. "After all your misgivings, CaoShen, he decided to disclose his secrets to you, not us!"

SuJin said, "When I next meet HeGan, I shall ask him what transpired between you."

"You won't find HeGan. He has left for an undisclosed location, and I have no clue where it is. There is no need to search for what has transpired between us; I am here to inform you."

Qian was shocked to hear that HeGan had left without telling them. Holding his bandaged arm, he exclaimed, "You mean we lost all our gold? Is that why you are so glum?"

CaoShen turned on him like a threatened snake and said, "Don't you dare talk ill of that good man!" The boys looked at each other, speechless. When did CaoShen drastically change his opinion of HeGan?

WoShi sagely motioned to CaoShen, "Get on with it."

CaoShen sat on the floor, folding his knees and tucking his legs behind them. First, he opened a silk-covered package. It contained a silver dagger with a large hilt and an ingenious scabbard.

Qian gasped, "Sheya! How did you get it?"

CaoShen said, "HeGan asked me to buy it for you. I paid sixty Jin coins for it—a fortune! After the blacksmith confirmed I was buying it for you, he demanded thirty Jin coins. HeGan asked me to double his payment as a reward for lending the knife to kill the boar from hell."

SuWu interjected, "The attack is not an accident. Someone threw blood on HeGan. Have you found out what happened?"

CaoShen said solemnly. "Yes, I did. It is betrayal!"

SuWu said, "Betrayal is part of all trades. That is why it is not a warrior's profession. It must be someone he knows."

Qian sat down opposite CaoShen and formally received the knife, bowing his head low and extending his arms. Then CaoShen said, "Tuhu has blessed it with the sacrificial blood of HeGan."

The gift overwhelmed Qian. He asked, "How do I thank HeGan?"

"No need. You have already thanked him for saving his life."

CaoShen looked up at SuJin and said, "Following Tuhu's advice, he will cease contacting all of you for a year." SuJin nodded his acceptance.

Qian animatedly showed the knife around, explaining the extraordinary features of the blade to ChenHe.

WoShi motioned to SuJin to take Qian's place. SuJin inquired, "Me? What for?" However, he sat down in deference to his master.

CaoShen handed over a silk pouch, a thick leather scroll, and a silk cloth with words written on it. SuJin looked at him with a questioning gaze.

CaoShen said, "You can read and hand over the silk cloth with names to SuWu and Qian to memorise it. I will burn it later. It lists men loyal to HeGan, mostly bureaucrats and jewellers along the Yellow River up to Panyu." SuJin extended the silk cloth to SuWu without looking at it.

SuWu said, "HeGan is supposed to come with us and help us reach Tianzhu. How is he going to do that with this one-year exile?"

CaoShen said, "He is working on it. Ships depart on monsoon trade winds once a year. We need to get to Panyu."

CaoShen extended another scroll towards SuJin. "This leather scroll lists how many Jin gold coins each imperial jeweller and bureaucrat holds." SuJin glanced at it and handed it over to SuWu.

SuWu smiled and told Qian, "We have the gold?"

SuJin held up the small silk pouch and asked, "What's this?" Since both CaoShen and WoShi remained silent, he opened the bag and pulled out a metal disc.

"The medallion?" SuJin turned it a few times, examining it before extending it to SuWu. "He said he would make one for me."

SuWu examined it closely and said, "It's a fair replica of the pendant that flashed before our eyes, but the workmanship is poor, and the white stones don't glitter!"

SuJin nodded but then scowled. "Does HeGan want me to switch this pendant with the one around WangMang's neck? I don't know how that can be done. Anyone can see this is a fake!"

SuWu asked, "What else, CaoShen?"

"Zhan, HeGan's closest friend and jeweller, made the assassination attempt. It appears that he does not wish to return the gold."

CaoShen looked at SuJin. "HeGan wants you to exact revenge on his behalf for the treachery."

SuJin's eyes gleamed. "Gladly, no one gets away with hurting our brother. Does he have a plan, or do we need to improvise?"

"No need for any violence. When you meet WangMang," CaoShen said, "hand over the leather scroll with the list of jewellers' names and the gold they possess."

With a frown, SuWu glanced through the scroll and said, "Yes, it includes Zhan's name." He burst out laughing. "HeGan will probably rob Zhan just before we hand over this list to WangMang! I am sure the gold written against his name is overstated, too."

WoShi stroked his beard and smiled. "That would be atrocious!" WoShi stroked his beard and said, "Zhan will find himself with insufficient gold while the others pay up exactly as per the list!"

SuWu told a crestfallen CaoShen, "Don't worry about losing the gold, CaoShen! Knowing that crafty man, this is the list of people HeGan doesn't trust. He gives out gold to trap his enemies. Once the imperial treasury captures and removes these gold traders and bureaucrats, Changan gold trade will belong to HeGan!"

CaoShen told SuWu, "Actually, we don't lose any money. All the gold on this list is pledged against gold ingots. Our gold has already been spent on the goods we purchased and traded. The jewellers must pay twice: once to the treasury and again to the ingot merchants. They will lose everything, even their Hezi!"

#27 SuJin Meets Empress Wang

Soldiers carrying the dowager Empress's banner led the way to the palace. SuJin and his companions, SuWu, CaoShen, and Master WoShi, rode behind in an imperial carriage.

Surprisingly, a large crowd from the city had gathered to cheer for them. Shouts of "Long live the Hero of Han! Lead us, Green Hunter!" Filled the air.

WoShi was upset. "How did this happen? How did the people of Changan know we were meeting the Empress Dowager?"

SuWu said, "Someone is concerned about our lives. With this level of attention from the city's populace, WangMang may be discouraged from attacking us."

CaoShen added, "Money is required to mobilise people. I guess HeGan is behind this."

SuWu disagreed. "HeGan is smart in trade; this is politics. It's somebody else, someone knowledgeable, but thankfully on our side." WoShi grunted.

They were waved through the gates, and CaoTeng, the eunuch in charge of palace administration, received them. He critically appraised SuJin and SuWu and said, "You boys are undeniably Lui stock. However, to claim lineage to the ruling family, we need documented evidence of conception from the archives. All false claims are punishable by death."

WoShi stated clearly, "We are not here to make any claims, eunuch! Now, you better be aware of that!"

CaoTeng looked sharply at WoShi and said, "Palace politics is your talent, Marquis; I hope your courtroom abilities haven't suffered from disuse. Be warned that any slight against the imperial clan or ancestors can separate your head from the body."

WoShi bowed slightly in gratitude for the friendly advice. CaoTeng smiled, "I must admit that the rousing of the peasants and townsfolk is a deft move." He scoffed at WoShi and added, "Now, your skill in outsmarting the machinations that await you inside will be the real test. Either you will emerge as a legend of political intrigue or lead yourself to death."

WoShi whispered to SuWu, "You are right about someone worrying about our lives. It is not an outsider but an insider, someone within the palace who is helping us."

SuWu looked at his master with a questioning expression. WoShi added, "This eunuch knows who has organised the people waiting outside, and he feels we are ill-prepared."

CaoTeng led SuJin and SuWu to a bathing area. The eunuchs stripped them and examined their noses, teeth, ears, and other parts for any concealed weapons. An elderly maid oiled and scrubbed them clean with bath beans made from soybean powder and fragrant herbs before bathing them in hot water.

Their teeth were cleaned with the stem of a sweet-smelling plant, and a maid handed over a bowl to gargle and wash their mouths. SuJin spat it out. "Ugh, what's this?"

She giggled. "Vinegar, cow urine, spices, and herbs to make your mouth smell sweet."

CaoTeng, overseeing the proceedings, apologised. "We rarely go to such lengths to clean up a visitor. However, in your case, the Empress wishes to see you up close. She is ailing, and you must be thoroughly cleaned. We cannot have unpleasant bodily odours disturbing her delicate constitution."

The attendants dressed them in a green linen pao, a one-piece dress, and a wide red silk sash that cinched the dress at the waist. They fastened their hair with thin leather strips, as combs were prohibited near the imperials.

The old maidservant, who scrubbed them clean, gathered their discarded dresses, and SuJin said, "I need the medallion."

The maid said, "I am sorry; I can't allow any jewellery."

SuJin insisted, "I need it to show to the Empress." The maid handed the medallion to CaoTeng.

He examined the medallion closely, holding it in his sleeve without touching it. "It's just a gold disc with embedded white stones and crude figurines." He looked up and said, "Trust me, this work won't impress her!"

He instructed the maid, "Boil the medallion and drop it in a pot with a fish. If the fish dies, inform me."

SuWu asked, "Why can't we wear our clothes?"

"Same reason, you may go close to the Empress, and we can't risk any illness to her," CaoTeng said.

As they were led out of the bath area, SuWu asked SuJin, "Why did you bring the replica medallion?"

SuJin said, "What if WangMang asks us to prove that we are talking about the same medallion? Let him compare the medallions before the Empress." He added, "I have no choice but to do what HeGan asked me. *Pull her out. She will obey the dragon-borne! The medallion is a vessel.* Jinshen told him."

SuWu asked, "*Dragon-borne?*" SuJin shrugged and looked away. He did not notice SuWu's deep frown as he gazed questioningly at the Prince.

They had to wait for an hour before their summons. CaoTeng handed over a gleaming medallion scrubbed clean as he led them into court.

"We are cautious with you. WangMang asked me to ensure that no ornaments with sharp edges are on you to ensure the safety of the Empress. It's good advice, especially after your heroics with the comb in the arena."

As they walked, CaoTeng added, "Your dress will be washed and kept in your carriage by the time you return from the audience hall."

SuJin laughed. "It won't dry out in the brief time we'll be inside. Not in this weather."

SuWu teased, "Unless the Empress takes a liking to us. Maybe she will invite us for dinner." They laughed together at the joke.

CaoTeng snorted boisterously, "Just don't stay here permanently! This is the palace of the dowager Empress, and your clothes will be dried on the hearth and freshened with steam and incense." The boys stared at him in disbelief while CaoTeng smiled, always eager to impress commoners.

The boys were dazzled by the magnificence of the imperial court. The hall smelled of jasmine and incense, and the walls had wooden panelling. Pillars were painted red lacquer and covered in golden figurines of dragons, flowers, and creepers. Despite the full-bodied imperial grandeur, the white and pink cherry blossom-coloured silk curtains gave the ambience a strikingly feminine touch.

The court hall was filled with Lui nobles and bureaucrats, each seated in a predesignated place according to their imperial and bureaucratic status. The boys were captivated by the shimmering gold and silk garments the attendees wore. A heavy medley of fragrances filled the air, creating a cloying atmosphere. A constant buzz of murmurs, like the trilling of insects in a spring forest, served as the backdrop as they entered.

Rather than sitting on the elevated imperial dais, the Empress chose to sit among the courtiers on a high seat adorned with plush cushions, her leg draped in bearskin. She appeared to be in high spirits, smiling and laughing gracefully with them. Defying tradition and protocol, she had invited WangMang to sit beside her, and everyone could see her frequently patting his arm tenderly.

The sheer opulence and grandeur left SuWu in awe. He moaned in bewilderment, "Prince, are we fighting against these affluent and powerful people, or are we fighting for them? Either way, I am drowning in diffidence!"

CaoTeng asked them to wait, and he hurried forward. Soldiers with crossbows and swords covered every exit, and SuWu looked up to see imperial archers on the rafters above. WoShi and CaoShen were made to stand apart from senior courtiers and loosely covered by soldiers, and more of them came in.

SuJin echoed SuWu's thoughts when he remarked, "The eunuch was right; they are taking no chances with us. Let's make an impression on the Empress and leave. I don't see any possibility of securing the medallion today. We need to pursue it another time!"

Overawed by the display of power, SuWu said, "Prince, did you genuinely consider an option to secure the medallion by force? Forgive me! I feel useless here and am unable to think coherently!"

Although the mass of soldiers tried to remain discreet, the packed court fell silent, and all heads turned towards the boys.

SuWu nervously babbled away, "I don't know what we are getting into. This expensive dress makes us look silly. Don't we look too clean to be warriors? WoShi looks so powerless here."

SuJin calmly said, "Relax, brother, breathe deep!"

The Empress dowager looked towards them across the large hall. She shaded her hand over her eyes to look at them and beckoned them forward.

They walked with their heads held high when CaoTeng stepped forward and asked them to kneel. Without hesitation, the boys kowtowed in unison in front of the Empress, who stared at them.

The Empress gestured with her frail hand at a maid. It was the same old lady who had bathed them. She kowtowed and said in a quivering voice, "I confirm! Twice, Your Highness."

The Empress's eyes narrowed slightly as she smiled, "Expected, but nonetheless intriguing!" She raised her hand and displayed three fingers to a eunuch, who struck a large gong three times, bringing the courtroom to order. As the bell's reverberations faded, she said, "Come closer, children."

The courtiers gasped. The Empress had familiarly addressed them as if they were family.

WangMang realised the Empress was up to something he was unaware of and tried to stop her. "Grand Empress, don't break protocol. They could be assassins?"

"My dear regent, they are Han heroes. They are not here to kill me or you! If they were assassins, they wouldn't have waited so long. Isn't one of them the same boy who killed the Hun champion with a comb? You stay out of this if you are uncomfortable."

WangMang wouldn't oppose the dowager Empress. Any affront to her would rally the cursed Lui clan and the people together. WangMang sat back rigidly, his eyes blazing with anger at the snub, yet he suppressed his indignation and smiled.

The Empress squinted and said, "There is no doubt that you are Lui boys, and it's unusual for both of you to have features of my..." She looked at WoShi and gave him a slight nod. She continued, "Hmm... different mothers... but..." She paused and took a deep breath inward in shock as realisation set in.

She covered her mouth and exclaimed, "Won't miracles cease? I shall wring the neck of that midwife Fang if I get my hands on her."

She questioned her maid again, "You confirm twice?"

The maid responded, "Yes, Empress; twice is correct."

She put her head down and shed tears. Concerned, WangMang leaned towards her and asked why she was crying. She lifted her hand and silenced him. She regained her composure and wiped her tears away, and the court waited with bated breath.

It was unusual to witness a feminine emotion from their Empress, a woman of bronze!

"Today is worth the effort and precautions I have taken to recover. WoShi, you old fox, you might be right. One boy could be an impersonation, but two! That's intriguing, isn't it, nephew?"

WangMang looked at the boys intently. In shock, he realised what the Empress was referring to, and his eyes widened in panic. He was looking at the children of Emperor Cheng.

Grand Empress Dowager Wang motioned her court crier and bureaucrat, "I am not sitting on the imperial dais, and nothing here shall be recorded. However, you have permission to repeat everything said here."

WangMang puffed out his chest and told the Empress. "Let me deal with them. Surely, they are fake Lui exploiting your kindness and, I dare say, your old age. WoShi understands your weaknesses and your relentless quest for your grandchild?"

The Empress told WangMang, "Oh! Do they remind you of my grandchildren? Nephew! Laotong mothers, fathered by my son." The audience collectively gasped.

With a sparkle in her eyes, the Empress said, "Don't worry! I will decide on your behalf!"

WangMang sat back, uncertain about what to do. Whatever was happening was unforeseen, and he could do nothing to intervene. The Empress Dowager was the most influential person in the empire, and her words were always a command.

The Empress asked the boys, "Are you here to claim your inheritance? How are you going to prove it, if I may ask?" The audience erupted in uproar, and WangMang stood up to confront the boys.

The Empress cleared her throat, and WangMang looked at her. "Not in my court," she told him sternly. "You will not interfere and ensure that your supporters keep quiet. This is a Lui matter."

WangMang abruptly sat back, but his face had turned black with fury. His sycophants quietened when they saw their regent disparaged.

People pushed and jostled to get closer to look at the boys, with some craning their heads to catch every word. A juicy court drama would be retold in every noble family in Changan before nightfall.

The Empress watched the boys while waiting for the court to settle down. As court decorum was restored and palace mandarins ensured silence, the Empress asked SuJin with mock earnestness, "Do I look like your grandmother?" Immediately, a murmur arose in the courtroom.

SuJin smiled and said, "No! Your Highness, such a beautiful woman couldn't be my grandmother."

The Empress laughed uproariously and said, "There goes your inheritance." The courtiers politely joined in the laughter. CaoTeng lifted his hand, and the audience quietened down.

The Empress dowager smiled approvingly at SuJin. "A nobleman with Lui blood, perhaps, but a Prince of Han; we shall see. We must agree on that, mustn't we?"

She addressed WangMang. "I summoned you and mostly your people..." She gestured wide at the gathered audience. "... As witnesses. If these boys pass all my tests, you shall present their acceptance to the bureaucrats."

WangMang protested, but she firmly stalled him. "I shall test the boy in my way. Of course, if they pass my test, you will get irrefutable proof." Court criers repeated her words.

"Acceptance from Empress Dowager Wang of imperial Han,"

"... as a Lui,"

"... as a Wang."

"... and on the instincts of a mother."

WangMang hesitated and said, "Irrefutable proof needs to be acceptable to all in this court, and we need documentation to verify their date of conception. Suppose all of this exists, we will immediately consider the request."

The Empress scoffed at the regent's words. "Don't worry about court and rules, nephew. I have been here longer than you. I have all the records to confirm their conception and know how to use them if one or both of these boys are my grandsons." The Empress warned WangMang, "Don't test me, nephew. I don't compromise on matters of the imperial clan." WangMang was distressed by the old lady's resolve and looked very uncomfortable.

WangMang said, "Empress, you are old. Wily WoShi is fooling you. I need to step in on behalf of the people of Han."

She agreed wholeheartedly. "It is possible. It would be treason if they cheated, and I will call it out. This is an imperial court, and there is no need to pre-empt verdicts." She sat straight and said, "I will let a mother's instinct guide me. The Han Empire has gone through turmoil for want of a true successor, and who better than the hero of Han if he indeed passes my scrutiny?"

"Times have changed, Empress. The bureaucracy and the chancellor must have a say in all this," cautioned WangMang.

"Is that a threat, Nephew? If so, be man enough to say it to my face—the one who brought you to this position as regent. I will demonstrate the power of an Empress here and now! My swords will cut deep; there shan't be any Wang standing beside you today. Remain calm until I am finished here."

Thoroughly chastened, WangMang said, "I am all for your safety and wise judgment."

WangMang whispered to the Empress. "You are deliberately checking the authenticity of these boys in front of me and my men." The Empress gave him a wide smile.

She said, "Precisely because you will call me an old mad woman outside this court. I must ensure that, if I am convinced, it will all end here today."

WangMang was shaken to the core as realisation dawned on him. "You informed the Lui clan to be in court in full strength and rallied the common people to support these boys at the palace gates."

She smiled and said, "Yes, I did that. Men outside are armed to the teeth to storm the palace and restore order under the rightful Emperor. They will get the revolution they want!" She glanced at her nephew and said, "Surely, you agree that I have my wits about me despite my illness. It's time for a proper Lui with the blood of the Wangs to ascend the throne."

WangMang's voice failed him, and he croaked, "The court needs proof beyond a mother's instinct. Our emperors had the company of many women. We can't make any child born outside the conceptual rituals become a Prince. For that matter, he can be any Lui, need not be an offspring of your lineage."

The grand Empress looked at WangMang and laughed, "You, my nephew, might be regent, but you have no idea what the true blood of Han can do to rally the people."

WangMang threw the last gamble. "There are many Lui in our midst. Maybe these boys are one of theirs."

The Empress held on to that and said aloud, "The regent has raised a question. There are many Lui by blood." She paused for effect and added, "However, how many Lui can claim lineage to the throne by marriage to the Wangs?"

The court responded in unison, "Just you, Empress!"

She nodded around and smiled at receiving unanimous approval. "Quite right. Since I do not have any other sons, my son's progeny should have my blood in them."

The court remained silent when the court crier repeated. "I will not test the boys here as a Lui. I am going to test them as a Wang. To be precise, my blood."

The court burst into discussions, and the Empress sat back in her highchair and beckoned for tea. She was in no hurry. As a seasoned politician, she had to convince the courtiers of her logic first.

Imperial bureaucrats and senior eunuchs set the court to order and updated WangMang on how to respond. He smiled at their reasoning. "The court documentation will verify whatever proof is professed by the boys. It will be allied with findings from both the Lui and Wang family records."

The Empress smiled at WangMang, "You are so predictable, nephew. I haven't had this much fun and excitement since I put on those dainty shoes for my marriage."

"Pray, my nephew! Pray that these boys are false. I find your defence obnoxious."

WangMang discussed the next course of action with his cousin WangYi, the commander-in-chief of his army, and his prime minister WangXun. WangYi said, "Don't worry, cousin. Whatever the Empress's decision, we will take care of them."

WangMang said, "Wait! For now! The Empress has her soldiers infiltrated throughout the court." WangYi, the armed forces commander, was shocked as he looked around suspiciously.

WangMang bitterly said, "Now I realise what she was up to all these days. She wasn't convalescing. She was building an army!"

WangMang was shaken to be outwitted by the Empress. "Let's make the boys fail the test, which would be in our best interest. She will mow us down if we attack her newfound pets. She is more Lui than Wang when it comes to palace matters."

WangYi agreed. "Surely, they will fail here and now. It's too far-fetched that they are imperial brats and survived hunger and deprivation on the streets."

WangXun cautioned WangMang. "They trained under that old goat, WoShi." The Empress beckoned WangMang back to sit beside her.

Grand Empress Dowager Wang began her interrogation. "Who is SuJin?"

SuJin dropped to one knee, and SuWu stepped back a few paces. The Empress stared at SuWu for some time before turning to SuJin. She asked, "Why have you come here?"

SuJin said, "I had a reason before I came here, but after seeing you and the people around me, I am done here." He looked around and remarked, "My destiny is not in the palace. I am certain of that."

The Empress smiled at him in amusement, suggesting he was no one to decide anything before her. SuJin stared back fearlessly, and CaoTeng commanded, "Lower your eyes, commoner."

SuWu's voice resonated loudly. "This is a family matter, eunuch. You will die if you command our Prince again."

WangYi stood up and yelled, "How? Do you think we will remain idle?"

The Empress motioned to her head of security, who hit his spear on the ground twice. Soldiers with the identifying mark of the Empress's bodyguards marched forward and shouted in unison. They forced all of WangMang's bodyguards out of the court. The head of palace security returned and respectfully placed an exquisite sword before SuWu. He returned to his position behind the Empress and hit his spear on the ground.

The Empress dowager gestured for a shocked CaoTeng to kneel. He fell to his feet and kowtowed before SuWu, apologising. SuWu did not take up the sword, and the petrified eunuch hurried back and blended in with the other palace servants. WangYi squirmed uncomfortably and looked around; no soldier he could call his own remained.

WangMang looked at the Empress in disbelief, and she said, "Mother's instinct."

WangXun smiled reassuringly at WangMang. This was the Empress's last public meeting. The Empress's dowager had to prove she was sane.

The Empress's trust in the boys surprised the court. Indeed, the dowager Empress had gone senile. Many bureaucrats shook their heads in dismay. The Empress was taking a risk by defending a hitherto unknown boy. Either she survived the day proving the boys to be her progeny, or she would be declared senile.

The Empress beckoned her maid, who rushed forward, holding a polished brass plate that reflected like a mirror. In a gentler tone, she asked WangMang, "Nephew, will you be my witness?"

A maid approached SuJin and asked him to roll up his hanfu to reveal his inner arm. She held a brass plate displaying a birthmark of a three-pronged staff - a trident. Empress Wang inhaled sharply, closed her eyes for a moment, nodded her head, and a tear fell.

WangMang asked loudly to include the courtiers. "Empress, what has a random birthmark got to do with proof?"

She replied, "Be patient, nephew."

WangMang looked flustered and asked directly, "You mean to say that he is the son of Emperor Cheng? It must be proven before this court. Moreover, we already have an Emperor on the throne!"

The Empress acknowledged his outburst. "I assure you that he isn't here for the throne. Nothing can stop him from taking the throne if he aspires to be the emperor, now or... later!"

An agitated WangMang said, "What's he here for?"

"Let's find out, shall we..." responded the Empress. She gestured to her maids, who helped her up. They led her to her favourite painting, which showed her husband, Emperor LuiShi, sitting with her and holding their infant son in her hands.

She said, "I should have believed you, son!"

In the meantime, after kowtowing to the Empress and Regent, an old and respected palace bureaucrat walked up to SuJin and checked his birthmark. The bureaucrat shouted excitedly, "It can't be... not in our lifetime." He licked his fingertips for saliva and rubbed the birthmark on SuJin.

SuJin pushed him away and said, "What are you doing, old man?"

"The mark."

"What mark?" Exclaimed SuJin.

"Do you not know that you have a birthmark on your inner arm?

SuJin responded, "What's special about that? My brother SuWu has the same inside his arm!" He gestured with his head towards SuWu, who looked vexed. SuWu had already figured out what was happening and was restless.

The bureaucrat opened a gold-embroidered yet old silk scroll and held it out for the other palace bureaucrats to inspect. "He has the same birthmark on his arm as Prince Ao, as recorded in the archives. He is an imperial Lui."

WangXun implored the Empress, "Highness, many of the Lui could have it, not just Emperor Cheng. I will immediately commission bureaucrats to check on every Lui family member to see if they have similar birthmarks.

"No, there is no need for that," said the Empress emphatically. The Empress returned to her highchair and held out her hand.

Her maid rolled the sleeve of her dress up, revealing her frail hand. A polished brass plate reflected her inner hand. WangMang and the courtiers witnessed the same birthmark of a long staff with three sharp prongs.

Someone shouted, "He is a Wang too!"

The Empress addressed the court, saying, "This birthmark is what led to my selection as the Empress of Han to fulfil the destiny of the first emperor. Not many know this, except for a few bureaucrats and astrologers. You can verify the archives."

Empress Dowager Wang declared, "Beyond documentation that could be missed, we have a God-given logic that can't fail! Haven't I given you that proof? Tell me!" All the senior bureaucrats nodded their heads fervently in agreement.

On a cue from the tired Empress, the old bureaucrat and astrologer relayed his words, stating that the mark of the trident cannot be found outside the bloodline of the progeny of Empress Dowager Wang. The boys were the children of Emperor Cheng. The court went into an uproar.

The Empress waited for the uproar to subside before she addressed her court, "What this proves is your collective failure." She looked around with blazing eyes and shouted, "You, responsible for the Emperor and the harem, did not know that not one but two boys had been born! What good are you as soldiers, eunuchs or courtiers? If this is what happens to the imperial family, what good can be expected from you for the peasants?" Not one courtier or bureaucrat moved. Everyone looked down at their feet in shame.

The Empress looked shaken and sad, and her maid asked, "Empress, you need to rest?"

She ignored her maid, looked around, and asked, "Does anyone here have any doubts about this boy? Can anyone here fake something like this?" She demanded, but the court remained silent.

She looked at WangMang and said, "Nephew, how about you?"

WangMang asked the court crier to step back. He leaned across the Empress and asked in a disturbed voice, "If he is not after the throne, what is he here for? We should give him what he wants." The Empress beckoned SuJin to sit on the floor beside her on her left side.

She ran her fingers through SuJin's hair and said, "You are different from your father, but you are alike, too. A better-looking, serious Prince, if I may say." "Do you chase after girls like Crown Prince Ao?"

SuJin was embarrassed. "No, Empress. At the moment, I want to embark on my voyage to Tianzhu for all our ancestors! For Han."

WangMang asked, "So, you are not after the throne or any official position?" SuJin nodded in agreement.

WangMang asked, "How about wealth? Gold?"

SuJin smiled. "I came here to give you some!" WangMang sat back, stunned.

Empress Dowager interjected, "So, what are you after, and why did you seek this old woman out?"

"I need the medallion."

"What?" WangMang exclaimed as he sat up. He stuttered, "What medallion?"

Empress Wang slyly glanced at WangMang and answered SuJin, "Whatever you want. How many medallions do you want? A hundred or a thousand. You can have it." SuJin laughed and squeezed the Empress's hand.

The Empress linked her hand with his and said, "So calloused, a warrior! Archer or swordsman?"

"Kind of both," SuJin said with a smile.

An agitated WangMang asked again, "What medallion?"

SuJin bowed to WangMang. "The one on your neck, Regent WangMang. It belongs to Zhang Liang, who has bequeathed it to me."

The grand Empress looked at SuJin and said, "That's all you want, a single medallion." She turned to WangMang and continued, "Hand it over, nephew! You can make as many as you need."

WangMang looked flustered. "Empress, this medallion is not for gifting. I found it, and I cannot give it to anyone." He reiterated firmly, forestalling further discussion. "All the gold in this city cannot buy it from me." He said this to thwart the Empress from making a counteroffer.

SuWu said, "What if I hand over more gold than this city has? Will you change your mind?"

The Empress and WangMang looked at him in shock. "That's a lot of gold!"

The Empress was impressed. "You are very resourceful. WoShi is right about you. We need you here!"

WangMang added with a menacing tone, "That's more than enough to start a revolution against the empire."

SuJin replied, "Perhaps! We aren't here to instigate a war. You can have it in exchange for the medallion. We secured the gold from a bandit."

The Empress smiled at SuJin, having reached her decision. "You shall become the Emperor of Han. Let the prophecy be thrown into the ocean."

SuJin held the Empress's left hand and said, "The medallion."

WangMang remained silent and looked at the imperial soldiers. None were his men. His aunt had outsmarted him comprehensively.

The Empress said, "Let me look at this medallion. What's so special about it?"

WangMang wavered, and the medallion began to heat up.

"Let me see your medallion, WangMang," she insisted, holding her right hand out. "What's wrong with showing me?" She exclaimed.

WangMang hesitated and said, "I shall hold it out for you, Empress, to see. I won't remove it from my neck." The Empress arched her eyebrows in surprise.

"You won't trust your Empress and aunt?"

Reluctantly, WangMang removed the medallion from his grand hanfu. The medallion hung from a leather strap around his neck. He leaned forward and stretched the medallion to the maximum ply of the leather strap. The Empress touched and flipped the medallion while SuJin held the Empress's left hand.

"It's hot to the touch. Are you running a fever, nephew?" WangMang had eyes only for SuJin, watching him closely. "Bright, shiny stones. These are constellations leading somewhere," she said.

SuJin sensed a dark presence pulsing and squirming like black smoke, shying away from him. He recalled HeGan's words and said, "Jinshen." Holding the replica medallion in his hand, he pulled at the dark spirit, coaxing and willing it to come to him.

He heard an unearthly scream in his mind; something was pulling back, afraid.

Time slowed as a strong presence bled from WangMang, expanded into the Empress and finally moved into his body with a warm, tingling sensation. The air was filled with an exotic perfume.

SuWu watched them closely. The Empress froze, her face displaying intense horror. WangMang looked at the Empress and SuJin curiously before yanking the medallion out of the Empress's hands. The medallion swung back onto WangMang's chest, and he quickly pushed it back into his ceremonial attire.

The Empress snapped back into reality, rubbed her fingertips, and said, "I felt something." She inhaled deeply and said, "What is that heavenly perfume."

WangMang jerked forward and exclaimed, "Ahh," as if something hot touched his chest. Leaning forward, he felt his chest to ensure the medallion was still hanging from his neck, and he was reassured by the heat it gave off.

He told the Empress, "I think you should leave the court now! It's been an exciting day for you."

SuJin told the Empress, "I agree with the regent, Empress. You need to rest."

SuJin told WangMang, "My destiny lies elsewhere, and I will leave for Tianzhu shortly." WangMang gave him a smile that did not reach his eyes but gave him a slight nod.

The Empress looked at SuJin and said, "Yes, I am convinced. You must go to Tianzhu and fulfil the oaths made by your ancestors." She looked at WangMang and said, "Let him take care of Han." WangMang exhaled in relief.

WangYi whispered something to WangMang. He told the Empress, "Your Highness, palace matters need my time. I request your permission to leave." The Empress nodded listlessly.

WangYi asked WangMang, "What about the gold?"

SuJin spoke aloud to SuWu, "Hand it over." SuWu took the leather scroll from CaoShen and handed it to WangYi, who tried to stare him down.

WangMang turned to SuJin and said, "So, you will be leaving for Tianzhu." He smiled, but his toughness was absent.

SuJin declared, "Yes, but I want to be left alone." WangMang agreed. "I promise your safety until you leave Changan." WangYi gave him a leering smile as they walked away.

SuJin said, "Grand Empress, we too should be leaving now." She clung to his hand.

"Wait! When I touched the medallion, I felt a presence. Did I imagine it? The spirit implored me to release your hand, and I heard the first Emperor!"

SuJin whispered. "The presence is now within me. It travelled from WangMang's medallion through your body into me, Grand Empress." She was shocked and stared at her grandson with wide eyes.

SuJin shrugged and said, "Frankly, I don't know how to deal with these powerful entities. I need to find a master, a spirit master!"

Empress Wang was thoughtful. "So, WangMang is now hanging an empty vessel on his chest? Isn't he?" SuJin nodded and added wryly. "It did not belong to him in the first place."

The Empress said, "WangMang was a simple, learned man, incapable of taking the decisions he made over the last few years. Now I know the spirit within the medallion made him devious and cruel." She frowned and stated, "He may return to his old self. I am unsure if that will help him or the empire."

"How about you, SuJin? Won't this spirit affect your judgment? Make you cruel like him."

SuJin's eyes flickered towards SuWu, who stood out of earshot before responding. "I will tell you because you are my grandmother!" She smiled, encouraging him to continue. "I hold a secret no one knows, not my teacher or trusted brothers." He looked around and whispered, "I already have a spirit within me, a powerful dragon spirit!

It saved me from drowning. The dragon spirit holds the dark spirit within its grasp, and together, they seem docile and quiet."

The Empress looked at him wide-eyed in shock. "Of course, the dark spirit within WangMang was a ferocious female Yang. It complements the energy of the dragon spirit, Yin, within you."

SuJin was taken aback by her deduction. "I haven't thought about it like that, but it does make sense." He asked, "How do you know this, Empress?"

She was cynical in her response. "Her scent! A woman knows another." She softly patted his hand and said, "The dark spirit filled me and screamed in a fury to let go of your hand. She seemed terrified of the dragon inside!" She looked at SuJin curiously and said, "No, it's you she is frightened of!"

SuJin's brow creased. "Me?"

The Empress elaborated. "Before I could pull my hand away from you, another presence, a bright one, filled me. I was held immobile, and after a brief struggle, I felt emptiness. She was looking past that spirit into you."

"I saw all your ancestors crowding around the first Emperor. I distinctly remember the first Emperor commanding me to let you go to Tianzhu." She said in wonder.

She looked at SuJin in awe. "What are you, my son? The astrologers were correct about you! You are a celestial being, holding two spirits within you: masculine and feminine, Yin and Yang."

She exhaled hard and said, "You must be immensely powerful to hold them both within you." With worry written on her face, she added, "I wonder what forces you are to face in Tianzhu! Surely, the gods are preparing you."

The Empress looked forlorn. "My instincts told me that you were my grandson at first sight. You walk in like my son Ao when he visits me to plead for my help. No one can replicate that subtle mannerism. A mother knows!"

"I thought about not letting you go and send your brother instead. He is the son of Mi, isn't he? Can't he stay back?" She motioned to SuWu, who was waiting patiently out of earshot.

SuJin smiled and was emphatic in his reply. "It is my destiny to go to Tianzhu, but without the cool head of SuWu, my elder brother, I will fail. I need him beside me, Empress. It's his destiny, too." He ruefully added, "You are right, though. He will make a mighty emperor."

The Empress gave up, and her shoulders drooped. "I understand. These are matters beyond me. No Empress, bureaucrats, priests, or army can stop you if you deal with spirits."

She said, "I will give you a ship." Empress Wang looked her age as she gazed wistfully at SuJin. "Go! Go now and come back victorious, loyal son of Han. Leave now before I change my mind."

She held the imperial seal and announced. "As the Han Empress, Wang, I fulfil our pledge to the gods by releasing our chosen bloodline to destiny on behalf of all Lui ancestors. I am entrusting my blood in free will and on behalf of the people of Han, past and present." She paused to breathe and continued, "As soon as SuJin leaves our shores, we deem the black vows complete to release all our ancestors from their bondage of unfinished promise."

She faltered and wept before composing herself to add, "May the gods bring you back to our lands, safe and sound."

Just as a sombre SuJin bowed and backed away, the Empress said, "Tell your elder brother that all the love and care I have for you includes him. I cannot hold him in my arms! My resolve will break."

****

They had a quiet dinner with WoShi, ignoring the staccato sound of ChenHe slurping. Qian had asked a hundred questions about their audience with the grand Empress dowager.

"I haven't been on a warship. I just heard that ships buck like a horse on the ocean?" Batu said and smiled, "I can handle that!"

Qian laughed and said, "Don't be too optimistic, barbarian from the sea of grass. People fall sick on ships. Unlike a horse, you can't get off in the middle of the ocean."

Batu looked miserable when he heard, "Is the ocean that big?" Qian laughed, adding, "With monsters many times bigger than the ship we sail, prowling in its depths." For a moment, ChenHe stopped chewing as he and Batu looked at Qian in horror.

ChenHe added, "We could fall off the edge of the earth too!" and Batu moaned, horrified.

SuJin told WoShi, "We will miss all of you. Now add the Empress to the list."

WoShi nodded. "Learn from her, all of you! She let her grandson walk away, not letting any emotions cloud her judgment. Now that is power!" WoShi added, "I can imagine the pain and hurt she is suffering as a grandmother looking at you boys. She never gave up searching and finally found both of you, only to say goodbye." SuWu fixed his gaze on WoShi.

WoShi looked at a troubled SuWu and said, "This is a sacrifice that no storyteller will tell, nor shall a bard sing."

****

Qian told WoShi that the ships from Tianzhu arrived during the final winds of the Meiyu monsoons and would depart with the retreating winds. Thus, just one crossing was possible in a year.

The warship gifted by the Empress required extensive modifications for ocean travel, which would require a few months.

Reluctant to wait longer, WoShi asked Qian, Batu, and CaoShen to leave for Dongying seaport to hire an experienced crew to man their ship to sail the oceans. He told them, "Your first stop should be Luoyang. The dwarfs shall hand over the bows there. The melted idols are already with the dwarfs."

Batu was reluctant to leave SuJin. "Let SuJin come with us. SuWu and you are capable of inspecting the ship."

WoShi convinced him, "Batu, the Prince, is safe with us. Moreover, the palace won't hand over the ship to anybody but SuJin."

****

WangMang returned after visiting the ailing Empress. "She won't last long! She demanded I shouldn't move against her pups until the river turns again!"

"Will that happen?" Asked WangYi

WangXun answered, "You cannot change destiny; it's not without reason that we call the Yellow River as "Han's sorrow". Our men are reporting an unusual pile-up of silt in the river with copious inflow from the mountains. As for the pups, accidents happen."

WangMang said, "The pups are the least of my concerns. The prophecy must unfold and herald the rout of the Lui. We have time to prepare a large army."

"Wang on the throne," said WangYi.

"Wang on the throne, with a mandate to rule," said WangXun. The three nodded gravely to each other and lifted their cups of rice wine in a silent toast.

WangMang wiped his wet moustache and said, "Commander WangYi, the Huns need to be decimated and driven back into the steppes. We need men. Secure the gold coins from jewellers and our knife money and mint copper Jin coins by the tens of thousands. Recruit thousands of peasants and deploy them at the borders."

WangYi nodded earnestly, and WangMang continued. "Return to Changan when I send word with battle-hardened and loyal soldiers. With the Empress dead, no one can stop the rout of the Lui."

"It will be done, cousin. With this gold, nothing can stop us." WangYi smiled and added, "While we recruit men, let me sabotage a battleship to sink in the Lui's Sorrow."

[THE END]

www.ingramcontent.com/pod-product-compliance
Lightning Source LLC
LaVergne TN
LVHW091611070526
838199LV00044B/757